SUNBOUND

SUNBOUND

BY

ALEX SPICER

ISBN-13: 978-0692392201
ISBN-10: 0692392203

First edition, May 2015

For my father,
whose boyhood imagination shaped the
foundation of this story.

And also my mother,
because I'll never hear the end
of it otherwise.

CONTENTS

For as long as the villagers of Illac could remember, the Earth Stone had been the center of their existence.

It is not surprising, considering it was the only thing keeping them alive on a world that had become a furnace.

PROLOGUE

The Earth Stone

"OF COURSE I'LL BE FINE. I have as good a chance as anyone. Better, actually."

Georg, tearing bread into thick chunks at the kitchen table, certainly sounded confident.

His younger brother, Klas, was not convinced. "You can out-sprint anyone, but this may be a test of stamina. You don't know how far the Earth Stone is from here."

Georg tossed an end crust to Klas and looked out of the kitchen window. He could see their father cutting wood beyond the barn, far from earshot.

"I think you'll be ready for it, though," Klas quickly added, not wanting to risk discouraging his brother. "Father has prepared you well for the initiation."

The two stood in an uncomfortable silence as they continued to break apart bread for a few minutes after that. The Stone's whereabouts was a mystery; the ritual demanded it. It was uncommon for siblings to discuss the initiation in depth with one another, especially brothers. To tempt fate and the favor of the gods was a dangerous game to play, and overconfidence more than often carried with it a shortened life expectancy.

Despite all that, it was then that Georg would speak the unthinkable.

"You know, I remember when I was a year younger than you are now, when I had to stay away the night the Three Yearlings set out," he told Klas as he fiddled with the miniature glass cube bauble that was attached to the necklace he had received from his father for his seventeenth birthday just four days earlier. "They left in all directions, at dawn."

"You watched?" Klas asked, shocked at his brother's actions. "How? Only the Elders are allowed anywhere near once they set out."

Georg glanced up at his intrigued brother and grinned.

"It rained heavily just before dawn that night. It was the first time in a long while and only lasted a short time, but it woke me up. When they allowed the children and women to come to the market circle after breakfast to await the Threes, I could see their footprints made during the downpour.

"Rumor has it that Jamic, the first to return, got back not long after midnight. If that's true, I figure the Earth Stone can't be farther than four or five miles away, and probably less than that," Georg pronounced proudly. "And it's somewhere towards the hills in the east."

Klas glared at his brother in disbelief. "You're full of it. How can you know that?"

Georg leaned in toward his brother and proudly explained.

"Because many of the returning Threes had white-pine needles stuck in their socks," he proclaimed, his grin widening. "When they grabbed a statue, they almost certainly would have taken the quickest route back."

"Stop it," Klas stated quickly, before turning away from Georg. "I've heard enough. I thought you were just joking with me, but what you're saying is—"

Klas pursed his lips as he looked back at his older brother. He could see in Georg's face that he already knew what he was about to tell him, and yet worryingly, his older brother did not seem to care.

"You'll be expelled from the village," Klas whispered, "not to mention the wrath of the gods... Please Georg, don't talk of this again."

Georg gazed intently at Klas for a moment before returning his attention to the chunks of bread on the table before him. Klas hated to be at odds with his brother about anything, but this time Georg had gone too far. He could only hope the gods would show forgiveness.

It was two evenings later that Georg was sent off to the temple to embark on his trek to the Earth Stone while the younger children slept and mothers prayed to the gods for their sons' return.

This time the Three Yearlings comprised seventeen boys, each having reached the age of sixteen since the last Earth Stone sacrifice three years ago. On a signal from the high priest they set off from the temple in search of the

Stone. Sixteen boys, at most, would return to the village as men. One, at least, would not return at all.

Sixteen clay figures had been placed at the base of the Earth Stone by the village priests. The task of the Three Yearlings was to discover the location of the hallowed structure, a secret withheld from them their entire lives and known only to adult men, retrieve a figure and return with it to the Illac market circle. Any Three Yearling who did not retrieve a figure and return to the circle was damned to the barren wastes, never to return to the village. In the heat beyond the sanctuary of the Stone they would not survive. Not finding the Earth Stone – or finding it too late – was a death sentence. Only the fittest, smartest, and toughest survived. The weakest was a sacrifice to the gods.

Starting at dawn the next day, Klas nervously waited for Georg with his mother and father at the market circle alongside the rest of the village. One by one the boys who were now men trickled in, each carrying a figure. Eventually fifteen returned. Two did not. One was Georg.

While most of the village celebrated the return of their sons, Klas and his family awaited Georg's arrival. The hours rolled by quickly with no sign of the sixteenth and final initiate, and as the sun began to set on the day, Klas watched his mother's hope give out as she returned home with tears in her eyes. To make matters worse he could hardly bear to look at his father, who had remained motionless with his eyes fixed on the road that led to the surrounding woods, his fists clenched tighter and tighter as the sun gradually set in the sky.

"I am sorry about Georg," a voice crackled behind them.

It was Ulises, a well-revered priest in the village.

For the first time in hours Klas' father's eyes strayed from the road to look at Ulises, and without a single word to either his remaining son or the priest, he trudged back home.

"The sacrifice the Illac people must make is not an easy one," Ulises sighed glumly to Klas. "It never has been."

"This is not the way it's supposed to be," Klas told him. "He knew—"

Klas caught himself as he noticed Ulises' right eyebrow rise slightly.

"He was the strongest, fastest," Klas corrected himself. "Everyone expected him to be the first back to the village…"

"The destiny the gods have set out for each of us is not always easy to accept or understand," Ulises explained as he placed his hand on Klas' shoulder, "but Georg's path has been laid out for him, as yours has for you. Everything happens for a reason, my child. Now come, you must be hungry. There is plenty of food remaining at the celebration."

"I think I'll stay here a little longer and wait for Georg," Klas replied.

Ulises took a deep breath and nodded. "Alright. Do not stay out too late, however. There is nothing you can do for him now."

As Ulises walked away, Klas began to think otherwise. Ulises had said it himself, after all – everything happens for a reason. What if Georg had been destined to tell Klas the general location of the Earth Stone? What if it was the will of the gods for Klas to go after his brother?

The moon had begun its ascension above the cut of the

tree line, gently lighting the eastern hills and beckoning him toward them. Klas looked around him – there was nobody in sight. If he left now no one would ever know, bar the gods.

Without giving himself a moment to appropriately think things through and possibly change his mind, Klas put his head down and ran as fast as he could. As he flew past the outskirts of the village and into the towering tree line, a sudden feeling of liberation overcame him. What he was doing went against everything that had been hammered into his head for as long as he could remember, but for some reason right now he didn't care about the consequences. He was going after Georg.

Surely Georg was injured and in need of help; no other explanation made any sense, and even if he were wrong about the direction he still would have had the same chance as any other boy.

The sun had already disappeared behind those distant scorched, gray eastern hills when he passed through the farmland that surrounded Illac and into the dense forest that encompassed the rest of the world as they knew it. The priests did not allow expansion of farmland past this point, and exploration of the forest much beyond its edge was regarded as pointlessly dangerous and insulting to the gods' gift of life to the people. Out there the forest eventually failed and gave way to barren wastes as all life failed in the heat of the sun, away from the island of affable air that was Illac.

The forest was cool, nearly cold, as the twilight gave way

to the full moon's delicate shine, stretching the shadows cast by the canopy of the trees above Klas down to the ground below. Shortly, the deciduous trees gave way to conifers as was common for the eastern side of the forest. Elsewhere, the forest tended to lead to seemingly endless dry scrubland and arid desert.

The white-pine conifers of this particular section of the forest were uniquely light green that glowed in the sunlight, and their branches were commonly used as decoration during one of the holy days. The needles even faded to white after falling and covered the forest floor like drifts of snow.

It was here that Klas stopped to reconsider his actions a first and final time. He held his hand above his brow and gazed deeply beyond the trees before him. This was the limit of common knowledge of what surrounded Illac.

ONE

Horton

"HORTON!"

Horton hazily popped his head up and wiped away the drool that had accrued between the corner of his mouth and the tabletop. As he rubbed his tired eyes the blurry figure that had abruptly awoken him slowly came into focus.

"Were you just sleeping?" his younger brother pestered him.

Horton leaned back in his chair and sighed as he discreetly attempted to stretch his arms.

"No, I wasn't sleeping. I was just resting... my face," Horton replied as he tried to avoid eye contact with his brother. "Sorry Deforest, we can't play boliball today – or ever, for that matter. I'm a man now."

"You're not a man yet," Deforest reminded him, tossing Horton's boliball mitten into his lap.

"No," Horton hissed as he threw the mitten aside. "Initiation is less than a week away. I need to focus on growing up. If Klas was still around to help me prepare then maybe I'd have time for stupid games, but he's not."

"Is it also his fault you're so lazy?" Deforest sneered back. "Father disappeared nine years ago and you still blame him for all your problems. When are you going to move on?"

"I wouldn't expect a child like you to understand," Horton scowled as he sunk his face into his arms atop the table.

Deforest shot back a remark as he stomped out of the room but Horton wasn't listening. His mind was preoccupied with the initiation.

"It *is* all his fault," Horton grumbled under his breath. "As if being practically half the size of the other boys my age isn't bad enough, I'm stuck without anyone to train me. I may as well sacrifice myself now and save everyone the effort."

Horton's heart sank into his stomach at the thought. His nervousness about the initiation quickly turned into anger.

In a sudden fit of rage, Horton slammed his fist on his desk, stood up and marched outside his home. "Argh!" he shouted at the top of his lungs to blow off steam.

He stood there for a moment breathing deeply, trying to regain his composure after the sudden upheaval, and as he did he imagined being able to run far away from the village and his problems. Along the horizon above the forest cropped up the dry, barren hills far to the east, and although he had seen them practically every day for much of his life, today they really caught his eye. As he briefly stared at them they seemed to call to him, wishing to emancipate him from his responsibilities and duties.

"Horton!"

His mother appeared in the doorway of their cottage. "What in the gods' names was all that commotion about? You need to grow up; you're acting like a child."

Looking around at his surroundings, Horton couldn't help but notice the neighboring villagers were all staring at him. To make matters even worse, laughing loudly at his expense from across the road was Thomas, the biggest and probably meanest boy his age, along with his mob of friends.

"Getting ready for the initiation, Horton?" Thomas yelled over, snorting with laughter. "Funny, I didn't realize they let little children participate."

"Oh yeah?" Horton shot back. "I didn't realize they let dumb people participate!"

Horton winced as he thought twice of his retort just as the words left his lips, and unfortunately for him, this only made Thomas and his friends laugh harder. Embarrassed, he hunched over and turned back to the house. As he stepped through the front door, he glanced back at the hills once more. He wished so desperately to be away from this place.

Shaking his head gloomily, Horton mumbled to himself. "At least I'm big where it matters. I should have said that, damnit."

That night Horton joined his mother and brother at the kitchen table for dinner. This was not a common occasion as they normally walked down to the temple and ate the communal food with the rest of the villagers, but tonight was special because his mother's crops had been more successful than usual that season.

"It seems like it's been many years since we have been blessed by the gods with a surplus," Horton's mother sighed to herself as they ate. "Back when the sun was a little more forgiving your father and I would often enjoy dinner together like this."

"Shut up," Horton coldly snapped at his mother. "Just… just shut up about father."

His mother's face creased fleetingly with irritation, but quickly relaxed.

"I – how's preparation for the initiation coming, Horton?" she asked, changing the subject.

Horton ignored her question for the moment because he didn't want to talk about it. In the back of his mind he thought she might drop the topic if he stayed silent long enough, but in truth he knew that was just wishful thinking.

Deforest instead seized the opportunity.

"If preparing means acting like a baby, then yeah, he's prepared."

Horton sneered and kicked his brother in the shin beneath the table.

"Ow! Damn you!" Deforest groaned. "It's not my fault you spend all your time feeling sorry for yourself, it's no wonder everyone thinks you're going to end up like father's brother."

"Deforest!" their mother gasped, appalled by her son's grim words.

Furious, Horton leaped up from his chair and grabbed Deforest by the arm. He pulled his brother out of his seat and threw him to the wooden floor.

"Stop it!" his mother screamed.

Both Horton and Deforest halted mid-tussle. The food their mother had labored all season to produce was spilled all over the floor. Horton expected his mother to scold them and send them to their rooms without supper, but she instead just looked at her two sons with deep disappointment. All Horton could do was stare back at her blankly, filled with shame. Then, without really thinking about it, he ran straight out the front door. Not stopping to look back, he ran down the lane, past the temple, over the dry creek bed and into the woods. He knew exactly where he needed to go to escape.

Peering between the trees, he could make out the silhouettes of the hills in the distance against the moonlit clouds. He knew he could never reach them, but something about heading toward them, even in vain, made him feel better.

As he ran he could feel his eyes tearing up. He knew he shouldn't – Thomas and some of the other boys called him a baby for crying after getting hit in the face with a boliball a few weeks prior, and he had vowed to never cry again. Still, he couldn't hold back his emotions.

"Grow up, damnit," Horton told himself. "Only children cry."

Horton wasn't sure how long he'd been running when he finally managed to pull himself out of his state, but the woods had begun to rapidly thicken, making movement increasingly difficult. He could still barely make out the eastern hills outlined against the silver-washed clouds through the tree branches above him, and despite the urge to stop and go back home, he kept marching deeper into the unknown.

And then, as though reliving a long-forgotten dream, the forest floor turned white. Stopping in his tracks, he reached down to pick up a handful of pine needles that carpeted the ground. As he stood there taking in his surroundings, he found himself reminiscing memories he didn't know he had. He wasn't sure how, but he felt as though he was very familiar with this place, and weirdly, he knew there was something of significance nearby. It was something sacred. Something forbidden.

Horton's heart skipped a beat when he caught sight of it.

Against the backdrop of the hills he had foolishly pursued loomed the most impressive and massive object he had ever seen. At first glance he wasn't sure if what he was looking at was there at all. The object's dark metallic shell camouflaged itself in the night, making Horton question whether he was just seeing things. However, his shock quickly turned into excitement as he inched closer through the thick brush.

"Brother!"

Horton practically jumped out of his shoes as he spun around in surprise. Through the trees behind him appeared Deforest, trying to catch his breath. Wearing the traditional Illac all-white garb, he was easy to spot in the moonlight.

"Deforest?" Horton called out. "What in the gods are you doing out here?"

"I came after you," Deforest explained, still panting. "Why did you run all the way out here? This is bad – we've got to get back right away."

Horton turned and looked toward the dark object just beyond the brush before them, leading Deforest's eyes toward it as well.

"Is that…?" Deforest whispered as he retreated a few steps away from the object.

Horton turned back to his brother. "I think it is. The Earth Stone."

"Please, let's go," Deforest exclaimed as he grabbed Horton's arm and tugged it. "If we're noticed by a priest out here – or worse, the gods – we'll be—"

"Hold on a second," Horton shrugged off Deforest as he pushed through the brush and into a wide clearing. At the center of the clearing was a pyramid, roughly the same height as the highest reaches of the surrounding treetops and the same dark color as the clear night sky overhead.

Deforest reluctantly followed closely behind Horton as they slowly walked up to the hallowed monument. Horton could feel frigid air emanating from it – he had never felt such coldness before – and yet adversely, as he pulled back the hood of his tunic and cautiously stretched his hand out to touch the Earth Stone's hard shell, he found it to be strangely warm. The foreign material it was composed of was hard, smooth and metallic, but unlike the ironworks he was familiar with, the composition of the pyramid was completely alien to him.

He smiled to himself slightly as he walked alongside the Earth Stone, his fingertips all the while maintaining contact with the pyramid's outer surface. Memories of his father flooded his mind as he made his way around its perimeter, and although he was unsure why, he felt soothed somehow. In fact, he felt more calm and relaxed than he had in years. He had imagined this moment, this contact with the Earth Stone, countless times throughout his life. Now, unbelievably, he was actually living it.

Then, out of the corner of his eye, Horton spotted something moving. He and Deforest jumped back as a startled fox ran out in front of them from behind a nearby bush and dived into a small burrow in the ground that led beneath the pyramid.

It was in that moment that reality switched back on in Horton's mind. He remembered where he was – far from home and in a sacrosanct place he should not yet have found. The serenity he felt just seconds before completely evaporated, replaced by the entrenching, unnerving darkness that now seemed to submerge him.

"You're right," Horton said to Deforest urgently, "we need to get out of here."

Horton put his back to the distant arid hills in the east and took off running through the forest once again, except this time his sights were set on returning home to the village.

The cold air shrilled past his ears and whipped through his hair. Branches scratched his face, causing him to stumble over a tree root and skin his knee, but he didn't care, nor did he cry. Fear overcame him. He tried to block it out of his mind but it was no use.

"Think of something bright," Horton told himself. "Think of something that makes you happy."

He suddenly remembered Deforest, and glanced back to see if he was following.

Oof!

Horton's head spun. He felt like he'd been run over by a grizzly bearpig. He looked up and saw the low-hanging branch he had run into face-first. Blood was gushing from his nose and onto his hands.

"Damnit, are you kidding me?" Horton muttered with the fresh taste of blood on his tongue.

He looked back to his brother who was now catching up to him. He could feel himself begin to cry.

"Brother!" Deforest called out.

"Go... go find me some brasys leaves to clean up my nose," Horton ordered his brother as he tried to keep his voice from wavering.

"Okay – I saw some over by the Earth Stone at one end of the clearing, I'll be right back," Deforest said before he ran off in search of a brasys plant.

Horton sat himself down against the base of a large tree while he waited for his brother to return. He couldn't believe how stupid he had been, coming all the way out here. Surely the gods would make him pay somehow.

A few minutes later Deforest returned with a fist full of brasys leaves. He stared as Horton wiped the blood off his face and shored up his gushing nose.

"What?" Horton said bluntly to Deforest with rolled leaves stuffed up each of his nostrils.

Deforest smirked as he tried to cover up his amusement

with his brother's appearance, of which the moonlight did little to improve. To his amazement, however, it was Horton who began to laugh at his less than flattering state.

"Now I know the gods are toying with me," Horton chortled as he wiped his eyes.

Deforest's smile quickly disappeared from his face. "Aren't you worried about what the gods would think of us being here?"

Horton sat further upright against the tree, sighed, and then looked up at his brother.

"You know what, I'm not," Horton resigned. "It's no secret that everyone in the village knows I'm going to be the sacrifice..."

Deforest attempted to intervene and tell him otherwise, but Horton ignored him and continued his rant.

"So what do I care? If I had never found it I'd be a dead man anyway. At least this way I already know where this damn Earth Stone is and maybe the gods will throw me the first break of my entire life."

It wasn't until Horton looked up at his brother again that he stopped talking. He could see his words were troubling Deforest, who had taken a few steps in the other direction and had his eyes fixed on the forest floor. Deforest then looked up at Horton with a half-smile on his face.

"For better or for worse, I'm actually glad we're out here together," Deforest suddenly said, to Horton's surprise. However, his demeanor quickly became sullen. "You're so concerned with your initiation, and with the way things are going, I'm worried we will never get to spend any time together ever again. We will never get to play boliball, catch spiderflies… be brothers. You know, just like we used to."

Horton opened his mouth to respond, but he had nothing to say. As much as he hated to admit it to himself, Deforest was right on all counts.

"I really didn't mean what I said earlier, but to be honest, you've been a completely different person lately," Deforest went on. "I've been really worried about you, but I didn't want to—"

Deforest cut himself off as he caught sight of Horton's wound gushing blood once more.

"Oh, your face," Deforest said, bringing attention to it. "I saw some more brasys leaves farther down the clearing by the Earth Stone. Wait here, I'll be back soon."

Horton nodded as he did his best to contain the blood flowing from his nose and face. After a few moments of fighting a losing battle, he carefully leaned his head back.

As he sat there with his head resting against the tree trunk, he felt his eyes getting heavy. He wasn't sure if it was exhaustion from everything that had happened that night or the sudden loss of blood, but ultimately it didn't matter.

Horton blinked his eyes open. The day's first light was thrown across the bright white pine-covered ground at his feet.

He looked around for a moment, trying to remember where he was. The sharp pain in his head quickly reminded him as he lifted himself up off the forest floor.

"Ugh. Uh, Deforest?"

Horton scanned the area as he rubbed his head. He couldn't see his brother anywhere.

"Deforest!"

He stood still for a short time, listening intently for a response, but it didn't come.

"Deforest!" Horton shouted once more.

"Where is that idiot?" he murmured.

He began to search frantically for any trace of his brother. His head throbbed and his eyes were foggy, but those were the least of his problems.

He ran back to the Earth Stone and scoured the perimeter of the clearing, all the while calling Deforest's name, but to no avail. He was not there.

"He must have gone home," Horton thought nervously to himself. "It's the only possibility. For help, I'm sure of it. But who can he trust to help and keep quiet about it? Why didn't he tell me, though? Maybe he didn't want to awaken me. Oh, gods help me."

The sun was quickly rising through the tree line. If he waited any longer he ran the risk of being seen reentering the village from the forest. Without any other options, Horton had no choice but to run all the way home and hope Deforest was there waiting for him.

As he raced through the long shadows of the early morning, he beckoned the remaining swathes of darkness to swallow him up and put him out of his misery.

Two

The Initiation

EVERY POSSIBLE SCENARIO ran through Horton's mind as he returned home.

"The gods are punishing me," he muttered between heavy breaths as he ran. "They took away Deforest. I was a fool to lead him to the Stone. Please gods, please let Deforest be at home. Punish me, not him."

Every step Horton took toward the village felt like one step closer to discovering what happened to Deforest, yet one step closer to the source of all his problems. The initiation seemed insignificant by comparison now, and despite how much he feared the terrible possibility that his brother was not at home, he ran as hard and as fast as he was able.

Growing increasingly exhausted both mentally and physically, he felt as if his legs were gaining weight underneath him with every stride. Although he tried to fight through it, eventually the humid morning air got the best of Horton, forcing him to break down into a walk as his lungs gasped for oxygen.

After a few minutes, Horton pulled his weary head up. Far in the distance between the tree line was the top of the Illac temple bell tower, reminding him of his ill-fated deed as it guided him back to Illac. Perhaps it was the exhaustion, but he couldn't help but gaze at it as he walked, as though begging it for mercy.

The remainder of the journey was a blur as Horton's mind became blank, too tired to think or focus any longer. He later vaguely recalled washing the blood off his face with water from a neighbor's well, but it wasn't until he found himself holding the door handle of his family's cottage that he realized he had made it home. The door creaked as he leaned his weight onto it to push it open.

Inside his mother was sitting on a chair next to a spent candle, her hand supporting her head against the armrest. It appeared she had been up all night waiting for her sons to return home. Her heavy eyes lit up as they caught sight of his face.

"Horton!" his mother said with an exhausted smile of relief. "Where have you been? I've been so worried!"

As his mother embraced him in a hug, he tried to peer around her, desperately hoping to see Deforest appear from his bedroom.

"Where's Deforest? Isn't he with you?" Horton's mother asked, gently pushing him away from her.

Horton's heart sank down to his knees. Everything he had feared had happened. His brother was gone.

"He isn't here?" Horton asked quietly.

"Didn't he catch up with you?" his mother pressed as her expression rapidly sank. "He ran right out through the front door after you – didn't you see him?"

Horton looked away from his mother's terrified face.

"No," he lied, unable to bear telling her the truth. "I never saw him."

"By the gods, Deforest!" Horton's mother shrieked. "We have to tell the elders that Deforest has disappeared!"

Horton watched his mother run out the front door and down the lane toward the temple. He wanted so badly to tell her the truth about what had happened, but it would surely tear her apart even greater.

He stood in the doorway for a moment, watching the hills to the east with a lost look on his face before slowly retiring to his bed out of exhaustion. As he lay there in silence he could hear men yelling in the distance as they searched for Deforest. He expected he would begin crying, but he never did. He had never felt so emotionless in his life.

Horton woke up some time later drenched in sweat. It had been hot lately – even more so than usual, but today was especially warm.

He pulled himself up from his bed and looked out the window. Judging by the sun's position it was midafternoon. He had been asleep for hours. Although he dreaded the likely bad news, he needed to know about Deforest one way or another.

Horton quietly made his way to the kitchen for water, all the while listening for any sign of his mother. The thought of possibly hearing her weep sickened him, but he knew it would be a sure sign his brother was gone.

As he passed his mother's room, he noticed the door was closed. Horton stood there for a moment as he considered opening it, but he couldn't. He didn't want to face his mother just yet.

Then, out of the corner of his eye, he noticed Deforest's door was also shut. This was unusual, as the only reason it would be closed is if his brother was sleeping in there.

"He's home!" Horton shouted as a rush of relief and happiness swept over him.

Without missing a beat he ran over to the door and swung it open with vigor, smiling ear to ear.

"Defor—!"

Horton stopped himself. His eyes carefully scanned the room back and forth, unwilling to accept what they saw. Nobody was there.

"They searched all day. They gave up on him about an hour ago."

Horton's mother had emerged from her room dressed in only a robe. She looked as though she had been crying.

"They say he's gone," she said as her glistening eyes pierced Horton's soul. "Eaten by a grizzly… or perhaps burned to ash beyond the protection of the Earth Stone. He couldn't have survived out there this long on his own."

Horton grabbed his mother and hugged her.

"This is all because of me – I'm so sorry."

His mother clutched him tighter.

"It's not your fault, Horton."

Horton shut his eyes tight. Perhaps he could escape

somewhere deep inside the recesses of his own mind.

No, it is my fault.

Horton spent the rest of the day moping around and staring blankly at the walls of his home. His conscious gnawed at him without reprieve as memories of the previous night whirled around incessantly in his head, despite his best efforts to block the ordeal out entirely. It wasn't that he didn't want to think about what happened, but rather that he was afraid to. He hated himself so much for what he had done. Nobody else knew it, but he was his own worst enemy.

Eventually Horton found the energy to go for a walk through the village. He figured the least he could do was repent at the village temple for what he had done. Perhaps the gods would take some sort of pity on him.

Along the way passing villagers paid their sympathies. He nodded to them in thanks, but paid little attention to their words. He didn't deserve or want their condolences.

Horton sat in the temple for what seemed like hours. At first he prayed to the gods for forgiveness, but after a while he just tuned himself out and gazed into nothingness, re-playing the previous day in his mind.

He remembered how content he had felt – even if for just a moment – when he and Deforest were out there by the Earth Stone. For a few minutes all his problems had washed away, and all that mattered was Deforest and him were being brothers once again.

"Hello, my child."

Horton jumped. He was so deep in thought that he hadn't noticed someone sit down next to him. He quickly relaxed, however, when he realized it was none other than Ulises, a high priest seemingly older than time itself. More importantly, though, he was a dear family friend and a great mentor. Horton kept it to himself, but he considered Ulises to be the closest thing to a father he had. In fact, he was the only man who had provided him with some training for the initiation – in secret mind you, since doing so is forbidden, especially for a priest.

Horton turned to face Ulises. He looked into his eyes for an instant then looked away.

"Hello, Ulises," Horton managed to muster up in a squeaky voice, before clearing his dry throat. He could sense Ulises probing him with his eyes, seeking the best way to comfort him.

"I am sincerely sorry for your loss, Horton," Ulises said after a brief pause. "Deforest was a good boy, full of spirit and a sense for adventure. I suppose that was his unfortunate undoing in the end."

"Maybe," Horton replied, turning to face Ulises again.

It was in that moment Horton decided to spill everything. He didn't care about the consequences; he just wanted to get all of it off his chest. He wanted Ulises to know that he had found the Earth Stone, that he was the one who had led Deforest to it, that he was the one that told Deforest to find brasys leaves on his own, that he was the reason the gods had taken his brother as punishment, that he…

"Every person is created by the gods for a reason, Horton," Ulises suddenly explained solemnly, interrupting

Horton's momentum toward coming clean. The priest articulated every word carefully as he spoke, as if each was being fed to him one by one by the gods themselves. "We live only to fulfill the destiny they have set before us. It may not be clear to you now – or perhaps ever – but Deforest did what he was meant to do, as you and I will too."

And then as quickly as he had arrived, Ulises stood up and began to leave.

"Blessings of the gods upon you, Horton." Ulises croaked as he walked away.

Horton sat there with mouth agape, watching the priest and his opportunity to let it all out head toward the door.

"Ulises?" Horton suddenly hollered, to which the priest stopped in his tracks and looked back with a half-glance.

And there he was, waiting for Horton to tell him the truth. Still, the young Illac simply stared at him, looking for the right words that never seemed to exist to begin with.

"May they be with you too," Horton finally called back as he covertly winced with disgust at himself.

Ulises nodded, smiled, and continued on his way.

Horton spent much of the next three days training alone for the initiation. He hadn't planned on going overboard preparing – in fact he had been rather lax about the whole ordeal, especially since he already knew the whereabouts of the Earth Stone, but he felt compelled to do so anyway. At first it was simply to take his mind off Deforest, but when he saw the way his mother looked at him over the last few days, he couldn't bear the thought of somehow failing the initiation and leaving her alone in the world.

Instead, he intended to be the first to return to the village with a stone idol and make his mother proud, something that would surely ease her heartache.

When the evening of the initiation finally came around, his mother and he joined the rest of the village at the temple for the pre-initiation festivities. The tension in the air was as intense as the sun's rays, and as Horton looked around at the other initiates and their families, he attempted to reinforce his flagging confidence by wondering which unfortunate Three Yearling would wind up being the sacrifice in his place. He couldn't help but notice other villagers staring at him and quickly glancing away when he made eye contact, but this was expected. Everyone expected him to be the one to fail, and he took some satisfaction in knowing they would be wrong.

"Horton," his mother said quietly, looking up from the plate of food she had spent more time prodding than actually eating, "I want you to know that whatever happens today, I love you and I am proud of you."

Horton took a deep breath and mustered together a confident smile. He could see his mother's eyes were beginning to tear up.

"Your brother was proud of you too," she added.

"I'll be fine, mother," Horton assured her, still putting on his bravest face. "I promise I'll be back."

His mother wiped the tears from her eyes. "I know you will."

Dong!

Heads shot upward in attention as the ring of the temple's bell signaled the initiates to gather at its altar. Horton could feel himself shaking slightly as he stood up from his seat. He quickly hugged his mother goodbye and made his way alongside the rest of the initiates. Standing at the podium in the middle of the altar was High Priest Eli, who motioned to everyone except the Three Yearlings to take a seat.

"Good evening, fellow Illacs," Eli began his speech "Today is a day in which we remember a time long since passed – a time when man disavowed its creators and indulged itself in sin in lieu of prayer. In retaliation, the gods razed the fertile ground and boiled the teeming oceans, sentencing mankind to death.

"However, while the gods plunged the forsaken into the darkest depths of existence, those few who remained faithful were blessed with a lifeline – the Earth Stone. In keeping with the ways of our ancestors and in gratitude of the gods' infinite generosity, we provide our creators with a sacrifice every three years. A single male child on the cusp of adulthood whose place on this earth is not to pass on strength to future generations, but give up his feeble life to the gods so that others may prosper."

Horton gritted his teeth as he saw villagers again glance his way out of the corner of their eyes.

"The rules for our young men are simple," Eli continued. "Find the Earth Stone, retrieve a clay statue from the site and return it to the market circle. There is a statue for every Three Yearling bar one, and that one is compelled to sacrifice himself to the gods by traversing the desolate wastes beyond the protection of our vaunted Stone."

The high priest paused for a moment to take a deep

breath, and as he did he looked into the eyes of each Three-Yearling, knowing the finality of the task he was about to bestow among them.

"And thus we send the sons of Illac away on their journey to the Earth Stone. May the gods guide your souls."

Dong! Dong! Dong!

It began. Some of the initiates instantly sprinted away erratically while others simply stood still and looked at each other, hoping to pick up on what direction seemed the most popular. In reality, none of the initiates except Horton knew where the Earth Stone was located. For everyone else it was completely up to chance.

After watching his fellow initiates for a brief time, Horton decided his best course of action would be to grab his satchel, casually jog out of the village and head toward the eastern hills and subsequently the Earth Stone while trying to not draw the attention of other Three Yearlings. Not surprisingly, when he did depart none of the initiates seemed to take any notice of what he was doing. After all, he was the favorite to be the sacrificed.

Once at the edge of the woods that surrounded the village, Horton sped up into a manageable running speed. He knew the landmarks he needed to find along the way and didn't want to accidentally miss any of them by moving too fast.

As he ran through endless trees, Horton's mind wandered back to when he made the same journey just a few days before. He had been so preoccupied with the initiation, he hadn't thought at all about his brother. Now that he had ample time to think, he began to replay the last week in his mind over and over.

He remembered how ashamed he had been of his behavior when he and his brother knocked his mother's harvest on the floor when they fought, how like a fool he had run blindly into the woods chasing distant hills he knew he could never reach, and how he had accidentally wandered into the location of the forbidden Earth Stone, all the while inadvertently dragging his younger brother to his untimely demise.

Yet, in spite of the heartache, it was the Earth Stone itself that brought back the strongest, most vivid memories. He could still feel the brisk, cool air emanating from it, its unnatural metallic composition, its warm smoothness upon his fingertips, the fox that had jumped out of the bushes and into the burrow beneath the Earth Stone, frightening him, the—

Horton suddenly stopped dead in place. Something wasn't right.

"A burrow? Under the Earth Stone?" he thought as he recalled the elders' teachings. "The Earth Stone is supposed to be an infinite pyramid that holds up the world; how can anything burrow beneath it?"

Horton's mind spun. Surely his memories deceived him.

"No, it couldn't be," he muttered. "But what if...."

Horton's eyes grew wide. A split-second later, he broke into an all-out sprint. He knew it was a long shot, but there was still hope for Deforest. He imagined his brother falling into the burrow and getting trapped. Perhaps he had broken his leg or couldn't climb back out.

After some time of retracing the path he had taken to the

Earth Stone a few days earlier, Horton could just barely make out its unmistakable shape between the sporadic gaps in the dense tree line.

As he cautiously approached the pyramid's clearing, Horton surveyed the area for fellow initiates. He kneeled down at the clearing's edge and ducked between two ferns. He watched and listened attentively, but there was only him and the sound of trees swaying in the breeze. As far as he could tell he was alone.

Laid out around the base of the Earth Stone was a single row of clay statues. There were no missing figures in the row, indicating that he was the first of the Three Yearlings to reach the Stone. He picked one up without a second thought and tossed it into his satchel, before making his way to where he thought he had previously seen the fox burrow.

It wasn't there. Horton ran along all four sides of the Earth Stone, painstakingly looking for a burrow, but there was no sign of one. He ran back to the initial spot he thought he had seen it just to be sure, but still nothing. Not only that, but the dirt was perfectly flat with no sign of any animal having dug into it. Horton slammed his fist against the side of the pyramid in frustration.

Scratch. Scratch. Scratch.

Horton took a step back. He could hear something rustling in the dirt below his feet.

Scratch. Scratch. Scratch.

Horton jumped back as a paw suddenly emerged through the hard dirt beneath him, before retracting back into the dark hole it had clawed out. A second later a nose appeared, followed by the head of a small fox. Stunned to see someone waiting for it, the fox stared at Horton for a moment before retreating back into the burrow.

It was then that Horton realized someone must have recently covered up the burrow, trapping the foxes while they were still inside.

Horton dropped to his knees and began to dig in order to widen the hole. The top foot or so of dirt was hard and dry, making it difficult to break through with bare hands, but fortunately the fox had already scraped away the bulk of it. To Horton's relief the soil just below the top layer was soft and slightly damp, making it easy to shovel aside with his hands.

Now that the hole was just big enough for his small frame to squeeze through, he crawled inside headfirst, about half way in. He stared deeply into the dark tunnel below him, hoping his eyes might catch a glimpse of something, but it was much too dark.

"Deforest!" Horton called out into the black.

He remained there for a moment listening, half submerged in a fox burrow leading beneath his people's sacred and forbidden pyramid.

No response.

Horton sighed. He started to pull himself back out, figuring at the very least he should still have time to be the first back to Illac with an idol, but then he saw a hint of something. Not a thing exactly, but at the right angle he could just barely make out the slightest sign of light, deep down in the tunnel. Horton rubbed his eyes, thinking he was seeing things, but upon second inspection it was still there – something beneath the pyramid. He wriggled himself lower into the burrow to give himself an even better vantage point.

All of a sudden the dirt beneath him gave way. With no time to react, he found himself tumbling down the hole and deeper into the unknown darkness for what seemed like an eternity.

Oof!

Horton finally landed – smacking the back of his head. As he pulled himself upright, he could feel that the ground was made up of the same hard metallic material as the outside of the pyramid. Turning around, he saw that the faint light was coming from the end of the passageway that lay before him. Horton peered back up to where he had tumbled from, but could see nothing. The entrance was surely caved in now. He stood up, rubbed the back of his head for a moment, and then looked down the hallway, his only option.

"Deforest, I hope you're in here," he prayed to himself.

Horton stepped carefully with his arms stretched out into the darkness around him as he walked towards the dim light's mysterious source somewhere at the end of the corridor. It was very cold. Horton opened his mouth in an effort to call out to his brother, but instead found himself gasping as a gust of icy air suddenly filled his lungs. He squeezed his hands then opened them. His fingers were beginning to numb.

"There's no way Deforest could have survived very long without proper clothing down here," he thought.

As he closed in on the end of the hallway, he discovered it broke off into two openings: one to the left and one to the right. The faint light originated from the opening on the right, partially revealing a large, apparently empty room that contained a raised platform. A solitary stone pedestal stood at the platform's center, with what looked like differently colored lights upon it. Before he entered the room, Horton pivoted around to look into the other doorway, but he couldn't see anything in the darkness. He gazed at it for a moment, hoping his eyes would adjust, but to no luck.

Horton turned back to the room with the pedestal and slowly entered. As he did, he realized he had no idea how big the room actually was. The pedestal's smattering of dim colored light just barely managed to splash beyond the doorway he just passed through, but was not nearly bright enough to reach any other surrounding wall or ceiling. Horton pulled his hood up over the back of his neck as he cautiously ventured deeper into the room, his eyes panning back and forth across the room impetuously, unable to shake the feeling that someone – or something – was watching him from the darkness. Clutching his satchel like a vice with his hands, he desperately wished he was somewhere – anywhere – else. At this point, to his dismay, he didn't have much choice.

Now within arm's reach of the pedestal, Horton averted his eyes from the darkness and looked toward the lights before him. There were four differently colored lights in a horizontal row, each lighting up a single square button. From left to right there was a green light, a blue light, a red light and a yellow light. Above each button were symbols – clearly a script of some type – but Horton had never seen anything like it before.

He looked up and gazed around once more into the semi-darkness and considered his options. He had no idea what the buttons did or if it was even safe to push them, so he stood there a moment, wondering whether it was worth exploring the darkness around him before doing anything he would regret.

Horton already knew the answer. He had no doubts that he ought to explore the room first, but the feeling of eyes watching him from afar meant straying from the light was not a possibility he could entertain, even if it was probably all in his imagination. Besides, one of the buttons might turn on more lights.

He looked back down at the buttons. He figured he would hit the green one first – it was his favorite color after all.

Ba-beep! Beep!

Horton looked around the room. His skin tingled a little bit, but as far as he could tell nothing happened. It must be broken, he guessed, so he moved on to the next one. Blue.

Ba-beep! Boop!

This time some light flooded in from up in one corner of the room. Horton could see what looked like sunlight, shining through a small window high up near the ceiling. He could make out more of the room now, but it still wasn't nearly bright enough. Horton hit the red light.

Ba-beep! Blap!

The sunlight coming through the window disappeared.

"This isn't right, why is it — Argh!"

Acrid air filled Horton's lungs. Now in a terrible coughing fit, he tried desperately to catch his breath, but the more he tried to breathe the more difficult it became. To make matters worse, the searing gasses that filled the room burned his eyes, forcing them shut. Disoriented, Horton staggered and tumbled down onto the floor below. Desperate to recoup himself, Horton forced his eyes open and frantically spun around in search of the lights. He saw the colored lights on the pedestal again now, but they were a few paces away.

Sensing himself on the verge of passing out, Horton propelled his body toward the lights, practically fell into them, and smacked the button closest to him – yellow.

THREE

Zeptus

"COME ON KID, you can't sleep here. This area is off limits to civilians."

Horton blinked his eyes open to find a man standing over him with his hands at his hips and dressed in the most unusual clothes he had ever seen.

"Let's go! Get up! This is your final warning, or there's going to be trouble."

Horton groaned as he pulled himself up off the ground. His head was still foggy and pounded in pain. After rubbing his eyes, Horton looked around at his surroundings. As far as he could tell he was still inside the pyramid, but what he'd thought it looked like was completely different from what he was seeing now. For one thing the large, dark room was completely lit up and flowers and statues lined its walls. Looking behind him, Horton found he had passed out against what looked like the pedestal – but there were no buttons or lights on it. In fact, it looked as though the top portion of it had been completely sheared off.

"Wha... what happened?" Horton grumbled, still grimacing from the sharp pain in his head.

The man glared at Horton as if he had asked what color the sky was.

"You damn kids are always finding new ways to push my buttons, aren't you? And is that what your generation are wearing nowadays? Forget it – I'd rather not know. Come on, you're coming with me."

The man grabbed Horton by the arm and yanked him toward an open doorway leading outside that had previously been submerged in darkness. Bright sunlight spilled from beyond it, and as they stepped through the door, Horton gasped at the sight before him.

The two emerged onto a ledge roughly half way up the pyramid. About forty meters below them sat a village of larger scale than Horton could have ever imagined possible, and it appeared to wrap all the way around the pyramid. Bordering the massive village in the distance ran a giant wall – even taller than the high trees in the forest that surrounded Illac. Horton shielded his eyes from the sun with his hand as he squinted to see what lay beyond the village, but a dreary haze of dust distorted everything that far out. He had often imagined what the wastelands looked like, and what he saw now outside those walls wasn't much dissimilar.

"Where are we?" Horton asked the man.

"We're in Zeptus City, you blithering idiot," the man

scowled back. "Watch your step now, boy. These stairs are steep and I don't want to end up having to carry you back."

Once at the base of the stairway, Horton stepped onto a road paved with stone. As he followed the man through the city's bustling streets, he quickly realized this place was nothing like Illac. Around him buzzed wheeled carts full of men, but unlike in Illac, these were not pulled by oxen. As far as Horton could tell, they seemed to magically pull themselves without the need of animals whatsoever. Furthermore, the people wore tight-fitting clothes of various colors and patterns, which was very unusual to Horton because he had only seen people wear uniformly loose-fitting white robes and tunics his entire life.

"Alright, here we are," the man announced, having brought him to a building not far down the road from the stairway that led up to the pyramid's entrance. "You'll be staying in a cell here until I figure out what to do with you."

The man opened the door to the building and pulled Horton inside. The two walked along a short hallway towards the back of the building to four jail cells. All of them were empty except one, which contained a young man sitting in a chair. He sat with his legs crossed and head rested back against the wall with his eyes on the ceiling. As he walked in, Horton noticed the man's eyes briefly glance down from their empty gaze before reverting back to their original position.

"You'll be in here," the man said as he led Horton inside a cell. "I'll be back to—"

"Constable Keen!"

A younger man dressed in similar dark blue clothes

came running down the hallway after the man who had arrested Horton.

"Constable, there's been another Vwari attack," the man gasped, still trying to catch his breath. "Aid has been requested at the northwestern gate."

"Another one already? Don't those things ever let up?" Constable Keen sighed as he locked Horton's cell. "Alright then, let's not waste time."

The men ran off and out of sight at a fevered pace. As Horton surveyed the alien building he had been brought to, he suddenly felt a long, long way from home. Worse yet there was still no sign of Deforest.

Horton paced his cell, trying to make sense of things. He pinched himself hard to make sure this wasn't all just some bizarre dream. It wasn't. He then noticed that the young man sitting in the cell next to him was watching his every move. Having been caught staring, the man sat up straight in his chair and put his hands on his knees.

"Hello there, I don't believe we've met," the man said, smiling. "My name is Penriding Blacksmith."

"Hi…" Horton quietly responded. His mother had always told him to keep away from the men who had been jailed in Illac, usually because they were belligerently drunk. Penriding seemed sober, however.

"Why are you in here?" Horton asked. "Are you drunk?"

Penriding laughed. "I wish I was. It would certainly make this more bearable."

Surprised Horton didn't laugh along with him, Penriding quickly cleared his throat and answered the initial question.

"Well kid, you know all about the Vwari attacks, right?"

Horton opened his mouth to tell him otherwise, but couldn't get a word out before Penriding continued. "You see, I think it's because they're after something, right here in the pyramid – surely of great power and importance.

"Unfortunately these *idiots*—" Penriding took extra care to ensure the guards could hear him, "are too stupid to realize it. So I decided I'd find out myself what it is in the pyramid the Vwari are after, and these buffoons locked me up."

"Oh," Horton replied, still trying to make heads or tails of the whole situation. "So did you find anything?"

"No," Penriding sighed deeply. "A couple of guards grabbed me right after I snuck through a door over by the grand chamber. There's something in there the High Council doesn't want us to find out about, I know it."

"Right," Horton responded with a nod, but in truth he wasn't paying much attention to what Penriding was saying. He was more concerned with how unusual this place was, and what kind of name is Penriding, anyway?

"What kind of name is Penriding, anyway?" Horton blurted. "And what's wrong with the way you talk?"

"Speak for yourself," Penriding laughed. "I don't think I've ever heard an outsider with an accent like yours before. As for Penriding, it was my grandfather's middle name – or so my father tells me – I never got a chance to meet the guy. As a matter of fact, my father says if it wasn't for him there would be no merchant union here in Zeptus. I'll have you know, the Blacksmith name happens to hold quite a lot of weight in this city."

"Zeptus…" Horton thought out loud. "I heard the man who brought me here say that. What is Zeptus?"

Penriding looked at Horton with wide eyes, as if he'd just said something incredibly stupid.

"What?" Penriding scoffed. "Kid, what is wrong with you? We're in Zeptus. Zeptus City? Everyone, even outsiders, know Zeptus City. Where exactly are you from?"

Before Horton could answer, heavy footsteps echoed down the hallway toward his and Penriding's cell. It was a guard accompanied by a tall, burly man wearing a thick black coat and a large, droopy hat that hid much of his head. The enormous man caught sight of Horton as he approached, causing him to pause for a split second before continuing his brisk pace. Horton shuddered as the man's eyes seemed to glow as they watched him intently.

"Mister Blacksmith," the guard announced in a somewhat malignant tone, "your father is here to retrieve you."

Horton watched as the guard unlocked Penriding's cell and opened the door. Penriding slowly stood up and walked out, noticeably avoiding eye contact with the man who Horton could only presume was his father.

"You are a fool and an embarrassment," the man's thunderous voice shot at Penriding. "Next time I will leave you here to rot."

Penriding's head swooned as low at it could go.

"Yes, father," he replied with trepidation.

Horton peered through the cell bars as the three of them walked away down the hallway. Then to his surprise, Penriding stopped for a moment to glance back at Horton.

"Guard, what will become of this boy?" he asked quickly so as to not hinder his father too greatly.

"I don't know, sir," the guard responded.

"Hurry up, Penriding!" his father's booming voice again rang through the corridor as he fired one last rigid glare back at Horton. Penriding winced for a second before spinning around to catch up to his father.

A moment later they were gone, leaving Horton alone. He turned around to survey his temporary home once more. In one corner was a sleeping mat on the floor with a single pillow for company. It didn't look very comfortable, but his body had no problem reminding him how tired he was. Reluctantly he lay down on it, but to his annoyance he couldn't fall sleep.

Thoughts of Illac, his mother, and Deforest filled his mind. He would have given anything to be back at home in his own bed.

"Ahem."

Horton rubbed his heavy eyes. He must have just nodded off. Standing in the doorway of his cell was the constable.

"Well, mister... uh – hmm...."

He paused as he perused the pages of parchment in his hands.

"Guard!" he abruptly shouted.

Moments later a guard came scampering down the hallway, clutching his helmet onto his head as he ran.

"Y-Yes, sir?" the guard's voice cracked.

The constable closed his eyes and clenched the parchment in his hand tightly. He was clearly reaching wick's end.

"Where is this young man's information? Have you fools done nothing while I was gone?"

"There was a... you see—" the guard rambled as he

struggled to find an excuse, but the constable was having none of it.

"Shut up you dimwit! Get his information before I throw you in a cell of your own. Actually, get lost – I'll do the damn paperwork myself."

The guard looked flustered for a few seconds, apparently unsure of what to do with himself before his orders eventually hit home, and he bumbled off from where he came. As he went his helmet flew off his head, causing a loud clanging noise that echoed through the hallway. Horton could see the constable was clearly not amused, as he fiercely yanked a pen out of his pocket and returned his eyes to the parchment.

"What's your name, boy?"

"Horton."

The constable peered up at Horton.

"Horton what?"

"Horton. H-O-R-T—"

"I don't want the damn spelling you idiot, what's your surname?"

Horton thought for a moment. He assumed this surname the constable referred to was the second part of a name, like Blacksmith. Illacs, however, do not have surnames, but Horton had a pretty good feeling that excuse wouldn't sit too well with the constable. Thinking on the spot, Horton used the first name that came to mind.

"Horton Deforest. My name is Horton Deforest," he said matter-of-factly.

The constable shook his head and returned his eyes to the parchment as he scribbled something onto it.

"Do you know what the problem is with your generation, Mister Horton Deforest? You all lack discipline. Agreed?"

"Uh, I suppose so," Horton replied, not really sure what point the constable was making.

"You suppose? Either agree or don't. There's no guesswork here, boy."

Horton stared at the constable a moment. In a weird way he reminded him of his father.

"Agreed," he concurred to appease the agitated constable.

"Okay, Horton," he began, not looking up from his papers. "What were you doing asleep in the grand chamber of the Rissa?"

Horton figured the Rissa was the name of the Zeptan pyramid.

"I was looking for someone. I must have hit my head and passed out."

"You say you were looking for someone? Who?"

Excitement overcame Horton as he realized the constable could be the answer to finding Deforest.

"My brother! I think he's here in Zeptus somewhere, his name is…" Horton gulped. He hadn't thought this through too well. "My brother's name is Deforest."

As quickly as it had come, Horton's excitement turned into dismay. The look on the constable's face told him everything he needed to know. That was the last straw.

"Oh, so your brother's name is Deforest Deforest?" the constable's face quickly turned bright red. "Okay, real funny. Everything's a joke to you kids, isn't it? The Vwari are taking the lives of brave Zeptans every day and kids like you are perfectly happy to waste my time. I don't have the patience to deal with this any longer."

And with that the constable balled up the parchment, threw it across the room and stormed off down the hallway in a huff. A few minutes later the clumsy guard returned to free Horton.

As the guard led Horton through the building, he noticed through the windows that it was nighttime outside. He wondered how long he had been in that cell – it was surely longer than he'd thought if it was already dark out. He'd have to find somewhere to stay for the night, but he had no leads and no friends.

Or perhaps he did.

"Excuse me, sir?" Horton asked the guard as he was led out of the jailhouse. "That man, Penriding Blacksmith, where about does he live?"

"Surely you know of Blacksmith manor?" the guard answered, visibly excited by the notion that he might actually know something that someone else didn't. "It's the biggest and tallest building in the city – apart from the Rissa, of course."

It was at that moment Horton stepped out into the Zeptus City night for the first time. His eyes could barely take it all in – it was the most incredible sight he had ever experienced.

Giant spheres of light were strung from the pyramid's peak and all the way out to the city's outer walls, illuminating Zeptus in a golden glow. Every building shone brightly from the inside too, but not by candlelight like in Illac; the light here was far too powerful. Still, the most breathtaking and impressive of all was the pyramid itself, which reflected the light like a massive beacon against the night sky. It seemed to emanate its energy and awesome influence down onto the surrounding city at its feet.

"It's there, over to the south."

The guard pointed toward a building like none other in the city. It stood at least three times taller than everything else around it, and upon its roof stood a great spire that looked as though it scraped the stars in the night sky above.

Horton flinched as the door suddenly slammed behind him. He was on his own in the city now – in a manner of speaking. Although it was nighttime, the streets were no less bustling than they were in broad daylight.

Standing on the tips of his toes, Horton hoped to catch a glimpse of what lay farther down the road before him. He stretched his head up as high as he could but it was no use. The manor's spire would have to guide him toward it.

As he made his way in search of Penriding, Horton noticed a lot of people staring at him as he walked past. He imagined it was probably because of his unusual garb, and so he tried not to think too much of it. Still, he couldn't help but be reminded of Illac – the way the villagers would stare at him in the days leading up to the initiation.

Horton picked up his pace a little as he began to notice the eyes of passer-bys glowering at him more and more. He could see them whispering amongst themselves as they gazed at him untrustingly, causing him to cower slightly as he felt the pressure around him intensify. Then, unable to withstand it any longer, he broke out into a sprint toward the spire.

Zeptans shouted and cursed as he shoved his way through the dense crowds, but he didn't care. He couldn't stop now. He had to reach the only Zeptan he remotely knew and who might be willing to help him.

When Horton eventually entered the area of the city that surrounded the manor, he immediately noticed the crowds of people had radically thinned out and were replaced by more men in the blue clothes he had seen at the jail. He also realized that meeting up with Penriding was not going to be as simple as he had originally thought. The exterior of the enormous Blacksmith home was protected by men outfitted in large and incredible black metallic suits, armor of some kind, with herculean swords that stood taller than Horton himself. Covering their heads were thick helmets that masked their identities. Compared to the ordinary soldiers in blue he had seen patrolling the city streets, these things were monsters.

Regardless, he didn't have much in the way of options. Horton scrounged together whatever courage he still had and made his way toward the manor's front gate.

"Halt, outsider! Your kind is not welcome here!" one of the guards yelled out at Horton from beyond the gate, prompting an armored gargantuan to heave its hefty sword off its back and point it at Horton, causing the young Illac to leap backward, eyes wide with terror.

"I'm sorry, I didn't know," Horton called out uneasily, unsure as to who exactly he was talking to. "A friend of mine is inside the manor, I need to see him. His name is Penriding Blacksmith."

One of the other soldiers appeared from behind the gate

to see what was going on. He saw the massive swordsman looking down on Horton and quickly intervened.

"Look boy, due to recent Vwari attacks all non-Zeptan residents are not permitted on the premises," he explained. "Even outsiders like you should know that. Remove yourself from the area or else we will."

Horton briefly considered pressing the man further, but wisely thought better of it. There was no way of getting into the building; he would have to figure something else out.

Suddenly shouts filled the air from somewhere close by. By the time Horton turned around to see what was going on it was already too late. The last thing he remembered of the incident was a scorching burst of pressure against his face.

"What are the chances? That's one lucky kid."

"We'll see. He's not completely out of the woods yet."

"You said you know him?"

Horton opened his eyes. He was lying in a bed somewhere, but he couldn't see. Something was covering his face.

"Yeah, we've met once before."

He knew he recognized that voice. It was Penriding.

Horton tried to talk, but his voice was muffled.

"Oh! Hey kid, you're awake! Doc, you think we can get some of these bandages off?"

"I suppose so. It's been a few days now, the ointment should have done its job."

Horton could feel someone removing the bandages from around his head and face, which stung when touched.

"There we are," the doctor said. "It doesn't look too bad, actually. How do you feel, young man?"

"My face hurts. What happened?" Horton replied softly. He felt weak.

"I would suspect so!" the doctor replied, ignoring Horton's question. "It's truly a miracle from Rissa that you survived a fire bomb attack from so close."

"Without a doubt. You were injured when the manor was attacked," Penriding added.

Horton turned his head to face Penriding.

"I need your help," Horton told him softly.

"And you'll get it my boy," the doctor interrupted, "but for now you need rest. Please leave him be, Master Penriding."

Penriding nodded, smiled at Horton and walked out with the doctor.

Horton didn't get to see Penriding over the next two days as he continued to recover, and although the doctor was friendly and the food was great, he was no closer to finding his brother. He did find out, however, that he was in fact inside the Blacksmith manor, having been carried inside for emergency medical attention following some sort of attack on the building. Annoyingly though, every time he pressed the doctor for more details about the attackers or the manor, he discovered his caretaker would hastily devise an excuse to change the subject.

After two more days passed without any sign of Penriding, Horton asked the doctor if he could see him. To Horton's surprise, the doctor seemed a bit taken aback by the request.

"Why on earth would you want to see the young master?" the doctor inquired.

Horton thought for a moment before deciding a half-truth might be a safer response considering the doctor's reaction.

"I'd like to thank him for putting me up in his residence."

The doctor stared blankly into space for a few seconds, then turned and began to make his way out the door. As he opened it he turned back to Horton.

"That is hardly necessary. I think we'll have you up and walking tomorrow, yes?"

Before Horton could respond, he was out the door. He wasn't sure why, but there was no doubt in his mind that something was up.

That evening as he ate his supper in bed, Horton found a note folded up beneath his teacup. He quickly opened it, all the while hoping with all his might it was word from Penriding. It was.

See me. Midnight. 11th floor. West wing. Don't be seen.

—PB

Horton's heart raced as he looked up from the note in his hands to the clock on the wall on the other side of the room. It read seven o'clock. He was five hours away from finally getting some answers.

It was five minutes to midnight when Horton made his

move. His room hadn't been visited for a few hours now, and the passing voices in the hallways outside seemed to have ceased as well. He hopped out of bed and dropped down onto the cold wooden floor. His knees buckled slightly when he put his weight onto them, but he caught his balance against the side of the bed. It had been some days since he had walked and his strength was sapped, but Horton straightened himself out, took a deep breath, and began to make his way to the door one step at a time.

Creak. Horton stopped in his tracks.

"Stupid floor," he groaned under his breath.

Now within arm's reach of the door, Horton grasped the handle and turned it as carefully and noiselessly as possible. He gave it a gentle tug to open it slowly, but worryingly it didn't move at all. It was an old wooden door – probably slightly warped over time – so he had to give it a bit more muscle. He pulled at the handle again, harder this time, but to his despair the door still refused to budge.

Horton sighed as his heart began to pound in his chest. One way or another, this door had to open. Horton put one hand on the wall next to the door to give himself some leverage and then pulled the door handle as hard as he could.

Whoosh. The door flew open, and as soon as it had, Horton wished it hadn't.

A guard standing right outside the door turned around and looked at Horton, who yelped from shock at the sight of someone. Without hesitation the guard rushed at Horton, grabbed him and covered his mouth.

"Shush!" the guard whispered. "It's okay, it's okay. Quick, go before anyone sees you."

Horton stared at the guard for a moment in confusion. Not just because there was a guard outside his door trying to help him, but also because this particular guard was a woman. He had never heard of a woman on guard duty before.

"I didn't see anything," the guard said with a wink.

Horton glanced back through the doorway toward the clock inside his room. It was two minutes to midnight and he had barely even left his room, let alone figured out which way was west.

"I don't suppose you know where—" he started to ask the guard, but she answered the question before he could finish.

"You're going to be late. Make a left at the end of the hall to reach the stairway," she quietly instructed.

Without time to question her further, he nodded to the guard and went on his way. He turned left and began his journey down the corridor.

The Illac stealthily made his way to the staircase and up to the 11th floor. He didn't run into anyone along the way, though he could hear people talking behind the closed doors he passed. While he quietly climbed the staircase he tried to figure out which direction was west, but he had no clue. Fortunately for Horton, as he found out upon reaching the 11th floor, it didn't matter. Penriding was already waiting for him at the floor's landing.

"There you are. You're late," Penriding said with arms crossed. "I was worried you weren't going to make it. Come on, follow me."

Penriding led Horton down a somber, unlit hallway in what appeared to be a remote and unused wing of the manor.

"In here," the Zeptan directed, opening a grimy old wooden door.

Inside was an old and derelict room, dimly illuminated by the flickering light of a solidary candle sat upon a dusty round table. A piece of folded parchment lay at the table's center, which Penriding walked over to and picked up.

"No problems with Linden then, I presume?" Penriding asked.

"Uh, who?" Horton responded as he surveyed the rest of the largely empty room.

"The leftenant, outside your room," Penriding said with a smirk. "She's an old friend of mine, figured you might need directions."

"Yeah, thanks…. You wanted to see me?" Horton asked, getting to the point.

"Yes," Penriding affirmed as he circled around Horton, examining him. "I've done a little bit of research. Those clothes you're wearing, they're not from any outsider tribes anyone around here has ever seen. In fact, the closest thing to those clothes I've found would be—"

Penriding paused mid-sentence. "Where did you say you were from again?"

"I'm not from anywhere around here as far as I can tell," Horton answered truthfully. "I arrived here through the pyramid – the Earth Stone – somehow, from Illac, my home – or at least it was my home…. I can't go back now."

"Through the pyramid?" Penriding's eyes darted back

and forth for a few seconds before his face lit up with excitement. "I knew it! I KNEW IT!"

As Penriding walked sprightly around the room, laughing none too quietly, Horton couldn't help but wonder if whatever emphasis on secrecy his host previously maintained was ever necessary.

"This is incredible," the Zeptan said, still elated.

"Listen, I'm trying to find my brother," Horton interrupted over Penriding's jubilation. "His name is Deforest. He may have arrived here through the pyramid too. Is there any way you can help me?"

Penriding stopped his rapid pacing. Horton could see the gears were turning in Penriding's head.

"You said you're from Illac?" Penriding finally noted. "Interesting. You're sure it was Illac and not somewhere else?"

Horton nodded, despite being unsure as to why where he was from was relevant.

"Yes. Yes, he may be here in Zeptus City," Penriding said assuredly. "If he's here I can find him. Definitely."

"Great!" Horton exclaimed. "He'd have been dressed like me. I suppose he looks like me a bit as well, except shorter, and we have the same accent, of course. He's only twelve years old."

"Hmm," Penriding said, his hand rubbing his chin. "Okay. You get back to your room. I'll talk to some contacts. If your brother is in Zeptus City, I'll find him."

"Thank you, Penriding," Horton said with gratitude.

The two headed back down the dark hallway toward the staircase.

"Your room is on the fourth floor, do you remember how to get back to it?" Penriding whispered to Horton once they reached the hallway landing.

"I do, thanks," Horton smiled as he reached out to shake Penriding's hand.

"You got it, kid," Penriding replied, grasping onto Horton's outreached hand. "By the way, I don't think I ever caught your name."

"It's Horton. Just Horton."

Not much transpired in the five days following Horton and Penriding's secret meeting. He hadn't heard from his new friend since, but was confident that Penriding would hold true to his word and help find Deforest.

Horton was recovering nicely from his burn injuries in the meantime, and the doctor generously provided him with Zeptan clothing and a special headscarf that would protect his head and face from the sun while they continued to heal.

Furthermore, he had been given free roam to certain parts of the manor, including its library, which Horton put to great use. He pleasantly discovered that Zeptans shared the same alphabet as Illacs, so besides some minor differences in dialect, he had little trouble studying Zeptan literature. While Penriding led the on-ground search for Deforest, Horton spent many hours each day reading about the city's history and the surrounding region, trying to figure out where his brother might have gone. Apparently countless hundreds of years ago Zeptus City's pyramid, which they refer to as the Rissa, had literally been a beacon for nomadic tribes clinging to life by the skin of their teeth as they passed through the great desert. Over time a city was erected in its shadow, and the Zeptan people lived in relative harmony ever since with the Rissa as their source of life and energy.

This made Horton think back to the pyramid near Illac, the Earth Stone, and how it gave the Illac people life, too. It did not, however, provide them with power and the same amenities the Zeptan people enjoyed. Perhaps the Earth Stone was broken, or possibly too far underground. He couldn't help but wonder what other mysteries the pyramids may be hiding.

He scoured through book after book looking for more answers, but there were none. Information about the Rissa itself was hard to come by in its own right, and what little there was revealed nothing about where it came from or who built it. He found this unusual considering the Rissa was the life-blood of Zeptus, but much like the Earth Stone, the Rissa was a sacred religious site to the Zeptan people and was for the most part off-limits to the public.

One morning while Horton was entrenched in a book about the edible delicacies of the outside tribes, Penriding stormed into the library.

"There you are! Come quickly, I have something to show you," Penriding said, grabbing the book from out of his grasp and tossing it onto a nearby chair. "Walk with me."

Horton followed Penriding out of the library and – to his surprise – straight through the front door of the manor. It was the first time he had been outside since the attack on the manor had injured him, and it felt good to breathe in fresh air once again. He didn't feel as out of place walking through the streets this time either, as he wore Zeptan clothing and the protective headscarf he was under doctor's orders to wear hid much of his face.

"He's not here," Penriding suddenly announced as Horton followed him through a busy street intersection.

"I'm sorry?" Horton replied, unsure to what Penriding referred.

The Zeptan stopped in the middle of the street and turned around to face Horton.

"Your brother," he glumly clarified. "I checked with all of my sources."

Horton swallowed hard and gazed blankly out beyond Penriding.

"So that's it then," he muttered.

"Not necessarily," Penriding said with a wry smile. "I think I know where we might find him."

Before Horton could question further, Penriding was on the move again.

"Wh-where are we going?" Horton called ahead as he weaved in and out of city-goers in order to keep up with the brisk-moving Zeptan.

Oof!

He had walked into Penriding, who was now stationary.

"Have you ever seen a wastewalker before, Horton?" he inquired.

"I think I saw them referenced in a book from the other day," Horton recollected, rubbing his now sore nose, "but no, I have never actually seen one. What is it?"

Penriding raised an eyebrow at Horton and smiled. "I'll show you."

Penriding led Horton to the very edge of the city, where they passed through a military checkpoint at the outer wall. To his fascination, on the other side of the wall was a long row of enormous vessels built out of what appeared to be the same material as the oxen-less carriages he had seen bustling along the city roads. These were quite different from the carriages, however, as they were monumentally grander in scale and had been docked on the edge of what looked like an ocean of unending desert sand as far as the eye could see.

The pair walked alongside the long row of immense contraptions, with each one seemingly more uniquely grand and formidable than the one before it. Horton trained his neck upwards as he gazed wondrously at them, until suddenly Penriding stopped him with a hand across his chest and pointed proudly at a docked contraption nearly twice as big as the temple in Illac.

"That," he said pompously with a large grin on his face. "That's a wastewalker. *My* wastewalker."

If anything, Horton imagined, the wastewalker looked like a giant metallic boat. Admittedly, he had never actually seen a boat before, but he had read in his mother's old fairy tale book about vessels that could travel across oceans of water, though he never would have believed anything like that could actually exist in reality. A wastewalker used 'some kind of electromagnetic hoopla,' as Penriding put it, to thrust itself along the sea of sand, and was complete with a large rudder at its rear so it could steer and two large stabilizers protracting from its mid-section on each side like feet to hold it upright. Two rows of circular electrodes ran along its bottom from the bow to stern, their current keeping the somewhat submerged vessel bobbing slightly in the sand.

"Her name is the Desert Storm," Penriding announced proudly. "My father named it after some ancient military conflict that was referenced in a text or something. Pretty good name, don't you think?"

"Yeah, I suppose so. So this is yours?" Horton asked.

"It is now," Penriding answered, grinning as wide as ever. "Come on, there's something else you need to see."

Horton followed Penriding up a long ramp that led from the docks up into the wastewalker. Once inside, Horton's jaw nearly hit the floor. Practically every wall was covered from top to bottom in gears and tubes, buttons and levers. It was all so incredibly unreal to Horton – like stepping into another place in time all together. Not even in his wildest dreams could he have imagined anything like this.

"All of our technology – the electricity, vehicles, weapons – they're all based on the remnants of artifacts found deep within the Rissa," Penriding said, noticing Horton's fascination with the vessel's interior.

"They say whoever built the Rissa had technology far beyond even this, but unfortunately we're stuck with these dregs," Penriding continued. "Some believe the Zeptan High Council is hiding technology from us for their own benefit, but if you ask me it's more likely they just can't figure out how to use any of it. Either way, they don't let anyone visit beyond the pyramid's grand chamber anymore, so it doesn't matter."

Horton remembered the pedestal with the lights that had transported him to Zeptus City. He briefly considered mentioning it, but Penriding gave him no chance to speak up.

"This is the Desert Storm's command room," Penriding showed off with his arms stretched out in presentation. "Take a look at this, Horton."

Penriding pulled out a folded piece of parchment. It was the one Horton had seen during their meeting back at the manor.

"This is your ticket to finding your brother," Penriding told him as he opened up the parchment, a map.

"Here," Penriding circled out a section of the map with his finger, which featured the Rissa at the center. "This is the extent of the explored world. At its heart are Zeptus City and the Rissa. It is common belief among Zeptans that the Rissa is the only pyramid in the world, but you are living proof that it is not. What this means is—"

"My people—" Horton blurted out, interrupting Penriding, "my people believe the Earth Stone, I mean, the Rissa, or, whatever the heck it's called – my people believe there is only one infinite pyramid. It is supposed to hold up the Earth."

Penriding cocked his head and stared at Horton with intrigue.

"I'm sorry to contradict your people's beliefs, but it can't be infinite; we know that," he eventually declared. "It is more likely that the two pyramids you and I have seen are both actually two corners of a single giant pyramid that is essentially the size of the world. That being the case, it should have five corners in all, right?"

Penriding didn't wait for an answer. He was on a roll. In his mind, all the pieces were starting to fall into place.

"All the pyramid's corners would have equal distance between them. Based on the rough size of the world…" Penriding continued on, mumbling to himself and scribbling on the map. One by one he drew circles around the Rissa and four additional locations on the map, then flopped himself down into a chair. He propped his chin up with his hand, eyes fix on some other invisible dimension that only he could see.

Horton could only stare at him in wonder. He had no idea what Penriding meant. After a few moments, Penriding snapped back into the real world and turned to Horton.

"Five corners, five wondrous pyramids spread throughout the world, right?" Penriding asked, to which Horton froze, his mouth half open and unsure whether the Zeptan would actually give him time to answer.

"Right?" Penriding repeated.

"Well uh, yeah I guess—" Horton stammered his response.

"Look Horton, it's quite simple," Penriding cut him off again. "We know about the pyramids at Zeptus and Illac, but the evidence points to there being three more pyramids out there waiting to be found. As a man of science it's my duty to seek them out, plus if anything it would stand to reason your missing brother is at one of them."

Penriding placed his hands on his hips and stared intensely at Horton for a moment.

"So what do you say kid, are you down for a little adventure?" he asked with a hint of excitement in his voice.

Horton bit his cheek as he thought about the offer. He wasn't sure what Penriding had in mind exactly, but he quickly came to a decision anyway.

"If it'll get me to Deforest, I'll go anywhere."

Penriding smiled.

"Perfect."

FOUR

Wastewalker

"THALES MAKES SEVEN, Farnsworth eight, and…" Penriding looked up from his crewman roster to Horton, "where in the Rissa's name is Ananke? I swear I couldn't have chosen a less reliable—"

"Sir!" A boy no older than Deforest appeared, running along the dock, knapsack clutched in hands.

"Sorry, I uh—"

"I have no time for excuses. Get on board," Penriding ordered the boy, who huffed with each step as he practically sprinted on board.

Penriding shook his head at Horton. "That damn kid. If my father catches wind that—"

"What is that, Penny?"

Horton recognized that thunderous voice. It was Penriding's father, who seemed to have appeared out of nowhere.

"Nothing, father," Penriding responded, sullenly. "We'll be underway momentarily."

"I should hope so," Mr. Blacksmith boomed. "Let us not have your first trade run fall apart before you even set off, yes? I am sure even a fool like you can handle a three-day trip."

Horton and Penriding's eyes locked for a split second before Penriding reassured his father.

"Yes father, all will be well. See you soon."

Mr. Blacksmith glared at Horton and Penriding for a moment, then swiftly spun around and walked off. Without a word, Penriding turned around and headed for the Desert Storm with Horton not far behind.

"Three days?" Horton yelled ahead to Penriding. "Penriding, this trip could take weeks – even months, for all we know."

"I do know," Penriding revealed. "I had no choice. I had to tell him I'd take the Desert Storm on a short merchant run; it was the only way he would let me go. We have enough supplies, don't worry."

"Don't worry?" Horton said in disbelief, stopping Penriding in his tracks. "Don't worry? Who are these sailors you've recruited? That last one was just a kid! We need soldiers and protection, not dock hands!"

"We have protection," Penriding solaced. "That's what Linden is for."

Penriding continued walking up to the wastewalker, leaving Horton to stand there fuming.

"Linden?" Horton again yelled over to Penriding. "Are you insane? What about the Vwari? I'm not leaving my life in the hands of a woman. No way! You can count me out of this."

At that Penriding stormed back over to Horton and confronted him, face to face.

"You don't want to come? Fine. Find your brother on your own," he said harshly, then turned his back to Horton. He only got as far as two steps, though, before turning around to face down Horton once again.

"Oh and another thing. Watch your mouth, kid. You say something stupid like that again and you'll find yourself in more trouble than you can handle."

Horton gritted his teeth and clenched his fists, but he knew Penriding was right. He had nowhere else to turn – he would have to take his chances on the Desert Storm. He took a deep breath and looked up at the wastewalker. He couldn't help but feel like he was digging his own grave.

"I guess I'm doing this…" he said to himself under his breath.

Horton walked on board the Desert Storm and made his way to the command room. Penriding and Linden were already there, and Horton did the best he could to avoid eye contact with them.

"Nice of you to join us," Penriding said sarcastically from a chair placed in the center of the room and perched a little higher than the others, the commander's chair.

"Pre-launch checks complete," Linden announced from the Desert Storm's control station at the front of the room. In front of her was a large window that provided a vantage point over the bow of the vessel.

"Very well," Penriding responded. "Take us out."

Horton grasped a nearby seat as the wastewalker's engines suddenly sprung to life. His eyes darted around the command room as unusual sounds reverberated through every square inch of the walls and instruments. Even more peculiar was the feeling he experienced when the wastewalker began to move, and although he had often rode oxen back in Illac, this was much different. Horton pulled himself into the seat he had clung on to for balance, and watched with wonder as the Desert Storm gradually pulled away from the Zeptus City docks. Once acclimated to the role and pitch motion of the craft, he climbed out of his seat and gazed out a side window at the brilliant city and its pyramid they were leaving behind. He had certainly come a long way from Illac.

"It's incredible," Horton muttered out loud, forgetting he was still angry with Penriding.

"The wastemen say the light from the Rissa can always be seen, no matter how far from home they travel, vigilantly reaching out to its children wherever they may be and ready to guide them home again," Linden said to the room.

"A beacon of life in a dead sea," Penriding said to himself, before looking over to Horton as if to say something, but instead he just sighed deeply and reverted his eyes to the front of the wastewalker.

Horton spent much of the next two days buried in the handful of books he had managed to carry on board with him from Blacksmith manor, and when he wasn't reading he found himself deep in thought on the wastewalker's upper deck, watching the rolling sand dunes endlessly break against the hull of the Desert Storm below. From there Horton could see the glint of the Rissa in the distance, holding true to Linden's word that it would keep watch over them. For some unknown reason, he felt safer knowing it was there.

He had only bothered to speak to Penriding once since the day they departed, and that was to ask about his duties as part of the onboard crew. Penriding had explained that he was a guest for the duration of the journey and was free to do as he wished, which Horton accepted begrudgingly; but it just so happened that what he really wished was for Penriding to give him some sort of job – any job – to keep him busy and subsequently keep his mind off Deforest and his mother.

On the third day of their journey during breakfast in the mess room, Horton ran into Ananke, the young wasteman he had seen on the docks. He watched Ananke sit down at the other end of the room to eat alone, so Horton, who had been conversing with one of the other crewmen at the time, excused himself and joined Ananke at his table.

"Hi, I'm Horton," Horton said as he sat down.

Ananke looked back at him quizzically, and then mumbled an inaudible response from under his breath.

"I saw you the other day on the docks," Horton went on. "You seem a little young to be working on board a wastewalker."

"I am not too young!" Ananke bursted, not minding the fact he still had a mouth full of food.

"No, of course you're not," Horton quickly relented as he averted his eyes down toward his breakfast. The two sat there for a moment in silence as they ate before Ananke eventually broke the silence.

"I heard about your brother, how you are looking for him," Ananke said in between shoving massive fork loads of his breakfast into his mouth. "The engineers were saying they would be surprised if he was still alive."

"Really," Horton said bluntly as he glared at Ananke, who seemed to realize after the fact that he could have been a little more sensitive. Horton noticed this, chocked it up to a dumb kid being just that, then leaned back in his chair and sighed.

"He's about your age, actually," Horton noted. "You remind me a little bit of him."

"I do?" Ananke raised his eyebrow as he swallowed his food, but before Horton had a chance to reply Ananke's eyes darted toward a clock on the wall.

"Damnit, I am late for my shift," he said abruptly. "Sorry."

With that he grabbed his half-empty bowl and flew out of the room.

As Horton looked around the room he realized he was the last one there. He ducked his head into his arms for a moment while at the table, and as he did he felt himself become overwhelmed with sadness. Part of it was homesickness, but mainly it was because he missed his brother. He could feel the urge to cry beginning to overcome him, but he fought it back. As he did he realized it had been a while since he had cried and it might not actually be such a bad thing, especially since nobody was around.

Right on cue Penriding burst into the room, making Horton's decision an easy one. Quickly pulling himself together, he looked up at the Desert Storm's commander standing in the doorway.

"Can we talk?" Penriding asked as he motioned for Horton to accompany him.

Horton agreed with a nod and followed Penriding to the wastewalker's upper deck.

"It's gone," Penriding told him when they got there.

"Huh?" Horton asked, wondering what he was talking about.

"The Rissa," Penriding answered. "We're so far away from Zeptus City we can no longer see its light. Very few have ever traveled this far from the city."

Horton looked around at the horizon in every direction. Penriding was right; it was gone. He suddenly felt very alone. It quickly sunk in that beside the wastewalker, nine crewmen, Linden and Penriding, there was nothing else out here but sand. His stomach churned as the feeling reminded him of the night Deforest disappeared, deep in the woods near the Earth Stone.

"I guess we're on our own now," Horton said in a bleak tone.

"We've got a good crew here, Horton," Penriding responded with a reassuring smile. "Although I do admit it wasn't easy finding Zeptans to accompany us on this journey. There are many who would consider what we're doing... heretical, but rest assured each member of this crew is out here for the same reason we are. While this might not be a military vessel, you have my word you'll be safe here. Despite what you might think, Linden is as tough as nails, and this crew is more than capable of—"

"Why do you have a child working on board?" Horton abruptly brought up out of nowhere and interrupted Penriding.

"A child?" Penriding repeated, but Horton just glared at him without response. He had no doubt that the Zeptan knew exactly who he was talking about.

"Ananke," Penriding finally admitted with a sigh. "Ananke is a special case. I know – it's a stupid idea to bring a child on a potentially dangerous trip like this, but…"

Penriding looked up at the bright blue sky, the sun forcing him to squint.

"But Ananke is a special case."

Horton raised his eyebrow at Penriding.

"I don't think I could ever begin to understand you, Penriding," Horton stated, reverting his eyes to the sandy wastes that surrounded them.

"My father is expecting my return today, you know," Penriding unexpectedly mentioned with a somewhat nervous look about him.

"You're afraid of your father, aren't you?" Horton commented, feeling confident that he had figured out their relationship. "You don't like him, I think."

However, Penriding looked at Horton as though he had spoken blasphemy.

"My father is one of the most revered men in the history of Zeptus City," he said vigorously. "I could only hope to be half the man he ever was."

Horton gave Penriding a dubious look.

"But…" Penriding continued as his vivacious defense of his father quickly waned, "we haven't always seen eye to eye. He wants me to follow his footsteps as a merchant, but I want to pursue scientific discovery. He's completely unwilling to compromise, unfortunately."

Horton fiddled with his headscarf and looked down at his feet.

"You've never mentioned your father before," Penriding pointed out. "Is he still in Illac?"

Horton took a deep breath.

"My father died years ago," Horton responded, his eyes still fix on his feet.

"I'm sorry," Penriding said with regret.

"It's okay," Horton muttered quietly before quickly changing the subject.

"Is there nothing at all I can do to help out while I'm out here?" he asked with just a hint of desperation. "It's pretty boring not having anything to do."

"If you really want to be put to work you should talk to Linden," Penriding recommended with a nonchalant shrug. "She's the duty officer. If there's a job for you she'll find it."

"Okay, will do," Horton replied with a slight smile.

Later that day Horton worked up enough courage to go see Linden in the command room. It was the first time he had ever really talked to her properly face to face, and frankly he wasn't sure what to make of her. In Illac the roles of women are set in stone: childcare, housekeeping, cooking and the like, so to be in the presence of a female soldier was unusual to say the least. Ultimately their conversation was brief and to the point, which made things considerably less uncomfortable for Horton. Linden told him to assist the chief mechanic in the engine room, which sounded pretty mundane, but he figured the least he could do was pull his weight during the trip, so he gladly accepted the job.

Over the next week Horton worked five hours a day cleaning and oiling gears, levers and pistons throughout the engine room, plus making bi-hourly coffee runs for the chief mechanic and his crew. In some respects he began to enjoy the job. It may have been dirty and monotonous, but it made him feel as though he belonged somewhere – a feeling he hadn't experienced in a long time.

Horton kept at this until one morning he woke up to the sound – or rather, lack of sound – of the Desert Storm's engines. Wondering what was wrong, he made his way to the command room, where he found Penriding and Linden in a heated discussion.

"It's not here!" Penriding yelled, slamming his fist on the map table.

"Are you sure you double-checked the coordinates?" Linden suggested.

"Of course I am! I double *and* triple-checked them," Penriding responded, now slouching himself over the map. "It's just not here. No pyramid, no answers—"

Penriding glanced up as he noticed Horton enter the room.

"And no Deforest."

Horton's heart sank. He looked at Penriding and then Linden, anticipating at least one of them to tell him "but" or perhaps "there's still hope," but instead they both simply stared blankly back at him. Unable to stifle his emotions, Horton turned around and ran up to the upper deck as fast as he could. He could feel tears streaming down his face. When he got to the upper deck he spun himself around, looking in every direction. Penriding was right, there was nothing here but sand as far as the eye could see.

Horton dropped to his knees. He felt so helpless. He thought for sure they would find another pyramid, or at the very least some kind of clue as to Deforest's whereabouts, but instead they had nothing. He could hear Penriding coming up the steps to the upper deck behind him. This time he didn't care if Penriding saw him crying.

"Things don't always turn out the way we plan, Horton," Penriding said. "The important thing is that we tried, though. Even though we were wrong – *I was wrong* – we at least gave it our best shot."

Penriding slowly walked over to the edge of the deck and looked down at the sand below.

"I've decided to take us back to Zeptus City," he said dolefully after a short pause. "We're right back where we started, and I don't suspect I'll be commanding my own wastewalker again anytime soon. I'll face the consequences alone. I guess my father was right, I was destined to be a merchant after all."

The Zeptan stood there for a moment in silence next to Horton, who all the while felt as though he should say something, but couldn't. All he really wanted was for Penriding to go away and leave him alone.

After a few minutes Penriding did eventually make his way back down the stairs, and not long later the wastewalker began to move again. All the while Horton stayed there on his knees, the sun's heat drying the tears on his face even through the headscarf.

"I'm so sorry, Deforest," he whispered. "I'm so sorry."

Horton passed the next two days keeping to himself inside his cabin. He didn't speak to anyone on board and he didn't bother to show up to help work in the engine room, either. In fact, the only time he left his cabin was when he ate with the rest of the crew in the mess room. He saw Penriding there one night, but the two simply exchanged glances and ignored each other. Horton figured they both needed their space at the time, and it seemed as though the rest of the crew agreed. The same mess room that had once been full of voices and laughter every night was now quieter than the Illac temple on Earth Day. It didn't bother Horton though, who was more than happy to pick a seat in the corner of the room and eat in seclusion.

He continued that regimen until one evening Ananke approached Horton as he sat in his usual spot in the corner while he ate. The young wasteman stood there for a moment watching Horton, who was doing his best job to ignore him. Eventually, though, Horton gave in.

"Do you need something?" Horton asked irritably.

Ananke didn't reply, and instead swiftly took a seat across from Horton.

"No, please, be my guest," Horton said sarcastically as he made room for Ananke to put his plate down.

Horton continued eating, but he could feel Ananke's eyes still staring at him. Tired of this charade he glanced up, only to find that Ananke was trying to say something but couldn't find the right words.

"Ananke," Horton reluctantly consoled, "what is it? Speak."

"I–I heard about your brother," Ananke finally managed to get out. "I know it is not easy to lose the people you care about. I recently lost my family too."

Horton's eyes opened wide.

"Who'd you lose?" Horton asked. "Your brother? Mother?"

"All of them," Ananke replied glumly as he seemed to gaze into nothingness. "My mother, father and two sisters were killed in a Vwari raid on my family's merchant barge a little over two months ago. A Blacksmith company wastewalker rescued me, took me in and gave me work to support myself, but my family is gone."

Horton could see tears in Ananke's eyes. He had no idea the boy had gone through so much.

"I'm sorry to hear that, Ananke," Horton said. "I guess we're going through the same thing then, huh?"

"Not really," Ananke said bluntly.

Horton's brow frowned as he looked at Ananke quizzically.

"How do you reckon that?" Horton inquired.

"You still have hope," Ananke explained. "Your brother may still be alive somewhere. You at least can hold on to that. This journey did not work out as planned, but that does not mean you cannot still find him. I would do anything to see my family again but I know that will never happen. Yet for you, anything is possible."

Horton looked at Ananke and smiled slightly. It amazed him that a kid so young could say something like that. It made Horton think about how selfish he had been lately, always worrying about his own feelings before considering those of others.

"You're right," Horton admitted. "You're exactly right. But we're both alone in the world right now, trying to find ourselves now that our lives have been turned upside-down. What we do have, though, are friends who are willing to look out for us, and that's as important as anything."

Ananke smiled, and it made Horton feel better to see him do so.

"You know, it is too bad we did not find a pyramid," Ananke told him. "I was really hoping to get to explore one. I hear you have been pretty deep inside one before."

"Yeah, pretty deep I suppose," Horton replied.

"What is it like?" Ananke questioned. "They say it is like nothing else in this world."

Horton laughed.

"Well, to be honest it was pretty dark inside," he explained. "I didn't really see much, but it's definitely different."

"I see," Ananke said, clearly disappointed.

"But," Horton continued on abruptly, "I did see a pedestal with four brightly lit buttons on it. When I pushed one of the buttons I found myself in another pyramid. That's how I ended up in Zeptus City, and I think my brother ended up in yet another pyramid too...."

Horton's voice trailed off as he finished the sentence, his mind putting his own words into context.

"Four buttons for five pyramids?" he repeated under his breath to himself.

Horton was almost certain the first button he hit – the green one – hadn't taken him anywhere. He now thought for sure that was the button for the pyramid in Illac.

He noticed Ananke was staring right at him, probably confused by the way he was acting.

"Sorry, was just thinking," Horton explained. "According to Penriding's map there's supposed to be five pyramids at equal distances around the world, yet there are only four buttons. I'm just wondering why there aren't five buttons."

"Maybe because there are only four pyramids?" Ananke suggested with a shrug.

Horton shook his head and looked at Ananke like he was crazy.

"Nope, that's not possible. There has to be five."

"Why?" Ananke pressed.

"Because a pyramid has five points, and so there must be five places where the corners protrude through the earth," Horton refuted. "Everybody knows that."

"Says who?" Ananke pestered. "There is an easy way to figure this out, you know."

Horton crossed his arms and sat back in chair. Ananke seemed like a smart kid, but he couldn't imagine him coming up with an answer to their problem so quickly.

"The Rissa has four sides," Ananke stated. "How many sides does the Earth Stone have?"

"Four, of course," Horton answered, still not sure what point the young Zeptan was trying to make.

Ananke leaned in. "How many sides are in contact with each of the five corners of a pyramid?"

Horton opened his mouth to answer, but quickly closed it as he thought twice about his answer. Ananke had made an incredibly intelligent point – the two pyramids he had seen so far each had four sides, but if the Earth Stone and Rissa were two points of one larger pyramid, at least one of them should have had only three sides. Horton tested the logic over and over in his head, but it always panned out the same. There had to be multiple, separate pyramids scattered across the globe.

His stomach dropped slightly at the thought, but it fell in line with everything he had been discovering lately. For as long as he could remember the priests had told that the Earth Stone cradled the world, so he never thought any differently. This notion, it seemed, was no more genuine than the shroud that had been thrown over Illac to separate it from the outside world for countless generations. For the first time it dawned on him that the stories and beliefs he had grown up with were probably not true.

"Sorry Ananke," Horton announced all of a sudden as he bolted up from the table, "you're exactly right – I need to go talk to Penriding."

Without looking back to see Ananke's reaction, Horton took off. The clangs of his footsteps echoed along the metallic corridors as he caromed through the Desert Storm toward the command room. There he found Penriding sleeping in his seat.

"Ahem," Horton coughed from the command room's doorway, trying to get his attention to no avail.

"Pen?" he called out a little louder as he slowly made his way over toward the commander in slumber.

Now standing right over the Zeptan, Horton extended his hand out to grasp Penriding's shoulder in order to shake him awake.

"Pen—ah!"

Next thing Horton knew he was staring down a silver barrel. Penriding had jumped awake and protracted some sort of mechanized weapon from inside his sleeve, then shoved it in Horton's face.

"Horton!" Penriding yelped as he realized what was going on. "Whoa, buddy! You can't just go around sneaking up on people like that – I almost blew your head clear off your shoulders."

Startled by what had happened, Horton staggered back. There was an undoubted smell of alcohol on Penriding's breath.

"What the heck is that thing?" Horton asked.

"This," Penriding began, still collecting himself, "is a firearm. Definitely not something you will see every day. I could kill a man from a good twenty yards away with this beauty."

"That's *if* you manage to hit anything," Linden butted in from the Desert Storm's helm. "I'd trust my sword any day over that gimmick."

Penriding rolled his eyes and returned his attention to Horton.

"Back to the matter at hand. To what do I owe the pleasure?" he asked him.

"I've been thinking," Horton told him. "Back when I was

inside the pyramid at Illac, there was a pedestal with four buttons on it. When I pushed each one I'm quite certain it took me to a different pyramid, and eventually left me at the Rissa in Zeptus City."

"Okay, and…?" Penriding asked.

"My point is there were four buttons," Horton explained with a hint of excitement made obvious by the fact he barely had time to draw breath between sentences. "Four buttons for five pyramids – it doesn't make sense. And another thing – Ananke made this point – both the Rissa and the Earth Stone have four sides, meaning they can't each be a corner of one larger pyramid. In fact, there may instead actually only be four pyramids, which would mean that they may not all be equally distributed around the world after all. It explains why there was nothing at your coordinates."

Penriding folded his hands behind his head, looked up at the ceiling and took a deep breath before sighing. He sat in that position for a moment while Horton watched him, hoping the Zeptan would have something insightful to say in response.

"Well that's annoying," Penriding eventually groaned. He then stood up and walked over to the map table, followed closely by Horton.

"Then we're right back at square one," he scratched his head as he looked over the map. "We have no other leads as to the whereabouts of the other pyramids."

"Ulises…" Horton said to himself, inadvertently catching the attention of Penriding.

"Excuse me?" Penriding asked.

He wasn't exactly sure why he had suddenly thought of Ulises, his mentor and priest back in Illac, but he had a gut feeling the Illac priests might know more about the pyramids than they let on.

"He was a priest and friend of mine back in the village I'm from," Horton revealed. "If anyone might know the secrets of the pyramids, I think it's him."

"Okay, that's great and all, but we have no idea how to get to Illac," Penriding pointed out.

"Right," Horton agreed, reluctantly. He knew all too well the pedestal inside the Rissa was damaged and missing the colored buttons, while a search for Illac by wastewalker would have been a near impossible task.

"Look, let's just get back to Zeptus City and forget about it," Penriding said with a sigh. "It's just not meant to be."

The Zeptan let out a giant yawn and walked over to his command chair to retrieve a bottle of liquor he had stashed beside it. "I'm calling it a night," he said to Horton between quick swigs from his bottle. "I'd suggest you do too."

Horton nodded and trudged his way out of the command room and back to his cabin. Along the way he thought about what Ananke had said about Deforest. However unlikely, there was still a chance his brother was alive and he took some solace in that. He decided he would get back to work in the engine room the next day and try to keep a brighter outlook on things.

Maybe everything will still turn out all right, he thought.

Horton was in better spirits for the remainder of the return journey, even though he dreaded the thought of what would become of Penriding, and subsequently himself, when they got back to Zeptus City. In the meantime, however, he returned to working in the engine room and was beginning to get a knack for engine maintenance. In addition to his own duties, he'd been helping out Ananke, including the less-than-enjoyable job of dishwashing after meals. He didn't mind it though; if anything it felt good to help others and free his mind of his own issues for a while.

The Desert Storm was intercepted by two military wastewalkers on the night the light from the Rissa reappeared in the distance. They stopped the vessel and sent two men aboard to meet with Penriding behind locked doors in the command room. Curious as to what was going on, Horton snuck up onto the upper deck and tried to listen in from above. He couldn't really make out much of what was said, although at one point the sound of a fist banging on a table and someone shouting reverberated up to him. The Illac actually considered marching down there and intervening for a brief moment before thinking better of it. Penriding was his friend, but the last thing he wanted was to get caught up in Zeptan politics.

It wasn't until a full half hour later that the two soldiers left the command room and returned to their respective wastewalkers. Ultimately, the Desert Storm ended up following them in tow for the rest of its journey home.

Penriding wasn't present in the mess room the following morning for breakfast, and when Horton stopped by the command room later that afternoon he discovered he wasn't there either. Linden was in her seat at the wastewalker's helm as usual, so Horton worked up the guts to ask her if she knew what happened to Penriding.

"If you must know," Linden answered, "Penriding's father is dead. Murdered, actually."

"What?" Horton asked, bewildered by how this could have happened. "How? When?"

"I don't know the details," Linden insisted. "All I know is that it was the Vwari."

Horton clenched his fists. He wouldn't say he liked the way Mr. Blacksmith treated his son, but the man had the decency to take him in and treat his injuries when he was caught in the firebomb attack outside the manor. He was sick of all the bad news lately – nothing had gone their way during the journey.

"Gods damnit!" Horton slammed his fist down on the map table, causing Linden to peer back at him from her seat.

Horton stormed out of the command center and to the upper deck. He looked out at the Rissa shining brightly in the distance and took a deep breath in an effort to calm himself down.

"A beacon of life in a sea of death," Horton said out loud to no one in particular. "What a load of bull. What the heck do the Vwari want with it, anyway?"

"It was my fault, you know," a shallow voice said from behind him.

Horton turned around to find Penriding had emerged from wherever he had hidden himself away. From the look of things, he was still shaken by his father's death.

"Are you okay?" Horton inquired, unsure whether Penriding was ready to talk about his father.

"He and a search party set out to find us when we didn't return after three days," Penriding said monotonously as if he hadn't heard Horton. "They looked and looked for days, and when everyone else had given up, he kept at it. His wastewalker ran into a Vwari raid cutter and… and I'm such an idiot."

"You were just following—" Horton began, but Penriding cut him off.

"Who was I to think I could uncover the mystery of the pyramids?" Penriding questioned, now laughing to himself. "I'm such a fool, Horton, such a fool."

As quickly as he had appeared, Penriding disappeared once more to the lower decks, leaving Horton standing there to absorb everything.

After a few moments Horton turned back to the ocean of sand and closed his eyes. He wanted to tear himself away from this place and back to the last time he was truly happy and at peace. He had to go back a long way, but eventually he found it. He and Deforest were playing a game of boliball out in the fields behind their cottage. It was an unusually mild day and they were laughing and enjoying themselves without a care in the world. He remembered in the middle of the game Deforest had paused suddenly, his eyes directed back to their home. As Deforest smiled and waved to a figure standing in the cottage's doorway, Horton had turned around to see who it was. He had to cover his eyes from the sun with his hands in order to see who it was, and as the figure came into clear view, his heart leaped in his chest with excitement. It was their father.

Horton clenched his jaw at the thought, and then made his way back to his cabin.

The Desert Storm arrived back at the Zeptus City docks late the following evening. The mood was fairly solemn among the crewmembers, and as they prepared to depart the wastewalker there was little more than a few quick goodbyes between them. As for Horton, Penriding had already offered him a place to stay at Blacksmith manor, which he gratefully accepted.

With not much in the way of belongings, Horton had been the first off the vessel, so he waited on the docks for Penriding and the others. One by one the crew made their way off the Desert Storm, with each silently nodding or quietly wishing Horton good luck in his future endeavors. Penriding and Linden were the last off with Ananke trailing not far behind, apparently on luggage duty.

"All set then?" Horton asked the group.

"I think so," Penriding responded while inspecting the bags that engulfed Ananke's small frame.

"Let me take some of those off you," Horton offered, seeing as how he had nothing to carry anyway.

The young wasteman seemed somewhat taken aback by the notion of Horton's aid as he peered around a bag's flap that had flopped over his face and was impairing his view. The confusion on his face quickly turned into a smile, however.

"Thanks!" Ananke gasped as Horton pulled a bag off of Ananke and lugged it over his shoulder.

The four of them were met at the gates that connected

the docks to the inner city by a motorized buggy waiting to taxi them back to the manor. Once the group loaded inside, Horton used the opportunity to get some answers out of Penriding.

"So what's going to happen now?" Horton asked.

"Well," Penriding began after a deep breath, "I have some meetings with the authorities, and then, of course, there's my father's will to deal with."

"You don't have any other family?" Horton inquired.

"Nothing immediate," Penriding said with his face squished tiredly into the palm of his right hand. "My father once mentioned something about extended family far out at a wasteland outpost, but otherwise no – I was an only child. My mother died when I was very young, I never really knew her."

Suddenly Linden clutched her sword, and as the other three turned to look at her the buggy began to rattle, followed by a loud explosion in the distance.

"Vwari," Penriding noted with a quick glance toward Linden.

A short time later the buggy came to a stop. They were outside the front gate to the manor now, which if anything had even more guards than Horton remembered. As they piled out of the buggy, the manor's gates abruptly swung open, giving way to a tall and lanky figure hastily running toward them. To Horton's surprise it was none other than Constable Keen to greet the group.

"Mr. Penriding," the constable said as he hurriedly ushered the group inside the manor. "I'm so sorry about your father, a most unfortunate turn of events."

"I must say it's curious to see you here, constable," Penriding replied.

The constable wiped his brow and let out a short sigh.

"Vwari attacks have increased as of late," he explained. "Cowardly hit and run tactics, primarily. However, we have reason to believe they may single you out as a target."

Penriding looked sharply at the constable. He appeared unsettled that such a thing was within the realm of possibility.

"The Vwari are dangerous, certainly," Penriding admitted, "but individual targets? They've never had any rhyme or reason to their attacks in the past."

"Mr. Penriding," the constable said, "these are clearly not the same Vwari we've dealt with out in the wastes in past years – they're too organized. It's as if they are prodding us for holes in our defenses."

Constable Keen looked around to see if anyone was listening.

"The High Council is getting nervous," he continued. "There are some who believe the Exetans play a larger role in all this than they have let on, and after what happened to your father—"

"A Vwari is no match for a Zeptan swordsman," Linden butted in. "The Council is foolish to think otherwise."

"It's the hordes that concern me, leftenant," Constable Keen replied with a frown. "When those damn hell-spawn gather in groups they can be ruthless."

"Then thank the Rissa for Reckoners, constable," Linden answered without batting an eyelid.

"I pray you are right, soldier," the constable replied with a hopeful smile. "Alright, hurry up inside now."

The constable herded the four of them through the front door with his hands.

"I see you brought the little jester along for the trip too," the constable said to Penriding as he guided Horton through the door. This irritated Horton a little and he considered saying something back, but when Ananke laughed he couldn't help but laugh too.

"A guard will escort each of you to your respective rooms," the constable declared as he waved his fingers at a group of nearby soldiers. "I'll make sure your baggage arrives in due time."

"I do not want to be alone," Ananke said from behind Horton. "I want to stay in Horton's room."

"Uh," Horton uttered, caught off-guard by the request. "I suppose that's fine with me."

The constable nodded and gave the guard new instructions before turning back to Horton and Ananke.

"Now get going; it's late," he said, shooing them away along with their armed escort.

They followed the guard to their room on the sixth floor of the manor. Inside there were two beds and a window with a magnificent view overlooking the city and its pyramid. The reflections of the city's lights off the pyramid's metallic surface made it look like something out of a dream.

"Do you ever wonder who built the pyramids?" Horton asked Ananke as he stared out the window at the massive structure.

"No," Ananke replied with a yawn, clearly not as impressed by the view as Horton. "My father told me that god created it so we could survive on this world."

"That's the same story where I'm from, except my people believe in many gods," Horton said, still looking out at the Rissa. "I'm not so sure I believe it anymore though. They must have a greater purpose, don't you think?"

Horton got no answer. He turned around to find Ananke already asleep on his bed. Horton smiled, put out the light, and went to sleep himself.

When Horton woke up the next morning he looked over to Ananke's bed to find it empty. Curious as to what became of him, he pulled himself out of bed and made his way to the door to peek outside. Standing guard just outside was none other than Linden.

"You must have been tired," she said. "You slept through breakfast."

"Where are the others?" Horton asked, rubbing his eyes.

"Penriding is in his father's – I mean *his* study," Linden replied. "He's been in business meetings with the trade authorities much of the morning."

"Ah," Horton responded, his eyes still half closed. "I guess I'll make my way over there once I'm ready."

It took only a few minutes for Horton to pull himself together, and when he reopened his door he found Linden still standing behind it, waiting for him. He followed closely as Linden escorted him to the study, which was all the way up on the manor's thirteenth floor. She lurched the large iron doors open to reveal a cozy room with Penriding sitting at the largest desk he had ever seen. In the room's opposing far corner sat Ananke, absorbed in a book in a reading chair that was about four sizes too large for him.

"Ah, there you are Horton," Penriding said dryly as he pulled his eyes up from a stack of papers laid out in front of him. "In the name of the Rissa, please distract me from this dull mess. If I had known inheriting a fortune as large as my father's would be this much work, I would have moved out into the wastes a long time ago. Please try to make yourself comfortable. I may be a while."

Horton smiled and nodded as he began to look around the study. The room's walls were lined with bookshelves and glass cabinets filled with all sorts of exotic and presumably priceless items.

"My father's collection of stuff," Penriding remarked, having noticed Horton eyeballing the room. "He accrued quite a lot of rare and valuable items over the years despite hardly ever actually leaving the city. It's as if he just vanished off to Rissa-knows-where and picked up random little trinkets. Feel free to look around."

Horton gladly took up the offer. As he slowly made his way around the room, he saw unusual looking skulls, brilliant minerals of every color and books that appeared to be as old as time itself. Stepping back to take in the entire collection at once, he imagined each object coming from some distant corner of the earth, all with its own mysterious back story.

However there was one item in particular that really caught Horton's eye, sitting all by itself on the top shelf of one of the cabinets, well out of his reach. It was weirdly familiar, as if he had seen it before in a dream.

"Penriding, what is that?" Horton called over, pointing at the specimen.

Tilting his head up from his stack of papers, Penriding squinted his eyes as he tried to see what Horton was referring to.

"Um," he said, pulling himself out of his chair, "that is... that is... that is something I am not familiar with, actually. It was my fathers, but I guess it's mine now."

Penriding pulled his chair over to the cabinet, stood on it and pulled the item down. Getting a better look, Horton saw that it was a piece of stone with four different colored gems – no, not gems – buttons. His heart skipped a beat. He was certain it was the same as the one he had seen in the Illac pyramid – the one that had transported him to Zeptus City.

"Looks like junk to me," Penriding shrugged. "Probably scrap off a wastewalker."

"No!" Horton shouted, surprising Penriding and causing Ananke's head to pop up behind his book.

"I know what this is," he continued, grabbing the stone piece out of Penriding's hands. "This is what I used back at the pyramid in Illac to get here."

Penriding raised his eyebrow at Horton as if he had lost his mind.

"Don't you see?" Horton went on. "This could be our way back to Illac. We'll be able to go there and the other pyramids."

"The only thing I see is that you're clearly confused," Penriding said, taking the piece back from Horton. "What are we supposed to do, plug this thing into the Rissa? There are no wires, no cables. This is just a piece of trash my father probably found out in the wastes somewhere, maybe even an extra wastewalker part. It's useless."

"Like I said, I know exactly what that is," Horton repeated, now a little annoyed. "Why would your father have had a piece of junk in his study? Everything else in here is priceless and one of a kind, so what's the point of having spare wastewalker parts in here? You've got to trust me on this, Pen."

Penriding rubbed his chin as he considered what Horton was proposing. His eyes darted back and forth between the stone piece and Horton as he thought.

"Okay," Penriding eventually conceded. "Let's say for a second this thing can somehow magically send us to another pyramid. The Rissa is heavily guarded and you and I are not exactly welcomed with open arms there. We would never get close enough to actually use it."

"Ahem," a loud cough echoed through the room's high ceiling. Turning around, Horton and Penriding found it came from a set of eyes peering over the top of a book in the corner of the room. Now that he had their attention, Ananke lowered the book onto his lap and grinned.

"It sounds like what you would need is a diversion," he told them as he set the book down onto the table beside him. "Horton, you still have your funny-looking clothes, right?"

"Uh, yeah… somewhere," Horton replied, not sure what Ananke was getting at.

"You get me those clothes and I will give the guards at the Rissa something else to worry about," Ananke explained. "If they see someone in those weird threads around the pyramid again they are sure to leave their posts to investigate. Meanwhile you two can slip inside and use that thing."

86

"No way, Ananke," Horton said sternly while looking at Penriding, hoping he would back him up. "It's far too dangerous. You could get in a lot of trouble for doing something like that, especially when the guards are on heightened alert for Vwari infiltrators."

"What do I care?" Ananke asked, now standing up from his chair. "What do I have to live for? My family is dead. The least I can do is something worthwhile. Do not take that away from me too. I will draw the guards away from the Rissa's entrance so you two can get inside."

Horton could see tears beginning to form in Ananke's eyes. In a way he felt as though he was looking back at himself. He had no hope. No future.

"He's right, Horton," Penriding said decisively. "We've got to do our part, Ananke has to do his."

Horton looked at Penriding in disbelief. He wanted to call Penriding an idiot for saying such a thing. He wanted to tell him he was cold-hearted and self-centered, that he should be looking after Ananke, not sacrificing him. But he didn't. He just stood there, bit his lip and didn't say a word more. He simply turned around and sat down in the nearest armchair, eyes glued to the floor.

"Then it's settled," Penriding decreed. He looked back at his desk covered in papers. "Let's get things in motion tonight. Horton?"

Horton's eyes disengaged from the floor and turned to Penriding.

"Give Ananke your old clothes from Illac immediately," Penriding ordered. "In the meantime, I'll cash in on some old favors. Meet at the west wing of the eleventh floor – Horton, you know the place. We're heading out at midnight."

Horton felt unsettled the rest of the day. On one hand he had an opportunity to go back to Illac and, possibly with the guidance of Ulises, be a step closer to finding his brother. Still, on the other hand, he felt what he and Penriding were doing to Ananke was wrong. He didn't deserve to take the fall for them. Horton didn't like it, but he knew it had to be done if they were to get to Illac.

He met up with Penriding and Ananke later that night on the eleventh floor as planned. There was little pleasant about the meeting spot, and even upon a second visit that part of the manor gave him the creeps.

"Alright, Linden is going to set off a false alarm on the north side of the building at ten-past," Penriding informed them once they had assembled. "That'll be our cue to sneak down to the bottom floor in the commotion, meet up with Linden, and slip past the front gate in her company. From there we'll make our way to the base of the pyramid."

"Isn't this your manor?" Horton pointed out. "Surely you can come and go as you please."

"Horton, the council knows why we were gone for almost two weeks on the Desert Storm," Penriding informed him. "Yes this is my home, but those guards out front are as much to keep me in line as they are to protect me. They won't let us get anywhere near the Rissa if they see us leave the manor."

Horton nodded in understanding.

Penriding then turned to Ananke, who was wearing a dark robe over Horton's white tunic. It was a little baggy on him, but it would have to do.

"You're all set?" Penriding asked Ananke.

"I am ready," Ananke confirmed.

Penriding looked back to Horton. He had noticed the Illac fidgeting nervously.

"We'll be fine, trust me," the Zeptan reassured. Horton certainly hoped so.

The three of them stood there in silence huddled around a single candle in a dark room for a few minutes while they waited for their signal. Horton glanced at Penriding and then Ananke. They both looked relatively calm. Somehow seeing them so relaxed made him feel a little more confident about what they were about to do.

"Everything will be fine," Penriding said again to Horton with a smile. "Who knows, it might even be a little fun."

The instant Penriding mentioned the word "fun" an alarm sounded somewhere in the lower levels of the manor. All three of them took a deep breath. It was time.

"Let's go," Penriding said boldly, then blew out the candle and whisked them away to the hallway and down the stairs.

The three of them stealthily made their way down toward the first floor, but when they reached the second floor landing, Penriding abruptly signaled them to stop a moment.

Horton could clearly hear shouting and the thumps of people running about on the floor below. A pair of preoccupied soldiers ran past the base of the stairs, but fortunately didn't look up at them.

Once the activity in their area appeared to settle down, with a wave of his hand Penriding signaled Horton and Ananke to continue on. Just when they reached the landing of the first floor, a door flew open right in front of them, revealing Constable Keen.

"Mr. Blacksmith?" the constable inquired. "What are you doing down here? Can't you hear the—"

"Sir!" a guard came running over. Horton recognized the voice beneath the helmet. It was quite muffled, but it was definitely Linden. "Sir, I'm in the process of escorting these three to the basement bunker – I was making sure the way ahead was clear."

The constable glared at her for a moment.

"Do not leave their side again, soldier," he boomed. "Now get on your way!"

"Yes sir, sorry sir!" Linden responded. She grabbed Penriding's arm and pulled him away from the constable with Horton and Ananke right behind.

"Way too close," Horton heard Penriding say under his breath as the four of them hastily exited through the manor's front door.

Outside, Horton could see that the alarm had effectively pulled almost all of the guards away from the front gate. All that was left were two youthful-looking soldiers, who quickly straightened themselves up at the sight of a now helmetless Linden as the group passed by.

Horton tried not to make eye contact with them as they passed, and for the first time he actually wished he had been wearing his protective headscarf to hide his face. He hadn't thought to put it on since it was nighttime.

Fortunately for them the guards didn't ask questions. It was clear by their deference to the leftenant that they considered her their superior. Linden guided the trio to an alleyway a few city blocks away from the manor and let them loose.

"Please be careful, all of you," Linden advised with a stern, almost motherly tone.

The three of them nodded and quickly went on their way. The pyramid wasn't any farther than a short walk from their location, but they knew things wouldn't be so easy once they got there.

FIVE

The Diversion

THE ZEPTUS CITY STREETS were quieter than the last
time Horton walked through them. Probably because of the
upswing in recent Vwari attacks, he figured.

The group was happy to discover it had no problems
getting to the base of the pyramid and then up the stairs
leading to the entrance of the Rissa. Once there, they concealed themselves behind a mound of crates off to one side
of the platform that extended along the southern side of the
pyramid, roughly half the way up.

Glancing over his shoulder, Horton witnessed an incredible view of the city he had seen only one time previously,
coming just after he'd been rudely awoken by Constable
Keen upon his accidental arrival at the Rissa. It was now late
evening, however, and the city's glowing hub spilled out
into the desert wastes that surrounded it, shedding some
light on the world beyond the city's walls in the clear night.

"Okay Ananke, let's figure out how—" Horton began, reverting his attention to the task at hand, but it was too late. Ananke, eager to fulfill his duty, already had thrown off his robe to reveal Horton's foreign white tunic and trotted himself out in front of a group of well-armed guards.

The guards eyed him suspiciously as he strolled past, and a few even began to slowly walk toward him, swords ready to be drawn.

"I don't think this is going to be enough," Horton pointed out to Penriding as the two peered out from between two stacks of crates. "There's way too many of them. We need to try something else."

"Relax, my friend," Penriding said, grinning. "If there is one thing my father taught me, it's that you always need a contingency plan."

Horton looked back over to Ananke, who was now walking almost directly in front of the pyramid's entrance. To his left was a small guardhouse with open supply crates outside it, waiting to be unpacked. Suddenly and without warning, Ananke reached into a pocket on the tunic and pulled out a small oblong object and threw it into one of the open crates before breaking out into a sprint.

"Hey you there, halt!" a guard that had been watching him yelled out.

Another guard ran over to the crate and looked inside.

"Bomb!" he shouted.

Horton snapped his head to look at Penriding who had begun to laugh. He couldn't believe what was happening.

Boom!

The bomb went off, taking out half the guardhouse

93

along with it. The guards who had not been sent flying in the blast took off in full chase of Ananke. Those fortunate enough to not take the full brunt of the explosion slowly gathered themselves and began to head after him too.

"Not bad for a kid," Penriding commented.

"Are you insane?" Horton screamed at Penriding, who quickly cupped Horton's mouth.

"Shut it! Someone will hear you!" Penriding whispered, fighting off Horton's attempts to pull his hand away from his face. He then shook the Illac to seize his attention before looking him right in the eyes.

"Look. The way inside the Rissa is clear. We need to move, now!" he said urgently, pointing to the entrance of the pyramid. "We don't have time to argue about what's already transpired. Let's go before it's too late."

Horton nodded reluctantly and Penriding pulled his hand away from Horton's mouth. Before anything else could be said Penriding bolted off toward the Rissa's entrance, leaving Horton standing there paralyzed momentarily. However, once he saw Penriding run through the now unguarded pyramid's entryway, he too put his head down and ran inside.

"Here, you've done this before," Penriding said once Horton caught up with him, the broken stone piece of the pedestal in his outstretched hand.

Horton snatched it away from Penriding and walked over to the broken pedestal he had woken up next to when he'd first arrived at Zeptus City. He examined the piece in his hand and what remained of the pedestal before him.

"It fits," he said to himself.

He wasn't sure how he was going to make it work, but he pushed the two pieces together like a jigsaw, hoping they would connect somehow. To Horton's relief, once they were pieced together he could feel each end pulling itself back into place with the other. Horton took a step back and looked at the now remolded but unlit pedestal, waiting for something to happen.

"Okay… and?" Penriding pestered as he paced back and forth behind Horton.

"I don't know!" Horton responded angrily. "I'm not exactly an expert on these damn things, okay?"

Suddenly the button on the far right of the pedestal's face lit up. It was yellow.

"Look!" Penriding whispered excitedly. "It's working!"

Then, in tandem, Horton and Penriding swiveled around to look back at the pyramid's entrance. There were voices approaching. Horton noticed a second button light up out of the corner of his eye, this time red.

"Quick, just push one!" Penriding said, running over to the pedestal.

"No!" Horton yelled as he used all his strength to hold Penriding back. "We've got to wait for the right one!"

The blue button lit up. Time was running out.

"Hey!"

A soldier leading a squad through the pyramid's entryway pointed at them.

"Quick, grab my hand!" Horton shouted to Penriding as the two hovered over the pedestal, ready to make the jump the instant the correct button was active.

Green.

Ba-beep! Beep!

The unlikely duo stood there hand-in-hand, breathing rapidly.

"It didn't work!" Penriding shouted, reaching out to the pedestal once again. "Hit another button!"

Horton grabbed the Zeptan's wrist just inches away from the red button.

"No, look!" Horton said, pointing behind them. A shroud of darkness had replaced the end of the room where the Rissa's entryway previously stood.

"We made it?" Penriding said, confounded for a moment before he realized they were, as Horton indicated, no longer inside the Rissa. "We did! We made— *oof!*"

Horton connected his fist squarely with Penriding's stomach.

"What in the gods is wrong with you?" Horton asked, grabbing Penriding by the collar as he keeled over in pain.

"Okay, okay, I deserved that," Penriding admitted as he winced in discomfort. "But hey – we're here aren't we?"

"Yeah we're here, but at what cost?" Horton fumed. "A simple diversion is one thing, but explosives? Ananke will be lucky if he's not executed for treason! I'm sick of you pulling these ridiculous charades behind my back all the time!"

"It's those ridiculous charades that got us here, kid," Penriding replied, trying to calm Horton down. "Look, don't worry about Ananke – he knew exactly what he was getting himself into. Besides, if it wasn't for me you would still be stuck in Zeptus City with no hope of ever finding your brother. You ought to be thanking me."

Horton released Penriding's collar from his clutches. He knew the Zeptan was probably right to some extent, but in the moment he was far too angry with him to ever admit it.

"I'm done talking to you," Horton announced in a huff as he made his way toward the door that joined their current chamber to the long hallway that led to the fox burrow and the outside world.

Penriding quietly followed a few paces behind, carrying an unusual cube he had brought along that looked like a miniaturized version of the lights Horton had seen hung throughout Zeptus City. It appeared to be some sort of torch, making it much easier to see where they were going as they walked down the pitch-black hallway.

"It's freezing in here," Penriding said, shivering, but Horton just ignored him and kept walking. With Penriding's torchlight he could already make out the end of the hallway, and as he expected, the entrance was still caved in with earth.

"Give me that," Horton sneered, snatching the cube of light out of Penriding's grasp.

"The surface is just beyond the top of this tunnel," Horton informed him as he shined the light as high up the burrow as he could.

"Simple enough," Penriding noted as he inspected the mound of dirt that had built up during the cave in. "I'm pretty sure I can make it up to the top. Keep that light pointed up there so I can see what I'm doing."

Penriding had already begun scaling the steep earth pile before Horton could respond in any way. Fortunately, the earth was soft and malleable, allowing him to gain a strong foothold by wedging his feet into it as he pulled himself up. Once he had climbed as high as he could, he began scraping at the burrow's ceiling with his hand, trying to break through to the surface.

"The earth is too hard and dry up here," he said after a couple of minutes with no success. "I can't get through without some kind of tool or—"

Penriding paused mid-sentence as he rifled through the satchel he had brought with him. After a few moments he pulled something out.

"Glad I brought another one just in case," Penriding shouted down to Horton, who could clearly see what the object was now. Not surprisingly, it was another bomb.

"May I please use this, your majesty?" Penriding asked sarcastically.

Horton bit down on his tongue. "Whatever. Just plant it and get down here quick."

"Yes, sir!" Penriding said enthusiastically as he dug a hole for the bomb in the softer dirt just below.

"Uh, you should probably get back," Penriding hollered down.

In agreement with Penriding for once, Horton retreated down the hallway to safety. He spun around as he heard Penriding sliding back down the mound, and a few seconds later the Zeptan appeared in his view, tumbling awkwardly down the side of the mass of earth and landing backside-first on the hard floor.

"Ouch!" Penriding yowled as he smacked into the metallic ground. He quickly pulled himself up and ran down the hallway to join Horton, all while rubbing his rear-end. Horton couldn't help but smirk.

Boom!

The sound of the explosion rang deafeningly through the hallway, causing Horton and Penriding to cover their ears. Temporarily disoriented, the pair stumbled around for a moment as they tried to recollect themselves.

"God damn," Penriding grimaced as he propped himself up against the hallway wall. "First you punch me and now this. I'm really getting beat up today."

"I'm glad you're enjoying it," Horton jibed.

Looking back down the hallway, Horton could see a beam of light had appeared, shining all the way down to the floor from the surface above. For better or for worse, Penriding's explosive devices were now two-for-two on the day.

Horton was the first to peer up from the hallway toward the now exposed world above. He could see leaf-filled tree branches gently swaying in the wind under the moon's soft glow. It felt good to be home.

One of the benefits of Penriding's bomb-contraption – besides blowing a massive hole in the ground – was that it had also thrown a tremendous amount of dirt down the fox burrow tunnel, making the climb up to the surface far less steep. Horton took the lead and climbed up first, followed closely by Penriding.

"Interesting," Penriding said to himself out loud as he gathered his bearings once topside. "The majority of the pyramid is underground, making it appear far smaller than the one in Zeptus. I wonder how deep underground they go."

Although Horton could hear Penriding talking, he wasn't paying attention to him. He was more concerned with figuring out which way his village was. He spun around a few times on his tiptoes as he searched for the distant hills he had previously used as a landmark to gauge direction.

"My village is this way," Horton announced as he caught sight of the hills between the treetops. "Let's get going. We don't have any time to waste."

After a short while of walking through the woods in awkward silence, the Zeptan decided to speak up.

"So the Illacs are the ones hogging all the damn trees," Penriding commented in hopes of getting some sort of reaction from Horton. "I think I can count every tree in Zeptus City with just my fingers."

Penriding stared at Horton as he awaited his response, but it didn't come. Not willing to just accept Horton's silent treatment, he decided to approach the Illac through a different avenue.

"So… are you excited to see your family and friends again?" he eagerly pressed.

Horton gritted his teeth. He had hoped Penriding wouldn't bring that subject up. He'd be damned if he was to acknowledge the Zeptan in any way at that moment, but he couldn't risk Penriding acting like an idiot once they reached the village.

"I think it'll be better if we aren't seen by anyone," Horton replied quickly.

"Don't get seen?" Penriding repeated, perplexed by his

request. "What do you mean? You haven't seen your people in weeks! I'm sure they're worried sick about you."

Horton sighed. "No, they won't be," he said quietly.

"What was that?" Penriding prodded.

Horton took a deep breath and stopped in his tracks.

"Look, the fact of the matter is I'm supposed to be dead," he reluctantly told Penriding.

"Dead?" Penriding asked, flabbergasted. "But you're not dead, you're alive! They'll be happy to see you!"

Horton laughed to himself and continued on his way towards the village. He didn't blame Penriding for not understanding, but it was amusing to hear him say something that seemed so naive.

"I'm assumed to be dead because I was supposed to be a sacrifice," Horton explained to Penriding as they carefully squeezed their way through heavy brush. "You see, every three years the Illacs hold an initiation for young men my age where we all have to make our way to the pyramid – we call it the Earth Stone – and return home with a small statue proving we found it. Unlike Zeptans, only initiated men in Illac know the location of the pyramid because it is in an area forbidden for anyone to travel except for the initiation. In my case I never returned and consequently became the sacrifice."

Glancing back at Penriding, Horton could tell by the bizarre face he was making that he was having trouble wrapping his head around the concept.

"Okay, so…" Penriding began, the gears slowly turning inside his mind, "without getting into the gritty details of your – I'm sorry – absurd religion, what would happen to you if you were to return to the village after being deemed the sacrifice?"

Horton thought to himself a moment. He had never considered that particular scenario.

"I have no idea," he told Penriding truthfully. "As far as I know, everyone who was supposed to be a sacrifice has never returned home, and quite frankly I don't plan on finding out. We're going straight to Ulises' home. No detours or sightseeing."

It wasn't until he said those last few words that he really thought about the possibility of seeing his mother again. Doing so would be risky and foolish, but then again it certainly couldn't hurt to at least check in on her without being noticed. As they trudged forward, Horton pushed that thought toward the back of his mind – for now, at least.

"I think I see something," Penriding pointed out from beside him.

He was right. There was a glimmer of light shining through the thick wall of trees ahead of them, coming from what was likely to have been the temple's bell tower. The two pushed their way through some deep thickets and found themselves standing at the edge of the village's clearing, just beyond the dry creek bed that ran along its eastern border.

"There – Ulises lives right next to that temple," Horton said to Penriding as he pointed to a thatched-roof building standing in the temple's moonlight shadow.

"We can't just walk up and knock, especially wearing these clothes," the Illac instructed. "We should go around and come in through those fields to the northeast."

"Exactly what I was thinking," Penriding agreed.

The two carefully made their way around the edge of the village, just beyond the boundaries of the clearing so as not to be seen. They hopped over an old wooden fence that held a small herd of sheepigs and quickly scurried across the field to reach the back side of the temple. They were just a stone's throw away from Ulises' home now and could see the flickering of candlelight through one of its open windows. With the area apparently clear, the pair sped over to the open window and crouched down below it. Unfortunately it was too high for either of them to see through on their own, so Penriding offered Horton a boost so he could take a peek inside.

"I can see a priest," Horton whispered to Penriding who was struggling to hold him up. "It's not Ulises though."

"Damn, you're a lot heavier than you look," Penriding grunted. "It's like trying to lift a midget-shaped block of iron."

"Shut up!" Horton hissed.

On the other side of the window was a priest reading a book near the front door to the priests' common room. Horton anticipated that Ulises was probably sleeping in his room at this point, but had no idea what time it was.

"Excuse me, what are you doing?" a voice called from behind them.

Both Penriding and Horton jumped at the sound of the anonymous inquisitor, sending Horton tumbling down onto Penriding and into a pile below the window with a giant thud. Horton looked up as he untangled himself from Penriding to find it was just a young Illac girl carrying a small pail of water. He hadn't known her personally but he recalled seeing her at school before. She was a few years younger than Deforest.

"We, uh… well," Horton began.

"Hey I know you," the kid said. "You're Deforest's stupid brother."

"Me? Are you crazy? Of course I'm not him," Horton insisted, "—and what do you mean by stupid?"

"*We*," Penriding interrupted, followed by a pause to glare at Horton before continuing, "are actually the Blacksmith brothers. We come from a very long and vaguely illustrious heritage of wood merchants, I'll have you know."

Horton raised an eyebrow at Penriding.

"We live deep in the forest you see, over yonder," Penriding explained as he flicked his finger in the direction they had come from. "That is why you have probably never heard of or seen us before. You see all the wood here in the village?"

The girl looked around and nodded.

"You are very much welcome," Penriding said with a cavalier nod. "Now, we have a very important delivery and mustn't be late. We need to speak with the good Priest Ulises, does he live here?"

She nodded once more.

"Wonderful. Now be a good girl and bring him out here to see us please," Penriding eloquently commanded with just a hint of desperation.

The kid looked at Horton and Penriding for a moment as if examining them, then shrugged.

"Okay!" she happily replied to their relief, before skipping off towards the front door of the building.

"Nice girl," Penriding commented as she disappeared out of sight around the corner of the building. "It's good to know not all Illacs are devoid of manners."

Horton rolled his eyes and leaned against the side of the building. A minute or so later the little girl returned with Ulises in tow.

"You said they live where? They work as blacksmiths? They are making a delivery of what?"

And then Ulises made eye contact with Horton. He stopped where he was and just looked at him for a moment, his eyes unblinking.

"Thank you, Vash, that will do," Ulises told the girl without removing his focus from Horton. "Please go home to your family now."

She nodded once more and sauntered away with pail in hand. As Ulises made his way toward him, Horton couldn't help but smile at the sight of his old friend.

"Horton," Ulises said quietly as he hugged him, "it is good to see you – and smiling too."

"You're not surprised to see me?" Horton asked. "I presumed everyone would think I was dead."

"Oh, I have lived long enough to know that nothing is impossible, my boy," Ulises replied, "but yes, the village – and your mother – believe you to be dead."

Horton's heart wrenched at the thought of his mother.

"And who is this with you?" Ulises said as he turned to examine Penriding, but before Horton could introduce the Zeptan, the priest was distracted by another thought.

"What happened to Thomas?" he asked.

Horton cocked his head. "Thomas?"

"Yes," Ulises said. "When neither you nor Thomas returned after the initiation we assumed you had both been sacrificed."

This was unexpected. Horton assumed that he had been the only sacrifice from the initiation. He bit his lip and tried to think back to that fateful day, but as hard as he tried, he could not recall seeing Thomas at all. It didn't make sense that he would have been a sacrifice too.

Then it struck him. He may have taken one of the statues before he entered the pyramid. Horton had a vague memory of grabbing one of the clay figures, but he could not remember definitively one way or the other. The only way to know for sure would be to look inside his satchel, but it had come loose and disappeared into the darkness the first time he had fallen down the fox burrow.

"I have no idea what happened to him," Horton eventually spat out a half-truth. By all means he despised Thomas more than anything, but he would never wish such a fate upon anyone, and the last thing he wanted at this point was more blood on his hands.

"This is highly unusual, Horton," Ulises said sternly. "First two sacrifices and now your return. Yes, the gods are surely up to something."

"Ulises, we have returned here because we need to speak to you," Penriding interrupted, cutting to the chase. "In private, please."

"Oh – yes, yes. Of course," Ulises uttered as he seemed to snap out of deep thought. "Please, follow me to my quarters."

Horton and Penriding followed Ulises inside. To their fortune the other priest who had been reading a book by the door didn't bother to glance up and see who had entered with Ulises. Horton didn't dare look too closely, but he suspected the priest may have fallen asleep.

"Would you like some tea?" Ulises asked once the three of them were in his room.

"Oh, yes please!" Penriding said enthusiastically.

Ulises raised an eyebrow at him, and then turned around to put the kettle in the fireplace.

"I suppose it would be simpler if I just ask you to start from the top, Horton," Ulises said as he stoked the fire. "Why this peculiar man is here with you, how in the gods' names you are still alive, etcetera, etcetera."

And so he did start from the top. Horton told him all about how he had fallen into the fox burrow on the day of the initiation, how he'd found the pedestal with four buttons that sent him to Zeptus City, how he'd been rescued and cared for by the Blacksmiths, how Penriding had taken him out on the wastes in search of the other pyramids, only to find that they weren't where they thought they were.

Ulises sat there with his hand pressed firmly onto his cheek for the duration of Horton's retelling of his travels, intently absorbing what he heard. He cast his eyes downward, staring deeply into his lap. Then, without warning, he closed them.

Not sure of what to do, Horton and Penriding glanced at one another.

"Is he asleep?" Penriding mouthed silently to Horton, who shrugged.

"Excuse me," Horton said gently, trying to regain Ulises' attention, "are you with us, Uli—?"

Then, in a split second, Ulises stood up from his chair.

"I am sorry – I was somewhere else entirely for a moment there," he apologized. "Please excuse me, I will return shortly."

Horton and Penriding looked at one another incredulously as Ulises departed the room.

"Charming fellow that Ulises," Penriding said in a sarcastic tone. "And I think he's forgotten about my tea."

Horton sighed to himself and wondered what Ulises was up to. He was beginning to think it may have been a mistake returning to Illac, that Ulises wouldn't have the answers they were looking for.

"I noticed you didn't mention anything about your brother to Ulises," Penriding quietly pointed out to Horton, but before he could say anything more Ulises reemerged through the door with his hands full of curled-up papers.

"These…" Ulises began as he plopped the stack down on the table, releasing a large cloud of dust into the air that caused Horton to have to fight back the urge to sneeze, "are older than I am, believe it or not. They are the only records of the outside world we Illacs have."

"Why haven't I heard of these before?" Horton inquired.

Ulises paused for a second before answering. "Frankly my boy, they were always thought to be fabricated, made-up lies. However, for reasons unknown to me, they have been kept and stored away."

The old priest pulled a few sheets of paper out of the pile and opened each one up slightly, just enough so as to catch a glimpse of its contents before swiftly setting it aside. He did this with a few of them before he found what he was looking for.

"Ah, here it is," he said before turning to walk it to another table against the back wall of the room. Horton and Penriding followed closely in his wake, their anticipation growing with every moment. Ulises then flattened the paper, spread it out onto the table and blew off the thick layer of dust it had accumulated.

Horton, meanwhile, had pulled himself in closer to get a better look, but couldn't make heads or tails of it. He could clearly see it was a map of some sort, but it was unlike anything he had ever seen before and was covered in written script he could not understand.

"What does it say?" Horton asked as Ulises scanned the map with his eyes.

"This is definitely some type of ancient Zeptan alphabet," Penriding pointed out, "but it's in a language I'm not familiar with."

"This map is many centuries old, my boy," Ulises noted. "There are very few who can read it."

"Hold on," Penriding said, pointing at a small symbol in the shape of a triangle on the map. "Look. *Zebitas*. That's got to be Zeptus City. And here – look."

Penriding pointed to another triangle, this one lying to the west at the far left end of the map.

"*Ilakium*," he read out loud before turning to look at Horton and Ulises. "Illac."

Penriding slid his finger to the east now, past Zeptus City. Eventually he came across another triangle.

"*Tiberonus*," he announced. "There's our third pyramid. They all lie in a line along the equator."

"And the fourth pyramid?" Horton asked.

Penriding scoured the map with his eyes.

"That's all there is," he eventually said with a look of disappointment. "There's nothing else here."

Horton looked over the map too. He looked up and down and in every corner, but there were no more triangles.

He had, however, noticed that Ulises' hand was covering a small section of the map right at the bottom. At first he wasn't going to say anything, but he figured it wouldn't hurt to be thorough.

"Excuse me, Ulises," Horton said. "Your hand is covering a bit of the map."

"My what is where?" Ulises asked quizzically, as if awoken from a stupor.

"Your hand," Horton said again, this time grabbing his old friend's wrist and pulling it away from the map.

And there it was, just as if it were trying to hide itself from them. The fourth triangle they had been looking for, sitting as far south as the map permitted.

"Oh my, that was silly of me," Ulises said apologetically.

Horton looked at Penriding. He could see the Zeptan staring at the fourth triangle with a disconcerted look on his face.

"*Exetus*," the Zeptan muttered in a shallow voice.

"What's the matter, Pen?" Horton asked. "We've found the locations of the pyramids, aren't you happy?"

"Huh?" Penriding responded, snapping out of a haze himself. "Oh, yeah, I'm very excited. Ulises, thank you very much for this. Do you mind if we borrow it?"

"The map?" Ulises asked.

"Yes, the map," Penriding replied. "We will return it once our journey is completed, of course."

Ulises sighed to himself and wandered over to his chair in the corner of the room and plopped himself into it. He stared blankly for a moment, his fingers twirling his old gray beard.

"You may," Ulises eventually confirmed, to which Horton and Penriding looked at each other, grinning ear to ear. "But only under one condition."

Their grin quickly transformed into a shared look of concern. They turned back to Ulises for the verdict, but instead found him with his eyes closed. Penriding lowered his head and sighed.

"And that condition is...?" Horton said loudly to rekindle Ulises' attention.

"I accompany you!" Ulises abruptly declared with a finger raised as he propped himself upright in his chair.

Horton noticed Penriding grimace slightly at the priest's request. He had a feeling the Zeptan wasn't entirely comfortable with bringing Ulises along, but in the end he simply gave Penriding a small shrug. They didn't really have any other option after all.

"You understand it will be dangerous," Penriding informed the old priest sternly. "I cannot be held accountable for your safety."

"Yes, I understand," Ulises said, smiling. "I am an old man and have lived within the same set boundaries my entire life, like all Illacs do. Yet I sit here wondering, now near the end of my tenure, what would or could have – or perhaps should have, been. Please grant an old man some happiness before his time is up. Please allow me to break free."

Penriding tiredly rubbed his face, clearly subdued by the priest's request. He rolled his eyes and threw his hands up in the air.

"Fine, fine," he reluctantly obliged, "but we are leaving right now. Grab your things."

"Oh my," Ulises uttered as he laboriously pulled himself up from his chair. "I will just be a moment, then."

Horton and Penriding sat at Ulises' table inspecting the map as the elderly priest prepared his belongings.

"We will first head east toward the pyramid at Tiberonus," Penriding said as he plotted a route with his finger.

"It's weird, these land masses don't match current Zeptan records at all," Penriding went on. "And these lines here, what do you think they mean?"

Horton looked over at the map to see what the Zeptan was referring to. He had no idea what the wavy lines could signify.

"I don't know, maybe water?" Horton suggested. "Like an ocean?"

"Water?" Penriding said, laughing. "Oceans of water only exist in children's fairytales. It's probably just changes in terrain or something."

"Yeah, probably," Horton said, regretting he had suggested it in the first place.

"Okay, I am ready to depart," Ulises reappeared with a small satchel flung over his shoulder.

"About time," Penriding remarked under his breath as he rolled up the map. "Let's get going then."

The three of them made their way to Ulises' door and slowly opened it. The priest who had been reading a book in the common room was still there. Initially Horton wasn't too concerned by this, but when he noticed the priest lift his hand to turn a page. Horton jumped back in retreat to Ulises' quarters.

Smiling, Ulises signaled Horton with his finger to follow close behind him, and acting as naturally as possible, he led Horton and Penriding quickly through the common room toward the front door.

"Do not stay up reading too late tonight, Diyah," Ulises commented to his fellow priest as they walked past. "I will be away for a short while. See you soon."

"Mmhmm," the priest responded, still refusing to lift an eye off his book.

The trio then vacated the building as briskly as they could, happy to have avoided detection so far.

"I really should have worn that damn head scarf," Horton said regretfully as they walked down the path from the temple to the eastern forest.

"You're supposed to be wearing it anyway," Penriding added.

"Just stay close my boy; you will be fine," Ulises reassured.

It was just when the group reached the edge of the village that Horton made a sudden decision.

"You guys go on to the Earth Stone, there's something I've got to do," he announced unexpectedly, and before Ulises or Penriding could stop him Horton had turned his back to them and was running at full speed back into the village.

"Are you insane? Get back here!" Penriding hissed, but it was too late. Horton had already made up his mind. He was going to see his mother.

Horton darted up the lane toward his home, all the while keeping his face hidden as best he could. He didn't expect to see anyone outside at this time of night, but he didn't want to take any chances. It wasn't long before he could see his house and the gentle flittering of candlelight through one of its windows. Normally it would have been very unusual for his mother to be up this late.

He approached the nearest window and carefully peered through. Inside was his mother sitting in her chair, fast asleep. Laid in her lap was an old book full of folk tales she used to read to Deforest and him when they were young. At the sight of this Horton seriously considered going inside so he could hug her and tell her he was still alive, that Deforest may also still be alive. He stood there contemplating the idea for a few minutes, but ultimately couldn't bring himself to do it. He couldn't bear to put her through saying goodbye to one of her sons once again. He promised himself the next time his mother sees him he will be staying for good.

Horton wiped his eyes and stepped away from the window. Not wanting to make this any more difficult than it already was, he spun around and ran back down the lane toward the edge of town. As he ran he could see those distant hills he had once wanted to escape to so badly, and he couldn't help but feel ashamed with himself for ever thinking like that. In fact, he would have given anything to be back home with his mother and Deforest once again.

SIX

AUI 2-318

HORTON CAUGHT UP with Penriding and Ulises near the edge of the woods, just past the dry creek. He expected they'd be angry and would tell him off for doing something so foolish, but to his relief, they didn't.

"So where'd you go?" Penriding questioned just after they had begun making their way through the woods toward the Earth Stone.

"Home," Horton said softly.

"Did you see your mother?" Penriding asked.

"Yes."

Horton noticed Penriding and Ulises quickly exchange glances with each other.

"She didn't see you, did she?" Penriding asked after a short pause.

"No, she didn't see me," Horton proclaimed loudly, catching his two companions off guard. "I…"

Horton started to explain himself, but he didn't know where to begin to express his feelings.

"I didn't know what to do," he finally said, solemnly. "It hurt too much to stay."

"You did the right thing, Horton," Ulises said as he wrapped his arm around Horton's shoulder. "Your mother has been a broken woman since you left. She has lost her husband and now both her sons in a very short time. It would be very difficult for her to let you go a second time."

Horton nodded to his old friend in understanding.

By the time the three of them reached the Earth Stone the sun was beginning to rise on the horizon. It had taken much longer than usual to return to the pyramid because Ulises was a slow walker, to Penriding's annoyance. That didn't bother Horton, though. He knew Penriding would probably never agree with him, but he was happy to have Ulises accompany them on their journey.

"What in the gods have you done?" Ulises groaned when he spotted the cavernous hole in the ground made by Penriding's bomb. "Do you know how long it takes to fill in those damn fox burrows? And now you go and do this?"

Penriding laughed, but Horton's curiosity was piqued.

"So the priests know there are holes leading into the Earth Stone?" he asked.

"Well, yes. I suppose so," Ulises answered abruptly, as if caught a little off-guard.

"And none of you ever went inside?" Horton pressed.

"Of course not – it is forbidden," the old priest explained. "Our duty is to keep these holes covered over so the initiates do not end up falling into them."

Horton noticed Penriding glance at him and snicker to himself.

"So nobody had ever ventured inside the Earth Stone before?" Horton continued.

"No," Ulises told him. "Not to my knowledge. Not until now."

Horton led the way down the earth pile and into the darkness of the pyramid. As they descended the incline, he motioned to Penriding to hand over the cube of light so he could take a quick look for the satchel he had lost the first time he'd fallen into the burrow. In the end he didn't have to look far to find it – a fox had dragged it into a corner of the tunnel and was using it as a bed. The fox appeared wary yet undaunted by Horton, who slowly walked over to it with his arms outstretched, ready to pull the bag out from under the lazy fox.

"Hey little guy," Horton uttered as if talking to a small child. "If you don't mind, I'll take tha—"

Just before he could grab hold of it, the fox seized the bag in his mouth and bolted off, dragging the satchel deeper into the pyramid. Reacting quickly, Horton followed in pursuit of the culprit, and despite briefly tripping over himself as he ran down the pile of earth leading to the hallway, he swiftly regained his composure and kept pace. The little fox struggled to reach getaway speed with the relatively heavy satchel snared in its teeth, yet still managed to keep just a few strides ahead of Horton.

Surprisingly, the fox turned a sharp left at the end of the hallway and in through the dark doorway Horton had not yet explored. With the cube of light in his hands, the Illac disregarded any short-lived sentiments of fear and barreled right in after him. He followed the fox for about fifty yards of twisting and turning through an empty maze of corridors until he unexpectedly stumbled across an open doorway in the wall and came to an abrupt halt. The fox, as though confused as to why their cat-and-mouse game had suddenly ended, glared at Horton through the darkness with its glowing, beady eyes. Then, as if to call a parley, it dropped the satchel from its mouth and scampered off.

Horton paid no further notice to the fox, however, because his focus was directed towards something far more interesting. Somehow in the midst of the Earth Stone's system of dark passageways, he had entered into a solitary room with an entirely separate pedestal of its own. He knew right away there was something different and perhaps special about this pedestal compared to the ones he had already seen. Squarely on its face sat a single, brightly lit button whose light adorned the small room that housed it with an almost dreamlike purple hue. So fascinated by it was Horton that he came within inches of pressing it without thinking twice of where it could have taken him without his companions.

"Horton!"

A faint call echoed through the corridors, snapping Horton out of his deep gaze as he hovered closely over the button. He yanked his body away from the pedestal and back into the corridor.

"I'm here!" Horton called out into the darkness. He shivered and watched his breath condense into a fog in front of his face as he awaited a response.

"Say again!" suddenly rung off the metallic walls, much closer this time.

"This way!" Horton shouted again.

A few moments later Penriding popped out from around a corner near the end of the corridor, and the instant he knew the others had found him Horton reverted his attention to the purple button in the room beside him. He could hear Penriding scolding him for running off as the Zeptan and Ulises joined him inside the room, but an air of silence came over them when they too saw it.

"It's incredible," Penriding eventually pronounced as he returned Horton's satchel to him, having picked it up in the hallway. "Should we push it?"

"I'm thinking about it," Horton replied, turning to look at Ulises for a verdict.

"I am just along for the ride," Ulises noted.

The trio approached the pedestal, ready to discover what secrets it held.

"Wait."

Everyone blinked out of their fixation as Horton pulled his companions away from the button.

"Before we do this I need to warn you," he said in a serious manner. "From my experience not all of these are safe to use."

Ulises and Penriding looked at each other.

"Make sure you hold your breath," Horton instructed. "We know nothing about where we're going. The air on the other side might not be breathable, so we may need to immediately jump back."

"A wise precaution," Ulises responded while Penriding nodded in agreement.

"Okay," Horton whispered and reached out to push the button. "Oh, and—"

Horton presented his hands for Ulises and Penriding to grab on to, which they did.

"Uh," Horton looked at his companions, realizing he now had no hands free to hit the button.

"I will do it!"

Ba-beep! Bom!

Before any of the others could react Ulises went ahead and pushed the button, and they instantly found themselves standing in an even smaller room with a four-buttoned pedestal at its center. Around them pale blue lights lined the base of the walls, lending the space an ominous aura.

They looked at each other with eyes wide and lips pursed before Penriding raised his hand up to signal the others that he would be the first to test the air. He sucked in a small mouthful at first, then a larger one, before exhaling.

"Perhaps a little dry, but seems safe to me," he shrugged nonchalantly.

Horton and Ulises then cautiously took in breaths of their own and confirmed the air was indeed safe.

"Oh and one question," Penriding queried Horton. "Do we actually have to hold hands when we do that or are you just doing it for your own sick pleasure?"

Horton laughed.

"I don't know why," he shrugged. "It just seems to make sense I guess."

Meanwhile, Ulises had begun to investigate the hallway outside the room.

"A most unfamiliar material," Ulises noted, grabbing

the attention of his companions. "I do not believe I have ever seen anything quite like it."

He was right – the walls here were not made up of the uniform dark metal Horton had seen at the other pyramids. They were light gray in color and slightly squishy to the touch, almost as if the walls were firm cushions.

"I guess we can go this way," Horton suggested, leading the group down the dimly lit corridor.

"Don't you go running off this time, kid," Penriding told him.

"Hey, I found this place, didn't I?" Horton retorted, shooting back a glance at the Zeptan. "Plus I got my satchel back."

It was the first time Horton had thought to take a look through his repossessed bag to see if it had a statue in it or not. It didn't take long to find out – as soon as he opened the satchel it was right there looking up into his eyes, as if taunting him.

What he had feared was true. He had in fact taken a statue during his initiation. It meant an Illac's blood – Thomas' blood – was on his hands. Horton looked over at the others and stuffed the statue deep down inside his satchel. He knew he ought to tell Ulises he had possessed a statue all along, but decided against it for the meantime. As they traversed their way through the labyrinth of alien corridors, he tried to block the whole Thomas ordeal out of his mind.

"I don't understand this at all," Penriding spoke up after a few minutes of what felt like aimless walking. "There are corridors upon corridors, yet no more doors or rooms. Why would anyone build such immense and bizarre constructs?"

"The gods," Ulises answered with a smile. "It is not always the destination that is most important, but the journey. Be patient, when we are ready we will find what we are looking for."

"What are we looking for?" Horton asked.

"That is up to each of us to decide for ourselves," Ulises replied, putting his hand on Horton's shoulder. "Sometimes we do not know what that is until we find it."

Horton wasn't sure he completely understood, but he smiled and nodded back at his old friend.

"Hey look," Penriding said as he pointed up the hall ahead of them. "I think there's a door up there, see it?"

He was right. Near the end of the corridor was an open door. Horton and Penriding sped up their pace as they marched towards it. Horton hoped he would spot some sort of colored light – or anything – as he approached the room, but unlike the minimally lit corridors, it appeared to be completely dark inside.

He was only a few steps away now. He took a deep breath and peered inside the room with the aid of his light cube, hoping to discover something of significance within.

Horton's heart leaped. He squinted his eyes and then rubbed them to ensure they weren't deceiving him. He looked at Penriding, and judging by the look on his face he was seeing the same thing too.

"Deforest!"

Horton broke out into a sprint towards his brother. Deforest was standing in the middle of a pitch-black room with his back to the door, his hooded white tunic radiating back the glow from his light cube as though he were an angel – or a ghost.

However, Horton quickly realized that something was awry and brought himself to a stop just a few steps shy of his brother. He watched intently as Deforest slowly turned himself around, revealing that he was not in fact Deforest, but a similar-looking boy probably closer to Horton's age. It also became clear to him that what he was looking at was not only someone else, but possibly some*thing* else. As he stood there face to face with the boy in white, he could see there was little in the way of emotion or expression in his face. His eerie, almost unnatural aura sent shivers tingling up his spine. It was as though he was a lifeless shell.

Ulises, only just now making his way to the door, gasped at the sight.

"It is him," he whispered under his breath.

Penriding and Ulises looked at each other and then made their way in behind Horton, who remained standing just a few yards away from the boy.

Then without warning the boy spoke to them. Horton leaned in slightly as he tried to make any sense of his soft voice, but he was clearly communicating in a language Horton had ever heard before. This prompted the young Illac to turn back to his companions in search of answers but he found none.

Suddenly the boy took a step towards Horton, whose instinct was to retreat, but to his own surprise he held his ground. He took a deep breath as he felt his heart thumping in his chest.

Horton flinched as the boy raised his hand up, palm outward toward him. He just looked at it for a moment, not exactly sure what the boy wanted him to do. Then, against his own best judgment, he put his own hand up to the boy's.

Horton expected the boy's hand to feel like something – cold, warm, soft, calloused – but it was none of those things. It was solid to the touch, but that was it. Horton looked into the boy's cold, dead eyes as they stood there in this peculiar connection, and as he did he could have sworn he saw some life return to them. Whether it was understanding, comradery, or perhaps even life itself he did not know, but there was something.

"Horton."

It spoke as it pulled its hand away from Horton's and back to its side.

"Son of… Klas," it said deliberately, as though examining everything it was saying.

"Yes," Horton said quietly, taken aback. "Are you… a god?"

It cocked its head slightly at the question.

"You are not the first to ask me that," it said. "I do not believe I am."

"Then who are you?" Horton asked.

"My designation is AUI 2-318," it answered. "I am Armstrong Station Six's artificial User interactant. However, my line of interactants are commonly referred to simply as 'AI.' You also may do so."

"So you're a person in the same sense we are, AI?" Penriding asked. "When you say 'interactant,' you mean you're a machine, don't you?"

"What you see before you is a holographic representation generated in order to facilitate the User's connection to this station's computer systems," it responded. "I am not a physical machine, but rather a rigid projection made up of light and photons to create the physical embodiment of what could be referred to as a machine."

"You're not alive?" Penriding continued to question Al. "You don't have a beating heart, blood, or anything?"

"No," Al replied. "My purpose is to fulfill my primary orders as directed by the User."

"So you will do anything you're ordered to do?" Penriding said as he formed a wide grin. "Stand on one leg."

"Any orders provided by non-User parties must be authorized by the User," Al replied.

"The User?" Penriding repeated. "Who is the User, Al?"

"Horton is this station's current primary User," Al stated.

"Me the User?" Horton suddenly blurted. "What makes me a User and not Penriding?"

Al cocked his head again slightly as he turned to Horton. "Are you not Horton, son of Klas, son of Jamic, son of Ober, son of…"

Horton and his companions stood there in disbelief as Al continued on naming Horton's descendants. Horton wasn't sure whether he should be terrified or impressed by this boy's – or rather, this thing's – incredible knowledge of his lineage.

"…son of Franklin, son of Commander Stephen P. Johnson?"

"Uh, yes. Yes I am," Horton warily confirmed.

"Then you are this station's User," Al declared.

"Okay," Horton said, looking at Ulises and Penriding. "Then what is the purpose of this station?"

"Armstrong Station Six is the operational headquarters of the Sunbound Initiative," Al responded. "This station is responsible for the sustention of its four sub-stations on Earth over the course of its operation, or otherwise until its primary objective is accomplished."

"Four sub-stations.... I think he means the pyramids," Penriding noted.

"What are the pyramids – I mean sub-stations – for?" Horton questioned Al as he continued his search for answers.

"User query is unknown," Al replied to their disbelief.

"You're in charge of the sub-stations, right?" Horton asked. "And you don't even know what they do?"

"I am unable to retrieve the necessary information from my database to answer that query," Al informed him. "Connection to non-vital data storage was severed after a runtime of 468 years, eight months to preserve remaining energy."

"468 years?" Ulises gasped. "I cannot believe it has been that long."

"How long has it been since that connection was severed, Al?" Horton inquired.

"User query is unknown," it replied again.

"This is incredible," Penriding mused to himself. "The greatest discovery of our time, surely."

The Zeptan then pulled out a cube of light from his satchel and began to inspect the area. As he walked he uncovered panels of buttons and screens with unusual circular seats next to them. As Horton watched Penriding make his way around the room, he imagined ancient humans bustling in and out of it while they worked on something that was surely of great significance. He just wished he knew what it was.

"Magnificent," Penriding said, examining the panels. "The technology of these people – sorry, of us – hundreds or perhaps thousands of years ago is mind-boggling. Al, what happened to the people who built all of this?"

"Non-User query is unknown," Al answered.

"Of course Alf doesn't know," Penriding said, rolling his eyes, and then he froze. Al had left the spot he had been stationed at and was walking over toward the Zeptan.

"Hey look, I'm sorry," Penriding said apologetically. "I was just joking with the Alf thing; I know your name is—"

"May I have your energy cell, please?" the hologram asked, holding out his hand. Penriding raised his eyebrow at Horton and then placed the cube of light into Al's hand.

In an extraordinary display, Al grasped the cube with both hands and pressed it directly into his chest, which absorbed the cube entirely. Horton and his companions looked at one another in disbelief while Al stood there motionless for a moment, glowing brighter than ever. Then, without warning, the lights and panels around the room suddenly clicked to life, revealing it to them. The room itself wasn't overly big – not nearly as large as the chamber that held the pedestal with the four buttons – but it was a considerable size nonetheless. Besides the door they had entered in through, the room was entirely enclosed.

"Well that's convenient," Penriding commented smarmily. "Though I wish he'd mentioned I wouldn't be getting it back. It's not like those things grow on trees, you know."

Clank.

Horton and the others jerked their heads in surprise as a heavy, metallic sound resounded through the air.

Click.

Whoosh!

A blinding light poured into the room as part of the wall in front of them mechanically slid away, revealing a window that provided Horton with a view he would remember the rest of his life.

"My god," Penriding mouthed with a slack jaw.

"I do not believe I – what is that?" Ulises asked, covering his eyes from the glare.

"Don't you recognize your own planet when you see it, priest?" Penriding responded with his face now almost pressed up to the window.

What Horton had suspected was confirmed. He could recognize that hazy brown color from any distance. They were looking down at the Earth from space.

"Please enjoy the view," Al said, smiling for the first time. "My previous User felt this kept things in perspective – when the sun is behind us, of course."

"We're in space?" Horton asked despite already knowing the answer.

"Yes," Al affirmed. "Armstrong Station Six is located inside the Plato crater on the Moon."

Horton watched Al closely as he spoke. It was inexplicable – he was almost certain he had seen him before somewhere, but he couldn't quite put his finger on it. He knew that it was impossible, though, and instead continued to press Al for any additional information that might help lead them to Deforest.

"So now that you've got some power, can you tell us what the sub-stations are for?" Horton pushed hopefully.

"I am sorry, I still do not have access to that data," Al replied. "I will need to regain full power in order to access all primary and secondary systems. I was able to access my hospitality sub-routines, however. Hopefully you will find me to be more personable."

"Fair enough," Penriding noted. "What needs to be done to restore full power?"

"This station is supplied power via its four sub-stations on the surface," Al said. "Unfortunately it appears all the sub-stations have fallen into disrepair. Sensors indicate that sub-stations Green and Orange are operating at low-level settings, but nowhere near full capacity."

"So that's it," Penriding said in a defeated tone. "They'll remain relics forever."

"Actually," Al interjected, holding up his finger. Horton, Penriding and Ulises then watched with fascination as Al reached into his chest with his opposite hand, pulled out a glowing blue orb and displayed it out in front of him. "There is something you can do. This is a diagnostic and repair tool that can be used to restore full operation to the four sub-stations."

"Isn't that a little flashy for a tool?" Penriding asked.

"The physical appearance of the tool is trivial," Al countered with a smile. "In fact, I fashioned this tool specifically as a facsimile of that tool you brought with you. I can adjust it to your own parameters if you wish."

Horton smiled. "That'll be fine, Al."

"Whoa, wait just a minute," Penriding blurted, stepping in front of Al. "We're not even sure what we're agreeing to here. Say we actually manage to fix the pyramids and restore power, then what? Who knows what this thing is capable of? For all we know Al could be lying to us. By Rissa, the pyramids could be some kind of super weapon left here by alien tree-beings to destroy us."

"You're overreacting, Penriding," Horton responded. "The pyramids have proven to be anything but weapons. As far as we know they're the only source of life left on Earth. Imagine if they were operational – they could possibly give new life to the entire planet."

"The User's hypothesis is rational," Al affirmed. "Though unfortunately, I do not have access to the relevant data in order to support the possibility of sentient tree life forms."

Penriding groaned and sat down in one of the circular seats by the panels. "Why do I feel like you're mocking me, Al?"

"That is not possible, non-User," Al replied. "My programming does not permit me to lie."

Penriding glared at Al for a moment before shaking his head and turning his attention back to Horton.

"Why do you even care so much about the pyramids?" the Zeptan questioned. "All you care about is finding your brother, right?"

Horton bowed his head. He had really hoped to avoid revealing the truth to Ulises about what happened to Deforest.

"What is this about your brother?" Ulises asked Horton. "Is he not dead? What happened to him?"

Horton clenched his jaw. He felt like punching Penriding in the stomach again.

"He... I'll tell you about it later, Ulises," Horton murmured. "I really don't want to discuss it right now."

"Oh, haven't you heard, priest?" Penriding spoke up. "It's Horton's fault that Deforest disappeared. He's out there all alone and Horton doesn't even know where he is."

"Damn you, Penriding!" Horton yelled as he stomped over to the Zeptan. "It wasn't my fault! And why are you suddenly so afraid of uncovering the pyramids' secrets, huh? You didn't even blink an eye when you lied to your father so you could search for a pyramid, and look what that got you!"

Horton stood there breathing heavily from his rant. He clenched his fists and waited for Penriding to say something back, but he didn't. Instead the Zeptan just turned his back to the others and sat there looking blankly into the computer panel before him.

"The map," Penriding said suddenly in a shallow voice.

"What?" Horton asked, confused.

"On the map Ulises gave us there are four pyramids," Penriding told them as he swiveled back around in his seat. "Three of them lay along the equator. Illac to the west, Zeptus City in the center and another to the east – Tiberus or something like that."

"Tiberonus," Ulises corrected.

"Sure, whatever," Penriding said, "but there was another to the south on its own."

"Exetus," Penriding and Ulises said simultaneously.

"Right. I had heard my father say that name once before in the company of the highest-ranking councilmen of Zeptus City," Penriding went on. "They said it's where the Vwari come from."

Horton slowly walked over to the window and looked out at the Earth. He wasn't going to give up on finding Deforest just because a wrench was thrown into their plans.

"Well we can't just throw our hands up and call it a day," Horton declared. "We have come this far, surely there is something we can do. We can take soldiers, heck, even Linden said they're no match for—"

"No, Horton," Penriding interrupted. "Please, no. It's too dangerous. I've already lost too many people I care about to the Vwari. I couldn't live with myself if I lost Linden or you. Damnit, even gramps," he said, nodding his head toward Ulises.

The group was silent for a few moments, taking in everything. Horton didn't know how he could respond to that. He didn't think Penriding was the kind of person to care about anyone other than himself. To his surprise, it was Ulises who eventually cut the tension.

"Al, why is it you present yourself as that boy?" he asked, apparently to change the subject.

"My appearance is merely a simulation of my previous User," Al explained. "My local memory currently only contains the visual records of my last two Users, with the other being Horton."

"Yes, stick to that one, please," Horton requested. "It's weird enough talking to a machine, let alone yourself."

"Very well, User," Al said, smiling.

"So how exactly does this thing work?" Ulises asked as he plucked the blue orb out of Al's hand.

"Ulises, we've already decided we aren't going to repair the pyramids," Horton told the priest. "We'll find another way. Believe me, I want to find Deforest again more than anything, but Penriding is right. Putting more lives at risk in the process is not the right way to do it."

"I know," he replied. "That is why I am going to repair them on my own. Now as I was saying, how do I activate it, Al?"

As Al began explaining how to operate the orb to Ulises, Horton sat down next to Penriding who had his hand covering his face as he tried to contain his laughter.

"You see? He has completely lost his mind, Horton," Penriding said with a sigh. "I told you it was a bad idea to bring him along. He's going to get us all killed."

Horton didn't respond to Penriding's comment. He didn't want to admit it, but he agreed with him. He knew Ulises' wit had withdrawn itself somewhat in his old age, but he hadn't expected anything like this from him.

"Ulises," Horton said calmly, trying to satiate his old friend, "let's not do anything rash. Penriding and I will take you back to Illac. I think you'll be much happier at home."

"Do not address me as though I am a fool, young Illac," Ulises declared with a look of graveness Horton had not seen in the priest before. "The time has come for me to break free of my shackles and do what needs to be done to help this world thrive. Whether you can comprehend that or not I do not care; either accompany me or do not. Al, please show me the way back to the portal."

"Of course, please follow me," Al said as he swiftly marched out of the room with Ulises. Horton and Penriding quickly exchanged glances with one another before jumping in closely behind, unwilling to let the old priest go on alone.

"Al, stop right there," Horton commanded the hologram, but despite his request it continued to walk on.

"He will not listen to you, Horton," Ulises explained as they twisted and turned through the maze of corridors. "Al is a servant to his orders – his mission takes precedent over everything. User or not, he will not permit you to interrupt his primary function."

"Damnit, please reconsider what you're doing, Ulises," Horton plead. "If you do this none of us will likely live to see it through."

Ulises stopped in his tracks and turned to Horton.

"Horton, I need you to trust me," he said passionately. "By the gods' will it is imperative that we complete this task that has been bestowed upon us."

With his piece said the priest spun around and continued following Al. Horton and Penriding looked at one another, giving each other an expression as though to say, "what can we do?" before catching up to Ulises again.

It wasn't long before they were at the pedestal with the four buttons once more. Al and Ulises stood over its four brightly colored lights while Horton and Penriding remained in the doorway.

"The portal's green button will return you to the western sub-station. Illac, as you call it," Al informed the priest.

"Thank you Al," Ulises said, and then turned back to Horton and Penriding with his hands extended. "Will you join me? I will not last long on my own, I am sure."

Horton took a deep breath and sighed. As he grasped his old friend's hand he was certain he would regret what he was doing, but deep inside he trusted Ulises more than anyone. Although he had all but abandoned his faith in his people's gods, he somehow felt as though this was the destiny they had laid out before him. Perhaps Ulises was right about this.

Horton and Ulises then turned to Penriding, who was still standing cross-armed in the doorway. The Zeptan looked at them sternly for a second, then closed his eyes and shook his head.

"You two won't get anywhere without a wastewalker and crew," he said as he made his way over to Ulises and extended his hand to grab the priest's. However, just before he did he stopped himself.

"Hold on just a second, I have to ask," Penriding turned to the hologram. "Al, it's not necessary to hold hands when we use this portal thing, right?"

"Of course it is," Al replied. "How else would it work?"

"I, uh – right," Penriding grumbled as he grabbed Ulises' hand.

"Hit the button, Horton," Ulises ordered. "Let us get that pyramid up and running again."

Horton smiled and pressed the green button.

Ba-beep! Beep!

The trio looked around in every direction. The pale blue lights that previously lined the room disappeared and were replaced by a purplish tint on the walls, emitted from the pedestal they stood around. They had successfully returned to the pyramid in Illac.

"I guess we should begin repairs here," Penriding stated, prompting him and the others to make their way through the dark corridors and back to the pedestal in the Earth Stone's main chamber. "I'm hoping you remember Al's instructions on how to make that orb work, Ulises."

"I am not as senile as you make me out to be, my boy," Ulises said firmly as he fumbled through his bag. The priest's eyes lit up as he pulled the luminous blue orb out of his bag and carefully handed it to Horton.

"Al told me exactly how to do it," Ulises went on. "To engage the orb, hold it in one hand while jumping in place. Yes, those were his instructions precisely."

Horton could see Penriding shake his head and roll his eyes behind Ulises' back. It seemed his old friend was farther in the clouds than he had thought.

"You're sure about that?" Horton prodded Ulises. "That seems a little unusual."

"Of course I am sure!" Ulises shot back. "By the gods I would do it myself if I could still jump at all. These hips are not as agile as they used to be."

"Right," Horton replied, still not convinced. "Well, here goes."

With the orb held tightly in his right hand, he took a deep breath and jumped as high as he could. When he landed back on his feet he froze for a moment, while his and the others' eyes darted around the chamber expectantly, waiting for anything to happen.

Nothing did.

"Um… let's try it again," Horton said as he tried to avoid eye contact with Penriding. He knew humoring Ulises was a waste of time.

Once more Horton jumped, this time with the orb in his left hand. When he landed back on his feet he stared at the orb, willing it to do something if even just for Ulises' sake.

But still, nothing.

"Maybe if we—" Horton began to suggest, but Penriding had seen enough.

"No more of this!" Penriding bellowed. "This is ludicrous. Ulises, thank you for the map. It is very much appreciated. However, we unfortunately do not have time to babysit the elderly. I will ask you nicely to go back to your little village amicably while Horton and I use the pedestal to jump back to Zeptus City. I don't care what you think on the matter – this decision is final."

Horton could not believe what Penriding had just said. He desperately wanted to defend Ulises, but quite frankly he didn't know how he could. Unable to bear watching Ulises' reaction, he slumped his head and looked down at his feet.

Ulises cleared his throat before croaking out a reply.

"I understand," he sighed.

Horton still couldn't bring himself to look up as he heard the priest slowly shuffle over toward him, and when Ulises hugged him he found himself caught off-guard. He was certain his old mentor would have been disappointed with him for not backing him up.

"You have grown into a good man, Horton," he said. "Your father would have been very proud of you."

It was not until Ulises let him go that Horton looked at his old friend.

"And I am proud of you as well," Ulises said with a smile. "If you do not mind, may I hold that orb one more time before I leave, please?"

"Yeah," Horton said as he handed it to Ulises. What was the harm in that, he figured.

"Do you know what I have found to be the biggest difference between an Illac and a Zeptan, boys?" Ulises asked out loud as he marched over to the pedestal with the four buttons. Horton and Penriding glanced at each other quickly before turning back to Ulises.

"Patience," Ulises declared as he hit the green button on the pedestal.

Horton couldn't believe he and Penriding hadn't seen Ulises' intent before it was too late. Clearly, Ulises was going to go it alone. At first Horton assumed his old friend had made a mistake. He thought perhaps the priest had meant to hit another button to go somewhere else, had attempted to seize the opportunity to take the orb and try his luck on his own, or maybe, as he had feared, truly lost his mind to old age.

As Horton and Penriding were about to find out, it was none of those things.

It all began with just a little twinkle at the center of the orb, but within a matter of seconds that tiny light had rapidly developed into a pulsating glow that filled the enormous darkened chamber with flashes of light that revealed all its secrets.

Ulises stepped back as the orb levitated itself out of his

hand and into a gyrating frenzy about half way up toward the room's high ceiling, before emitting thin red lights that seemed to probe every crevice of the pyramid around them. Lights around the chamber blinked on and off and strange clanks and grinding noises reverberated throughout, as though the orb was desperately trying to resuscitate the Earth Stone. Then without warning, the fantastical array of lights retreated back within the orb and condensed into a miniscule red dot at its center before the orb fell down to the hard floor with a loud thunk.

The three companions looked at one another timidly for a couple of seconds before slowly working up the nerve to inspect the orb closely. Together they tried to peer inside it, all the while wary to maintain their distance. Horton could just faintly see a pinprick of red light still inside it, encompassed deep within the orb's usual soft blue gleam. But then he blinked and it was gone.

Waiting for the first sign of life from the pyramid, the trio stood there in quiet darkness for what seemed like an eternity. Unusually, the different bright colored lights that had previously been cast out by the pedestal's buttons were now dim. None of them wanted to be the one to suggest the orb had not only failed, but possibly damaged the pyramid even more.

Clank.

The sound of thick, heavy metal begrudgingly shifting somewhere deep below resonated up through the pyramid and into their bones. A moment later, the Earth Stone sputtered back to life. Startled, Horton flinched as the room flooded with light, instantly revealing its incredible size.

To his disappointment there was nothing in it, however, except the portal and four support pillars.

"Oh," Penriding chuckled, breaking their shared silence. "Jump in place. You see, it's not literally jump in place, it's—"

"Yeah, yeah, we get it," Horton remarked, cutting off Penriding's pointless explanation as he turned to look at Ulises. "At least now we know how to fix these things. It's about time we finally made some headway."

"Well, I am glad to be of service for once," Ulises replied, all the while glaring at Penriding.

"This is quite different from the grand chamber in the Rissa," Horton quickly pointed out, having noticed Penriding preparing to fire off a surely unconstructive response toward Ulises.

"Not necessarily," Penriding replied after a brief pause to properly inspect the enormous room. "To an extent we've made our own modifications to the chamber. I'm sure it was once like this."

Horton could hear a low humming sound radiating through the ground below him. He kneeled down and put his hand on the cold metal floor.

"I can feel it," he said, looking at the others. "I don't know what, but it's definitely doing something."

"One down, three to go," Ulises croaked as he pulled his hood over his head. "Now to resume the task at hand — that is, assuming I am still wanted."

Horton looked to Penriding. An answer from him would mean a lot more than anything from Horton.

The Zeptan rubbed his chin for a bit then gestured to

Ulises with his head as if to say "let's go." It wasn't exactly what Horton had hoped for in the way of an act of contrition, but it would have to do.

"Where to next then?" Horton asked as he picked the orb up off the floor and carefully placed it in his satchel.

"What about the other buttons on here?" Penriding inquired as he inspected the pedestal. "They'll take us to the other pyramids, right?"

Horton walked over to the pedestal and looked at the buttons, trying to remember which went where.

"The yellow button is definitely Zeptus City," he said while scratching the back of his head. "The blue button took me somewhere – I'm not sure where exactly, I didn't take a good look around. It seemed safe though."

"And the red button?" Penriding asked as his finger wavered dangerously close to pushing it.

"Don't touch it," Horton instructed, covering it with his hand. "The air in the portal's chamber there isn't breathable. I almost didn't make it back."

"Okay, that makes our decision an easy one," Penriding said. "We're going blue."

"Hold on, I will press it," Ulises interjected as he bursted in between Horton and Penriding to get to the portal. "Assuming you two do not mind – we really should be on our way."

Horton was taken aback slightly by Ulises' sudden vigor, but he nodded and held out his hands for his companions to grab on to. Once joined, Ulises did the honors and pushed the blue button.

Ba-beep!

"Uh, looks like this pyramid is already on," Penriding said as he looked around the already lit room.

"You did hit the blue button, right?" Horton asked Ulises, who seemed to snap out of a blank daze when he did. "Did you hear what I said, Ulises?"

"Yes, yes," he quickly replied as he shook free the cobwebs in his mind. "It was the blue one."

"That's weird," Horton noted, simply chocking up Ulises' sudden lack of focus to old age. "Last time I was here the chamber was dark."

"I definitely saw him press the blue button," Penriding refuted. "The pyramid here is already operating. Someone must have beaten us to it."

Horton looked around the room, trying to spot something different from the pyramid back in Illac, but as far as he could tell it looked exactly the same. He made his way back over to the pedestal. The blue light was no longer shining – something was wrong.

"Hang on a second – stand right there," Horton directed the others, pointing to a spot a few paces away from the pedestal. "I'll be right back."

Ba-beep!

Horton hit the green button, expecting to see his friends vanish as he traveled to a different pyramid, but they didn't. He hit the dimmed blue button again.

"No sound that time," Ulises noted.

Penriding put his hands on his hips and shook his head.

"Well old man you've gone and broken the damn thing," he remarked to Ulises.

"Hey!" Horton angrily shot at the Zeptan.

"Relax, it was only a joke," Penriding replied, waving his hands in surrender. "Obviously the old geezer didn't actually disable it himself. Well, at least not on purpose."

"We are off to repair the pyramid at Zeptus City then, I suppose," Ulises said, ignoring Penriding. "And this time I will let the Zeptan take care of travel arrangements."

Penriding glared at Ulises as the trio joined hands once again around the podium.

"I was afraid of this. Returning to Zeptus is a probably a really bad idea, you know," Penriding sighed as he prepared to hit the yellow button.

"Why is that?" Horton asked a moment before Penriding pressed it.

Ba-beep! Beep!

"Wha—? Hey! Put your hands up!" a soldier yelled out before pointing his sword at Ulises' face. Before any of them knew what was going on, the three were encircled by what seemed to be half the Zeptan military with their weapons drawn. Horton turned to look at Penriding, who glanced back at him with a nervous-looking smirk.

"This is why."

SEVEN

Fairytales

HORTON GLANCED OVER at the fast-asleep Ulises in the cell to his right and then at Penriding to his left. He and the others had been locked up for quite a while now, and it was not until just then that he came to the realization they had now come full circle. As if repeating history, there was Penriding, sitting in the same position he had found him weeks earlier when their paths had first crossed. He snickered and shook his head to himself at the thought.

Having noticed this, Penriding leaned his head forward slightly and opened a single eye at Horton.

"What are you laughing about?" the Zeptan queried.

"Nothing," Horton replied. "Just thinking about how hapless we are."

"Why do you say that?" Penriding asked while rubbing his eyes.

"Isn't it obvious?" Horton scowled. "Look at us."

Penriding laughed and leaned his head back against the wall with a grin on his face.

"It just so happens I like it here," he said before turning to wink at Horton, who responded with a fatigued sigh.

Knowing he desperately needed to get some sleep, Horton closed his eyes. Just as he began to nod off, however, he was awoken by footsteps echoing down the corridor outside their cells. He opened his eyes to see a very stern looking Constable Keen marching his way towards them.

"I'm not sure even your father could have gotten you out of this one," the constable told Penriding as he approached the cells. Then to Horton's surprise, the constable's stern face instantly transformed into a nervous one.

"The council will not overlook this, Mr. Blacksmith," he said as he pulled his body up to the bars of Penriding's cell so tightly it appeared as though he was trying to pull himself through them.

"I need an answer," he whispered, as if trying to avoid anyone overhearing. "Were you involved?"

Penriding perked himself up in the seat.

"Involved in what?" he asked.

The constable lowered his head and glared at him through his eyebrows.

"In the attack," the constable hissed. Horton noticed the constable glancing over at Ulises and him. "That boy, Ananke, wore the same clothes that old man is wearing, and that boy there wore them before as well. There are stirrings that you've allied with the enemy."

"Completely untrue," Penriding refuted. "Ananke acted

entirely on his own accord. We had absolutely nothing to do with him."

The constable took a deep breath and stepped away from the cell bars.

"Very well," he said with a nod. "I shall inform the council that they need not worry about young Mr. Blacksmith and his companions."

The constable turned to make his way back down the corridor, but Penriding stopped him.

"Constable," he called out, grabbing his attention. "I would prefer to address the council myself. I have a matter of great importance to discuss."

"You do?" the constable asked with a tentative look on his face. Horton could tell the constable wanted to question Penriding as to why he wanted to speak to the council, but he seemed apprehensive about doing so – at least in the moment. "Well, I shall see what I can do, I suppose. Good day."

While Constable Keen whisked away back down the corridor, Horton stared at Penriding ceaselessly, bewildered that he could so calmly damn Ananke without a second thought.

"What?" Penriding asked Horton when he caught his eye.

"I'm just amazed that you can so readily condemn a child you once claimed to have rescued out of pity," Horton replied with a hint of agitation in his voice.

"Don't worry about him – that kid'll be fine," Penriding quickly answered with a hoity-toity wave of his hand.

"Really," Horton said, gritting his teeth. "I bet you would do the same to me given the chance."

Penriding froze momentarily, then leaned forward in his seat toward Horton.

"Horton, my friend," Penriding said with an appeasing smile. "You misjudge me. You underestimate the power the Blacksmith name carries in this city. The fact we're jailed right now is purely a facade. I guarantee Ananke's safety, I promise."

Horton gazed blankly at his feet. It was true that the Blacksmith family seemed to have Zeptus City under its thumb, but for Ananke's sake he could only hope Penriding would keep his word. He groaned to himself and shuffled his way over to the makeshift bed on the floor of the cell and lay down.

He wasn't sure how long he had been asleep, but Horton woke up to discover the cell to the left of him was empty. He sat up and looked over to the cell on his right to find Ulises sitting in a chair with his hands on his knees, watching him.

"They took him away about an hour ago," Ulises told him. "I have no idea where."

Horton lay back down on his back and stared at the ceiling.

"He's likely meeting with the Zeptan High Council," Horton replied. "Probably trying to get us out of trouble."

"This Blacksmith boy, do you trust him?" Ulises asked.

"Yeah, I suppose so," Horton answered, somewhat curious as to why Ulises would care to ask him that. "Why, have you heard of that name before?"

"No," Ulises said abruptly. "Not before today, anyway."

Horton remained silent for the next few minutes as his eyes followed the lines made by the cracked walls of his confines. He wondered how long it would be before Penriding returned.

"Oh, I meant to ask earlier," Ulises went on. "Why is it we have been arrested? Did we do something wrong?"

Horton glanced over to his old friend. The question caught him a little off guard since he hadn't thought twice about Ulises wondering why they had been arrested upon their return to Zeptus. It was bad enough having to confess about what had happened to Deforest, so there was no way he was going to bring up Ananke just yet.

"The Zeptans have rules about accessing the interior of the pyramid here or something," Horton explained. "Nothing big. I'm sure Penriding will have us out of here in no time."

"Well I do hope so," Ulises responded. "The punishment for entering the Earth Stone back home is banishment, naturally. I suppose we are fortunate the Zeptans do not judge quite as harshly as us Illacs."

"Yeah," Horton said with a nervous laugh.

"You better get us out of this, Penriding," he muttered quietly to himself away from Ulises' earshot.

Horton suddenly perked up as muffled voices materialized at the end of the hallway, conveniently diverting his attention away from his conversation with Ulises. A moment later Penriding and Constable Keen appeared side-by-side, walking down the hallway towards them with Linden trailing closely behind. It was the first time Horton had seen the leftenant since she had snuck Penriding, Ananke and himself out of the Blacksmith manor a few days earlier. He was glad to see the Zeptan soldier again, even if it was still unusual for him to see a woman in such a masculine role. Horton's cheer quickly ceased, however, when he saw the glum look on Penriding's face as he spoke with the constable. He couldn't hear what they were saying, but it looked as though it didn't bode well. Yet to Horton's revelation, when Penriding and he made eye contact, his entire demeanor swiftly altered.

"Hey you two," Penriding addressed the jailed Illacs with a smile. "We're all free to go. Better yet, the High Council has taken such great interest in our little errand to the pyramids that they're officially sanctioning it. We've been tendered an outfit of soldiers to accompany us. We're heading off for the next pyramid right away."

"Just like that?" Ulises asked.

"Just like that," Penriding confirmed.

"That's great!" Horton professed as the constable unlocked his cell. "How did you get them on our side?"

Penriding glanced at Constable Keen before answering.

"We made a little deal. Nothing exciting, really."

"Well done, Penriding, well done," Ulises praised as he, too, was released from his cell. "What is our next course of action then?"

"Your next course of action is making your way to the Desert Storm with Mr. Blacksmith," the constable interjected. "Immediately."

"Yes, yes, the constable is of course very right," Penriding responded, looking as though he had skipped a beat. "It's important we depart right away. No time to lose, after all."

"The buggy is here, sir!" a voice shouted down the hallway, followed by the clang of metal hitting the floor. To nobody's surprise it was the same gormless guard Horton had seen when he had been jailed weeks before. From the looks of it, he still hadn't been issued a properly sized helmet.

The group discovered during their ride to the docks that Linden had just been promoted, and would be the commanding officer for the duration of the mission now that the Zeptan military had become involved. Constable Keen escorted them out of the building and to their awaiting ride outside the manor, but did not accompany them further.

Horton lifted himself out of his chair a little so he could see out the small window on the side of the buggy as they traveled through the city streets. To his astonishment it appeared Vwari attacks had ramped up even more. Columns of black smoke spotted the vast city's expanse and soldiers seemed to outnumber civilians now on the streets. He couldn't help but wonder what would influence the Zeptan High Council to willingly hand over soldiers to their cause during a time of such peril in the city. He had an inkling it all had to do with the Vwari and Exetus, though.

Then Ananke popped into Horton's head. Penriding hadn't mentioned what had become of him.

"Ananke?" Horton asked Penriding vaguely, trying to avoid going into any specific details in front of Ulises.

Penriding puckered his lips and sighed. Then, to Horton's dread, he remorsefully shook his head. Horton quickly turned to look back out the window and clenched his fists tightly. He didn't want to believe what he just saw from Penriding. Remembering that the Zeptan had promised Ananke's safety only made him angrier. He turned back to Penriding and opened his mouth to speak, but words failed him. He wanted to press Penriding further and figure out what in the gods' names had happened, but he just couldn't bring himself to do it. Instead Horton pressed his mouth into the palm of his hand and closed his eyes. He took a deep breath and tried to block the entire episode out of his mind. He had become accustomed to having to bottle up his feelings as of late.

"You okay?" Ulises asked Horton, putting his hand on his back. He obviously hadn't hidden his distress well enough.

"Hmm? Yeah," Horton replied as he tried to regain his composure. "Just tired, that's all."

Horton glanced over at Penriding once more as he straightened himself up in his seat, but the Zeptan took no notice. He was busy gazing blankly at the space above Ulises' head.

There was a great deal of commotion going on outside as their buggy approached the docks, prompting Horton to stand up slightly and peer out of the window once again. Outside he saw a man yelling out orders to a throng of soldiers that were running about fervently. Then without warning the buggy came to an abrupt halt and a soldier swung the door open.

"Commander, you and your company need to get to your wastewalker and set off immediately," the soldier said, motioning to them to step out of the vehicle. "Forward scouts report a Vwari attack is inbound on this location."

"Alright get out, get out," Linden asserted.

As they piled out of the buggy, Horton overheard the soldier brief Linden on the situation.

"Your outfit has the Desert Storm ready to depart, sir," he said. "If I may say, I think it would be wise to postpone the mission until the immediate threat is dealt with."

"Thank you soldier, that'll do. We have our orders," Linden responded. "We're heading due east, so we should be able to avoid the brunt of it."

"East?" the soldier repeated with a confused look on his face, but Linden ignored him and briskly led their group toward Penriding's wastewalker.

A soldier in dark and bulky metallic armor met them at the foot of the bridge to board the Desert Storm, and he saluted Linden as they followed her past him and onto the wastewalker. Horton had seen other soldiers in similar armor surrounding the Blacksmith manor, and he speculated whether they were the ones who would be coming along with them on their mission. In a haunting way they reminded him of the demons his mother would describe to him in fairytales when he was a child. Them being around made him feel a little uneasy, but he tried not to think about it. They were just fairytales after all.

Just as Horton was about to step onto the wastewalker, he heard the sharp crack of a cannon being fired. His attention turned up to the city's high walls, which had rows of cannons mounted atop them. The fire began slowly at first with a sporadic blast every few seconds, but the rate quickly accelerated. Before Horton knew it the air was rife with the popping sound of heavy artillery fire, forcing him and the others to hurry themselves onto the Desert Storm and into its command room.

"Rotors one and two prepped, sir!" a soldier manning the helm yelled out as Linden sat in what was previously Penriding's command chair. It was weird seeing so many soldiers filling out the command room – the last time he was in here there had been just two or three operating the wastewalker, and now there was at least three times that. The soldiers manning the Desert Storm's controls were in regular military garb, but the two standing at each side of Linden were in that hulking armor Horton had seen outside a moment earlier. He was able to get a good look at their hellacious swords now, which were strapped to their backs. They were as ornate as they were massive, and if anything, looked as though they were more for display than whatever else, primarily because he couldn't imagine anyone actually being able to wield something so enormous effectively in combat.

As he scanned the room with reserved curiosity, Horton looked over to find out what Penriding was up to. He expecting the wealthy Zeptan to be hollering out orders of some kind since it was his vessel, but strangely he wasn't. Instead, he had slowly crept his way to the back of the room and leaned up against the wall with his arms crossed. It was very apparent that this was no longer a simple merchant barge.

Amidst all the commotion a soldier tapped Horton on the shoulder and motioned to Ulises and him to follow. He led them down to the bowels of the wastewalker, and as they passed through one of the stairwells Horton caught sight of what he believed was a Vwari cutter through a port hole. It wasn't anywhere near as spectacular or flashy as the Zeptan wastewalkers he had seen, and its exterior was rugged-looking and markedly smaller in size, but definitely more mobile over the sand. If he had to guess, he would have said the Vwari cutters were made up of scrap metal and other assorted components scrounged from the debris of raided Zeptan vessels.

"Stay close, Horton," Ulises said, noticing that Horton had paused in the stairwell.

Creak.

Horton jumped. The Desert Storm had begun to move. As Horton quickstepped down the stairs to catch up to Ulises and the soldier, the engine groaned as it toiled to get the heavy shell that housed it in motion.

"You two stay in here until things clear up top-side," the soldier ordered as he herded them into the room Horton had stayed in the last time he had been on board. An additional bed had been added on the other side of the room for Ulises.

Exhausted, Horton plopped himself down on his bed and Ulises did the same. He could feel the wastewalker really ripping through the desert now. Judging by the deep, rough sound of sand breaking against the bow of the Desert Storm, he estimated they must already be close to top speed.

Over the next few minutes the two Illacs sat in silence as they listened intently to the fading sound of cannon fire. Whether by dumb luck or destiny, they seemed to have escaped the Vwari assault completely unscathed.

It wasn't long after the sound of cannons completely dissipated that Ulises broke the silence by clearing his throat, prompting Horton to turn and look at him.

"We are knee-deep in it now, are we not?" the old priest said with a wry smile.

"Yeah, we are," Horton confirmed. He could see his old friend was on verge of saying something, but struggling to get it out.

"You okay, Ulises?" he asked.

"Horton," Ulises began, his tongue clearly still looking for the right words. "Whatever happened with Deforest, whoever is to fault or blame, understand that it does not lie with you."

Horton looked at the ground. He really didn't want to talk about what happened to his brother. Not yet, anyway.

"I appreciate that, really, but I don't—"

"I know you do not want to talk about it," Ulises interrupted, "and we will not. I just… I do not want Deforest's fate – whatever it may be – to affect your…"

Ulises brushed his beard with his hand as he chose his words carefully.

"Decision making."

Horton nodded his head. He had no idea what Ulises was going on about, but he figured if he just agreed with him he would drop the subject and they could move on.

"Klas and Georg were so much like you and Deforest, you know," Ulises muttered. "I would hate for you to end up like them."

"What's that supposed to mean?" Horton fumed as he stood up from the bed. "End up like them? What, dead? If

Deforest is still alive out there somewhere I'm going to find him, and if I have to die trying, then so be it."

"I am sorry, Horton, I did not mean it in that way." Ulises said apologetically. He stared sorrowfully at the angry, young Illac for a moment before gently sighing and lying down to rest. Horton quietly scowled as he lay himself down as well.

"Why would he even say that?" Horton thought as he rolled onto his side. He would fall asleep angry that night.

Horton woke up a number of hours later, though he was unsure of how long he had been out. There were no windows in the cabin, so he sluggishly made his way to the upper deck to take a look outside. The sun was just beginning to scrape the horizon when he got topside – he had slept straight through to the next morning.

He walked over to his usual perch against the railing, overlooking the vast, empty sea of sand below the Desert Storm's bow. As he stood there, the morning breeze running through his hair, he thought back to his conversation with Ulises the previous day.

It had been the first time he had heard Georg's name in many years and he couldn't figure out why Ulises would bring up his father and uncle so suddenly. As far as he was aware, Georg had died as a sacrifice during his initiation, but beyond that Klas had very rarely mentioned him so Horton assumed his father had always been ashamed of his brother. Of the little he had heard about Georg, he knew he wasn't like Klas and his sons – he was charismatic, physically well-built and agile. As a matter of fact, he was actually expected to excel in the initiation – perhaps even be the first Three Yearling to return back to the village. In a twist of fate, it was Horton's father who succeeded.

"The doctor said you still need to wear this when you're outside," a voice from behind him said. Horton turned around to see Linden holding out his protective head scarf.

"You alright?" Linden asked as Horton reluctantly grabbed the scarf out of her hand.

"Yeah, just thinking to myself," he replied while adjusting it onto his head, before leaning back over the railing.

Horton expected Linden to walk away at that point as she normally would have, but this time she joined him at the rail. He glanced at her quickly before returning his attention to the wastes. The glint of the Rissa in the distance had become more discernible now that the sun was rising.

"No problems getting away from the city?" Horton asked after a few moments of silence.

"None, fortunately," Linden answered. "The cannonade opened a gap in the Vwari forces just wide enough for us to sprint through. It is likely they let us get away because they believed we were a simple merchant barge. We should be in the clear now, Vwari raiders aren't known to travel this far eastward."

"Good, good," Horton mumbled. He felt a little awkward trying to make conversation with Linden, so he mentioned the first relevant thing that popped into his head. "By the way, who are those soldiers in the black armor?"

Linden smiled slightly in the corner of her mouth. "They're the best of the best. Specialized Vwari killers, trained from a young age. They are known as the Reckoners."

"But that armor... and that sword," Horton said in disbelief. "The weight must be incredible. I don't think I've seen a Zeptan big enough to handle anything like that."

"A Reckoner isn't any ordinary Zeptan," Linden explained as she stepped away from the railing. Horton hoped she would clarify further but to his disappointment she didn't.

"Breakfast should be almost ready," she said instead. "Why don't you head down to the mess room, I'll be heading there shortly myself."

Horton nodded diffidently as Linden disappeared below to the lower decks. He felt a little better knowing these so-called "Reckoners" were there to protect them from the Vwari, but he still didn't want to run into one while alone in one of the Desert Storm's narrow corridors.

The next week and a half felt like the longest of Horton's life. Now that the Desert Storm was under military operation, he was restricted from the most interesting areas of the vessel. He had offered his help in the engine room but was turned away, and attempts to check in on Penriding and Linden in the command room were denied by a soldier standing guard of its door. He had no books to read or friends to talk to – apart from Ulises, but the priest was more interested in sleeping on the upper deck or writing in his journal. Besides, things had been a little awkward between Ulises and him since their conversation that first evening back on board the wastewalker. They had both tried to play it off like everything was fine, but in truth it seemed as though they had been avoiding one another as much as possible.

To pass the time one morning, Horton decided to write a letter to Deforest. Normally he hated writing and avoided it if he could help it, but he had become so fed up with the lack of things to do that he borrowed a page from Ulises' journal and got to it. He knew it was all probably in vain, but he wanted to apologize to Deforest for what had happened, tell him about his journey to find him, and describe Zeptus City and his new companions. After he finished writing the letter he stared at it for a moment, rereading bits of it in his head.

"This is stupid; what am I doing?" he muttered to himself.

Without giving it a second thought he decided to rip it up and throw it away. He held the letter in both hands and began tearing it in half. He had gotten half way through the letter when the Desert Storm lurched to a sudden stop, almost sending him hurtling over the table where he had been sitting. He pulled himself up out of the chair, stuffed the half-torn letter into his satchel beside the bed and swung the cabin door open. With barely a foot through the door, Horton froze. The sound of men hollering and shouting rang down through the corridors from the decks above. He quickly threw on his head scarf and sprinted down the hallway and up the stairs to see what all the commotion was about. When he reached the upper deck, he found most of the crew laughing and celebrating.

"Horton!" Penriding called out through the crowd having spotted the Illac. "Come here! Take a look at this!"

Horton squeezed his way through the mob of soldiers and to the railing at the edge of the deck. Then his jaw dropped.

He couldn't help but do a double-take when he saw it. He even had to pinch himself to make sure he wasn't dreaming, but the pain told him it was real. The Desert Storm was beached at the edge of the most beautiful, blue-green mass he could have ever imagined.

"You were right about the map," Penriding said, putting his hand on Horton's shoulder. "It is an ocean."

Horton tried to say something – anything – but he couldn't find the breath to speak. Fishes of every color imaginable swam in schools over the glimmering, gold-like sand beneath the calm waves below. It was as though he was living in one of the old stories his mother used to tell Deforest and him back in Illac.

"I think we've stumbled into a fairytale, Horton," Penriding said with a laugh.

One by one the crew clamored down off the wastewalker and onto the fine sand on the beach below. A couple of them ran straight into the sea, overjoyed at the experience of being able to submerge themselves in something as precious as water. Horton too climbed down, and stood there watching them in the wastewalker's shadow on the sand as he considered joining them.

"What are you waiting for?" Ulises croaked from behind him with a smile. "You have been cooped up in that damn contraption far too long. Go enjoy yourself."

Horton pulled his scarf away from his face and smiled back at his old friend. He was more than happy to oblige him, and made his way to the edge of the ocean. His excitement grew with each step he took toward it, and when he finally stepped into the water all he could do was burst into laughter.

The waves serenely broke around his ankles and the cool water soothed his dry feet. Little kaleidoscopic fish nibbled on his toes as he waddled deeper and deeper into the blue. Never before in his life had he felt so alive. Then, as if lured in by the sweet call of the water's gentle siren waves, he yanked off his head scarf and dove underneath.

As he floated there, completely submerged in a fantastic alien world filled with shades of colors he had never seen before, he couldn't help but grin ear to ear.

One day, he thought, Deforest would have to see this too.

Suddenly something latched onto Horton's arm and lurched him backward with great force. He twisted around to see what it was that had apprehended him, but the slew of bubbles created as he thrashed to break free obstructed his view. Next thing he knew he was yanked above water and face to face with the apparent foe.

"Hey, buddy! Relax!" Penriding said, laughing. "Good god kid I thought you had drowned. Please stay close to the others – the last thing I want is you getting gobbled up by a sea monster or something."

Horton nodded as he wiped the salty water from his eyes.

"And put that damn headscarf back on," Penriding called back to him as the Zeptan waded back toward shore. "You're going to be in a world of pain if your face gets damaged by the sun."

Horton pulled the headscarf out of the water and rung it out before wrapping it back around his head. He would spend the next few hours relaxing in the shallow waters, protected from the sun by the shadow of the wastewalker. He watched the fishes as they swarmed around him, evidently as curious about him as he was of them. Not far away, a handful of the Desert Storm's engineers debated with Linden over the wastewalker's ability to travel over water.

"Theoretically it should operate just as it does on sand, so it'll be no problem," one of them said.

"No, no, it's far too heavy. It will sink straight to the ocean floor," another one shot back.

"Well we can't just stop now – we have to at least try."

"Yeah and what if it doesn't work? We'll all be stranded out here to die."

Between them all stood Linden, her hands at her hips as she absorbed their advice. Eventually she cut them off and made a decision.

"Dump all unessential weight on the beach and prepare the wastewalker for departure," she said audaciously. "We'll pick it back up on the return trip."

"Yes, sir!" the engineers declared simultaneously and filed back onto the wastewalker, but even after they left Linden continued to stare out into the ocean, not budging from her original pose.

"You sure it'll work?" Horton shouted over to her, knocking Linden out of her lull.

Linden looked at him for a moment and then shrugged. "No, but we won't find out unless we try. We've got a mission to complete."

Horton nodded in agreement. Linden was starting to grow on him. He felt good knowing that she was the one heading up the mission and he trusted her judgment – even if she was a woman.

"Get back on board, Horton," she called over. "It'll be dark in a few hours, and we need to get this behemoth floating before sundown. Oh, and grab your friend too."

Horton glanced over at Ulises. The old priest had been passed out in slumber for the last few hours on a makeshift beach chair. He walked over to the priest and tapped him on the shoulder.

"Ulises," he said gently to garner his attention. As Ulises opened his eyes he looked as though he was waking up into dream world. He surveyed his surroundings for a moment before remembering where he was.

"Oh my," he muttered as he pulled himself out of the chair. "I was having the most wondrous dream."

Horton smiled and shook his head. He grabbed Ulises' chair and accompanied his old friend back to the Desert Storm.

"Hey, uh, I'm sorry for snapping at you the other week when you mentioned my father," Horton said quietly as they walked. "I've just been a little stressed out lately."

"There is no need for remorse, my boy," Ulises replied, putting his arm around Horton's shoulder. "I already told you that."

Horton spent the next hour or so helping the rest of the crew dump excess weight off the vessel. The majority of it was boxes of munitions for the wastewalker's cannons, with the rest being primarily assorted bits and pieces: a dresser here, an end table there. When the Desert Storm was finally ready to push off from the ocean of sand and onto a real one, Horton made his way up to the top deck to get a good view. He looked around and found to his wonder that nobody else had thought of the same idea. It didn't matter now though, and as the engines began to buzz below he grasped onto the railing.

"Here we go," he said to himself.

Slowly but surely, the Desert Storm staggered forward toward the water. Leaning over the railing, Horton could see waves sloshing up against the bow as it trudged deeper and deeper. About forty yards ahead the hue of the sea changed from a bright aquamarine shade to a deep, dark navy blue where the coastal shelf suddenly dropped off. That was where they would discover once and for all if their journey – and likely their lives – would come to an end.

Horton readjusted his sweaty grip on the railing as the wastewalker approached the edge of the coastal shelf. His heart pounded as he looked directly over the front of it and into the dark void of the ocean below him.

It wasn't long before he began to have second thoughts about his positioning as the wastewalker began to list, its front-end depressing deep into the water, forcing the young Illac to hold onto the railing as tightly as he could. Somewhere beneath his feet the vessel's hull clanged and popped as the water's pressure asserted itself upon it.

"Oh gods, please don't let us sink," he plead.

A second later the Desert Storm's rear-end plunked into

the water, leaving the vessel entirely at the ocean's whim. Horton experienced a free-fall feeling for a moment as it sank almost entirely under water, and for a split second, he could have coolly stepped off the top deck and onto the surface of the water – it had come that close to being completely submerged. However in the same manner of time as it took to sink, the wastewalker quickly ascended back up toward the surface of the water and to safety. Horton could hear cheering from the decks below. It had worked. The Desert Storm was afloat.

Horton let out a deep sigh of relief. He chuckled to himself as he thought in hindsight what a stupid idea watching from the upper deck was, and now all he wanted to do was get back inside.

The vessel rolled back and forth as it went, inducing him to hold onto the railing as he made his way over to the stairwell that led to the lower decks. Once below, Horton ran into a beaming Penriding along his way back to his cabin.

"How was that for a show?" he laughed. "I'm sorry you didn't get the view we got from the command room, we were under water for a second there."

"That's quite alright," Horton replied, purposely neglecting to mention the fact he had almost had a firsthand account of being under water himself during the ordeal.

"Is the hull going to hold?" Horton asked, making note of the fact the metal walls that housed them had been popping and panging for the last few minutes.

"Once the pressure balances out it'll stop groaning so much," Penriding assured. "The Desert Storm is not used to getting its feet wet, but she will be fine."

"Okay, good," Horton replied, feeling better. "So how far are we from the pyramid now?"

Penriding scrunched his nose as he made the calculation in his head. "Well, we're moving at a slightly slower pace on water, but it shouldn't be more than a few more days now. I'll try to keep you in the loop, but frankly I'm not getting much in the way of details either. Those military bozos are being real tight-lipped about everything. It's those damn Reckoners you know – they're no fun at all."

"Reckoners," Horton repeated, his eyes lighting up with interest. "What do you know about them?"

"Those things? Not much at all, to be honest," Penriding answered. "They're a pretty secretive group, only answering to the highest-ranking Zeptan officials. Now that I think about it, I don't believe I have ever seen one without his full armor on – I bet they're all hideous monsters underneath or something."

Horton could tell Penriding was joking, but he wasn't so sure he was that far from the truth.

"They must be pretty strong to lug around that giant sword and armor all day," Horton added.

"Yeah, I suppose so," Penriding said, nodding his head. "I'm just kind of used to them; there's usually a couple around the manor. My father held quite a bit of influence over their little band."

"What about you?" Horton pressed.

"Me? No, not really," Penriding said glumly. "They seem to respond to Linden though, so that's something."

"Yeah," Horton replied with a nod in agreement.

"Alright kid, I need to get to sleep. I'm feeling pretty

worn out after today," Penriding said as he rubbed his face with his hands. "I'll catch you later."

"Sure, goodnight," Horton said as Penriding walked on past him.

Horton then legged his way down the corridor to his cabin, where to no surprise he found Ulises asleep in bed. He sighed to himself and sat down on his hard bed. By his feet lay his satchel with a corner of the letter he had written to Deforest earlier sticking out of it. He pulled the half-torn paper out, stared at it for a moment, and then walked it over to the desk in the corner of the room. He laid it down, carefully flattened it with his hand and continued writing.

Deforest you won't believe what we saw today. An actual ocean of water, as far as the eye could see! It was just like in the fairytales mother used to read us...

EIGHT

The Reckoner

HORTON PASSED THE BULK of the next few days staring out into the ocean with Ulises, and the farther out to sea they went, the larger the fish seemed to become. Once in a while some would follow alongside the wastewalker and briefly pop up above surface, as if to acknowledge them. Ulises was always busy writing in his journal, keeping a record of the different sea life they came across. He would scribble down notes and quick sketches while Horton shouted out each fish's attributes and scale colors.

This had kept the two Illacs fairly busy, and for a short while Horton completely forgot about their mission at hand. However, early one morning he made his way up to the upper deck to watch the fish as he normally did, but instead saw something rather unusual. At first glance he thought he imagined it or perhaps saw a strangely shaped cloud, but as he covered his eyes from the sun and squinted, he could see with strong certainty what it was he was looking at. Just above the horizon was the pinnacle of a pyramid.

Horton pushed off the railing and catapulted himself down the stairwell to the lower decks. He squeezed between two soldiers as he made his way through the corridors to Penriding's cabin and knocked on his door excitedly, ready to tell him the big news.

"Yes?" Penriding's muffled voice asked through the door.

Horton swung the door open and burst inside.

"We've found it! We've found—"

Horton cut himself off mid-sentence with a gasp. Staring down at him were two Reckoners. He took a step back towards the door, his hand reached out behind him as he tried to find the handle.

"Horton, good morning," Penriding greeted him as the Zeptan appeared from out behind the two daunting fortresses of armor. Linden was there with him, too.

"The uh, the pyramid…" Horton began, trying to remember what he had come there to say.

"The pyramid, yes, I'm happy to say we've found it," Penriding said with a smile.

"Oh, you already know?" Horton asked as he made his way around the edge of the room to Penriding, choosing the path farthest away from the Reckoners.

"Yes, we were just discussing it," Linden confirmed. "We'll be arriving at the site of the pyramid in about three hours. Why don't you go prepare your things?"

Horton nodded and made his way back through the

room toward the door, trying his best to avoid eye contact with the Reckoners, which he found considerably hard to do. As he walked past them, he could sense the Reckoner closest to him tracking him with his head.

"You're an Illac," he suddenly grunted. Horton jumped back slightly, stunned to hear him speak. The Reckoner's voice was harsh and muffled through its thick helmet. He could only stare back at the juggernaut as he tried to find the words to respond.

"Where is Illac?" the Reckoner pressed.

"That's enough," Linden suddenly barked at the Reckoner. "Horton, go prepare your things."

Horton quickly left the room, more than happy to oblige Linden's order. He felt relieved to be spared from the Reckoner's grave snare. Despite everything, he still couldn't figure out why the Reckoners intimidated him so much.

When Horton returned to his cabin, Ulises was awake and writing in his journal.

"Good news, Ulises," Horton told him. "We've found the Tiberonus pyramid. We'll be landing in a few hours."

"Oh, that is very good," Ulises said, smiling at Horton as he peered up from his journal.

Horton sat down on his bed, grabbed his satchel and set it on his lap. Still inside it was the orb Al had given them. A blue glow radiated onto Horton's face as he looked at it in his hand.

"Deforest might be in this pyramid," Horton told Ulises, his eyes still focused on the orb.

"Mm," Ulises hummed in agreement.

"And if he's not..." Horton whispered quietly under his breath.

Horton sighed. He didn't want to finish that thought. It wasn't something he even wanted to consider. Instead, he carefully placed the orb back in his satchel, slung it over his shoulder and made his way back to the upper deck to watch as the wastewalker approached the pyramid.

Ulises came up and joined him shortly after, and by this point it was clear to Horton the pyramid was sitting on a lush tropical island that was part of a larger archipelago. He estimated the Tiberonus pyramid was only about half as exposed above the ground than the Rissa, which was still considerably larger than the Earth Stone. It was difficult to get a good look at it, though, since the pyramid's base was surrounded by a dense forest with the largest trees he had ever seen. This was all good news to Horton however, because if Deforest had ended up here, there was a real possibility he was still alive.

It wasn't long until the majority of the crew congregated on the upper deck as the Desert Storm approached the island the pyramid called home. Linden came over and informed Horton that they would be deploying a relatively small group to investigate the pyramid since the area appeared to be safe. Horton, Penriding, Linden and a few soldiers comprised the group, plus the addition of a lone Reckoner tagging along – just to be on the safe side. She also recommended Ulises stay behind, and to Horton's astonishment, the priest agreed.

"I am far too old and slow for such a trek," he had told Horton. "Besides, I can see fine from right here on the wastewalker."

By the time the Desert Storm beached itself on the island's shore and the group set out, the sun was at its highest point in the sky, making Horton glad to have his head scarf on for a change.

They tread single file through the thick forest toward the pyramid as Linden led the way, her sword fiercely swatting at branches and brush as she blazed a trail. Penriding shadowed closely behind her, followed by Horton. Three Zeptan soldiers brought up the rear behind Horton, with the lone Reckoner tailing the group by a few meters, clunking with every step as he went. Every few minutes Horton would glance back at him, and despite his massive armor, the Reckoner seemed to have no problems maintaining pace with the rest of them.

The incessant sound of cooing birds and hollering primates kept the group on their toes as they went. Beady eyes watched them ominously from high in the canopy, prompting Horton to take a few steps closer to Penriding as they walked.

As they closed in on the pyramid, they could see that much of the exposed lower section of the pyramid was covered in vines and vegetation. The group circled the pyramid looking for an entrance, and it wasn't until they got about half way around the structure that they came across a staircase leading up to its entryway, just as there was in Zeptus City. They had actually almost not seen it entirely – the stairs were completely overgrown with vines, so badly in fact that Linden instructed the Reckoner to lead the way up it. His heavy boots sank deep into the vines as he walked, effectively creating a fresh stairway of flattened vegetation for the rest of them. Once at the top, the group walked over to where they expected the entrance to be, only to find a solid wall in its place.

"This isn't right," Penriding announced as he ran his hands over where the door should have been.

Horton followed closely behind Linden as she, too, examined the wall of the pyramid. It was true; there was no apparent opening.

While the others discussed going back to find another way in, Horton walked over to the wall to investigate it closely himself. Looking over the pyramid, he thought back to when he first discovered the Earth Stone's portal and travelled through it to the different pyramids. He remembered the blue button had sent him to a pyramid that was dark inside – there were definitely no open doors nearby.

"But there was a light shining in…" Horton muttered to himself as the memory resurfaced in his mind.

He clearly recalled a stream of light pouring in from somewhere up above. Horton took a step backward and surveyed the panels higher up the pyramid's exterior. Sure enough, there was a small square opening, roughly twenty-five feet above them.

"Hey, guys," Horton announced, pulling the groups' attention away from their discussion. "I think I found something."

He pointed up to the gap in the shell of the pyramid, just fractionally large enough for Horton's small stature to squeeze through.

"Do you think you can get up there?" Penriding asked as he covered his eyes from the sun as he looked up.

"I think I might," Horton answered. He put one foot up against the pyramid's sloped exterior and attempted to climb up the side of it toward the opening, but it was no use. The angle wasn't all that severe, but the metallic panels that made up its sides were too slick for him to get any kind of grip.

"Never mind. I guess not," Horton said in a subdued tone.

Then Linden motioned to the Reckoner with her hand.

"Uh," Horton gaped as the monster trod over toward him, and before he could say anything otherwise, the Reckoner picked the Illac up and lifted him above his head.

"I don't see what good this will do, we're still nowhere near—whoa!"

The next thing Horton knew he was sailing through the air in the direction of the opening. As he approached it, he stretched out his hands to grab on to the ledge.

Oof!

Horton hit the wall hard, but managed to hang one of his arms through the small opening. His satchel slid off his opposite shoulder when he slammed into the wall, but fortunately, he was able to catch it with his free hand just before it fell.

"Alright! Looking good, Horton!" Penriding yelled up with a grin on his face.

"Easy for you to say," Horton griped.

Horton rearranged the satchel over his shoulder and pulled himself up and through the gap. As he viewed through it he found his memory had served him well: He was looking down into the chamber that held the portal. Unlike before, however, the portal's normally brightly lit buttons were dark, and the only source of light in the room was through the space he was currently perched. With the need to investigate further, Horton vaulted himself over the ledge and carefully dropped down to the floor below.

"Deforest?" Horton called out into the dark chamber. Besides the thin beam of sunlight shining in through the opening, the room was pitch black.

"Deforest it's me, Horton," he called again.

No response.

Remembering the glow of the orb, Horton reached into his satchel to retrieve it. He held it out in front of him like a torch as he gingerly walked over to the portal and inspected it. He could feel the orb softly buzzing in his right hand and as he stood over the portal, the blue button blinked back to life, flashing slowly and softly as if inviting him to resurrect it. Horton had no reason not to obey – repairing the pyramid was the reason he was there after all, plus finding Deforest would be a lot easier with the lights back on.

He stared at the blue button for a short time, took a deep breath, and then pressed it with his left hand.

Ba-beep! Boop!

Just as it had back at the Earth Stone in Illac, the orb's glow rapidly intensified. A few seconds later it began to gyrate in his hand, then in the same fashion as before, it rose up out of his grasp and emitted thin red beams that seemed to be examining every nook and cranny of the chamber that housed them. It did this for a moment or two before suddenly shutting off and falling to the floor.

Horton stood there for what seemed like minutes in the

silent darkness, waiting intently for some sign of life from the pyramid.

Clank.

Although expecting it, Horton flinched. A few seconds later the floor beneath him vibrated as some incredible and unknown machinery breathed new life. Not long after the lights flickered on throughout the chamber, exposing it to him. A lone bird that had been nesting in a dark corner of the expansive room squawked with discontent as it flew out through the opening Horton had climbed through. He looked around, trying to find any sign that someone had been there, but just like in Illac, the chamber was completely empty.

Horton dropped his head in disappointment, but quickly his frown turned into intrigue. Under his feet was a small scattering of leaves he had unknowingly stepped on in the darkness. He picked one up to examine it.

"Brasys leaves!" he shouted out loud with giddy excitement.

Horton finally knew for sure what had happened to his brother. He had traveled through the portal and come here.

"Deforest!" Horton yelled out as loud as he could.

Whoosh!

The wall where the chamber entrance should have been suddenly slid away, revealing his companions.

"Pen! Linden! I found—"

Horton stopped himself when he saw their terror-filled faces turn to face him. Something was wrong.

"Quickly, get inside the pyramid!" Linden ordered, her sword drawn.

Penriding and one of the Zeptan soldiers were the first to comply, carrying another soldier who had been severely wounded somehow. And then Horton recoiled with dread. From beyond the entryway came the most spine-chilling shrills imaginable.

"We need to get out of here," Linden announced. "Use the green button to return to Zeptus. The green button!"

Just then the lone Reckoner appeared in the doorway, apparently falling back to Linden's position. He had his mammoth sword in hand, dripping with fresh blood.

It was right then that Horton finally saw them. Nothing could have ever prepared him for the nightmarish sight of this gruesome horde, flowing through the doorway and into the chamber like a cascade of phantoms.

"Vwari inbound!" Linden shouted, but Horton already knew what these things were.

His heart dropped into his stomach as his eyes gazed upon them. Their sunken faces and boney hands were as pale as the moon, with each Vwari haphazardly wrapped in grey linen to cover its slender frame. They seethed with anger beyond measure, and moved in gangly, inhuman strides that allowed the creatures to cover ground frighteningly fast. Yet the worst of it all was their ear-piercing shrieks, which alone were enough to incapacitate a man.

"Everyone get back to Zeptus!" Linden screamed as she prepared to face the swarm alongside the Reckoner. "We'll hold them off and destroy the portal. We can't let them get through to the Rissa!"

Penriding let go of the wounded soldier, who a second later vanished into thin air along with the other soldier through the portal to Zeptus City. Horton could only imagine what had become of the third trooper.

The clash of iron and flesh suddenly filled the air. Turning away from the portal and toward the scene of the battle, it became immediately apparent to Horton why Reckoners wore such extravagant armor. Linden was remarkable with a sword in her own right, handling one or two Vwari at a time with brilliant finesse, but the Reckoner was incredible.

A dozen Vwari surrounded the goliath in an effort to overpower it. They clambered daringly onto his back in an attempt to bring him down, but the tactic had seemingly no effect. The Reckoner was an absolute machine of destruction as his supersized sword pulverizing multiple Vwari with every swing. Horton could only stare and witness the brute with mesmerized fascination.

Yet despite their combined struggle, Linden and the Reckoner were gradually being pushed deeper and deeper into the chamber toward the portal. The torrent of Vwari through the exposed entrance appeared endless.

"Penriding, Horton, go!" Linden yelled back to them mid-tussle.

"You go on, I'll stay," Penriding said as he seized Horton by the arm to garner his attention.

"No way, my brother might still be here somewhere," Horton replied defiantly. "I'm staying, too."

Linden glanced back to find that the two weren't budging.

"Damnit!" she yelled out. "Destroy the portal!"

The Reckoner got the message. He let fly a mighty blow

of his sword, sending countless Vwari hurtling away, giving Linden and him a few precious seconds of breathing room to run over to the portal.

"This is your last chance," Linden warned Horton and Penriding.

"I'm not giving up without Deforest," Horton insisted.

"And I'm not leaving without you," Penriding added, looking at Linden.

She puckered her face in silent dismay before motioning to the Reckoner to destroy the pedestal. The group took a step back as the portal was obliterated in one swift stroke. That was it. Their only way back to the wastewalker was through the Vwari.

The situation looked increasingly dim, however, as countless more Vwari made their way into the chamber and encircled the group around where the portal had stood. Horton and the others' adversary stood there waiting, mere feet away, as if calculating their final onslaught.

Already regretting his decision to stay behind, Horton could hear his heart beat pounding in his ears now, thumping louder and louder with every passing moment.

Clang. Clang. Clang. Clang.

As Vwari continued to fill the massive chamber, he realized this was it. He was going to die.

Clang. Clang. Clang. Clang.

He slowly crept behind the Reckoner for protection. The once demonic figure he had feared was now his acting guardian angel.

CLANG. CLANG. CLANG. CLANG.

Or rather, guardian angels.

Sprinting in through the chamber's entrance like runaway wastewalkers appeared two Reckoners to their rescue, plowing a path for themselves through the sea of Vwari toward their trapped comrades. The trinity of Reckoners quickly gathered around Penriding, Linden and Horton, creating a bastion of black armor that was the only barrier between the bleached swathes of foes now closing in on them.

Horton couldn't tell which side threw the first blow, but once the fighting began it was as though Pandora's Box itself had been opened. As expected, the ensemble of Reckoners was devastatingly effective. Shielded between Penriding and Linden, Horton watched with grim enamor as wave after wave of enraged Vwari jarred against their protectors' improvised garrison, only to be violently denied access by their blades.

It felt like a terrible, long-forgotten dream as he stood there with little else besides his rejected Illac gods to pray to, wishing that the Vwari would cease their apparent martyrdom. An eternity passed in Horton's mind before the immense invasive assault eventually began to thin out, leaving behind only the mangled dregs of the Vwari bombardment.

"We need to move right now," Linden ordered as she seized their opportunity to escape. "The Vwari will return with far greater numbers."

"No, I've got to find Deforest first," Horton decreed.

"Do what you want, but we're leaving with or without you," Linden stated with a quick, callous glance at Horton before turning back to the trio of Reckoners. "Let's go."

In an instant they took off running, leaving Horton

standing there on his own with countless dead Vwari piled at his feet. He looked around for a moment in disarray, trying to figure out what he wanted to do.

Now half way to the entrance, Penriding stopped and turned back to look at him.

"Horton," he pleaded, shaking his head.

It was only then that the truth of the situation finally took hold of him. The island was swarming with Vwari that had presumably been trying to figure out a way inside the pyramid. If Deforest had left somehow – perhaps through the opening Horton had entered through, he was surely dead. Alternatively, if he had stayed he would have starved to death. He wasn't in Zeptus, he wasn't in Illac. Even worse, if he had hit the red button on the pedestal he would have suffocated.

A tear ran down his face beneath his headscarf. It was over.

Penriding grabbed his arm. He had ran back to Horton to retrieve his friend.

"Come on," he told the young Illac.

Snapped out of his daze, Horton joined Penriding and hurriedly ran to catch up to Linden and the Reckoners ahead of them. In a turn of fortune, the group's path to the forest below appeared to be temporarily clear as they descended the stairway to the forest floor. The Vwari had apparently retreated all the way back into the thick foliage.

Taking the lead, the team of Reckoners formed a battering ram of sorts as they ran through the forest toward the Desert Storm, effectively bulldozing the overgrowth in front of them and allowing the group to withdraw quickly.

Nevertheless, it wasn't long before the debilitating sound of screeching Vwari filled the air from all directions once more, closing in on them as they ran. Thoughts of being picked off by one of the monsters through the brush around them filled Horton's head, unnerving him. He fixed his eyes on the Reckoner's dark armor in front of him to combat the harrowing notion, but it was no use. He could feel the forest and Vwari engulfing him, submerging him. With nowhere else to hide, he squinted his eyes almost entirely shut.

Everything happens for a reason.

Ulises' words echoed in his mind, but he refused to accept them. Surely there was still hope. There had to be.

Deforest's path has been laid out before him.

He saw his brother's face in his mind, as plain as day. It killed him to think he had failed Deforest.

A sudden cool breeze washed over his face. He opened his eyes to find the Reckoners had breached the edge of the dense forest and returned them to the beach where the Desert Storm was waiting, ready to depart. If it left quickly, they stood a chance to make a clean break.

Then, just meters away from the wastewalker, one of the Reckoners stopped inexplicably, causing Horton to nearly run into his back. Confused, Horton looked around to find that all three Reckoners had abruptly halted in unison.

"Get on board!" Linden instructed, waving at Horton to follow Penriding and her. "We're leaving right now!"

"What about the Reckoners?" Horton asked Linden as he ran up the ramp to the wastewalker. She didn't reply, but her gaze toward the beach answered the question on its own.

Hundreds upon hundreds of Vwari poured out of the forest and onto the beach. As the creatures encroached upon the Reckoners, they heaved their herculean swords off their backs and stood their ground at the water's edge.

"Tell the helmsman to pull out immediately," Horton overheard Linden instruct one of the nearby soldiers. "We're done here."

"Yes, sir!" he replied before running off, but Horton wasn't planning on letting this go so easily.

"You can't leave them – they just saved our lives!" he contended.

"Sorry Horton," Linden replied flatly. "They're doing their jobs, and we need to do ours."

Horton wanted to press further, but Linden didn't stick around to hear his opinion. He could only stand and watch powerlessly as the boarding ramp was pulled up and the Desert Storm propelled away from the shore.

They're doing their jobs, and we need to do ours.

Linden's words replayed in his head over and over as he stared blankly back onto the beach. He had heard Penriding say something similar to rationalize Ananke's perilous diversion back at the Rissa.

"It is not a fair world, Horton," a voice said from behind him. To his surprise it was Ulises. "Sacrifices must be made for the greater good. Being an Illac you should know that as well as anybody."

Horton didn't respond. Back on the beach, the forsaken Reckoners fought valiantly, but in vain. One by one they fell, seeming to tire as their resistance did little to deter the ceaseless plague of Vwari. They were helplessly over-whelmed. He closed his eyes, unable to bear watching their sacrifice any longer.

He couldn't help but think that Ulises – and everyone else for the matter – was wrong. Just as the priest began to put his arm around his shoulder, Horton pushed him away and silently walked back to his cabin.

It was early that evening when Horton went to bed. It wasn't that he was tired; he just didn't want anyone's com-pany. Laying there with his eyes fixed on the ceiling, the Desert Storm creaking as it traversed the ocean, Horton couldn't stop thinking about what had happened back on the island that day. He thought about Deforest, the Vwari and the Reckoners.

"Why would a Reckoner blindly throw away his life in the name of duty like that?" he uttered under his breath. Before today Horton had seen Reckoners as nothing more than a mysterious and heavy chunk of black armor, their semblance merely a physical portrayal of the faceless dark-ness he'd been running from for so long. Now, though, they were different.

"What drives a person to that end?" he wondered.

NINE

Exetus

HORTON WOKE UP the following morning with one clear goal set in his mind. He needed to talk to a Reckoner.

Quite frankly, however, he didn't even know where they resided on the Desert Storm, let alone if they would actually talk back to him. The only thing he did know was they spent the majority of their time alongside Linden in the command room, but beyond that he had never bothered to see what they did with themselves during downtime. In fact, he was almost completely certain he had never even seen one relaxing on the upper deck or eating in the mess hall, for that matter. The more he tried to figure them out, the more questions he had.

Ultimately, Horton concluded that his best shot would be to try talking to Linden about them, and so he did so during breakfast that day. He decided he would take a chance at sitting down alongside Linden and Penriding for once with the other higher-ranking soldiers at the officer's table in the mess room.

"Mind if I sit here?" Horton asked timorously as he stood at the end of the table closest to them.

Penriding tried to hide his smirk by quickly taking a swig from his cup, but Horton caught it, causing him to immediately begin to have second thoughts. To his disbelief, however, Linden looked up at him from her meal and gave him an apathetic half-nod of approval.

"Thanks," Horton said with relief as he sat his plate on the table, forcing two soldiers to shuffle down the bench to make room for him.

"Feeling better today Horton?" Penriding asked right before swallowing a mouthful of food. "Sorry about Deforest by the way. You never know though. He might still show up somewhere."

"I'm fine," Horton replied with a half-hearted smile. He had been trying his hardest to completely block the whole fiasco from yesterday out of his mind. It had not yet fully sunk in that any realistic hope of finding his brother alive was now completely doused, and if he had his way he would rather defer that pain for as long as possible.

Horton sat there eating at the table in silence for the rest of breakfast. He had hoped to question Linden a bit about the Reckoner, but while she ate she seemed so distant that he couldn't bring himself to disturb her.

One by the one the soldiers at the table picked up their plates and left, and as fate would have it, Horton ended up sitting there with just Penriding and Linden left for company. This was his best chance.

"Hey, Linden?" Horton cautiously solicited. "Where are the Reckoners—"

Linden and Penriding's eyes swung away from oblivion's grasp and locked onto Horton's at the mention of Reckoners, causing him to nervously gulp before continuing.

"...staying on the wastewalker? I would like to talk to them – if possible, I mean."

Penriding's eyes lit up in intrigue. He seemed to take some degree of underhanded pleasure with Horton's request.

"Why would a young Illac like you take such a sudden interest in Reckoners?" Linden asked listlessly as she threw her napkin on her plate.

"I'm not sure exactly," he said half-truthfully. He knew what he wanted to ask the Reckoners, but he wasn't sure why he felt so inclined to do so. It was as if they held some empirical truth that he was resolved to discover.

"I'd just like to talk to them," he told her, not beating around the bush. "That is, if I may."

Linden stared him down for a solid five seconds. Horton was certain she was on the verge of accepting his request.

"No."

Horton was taken aback.

"No?"

"No," Linden said decisively once more. "Do not ask me again."

The commander then stood up and left before Horton could fight it any further, which was probably a good thing.

Horton glared at Penriding, who had returned to snickering behind the guise of drinking from his cup.

"Oh come on," Penriding said with a grin, giving in to Horton's clear displeasure in the Zeptan's apparent amusement.

"What?" Horton prodded. "What's so funny about that?"

"Nothing, nothing at all," Penriding replied as he continued his attempt to keep a straight face. "It's just a little weird that you would have a sudden fascination with those things. Normal people make it their business to disassociate themselves from the Reckoners if they can help it, not befriend them."

"I'm not trying to befriend anyone," Horton insisted. "I just want to talk to one, see what make him tick. I don't know – something like that."

Penriding leaned back in his seat and fished deep in his pocket, all the while shaking his head and smiling.

"Here," the Zeptan said as he discreetly placed something on Horton's knee beneath the table. He reached under the table and grabbed it. It was a key.

"I didn't give you that," Penriding added as he looked around the room beyond Horton.

"How did you get this?" Horton whispered as he squeezed the key into his palm.

"Have you already forgotten whose wastewalker this is?" Penriding asked brazenly. "There's a room in the back of the cargo hold – I'm quite certain they're being housed up in there. Although I don't know how well they take to random visits – or he, rather."

"He?" Horton repeated.

"Well yeah, there's only one of them left on board now that the other three are gone," Penriding explained.

"They're not gone, they were killed," Horton corrected.

Penriding raised an eyebrow. "Gone, dead. It's all the same thing."

"Those three Reckoners died holding off the Vwari so we could escape," Horton said firmly under his breath, now feeling a little aggravated. "They don't deserve to be treated as though they never existed in the first place."

"No you're right, you're right," Penriding reconciled as he stood up from the table and adjusted his belt. "Just be careful, okay? I'll catch you later."

Horton rubbed his eyes in exasperation as Penriding walked off. Sometimes it felt like the entire world was against him. Still, on the bright side he got what he had wanted. He looked down at his hand. Nestled in his palm was the key to a Reckoner.

It was late that night when Horton decided the time was right to sneak down to the cargo hold and try to confront the Reckoner. By this time much of the crew would be asleep, he imagined, making it far less likely he'd be caught skulking around.

He began his trek by tiptoeing to his cabin door, careful not to wake Ulises. He opened it and peered out – fortunately the corridor outside was vacant. The hard metal floors made it easy for Horton to soften his footsteps, allowing him to move in virtual silence alongside the walls toward the stairway. He held onto the guardrail to support himself as he gently footed his way deep down into the lowest levels of the wastewalker toward the cargo hold, which was located beyond even the engine room he had once regularly frequented.

Once at the unlit landing at the base of the stairs, Horton could just barely make out the contours of a lone iron door. He examined it carefully with his hands in the darkness until he found its handle, but when he tried to pull it open the door refused to budge. Anticipating this, Horton inserted his hand into his pocket and pulled out the silver-plated key Penriding had provided him, and then felt with his other hand for a key hole.

"There you are," he whispered once he found it.

Horton quickly glanced back up the empty stairwell one last time to make sure the coast was still clear, then pushed the key in and turned.

Click.

Following a deep breath, he slowly pushed the door open.

Horton peered into the room beyond the locked iron door. Just as Penriding had told him, inside was the Desert Storm's cargo hold. The room was crammed to the ceiling with crates of food and other supplies, and it surely would have been filled to the absolute brim prior to when the crew unloaded most of their munitions before taking to the ocean.

Above him a single source of light swung from the ceiling to the tune of the wastewalker rocking back and forth on the waves, providing erratic silhouettes throughout the voluminous room. Horton noticed a door at the far end of the hold between two tall stacks of crates, but it hardly seemed large enough for a Reckoner to fit through in full armor. Regardless, he carefully navigated the maze of crates to reach the back wall that held the door, his eyes all the while twitching back and forth as the shadows teased him in a game of hide and seek.

As he approached the door at the far end of the hold, Horton slowed himself down to a deliberate and cautious pace. Turning his ear toward it slightly, the Illac tried to catch any sign of life from beyond its keep.

"What do you want?" a heavy voiced asked out of nowhere from the shadows nearby.

To Horton's own surprise he hadn't recoiled at the sound of this unexpected demand. Instead he stood fast in his place and gazed into the darkness from where it came as he attempted to decipher its source.

After a few seconds of staring into nothingness, the ever-changing light deviated to just the right spot, revealing a Reckoner sitting against the wall, still completely adorned in his heavy ebony cocoon. Horton just managed to catch a glimpse of his sword resting against the wall nearby, briefly manumitted from its master, before the light swung away and drenched the mysterious being in darkness once more.

Horton heard the Reckoner pulling himself up in the umbra, the light seemingly eluding his domain as much as possible. He let out a low groan as he approached, the burden he carried clunking with each step, but Horton held his ground.

"You're an Illac," the Reckoner stated sluggishly from behind his masked face as he reluctantly exposed himself to Horton, who couldn't help but stare at the goliath, and who, in the moment, didn't look dissimilar to a poppy growing in the shadow of a monolith.

"Where is Illac?" he boomed, this time prompting Horton to take a half step backward.

"I—I don't know," Horton answered warily, unsure of why he seemed so intent on knowing his village's location. "I mean, not from where we are right now, but yes, I am from Illac."

"You shouldn't be here," he said with a note of disdain in his voice.

"They saved my life – the other Reckoners – they saved everyone's lives," Horton blurted, afraid of what might happen if he stopped talking. "I just wanted to thank you. I noticed you and the others don't seem to get much respect from anyone."

The Reckoner scoffed as he walked over to a well-lit wall and sat down against it in a series of clangors. "Fear... fear of the unknown. We are not like the other Zeptans. We are different."

"Different?" Horton asked, uncertain of where to begin his line of questioning. "You mean your size? The armor? Why don't you ever take it off?"

The Reckoner took a deep, wheezy breath.

"Those blessed with the ability to wear this armor come only from the Diamond Eagle tribe that resides in the wastes far to the west of Zeptus City. From a young age the men of our tribe are trained in combat so that we may one day serve the Zeptan High Council. A select few earn the honor of wearing the armor endowed to us by the Rissa itself. Once it goes on, it doesn't come off."

"What makes the armor so special?" Horton pressed.

"A Reckoner's armor is a gift from God herself," the Reckoner told him. "Retrieved from deep within the bowels of the Rissa, this armor provides me with divine strength and speed to vanquish our foes. To fight and die in the defense of Zeptus in the name of the Rissa is the highest honor a man from my tribe could ever achieve. There is no need to thank my former cohorts for their service."

"I see," Horton noted. "And so you use that power to fight the Vwari?"

"They are the greatest threat to Zeptus," the Reckoner confirmed.

Horton walked over to one of the smaller crates and sat down on it. He stared down the Reckoner, his elbow on his knee as his hand supported his head. A few months ago he would have laughed off a story about supernatural armor – blessed by a God of all things – but from what he had seen on his journey so far it didn't surprise him. Plus, he had seen the Reckoner's devastating ability with his own eyes.

"My name is Horton, son of Klas," Horton announced after a moment of silence. "What's your name?"

Horton continued to stare at the Reckoner with great intrigue as he waited for a response, but it never came. Instead, the Reckoner pulled himself up off the floor and lumbered over toward Horton and stood over him. Then, without warning, he grabbed Horton by the scruff of the neck, pulled him up off the crate and held the Illac at face level.

"Illac..." he groaned as Horton felt the Reckoner's grasp tighten. "I know all too well who you are."

Then, as if abruptly coming to his senses, the Reckoner slowly let Horton down onto his feet.

"It was a mistake coming here," he bellowed as he turned his back to Horton. "Do not return."

Horton was stunned by what had just transpired. Just as it seemed he was getting through to the Reckoner, he turned on him. Nevertheless, Horton heeded his request and quickly returned to his cabin without another word said.

As Horton snuck back up the stairwell, all he could do was replay the Reckoner's confounding and volatile change in personality again and again in his head. All he had done was ask the Reckoner his name – what was the problem with that, he wondered.

He tossed and turned in his bed for hours before he fell asleep that night. He was glad he found out why the Reckoners had so readily sacrificed themselves for him and the others back on the island, but the fact that the man had turned on him so suddenly bothered him. Perhaps that is just how they are, he figured. Maybe that was why Linden didn't want him to see them.

Horton returned to his usual spot in the mess room the next day for breakfast. He was feeling especially groggy that morning and the last thing he wanted to do was talk to Penriding, who undoubtedly would want him to provide a comprehensive synopsis of his powwow with the Reckoner from the previous night.

He did well to avoid eye contact with the Zeptan as he swiftly entered the room with his plate, hoping to glide in undetected. However just as he was about to sit down he noticed Penriding out of the corner of his eye, rapidly encroaching upon him from the other side of the room like a waste fox stalking its prey.

Horton shut his eyes and took a deep breath when Penriding sat down across the table from him with a grin on his face.

"Well?" he demanded.

"Well what?" Horton replied lethargically.

"Don't you even," Penriding shot back half-seriously as he took a quick audit of the room to see who was within earshot. "You know exactly what I'm talking about – don't make me spell it out for you."

Horton reached down and pulled out the key Penriding had loaned him and placed it on the table.

"Nothing happened," he lied. "I went down to the cargo hold like you said but he wasn't there."

"You're kidding," Penriding lamented. "Well, try again tonight then."

"No," Horton said hastily. "I mean, I don't really want to talk to him now. Thanks for the key, though."

Penriding sighed as he picked the key up off the table. "Damn, I was really looking forward to hearing about your little picnic, too."

"Why don't you talk to him?" Horton inquired.

Penriding chuckled. "Believe me I've tried, but those damn things always ignore me."

He leaned across the table toward Horton as if to whisper a secret.

"Between you and me, I don't think they like me," he said with the gravest-looking face he could pull off. "I think they're jealous of my dashingly good looks."

"Nope, it's definitely not that," Horton quipped with a smile.

As Penriding chuckled and leaned back in his seat, Horton caught Linden eyeing him from across the room with a cold look on her face. He suddenly got the terrible feeling that she knew what he had done, or perhaps the Reckoner had mentioned his late-night visit to his superior. All he knew was the last thing he wanted to have to do was try to explain himself to her after she had told him no.

Horton spent his time after breakfast that day up on the upper deck staring out into the boundless ocean. Ulises was up there for much of the day too, still cataloging fish in his journal. Normally Horton would volunteer to help, but today he couldn't find the appetite for it. Instead he thought about his brother.

It was the first time since he left the island that Horton gave the subject of Deforest a chance to really sink in. He had been afraid of how he would take it because he wasn't really sure how well he knew himself anymore. Still, as much as his heart ached for his lost brother, it didn't break. Horton wasn't sure if it was because he'd subconsciously become used to the fact that Deforest was likely gone forever or if he had simply hardened emotionally over the past few months. Either way, he definitely wasn't the same Illac who had tumbled down a fox hole and into the Earth Stone.

Horton jolted awake that night to the crack of thunder. The Desert Storm seesawed on the waves as the sound of pouring rain droned down upon its hull, and it creaked with anguish every time it rolled on the water. The vessel's weary body was clearly not fashioned to withstand the turmoil of a storm such as this.

He sat up and listened. Never before had he experienced weather this intense. Rain was not unheard of back home, but it wasn't exactly a common phenomenon either.

Horton shuddered as the sound of thunder rang out once more. He looked over at Ulises to see if he, too, was awake, but as typical the old priest was still asleep. The young Illac sighed to himself and lay back down, his eyes fixed on the wooden beam above his head. He could feel his heart pounding in his chest.

"It's okay," Horton quietly mumbled to himself. "Everything is okay. We're fine."

Horton closed his eyes and tried to relax. He breathed in and out for a bit, trying to slow his heart rate. It was childish to be afraid of a thunderstorm.

"Everything is going to be okay," he told himself again.

Pop!

Horton shot his eyes wide open. That last blast of thunder sounded weirdly like cannon fire.

Pop! Pop! Pop!

"That *is* cannon fire!" he said out loud.

Horton sat up in his bed once again. There was no doubt about it – the Desert Storm was engaged in battle.

"Ulises!" Horton hissed as he climbed out of bed and over to the button on the wall that illuminated the room. Ulises mumbled gibberish as he awoke from his sleep to see Horton's frantic face looking over him.

"What in the gods is it, boy?" Ulises murmured as he

tried to rub his eyes, but Horton grabbed the priest's wrist and pulled his hand away from his face.

"Listen," he said, eyes pointed toward the ceiling.

Ulises' eyes unfurled as he too heard it – the sound of cannon fire had clearly escalated.

Boom!

Horton found himself thrown to the floor as the Desert Storm took a jarring punch. The voices and footsteps of frenetic soldiers echoed through the corridor outside their cabin.

Bang!

A second blow slammed the wastewalker before Horton could collect himself from the initial hit. He looked up at Ulises to find him thrown back onto his bed with his hands gripping onto the headboard for dear life. After pulling himself up, Horton raced to the cabin door to peer outside.

"Stay inside!" a lone soldier running down the corridor shouted over when he caught sight of Horton's head poking out from behind his door. "Don't leave your cabin. Everything is going to be okay."

That did little to comfort Horton, who quickly slammed the door shut. He hated to consider the possibility, but he had a good idea of what was attacking them. He turned back around to survey the room before looking at Ulises. They needed to bar the door.

"Here, help me with this," he motioned to Ulises as he pulled the desk out from the corner of the room. Together the two Illacs frantically threw everything they could in front of the door while the ominous cries of death and despair filled the air from elsewhere on the vessel.

"Who do you think it is?" Ulises wheezed as he heaved a chair on top of the hastily erected stack of furniture in front of the door.

Horton turned and faced Ulises in order to answer, but instead froze in place. With a heavy desk chair in arms, his eyes shot wide open as his heart suddenly skipped a beat. He was sure he heard footsteps from down the corridor outside, and they were not the hard, rugged footsteps of soldier boots, but rather something else – something that resurfaced terrible memories from his time inside the Tiberonus pyramid. Swiftly, Horton climbed over their makeshift furniture barricade to push the button that turned off the light source, leaving them blanketed in darkness. He and Ulises then shifted to the back corner of the cabin and waited.

Horton's heart was now relocated in the bottom of his throat as the pitter-patter of flesh upon metal wandered down the corridor towards their cabin. He willed as hard as he could for the lone Reckoner on board to suddenly storm down the corridor and rescue them, but he almost certainly was holed up fighting elsewhere on the wastewalker.

He gasped as the light scratch of fingernails resonated through the cabin door as the intruder grappled with their cabin door's handle. Once solved by the invader, the door squeaked as it slowly opened, only to be denied by the tower of furniture he and Ulises had constructed.

Then he heard it; the paralyzing screech he had agonizingly endured once before. He prayed under his breath that these unknown besiegers had been something else – anything else – but alas his plea was ignored. It was the Vwari.

Crash!

Furniture tumbled down onto the floor as the monster threw its body recklessly against the door like a battering ram. Light flooded the room as the door slowly crept open with each bash from the inhuman creature. The makeshift defense would not hold out for much longer.

And suddenly, there it was. No match for the unrelenting onslaught of a lone Vwari, their barricade was leveled and cast haphazardly across the cabin floor. The door creaked pitilessly as the creature slowly pressed it wide open, revealing the monster's featureless silhouette to Horton against the lit backdrop of the corridor outside. As the Vwari took its first step through the doorway towards them, Horton shuddered slightly, realizing the Vwari was staring right at him. Its golden eyes shone like miniature suns in the darkness, fervent with enigmatic hatred.

Horton gasped as Ulises took hold of his shoulder and swung him behind the priest. Surely his old friend and mentor would vainly be the young Illac's final line of defense, Horton thought. His eyes squeezed shut as the wretched being trod ever closer, berating them with its audible wheezing. He would have given anything to be anywhere other than where he was at that moment. He wished he was safely back in Illac with Deforest and his mother. He wanted to see his father again.

It was then that something clicked inside Horton. Whether it was adrenaline, hormones, the desire to survive – who knows, but the underlying fear he had carried with him since his father disappeared those nine long years ago instantly dissipated.

"Aaaah!" Horton screamed as he pushed Ulises aside to take on the Vwari. In a brash influx of courage and stupidity, he found himself determined to inflict as much pain on that damned thing as he could, even if it cost him his life. However, when Horton looked out at where the Vwari had stood just a few seconds before, there was nothing.

"What happened? Where did it go?" Horton asked between heavy breaths, his eyes scanning the room.

"I—I am not exactly sure," Ulises croaked, clearly shaken up by what had just happened. "It entered in a fit of rage, but when it saw me it seemed to immediately settle down. It was almost as if it trusted me. I cannot explain it, Horton. It just turned around and walked out."

Horton dashed over to the door, high-stepping overturned furniture along the way. The corridor outside was completely clear and the wastewalker was silent. For better or for worse it appeared the fighting was over, and more importantly, for the time being Ulises and he were still alive.

"That soldier told us to stay in here," Ulises cautioned as he too poked his head out into the corridor a moment later.

"It's far too quiet," Horton pointed out as he cautiously stepped out of the cabin. "I need to find out what's going on."

"Well in that case I am coming too," Ulises insisted.

"Fine," Horton replied as he doubled back to his bed to retrieve his satchel from underneath it. He reached into one of its pockets, pulled out his head scarf and wrapped it on before throwing the satchel over his shoulder.

"Let's go."

The two of them quickly scurried toward the stairwell at the end of the deck. Horton could tell that the Desert

Storm's engines had been disengaged and the vessel was listing onto its starboard side. There were signs at the base of the stairwell that a struggle had occurred there. A large pool of blood had accrued on the floor, but no body to go with it. Oddly, as Horton and Ulises snuck their way to the higher decks of the wastewalker, the command room being their target destination, they found no bodies at all, despite the bountiful evidence of hand-to-hand combat that had taken place throughout. The two Illacs pushed on, however, and eventually found themselves outside the command room having faced, to their relief, no resistance at all.

Horton perked up at the sound of muffled voices coming from behind the door. This was a good sign – he was fairly positive the Vwari could not speak. However, as he carefully leaned himself against it to listen for a familiar voice, he paused. It wasn't Penriding, Linden or anyone else he recognized. Horton took a deep breath – he would need to get a better look. Emboldened by Ulises' surprisingly calm demeanor, he slowly pushed the command room's door open a hair, giving him just enough of a view to see a hooded man in a black cloak standing over a kneeling Linden, who had each of her arms restrained by a Vwari.

"What in the gods? Who is that man?" Horton muttered under his breath.

Also knelt alongside Linden was Penriding, his face swollen and bleeding from the nose. Curious, Horton opened the door slightly wider to reveal a handful of Zeptan soldiers sitting cross-legged on the other side of the room under the watchful guard of Vwari. Leaning up against the wall behind them was the Reckoner's sword.

Horton covered his mouth to muffle his gasp. He could not believe that the Reckoner had fallen.

Then the man in black moved out of view, prompting Horton to shuffle his feet slightly to get another look at him. As far as he could decipher, he appeared to be the Vwari ringleader. He would have thought it impossible to tame a race as volatile and wicked as the Vwari, but they seemed to follow the orders the mysterious man barked at them with complete and unwavering submission.

Suddenly the hooded man turned for a brief instant in Horton's direction, and as he did Horton saw part of his face from beneath his veil, revealing to his dismay a man hidden further still behind a coarse black beard. More interestingly, however, was the white clothing he wore beneath his cloak, though Horton was unable to get a good look at it.

"Take a look, Ulises," Horton whispered back to the priest. "Do you recognize that man in the black cloak?"

When Horton got no response he asked again.

"Ulises?" he whispered, this time blindly stretching his hand out behind him to garner his old friend's attention, but he only felt air.

Horton spun around.

"Uli—?"

Ugh...

"Whoa, easy kid," Penriding's voice seemed to materialize out of nowhere as Horton came to. "You were in quite a heap when the Vwari threw you in here. Are you okay?"

Horton opened his eyes to find he was not on the Desert Storm anymore. Sitting himself up and removing his head scarf from over his eyes, he further discovered that some of the remnants of the Desert Storm's crew were also there with him, sitting against the cold, black walls that surrounded them in that alien room. Judging by the discordant hum of the engines and uneven ride, he guessed they were on a Vwari vessel.

"What happened?" Horton asked as he scanned the room, finding that Linden, Ulises and the Reckoner were the only ones not among them from those he had seen in the command room.

"A Vwari raid party intercepted us in the middle of the night," Penriding explained. "They were there waiting for us – must have found all the supplies we dumped on the beach."

"What about Ulises and Linden? What about the Reckoner?" Horton suddenly boomed, as if interrogating the entire room.

"Linden was gravely wounded during the fight," Penriding said shallowly. "There was a man in a black cloak... I can't explain it. It was as if he commanded the Vwari, their every movement. She never had a chance. Those damn things seized her, and that bastard demanded the Reckoner stand down or else he would end Linden's life. The Reckoner refused, so I ordered him to."

"And did he?" Horton asked.

Penriding nodded slowly.

"They took Linden and the Reckoner away. I don't know where," Penriding said sadly. "As for Ulises, I have no idea. I never saw him."

Horton took a deep breath and sighed. Everything had fallen apart.

"Oh, you had this on you when the Vwari dragged you in," Penriding said, tossing Horton his satchel. "It was tied up so tightly around you I thought it might have suffocated you to death."

Horton wearily opened it up to find that all of the satchel's contents remained intact. Amazingly, that included the blue orb Al had given them to repair the pyramids, tucked away into one corner of the deepest pocket.

"At least we still have the orb," Horton said listlessly as he closed the satchel up and placed it at his side. "Though who knows what good that will do us now. Do you have any idea where they're going to take us?"

"I don't know," Penriding replied as he slowly shook his head. His eyes were glazed over, deep in thought. "I just don't know."

Horton wasn't sure how much time they had spent in that room without food or water when the Vwari vessel finally came to a stop, but he groggily estimated that it must have been at least twenty-odd hours.

Eventually a door swung open, revealing a different, shorter man also adorned in a black cloak. He, too, to no surprise, was surrounded by his own legion of Vwari. The man entered the room and casually circled it two times, inspecting each of his prisoners before pointing at one of the Zeptan soldiers. As quickly as the man singled him out, his group of Vwari pounced on the soldier and dragged him out of the room kicking and screaming, while the others could do little more than look away or stare in horror.

"If any of you fall out of line, your fate will be the same as his," the cloaked man decreed. "Now come with me."

Horton and Penriding looked at each other and the other imprisoned soldiers. They had no other option but to do as he said. Reluctantly, Horton pulled his headscarf on and joined the Zeptans as they followed the man out of the room and down a short corridor, all the while closely watched by a swarm of Vwari that were quite evidently restraining themselves from assaulting them right then and there.

The man then stopped the group in front of the vessel's boarding hatch, turned around and looked at them with a devilish grin before addressing them simply.

"Zeptans, welcome to Exetus."

As the mechanical hatch began to lower, the Zeptan prisoners were forced to shield their eyes with their hands as the glare from the bleached-white outside world unveiled itself.

Stepping off the ramp, Horton's squinted gaze turned into astonishment as a freezing wind blew over him. White particles blew into his eyes through his head scarf, causing him to lose balance momentarily on the unusually-textured sand they were walking on. He looked ahead to see where the man was leading them, but in that weather he couldn't distinguish anything beyond just a few meters in any direction.

"Horton!" Penriding yelled as the wind howled around them. "I think I know what this stuff is! It's snod!"

"What?" Horton shouted back. Penriding was only a couple of short paces away, but the howling wind drowned out his voice.

"Snod! Or is it snow? Actually, I think it's snow! Either way, it is basically frozen rain!" Penriding continued to shout. "We must be somewhere near the southern pyramid!"

Horton heard him this time, but he had already figured out what Penriding was trying to tell him on his own. From directly in front of them emerged a dark, frostbitten pyramid, having been hidden in the intense blizzard of "snow," as Penriding put it. Much like the Earth Stone, almost the entire pyramid appeared to be encapsulated underground, with only the final ten meters or so below its peak revealing itself above the snow-covered surface.

The stranger in black led the prisoners and his Vwari guard through a small entrance in the pyramid's side that looked like it was probably not an original part of the structure's design. If anything, the entryway appeared as though it had been crudely carved into the side of the pyramid relatively recently. Regardless, it divulged a dark, makeshift staircase that led down to the structure's lower levels. Horton could feel his pulse rising again as they creaked their way down the jerry-rigged winding staircase and toward the unknown fate that awaited them in the pyramid's stygian depths.

As a gust of frozen arctic air blew down past them, Horton pulled his headscarf on a little tighter. He was glad for it too – for some reason he felt safer with his head hidden behind that thin shroud, especially considering that from somewhere close behind him came the grisly sound of a wheezing Vwari, prickling the back of his neck despite his covering.

Flaming torches spotted the walls as the last remnants

of sunlight pouring in through the top of the pyramid gave way to the darkness that entrenched its deep interior. Unusually, the air seemed to get warmer as they descended. This was abnormal compared to the other pyramids he had visited, prompting Horton to note to himself that this was possibly the first time in his life he was happy to be getting away from cool air.

Peering over the edge of the stairs' railing, Horton spotted a wide doorway down below that contained within it a brightly lit chamber. Long anonymous shadows slithered through the opening and across the floor, and as Horton tried to discover their source, he found them unwilling to betray who or what had created them. When the group got closer to the bottom of the stairs, he found himself squeezing his satchel ever tighter against his body. It still contained the repair orb Al had given them, and their escape from this place likely hinged on whether an opportunity to employ it should arise.

As Horton, Penriding and the surviving soldiers were led through a doorway and into a large hall, Horton realized where all the warm air was coming from. Large cisterns of fire lined the walls, filling the room with heat and light. At the back of the room was a rostrum, upon which eight beings stood in black cloaks and hoods, their faces sequestered from view. Even more curious still was a long-bearded man seated upon an apparent throne of sorts, his black cloak cast over one shoulder, divulging part of the white tunic he wore underneath that was not so much unlike an Illac's.

All around them legions of Vwari girdled the walls and

balconies of that hall deep within the pyramid, their numbers seemingly infinite. Each Vwari's eyes gazed attentively toward the altar of cloaked men, ostensibly hanging on their every word and action.

Eventually the cloaked man who had led them to this place came to a sudden halt, just ten strides short of the man in a chair. Then, without getting up, the seated man shot out his right arm and formed a fist with his hand, somehow prompting the Vwari escorts to reflexively seize the arms of Horton and the other prisoners. Horton shivered slightly as the repulsive creature's long, boney fingers held him still.

"Welcome to the somber abode of the bygones, Zeptans," the seated man suddenly announced, silencing the undertone of wheezing from the Vwari. His voice was harsh, apathetic and as worn down as his appearance.

He looked at his captives for a moment and then flicked his wrist slightly, which apparently was enough to signal the Vwari to release Horton and the Zeptans from their scraggy grasps, to Horton's relief. The man then lethargically pulled himself up from his chair before turning to one of the other cloaked individuals at his side.

"Bring in the others," he commanded, at which one of his minions walked away and exited through another doorway to the right side of the platform. A gang of Vwari spontaneously fell in behind him as he disappeared.

Just a few moments later he returned, followed closely by Linden and the Reckoner, whose thickly armored arms and legs had been chained together and his sword still separated from its wielder. Horton looked around as the two of them were led over beside him and the others. He was glad to see Linden and the Reckoner again, but to his dismay there was still no sign of Ulises.

"Isn't this an interesting development," the shadowy, bearded man said as he slowly lumbered his way toward the Reckoner. Horton tried to catch a glimpse of his face, but it was too well hidden beneath his dark beard and hood.

"After all these years, I have never had an opportunity to meet a Reckoner face to face before," the man went on while clearly keeping his distance from the enormous brute.

"Reckoner... vwari killer," he mumbled to himself as he inspected it from afar, before addressing the Reckoner with his grating voice. "But what are you really? Nothing more than a plain and simple man wearing mechanized armor, allegedly gifted to the Zeptan people by none other than the Rissa itself.

"You know, I've heard that only a person of certain blood – a very specific blood line – can wear that armor and remove it once it's on, but they never do. That really is quite fascinating. I suppose, therefore, I couldn't coerce you into kindly removing your helmet for me?"

The Reckoner stood motionless and silent.

"Why would a Reckoner listen to scum like you?" Linden spat out, her right hand all the while clasped onto her abdomen as she grimaced with intense pain. Horton could tell that her ailing condition had not improved any while in captivity. "Save your breath, you will never get that helmet off him. None but their own kind can."

The man stared at Linden from beneath his hood for a moment, before slowly nodding his head in agreement.

"And why should he do such a thing for me?" he asked. "By all means, in that armor he is no longer a mere man, no – he is something much more.

"Perhaps a god?" he said out loud with a laugh. "No, not quite a god. A god is immortal, all-knowing, and most of all, not under the control of another.

"You know, Mister Reckoner, you and I are not much unlike one another," the man went on. "In fact, beneath all those gears and thick armor, you and I share the same blood – the blood your Zeptan puppeteers use to their own advantage."

"Your words are nothing short of drivel and lies," Linden sneered at the man. "You're completely full of it."

"Am I?" the man responded as he glared at Linden once again. "Then I suppose the Reckoner won't mind if I try to remove his helmet?"

The man quickly turned his attention back to the Reckoner, who had all the while remained like a statue. Horton watched with great intrigue as the man slowly and cautiously approached the hulking soldier, his hands all the while out in front of him as if he were approaching a rabid animal.

"Kneel," the man commanded as he closed in on the behemoth, but the Reckoner persisted in holding his position.

"Kneel!" he shouted once more, but the Reckoner still refused to submit. The man turned to the Vwari standing nearby and directed them with his hand toward the Reckoner. In a split second a swarm of Vwari had forcefully attached themselves to his armor, forcing the Reckoner to buckle down onto his knees.

"That's much better," the man said with a scratchy chuckle. With the Reckoner completely immobilized, the man brazenly walked over to him and began to feel around the seam between the helmet and the body armor.

"Ah, here it is," he said after a few seconds. Horton heard a clicking sound, followed by the hiss of air escaping from within the armor. The man twisted the helmet slightly before pulling it up and off the Reckoner's head and throwing it aside, exposing a pale-skinned man with a long, thin face.

"You see?" the man said gently to the Reckoner, who squinted as his eyes adjusted to the light of the room. "You and I, we're the same. It's the Zeptans that are the enemy, not us."

Horton watched the Reckoner curiously, stunned to see that the man inside the brutish armor showed no apparent anger or ill-regard toward the bearded man, despite what he had just done. He could only imagine what was going through the Reckoner's mind as he kneeled there, his gauntlets touching the skin on his bare face for the first time in only the gods knew how long.

"Let him go," the man then commanded the Vwari, who quickly clambered off the helmetless Reckoner before scurrying back toward the edges of the hall.

The man then pulled his dark cloak back over his left shoulder and spun around to step away from the Reckoner, evidently leaving him there to assess what had happened on his own. As he turned his back to the prisoners, Horton noticed that Penriding was clenching his fist and fidgeting next to him. By the time he turned to see what was wrong with him, the brash Zeptan had engaged the hidden mechanical firearm from beneath his sleeve and pointed it at the mysterious bearded man.

Bang!

Horton jumped back as the gun went off in a large cloud of smoke. The long-bearded man instantly spun around in astonishment, all the while feeling around upon his chest as he searched for a wound, but there was none. Instead, once the smoke cleared and he saw what had transpired, his stunned look transformed into a grin. Penriding was standing there wincing in pain as the Reckoner held the Zeptan's wrist in his hand, having managed to push the firearm's trajectory away from the Exetan just in the nick of time.

The man broke out into a deranged laugh at the sight of Penriding in the grip of the Reckoner.

"What a cute, yet incredibly foolish trick," he said abhorrently before pausing a moment to glare intensely at Penriding. He seemed to be trying to figure the Zeptan out. "Only once before have I seen such a device as that...

"Who are you, boy?" the man interrogated Penriding harshly. Horton could make out the man's eyes now from this distance, which caused him to recoil somewhat. They seemed strangely familiar.

"Penriding Blacksmith," Penriding said without missing a beat. Horton couldn't help but notice Linden's face grimace as he did so.

The man laughed to himself once again.

"Penriding?" he repeated to himself in amazement. "Son of Nestor Blacksmith and heir to the Blacksmith Merchant Union?"

Penriding nodded as he stared past the man with stead-fast resolve.

"Why am I not surprised that a Blacksmith, a family built on underhanded promises and lies, would pull such an imbecilic stunt," the man remarked. "I will enjoy killing you, Penriding, just as I did your self-serving father."

Rage filled Penriding's eyes, forcing the Reckoner to tighten his grip on the Zeptan as he tensed up. Meanwhile the man had positioned himself right in front of Penriding's face.

"Do you not know who I am, Zeptan?" he asked with a snarl. "Surely your father told you why the Vwari long for Zeptan blood, or did he and your almighty High Council keep that little detail to themselves for all these years?"

Suddenly the man flung back his hood, revealing his de-faced appearance. Horton shuddered at the sight of him, as it looked as though he had been seriously burned at some point. However, despite the fact Horton couldn't immediately recognize him – his features were far too ruined – he still felt as though he had seen his eyes somewhere, as if from a distant memory or dream. Then, without warning, the man grabbed Penriding's neck with his hand.

"You see my face, Blacksmith?" the man growled. "Your father did this to me."

As he held Penriding, the squirming Zeptan all the while turning a shade of blue in his grasp, the man suddenly turned his eyes toward Horton, whose heart instantly stopped. Frozen, the Illac could only stare unwaveringly back at him from beneath his cowl, unable to bring himself to react in any way. Then to Penriding's relief, he released the Zeptan from his grip and averted his attention to the Illac, who now clutched his satchel so tightly it was beginning to hurt.

"Who is this boy?" the man questioned in an abrupt but calm manner. "Is this a relative of yours, Blacksmith?"

Horton noticed Penriding glance at him nervously as he tried to catch his breath, but the man didn't wait for an answer.

"What is that you have there?" the man now asked as he pried the satchel from Horton's clutches. His eyes immediately lit up when he opened it, the gentle blue glow of the orb shining across his face. He reached inside, pulled it out and then gazed into it for a moment before smiling to himself. "This is a very impressive toy, Zeptan. I'm sure you won't mind if I give it to my son – he doesn't have much to keep him occupied in a brutal place such as this, I'm afraid."

Horton didn't respond. Instead he just stood there like a stone figure, his eyes looking squarely ahead of him as he prayed to the gods that the man left him alone.

To Horton's relief, he did. The man stashed the orb inside his cloak, let go a harsh cough, then pulled his hood back over his head before making his way back to his throne and seating himself.

"Lock them all up," he warily ordered, and as soon as he had done so Horton found himself tightly squeezed as a multitude of hands whisked him away within a wave of Vwari, dragging him through a maze of dim torch-lit corridors and eventually into a cold, dark cell.

Horton stared off into nothingness when the barred door

slammed shut behind him and the Vwari scuttled away. His emotions were numb and his mind was completely blank, despite everything that had just happened. He dropped his satchel on the ground and sat down in the corner of his hard and barren prison before closing his eyes.

When Horton woke up some time later, he immediately recalled an apparent dream he had experienced while he slept in those gloomy confines. In the dream, a small figure was standing there in the shadows of the passage just outside his cell, watching him with distinct fascination. It had seemed so real to him, but as hard as he tried Horton could not remember if what he had seen was an actual account or something his jaded mind had procured on its own.

Someone had definitely been to visit at some point, however, because a copper bowl and cup had been placed through the bars of his cell during his slumber. Slowly shifting his body across the floor toward them, Horton found that the cup contained water and the bowl some sort of stew. He quickly gulped down the water, somewhat quenching his bitter thirst, but he thought twice about the food. He was certainly hungry, but the sour odor of the stew's unknown ingredients made him cast the bowl aside.

Horton properly inspected his cell for the first time as he slowly stood up. By comparison, the cell he had grown to know all too well back in Zeptus City was a palace. Here there were no windows and no amenities, just an empty cage. He had no way of telling what time it was and the hallway outside had been lit only by small torches spaced too far apart to be adequately illuminated. As he feebly stepped towards the cell door to take a look down the corridor, a sudden spell of dizziness overcame him, forcing him to trudge back over to the corner of the cell and sit down once again.

For some time he simply stared at the flickering light of a torch on the other side of the bars, his head still devoid of thought. He felt incredibly weak and didn't want to expend the effort to consider what was going to happen to him and the others next. For that matter, he didn't even know who the people were that held him captive. All he knew was they had complete control over the Vwari.

Horton slowly blinked his heavy eyelids open. He had fallen asleep again, and as he pulled his head up off his shoulder he could see the outline of a figure watching him from outside the cell, just as he had before. He quickly pinched himself to check if he was dreaming, but he was not. Horton gazed at the silhouette for some time, trying desperately to make out the face of who it was before him, but it was too dark.

"Hello?" Horton asked softly, his voice quavering slightly in his deteriorated state.

The small darkened figure seemed to want to flee for a moment before quickly reconsidering. Unexpectedly instead, a blue glow began to emanate from within its body.

Horton froze as he realized what the glow was coming from. The being pulled out from beneath its cloak the repair orb that had been taken from him earlier, and then set it down on the floor just inside the cell.

"Th-This is yours," the figure said timidly. "I just wanted to return it to you."

Horton practically choked as his throat swelled up. Carefully and deliberately, he lifted himself off the cold floor. He could see the figure was apprehensive and ready to bolt away down the hallway, but he couldn't let that happen. He gulped hard as he tried to clear his throat, preparing himself to address the individual.

Suddenly Horton's knee buckled, causing him to stumble into the bars that separated him from the person just outside. He grabbed onto the cell door to prop himself up with all the strength he could still rally, but it was too late. As Horton tore off his head scarf and took a deep breath, he heard the pitter-patter of feet running away down the hallway, quickly disappearing into the darkness. He was undoubtedly on his final legs now, and could feel tears ready to cascade from his eyes.

"Wait!" Horton shouted with all the voice he could muster.

"Please…" he uttered futilely.

Horton dropped down onto a knee as he let go of the bar, unable to support himself any longer. Beneath him lay the brilliant blue orb, suffusing the floor around him with its radiance. He sluggishly picked it up off the floor, held it close to his face and stared into it, praying to the gods he would return.

Please, please, please…

His plea echoed in his head while his eyes became transfixed on the orb as if it was the final lifeblood holding him conscious.

And then he felt it – a warm hand, pulling his own and the orb down and away from his face. Horton looked up over it to see another sapphire-lit face he did not believe he would ever see again, gazing back at him with equal astonishment.

Deforest...

"Horton!"

TEN

Georg

KLAS SQUINTED as he searched for the sun's location in the sky through a break in the tree cover. He could feel it beating down on the top his head, despite the protection of his white hood. He knew he was getting closer – snow-white needles covered the ground here like permafrost, though he dared not call out for Georg. If the wrong person should hear him out here, the consequences for being this far out from the village would be dire.

Far ahead in the distance stood the eastern hills Georg had directed him toward to find the elusive Earth Stone. In the back of his mind Klas could feel the hills judging him with their invisible eyes, just as the gods were surely doing at that very moment for the heretical act he was undertaking, but by now it didn't matter. It was far too late to turn back.

Far too late.

It wasn't much longer before the enigmatic Earth Stone appeared to Klas from beyond the sheen of mist that concealed it. He was relieved at the sight of it to say the least – Georg had been right about the Stone's location, which ruled out the possibility he had gotten lost. Still, Klas approached the sacred site with caution, well aware his brother wasn't the only Three Yearling that could still be roving the area.

Having discovered a good, hidden vantage point from behind a tree, Klas peered into the pyramid's clearing for any sign of his brother. It didn't take long.

He almost choked when he saw it – a boy lying face-down in the dirt near the edge of the pyramid. Klas' heart sank.

"Georg..."

With complete disregard to his preceding determination for covertness, Klas broke into a full sprint, leaping over the small shrubbery at the edge of the clearing to reach the motionless body. Dark red blood soaked the hood that covered the boy's head.

"Georg!" he called out quietly as he slid down onto his knees next to the body. He held his breath as he carefully pealed back the hood, all the while desperately praying and pleading to the gods to not reveal his elder brother beneath it.

Klas let out a sigh of relief as he discovered it wasn't. The boy was the other missing Three Yearling, Tedward, apparently bludgeoned in the head to death. He scooted back away from the body as the realization of what had transpired sunk in. It seemed all but a certainty that Georg had dealt the fatal blow.

"Klas?" a shaky voice said from over his shoulder. He spun his head around to find an anguish-stricken Georg awkwardly limping toward him with a sharp rock in one hand and a long stick supporting his weight in the other.

"Georg!" Klas exclaimed, looking back to the body that lay at his feet. "What in the gods happened? Did you...?"

Georg nodded remorsefully.

"I tripped over a tree root on my way to the Earth Stone and badly injured my ankle," Georg explained. "I found this stick and continued on to the Earth Stone as quickly as I could, but by the time I got here all that was left was one statue... and him."

"And so you..." Klas said, trying his hardest to not look at the fallen Illac.

Georg scrunched his face and nodded again.

"I need to bury him before I return to the village," Georg said quickly, "but the dirt around here is too hard to dig into with only my hands."

"I can go back to the village and get a spade or something," Klas suggested as he stood back up onto his feet.

"Okay, but be swift," Georg said, his eyes scouring the tree line surrounding the clearing. "I don't know how much time we have before the priests come back and find what happened."

Klas nodded tepidly.

Georg put his hand on his younger brother's shoulder just as he began to leave.

"Everything is going to be fine," the elder Illac brother

reaffirmed with the bravest face his could conjure. "There is nothing to fear, nothing to doubt."

The day's sunlight was waning by the time Klas returned to the Earth Stone from the village with a spade in hand. As he came upon the clearing, he immediately noticed that the body had disappeared and was replaced by a small, dark hole in the ground close to where it once lay.

He looked around, scanning the area for his brother, but there was no sign of him. Peering down to inspect the hole, Klas realized it wasn't just a hole, but a long, dark tunnel. Its edges near the surface were rough and uneven, presumably where Georg had begun to dig into the hard ground with a rock.

Dropping down to his knees for a closer look inside, Klas could see that the dry surface had broken away to reveal the small underground crawlway after not much more than a foot of burrowing. Chilly air numbed his face as it expelled from the tunnel below him.

"It's him, I swear!"

Horton slowly opened his eyes as the sound of voices and footsteps echoed down the corridor outside his cell.

His mind was foggy. Just a moment ago he could have sworn he was back outside the Earth Stone, but now he was lying on his stomach with his face pressed against the cold hard floor. Eyes still heavy, he rolled over onto his back.

"There's no way. It's impossible. Thomas was the sacrifice, not him."

Horton fought the urge to slip away into sleep once again as the voices drew closer. He remembered now. It was Deforest. He had seen his brother.

The cell door clinked as a dark, hooded body unlocked and opened it, reigniting the fire of his tapering consciousness a spell longer. He could feel a presence hanging just over him for a moment before a hand gently propped his head up off the ground.

"Horton..."

Klas put his hands on his hips and reexamined the clearing around the Earth Stone. The long shadows that had been spilled across the ground just a few minutes before had now disappeared and given way to a flood of darkness. Only a thin orange beam from the sun setting beyond the horizon offered him the benefit of visibility now.

"Georg?" Klas called into the hole, but received no response.

He could feel his stomach tingling as nerves kicked in. He wasn't sure if Georg had wandered off into the woods or explored the tunnel, and there wasn't time to wait for him to return.

Klas stood up and looked to the east. The distant, barren hills beyond the forest seemed to be swallowing the last rays of the day's sunlight. He should really be getting back to the village. If he didn't return home soon, someone would notice he was gone.

"Klas!" Georg's stifled voice suddenly called from below him.

Spinning around, Klas spotted a hand emerge from the small opening in the ground, reaching out to him.

"Follow me, brother," Georg said from the darkness. "I have something incredible to show you."

Klas began to reach out to grab his brother's hand but stopped himself.

"What is it? What is it that's down there?" Klas asked hesitantly.

"Heaven," Georg replied after a pause, prompting Klas to grab his brother's hand.

He could feel Georg's grip tighten as he guided him into the tunnel, entrenching them both in complete darkness.

"And Hell."

"You alright, Horton?"

A familiar voice sent Horton suddenly hurtling back into consciousness. He gazed wide-eyed at his new surroundings for a moment as he rekindled his bearings. He was sitting up on a bed in a room he did not recognize, but judging by the walls he could tell he was still inside the Exetus pyramid. There was a wooden door at the other end of the room that looked as though it had been installed somewhat recently.

"I was just at— Ulises?" Horton stopped himself as he realized who was in his company. "What happened to you? Where am I? I was just at the Earth Stone – Georg was there too – it was so real, I—"

"Calm down, calm down," Ulises said softly as he turned around to pour Horton a cup of water from a jug sitting on the table next to him. "You are still dehydrated. Drink this."

Horton was more than happy to comply as he quickly downed the cup of water.

"Ulises," Horton said as he wiped his mouth with his sleeve, "what in the gods is going on?"

Ulises opened his mouth as he began to answer, but Horton cut him off as the last memories from before he blacked out reemerged.

"It was Deforest. I saw Deforest," Horton proclaimed as he began to pull himself up and out of the bed. "He's here, I know I saw him. Where is he?"

Ulises jumped up to grab Horton before he could get onto his feet.

"Horton, hold on, there is something you need to know about—"

The wooden door at the other end of the room suddenly swung open, crashing into the wall next to it with a rickety thud. Standing in the doorway was one of the black-cloaked men.

"Is he awake yet?" the man asked as he pulled back his hood to reveal a strangely familiar face to Horton.

"See for yourself, Asa," Ulises replied as he sunk back into his seat with a sigh.

"Asa?" Horton repeated with a shocked look on his face. "I remember you.... You're from Illac. You were the sacrifice from what, nine years ago? But you're supposed to be..."

"Dead?" Asa said sullenly. "No, I have not been so fortunate. You will come with me now, Horton."

Horton turned to Ulises in search of some sort of counsel or reassurance, but instead got nothing more than a vague nod from his old mentor.

"Alright then," Horton said skeptically as he slid off the side of the bed and onto the floor. His balance felt a little off, but he didn't think he would have any problems walking. As he approached the door to join Asa, he turned back to the old priest.

"What about Ulises?" he asked the cloaked Illac.

"He will stay here – his fate is yet to be decided," Asa responded coldly. "Now come, he has been waiting."

Horton stared back at Ulises as Asa guided him through the doorway. He couldn't help but wonder what it was Ulises was about to tell him. It was surely something important.

Horton stared at the back of Asa's head as he followed closely behind the implausibly resurrected Illac. None of what was going on made sense. He couldn't figure out what Illacs were doing in Exetus – or what his brother was doing here, for that matter.

"He has been looking forward to your awakening," Asa commented as the two approached another wooden door a short ways down the corridor. "To say he was surprised to see you and Deforest appear in Exetus so suddenly is an understatement."

"Who is 'he' exactly?" Horton asked as Asa pushed the door open, but as he set his eyes upon the two figures inside the room, it instantly became all too clear.

Near the middle of the room was Deforest, leaning up against a large table covered in maps, adorned in the same garb as the other men here – black cloaks over white tunics. To his immediate left was the scarred man with the beard who interrogated him and the Zeptans when they first arrived. He knew he had recognized his weary eyes before, and now, as Deforest's smiling face beamed back up into them, he knew exactly who they belonged to.

"Klas," Asa announced as he slammed the door closed behind them. "Your *other* son is here."

Deforest immediately spun around, his eyes wide with excitement.

"Horton!"

As his younger brother bolted over to give him a hug, Horton could only smile in return.

"I'm so glad you're okay, Horton," Deforest said with his face buried in Horton's chest. "I didn't think I would ever see you again."

"Me too, Deforest," Horton replied in a reserved manner.

It was an unusual moment for Horton as he stood there finally united with his brother once again. He expected he would be overcome with joy at the sight of Deforest, having toiled for so long in search of him, but instead a dark cloud loomed over him as his and Klas' eyes locked together from across the room.

"Asa, please take Deforest with you," Klas said when he finally peeled his eyes away from Horton's. "I would like to speak with my eldest son in private."

"But father—" Deforest began, but Klas was having none of it.

"Go!" Klas ordered, to which Deforest reluctantly released Horton from his grip. He looked up at his brother and smiled slightly, before skulking away with Asa from the room.

When the door slammed shut leaving Klas and Horton alone, the father and son stood still like statues for a moment in silence. Horton wasn't sure what to say or even what to feel, as all the questions he had always wanted to ask his father seemed to dissipate from his mind, replaced by numbness. He had never anticipated the possibility of seeing his father again, and to make matters worse, he couldn't deny the inkling in the back of his mind that he wasn't sure he had wanted to.

Eventually, it was Klas who spoke up.

"Do you know what separates men from gods, Horton?" his raspy voice asked.

"Don't, Klas," Horton quickly shot at him.

"Don't call me that, I'm your father," Klas replied softly, but Horton offered him no sympathy.

"You're not my father," he told him stubbornly. "My father died nine years ago when he deserted his family."

Klas let out a deep sigh.

"I understand how you feel," he reasoned, "but you must believe me, I never meant for any of this."

"Who are you?" Horton shouted back, his anger toward his father beginning to resurface. "Why are you and other Illacs here? Why are you in command of those monsters? Why did you leave mother and us all alone?"

"Please, Horton," Klas plead. "I'm truly sorry for what happened, I really am, but you need to listen to me."

Horton didn't respond. Instead he crossed his arms and leaned up against the cold metallic wall.

"I don't know what you were doing with those Zeptans, but you need to know that they are liars," Klas contended. "Every word out of their mouths is deceitful and meant only to twist you to their will."

"What the hell are you talking about?" Horton spat.

"Do you know what happened to your uncle, Horton?" Klas asked as he slowly made his way across the room toward his son.

"Yeah, Georg was a sacrifice. You told me that."

Klas shook his head slowly.

"Everything I told you was to protect you from the truth until the time was right," Klas explained. "The truth the Illac priests have hidden from us, the truth the Zeptans will go to any length to destroy."

"What truth?" Horton asked as he gave his father a dubious look.

Klas placed his hands on Horton's shoulders. "That you, me, Deforest and all the other Illac men and women are the direct descendants of gods."

Horton coughed as he nearly choked at the thought. Surely his father had completely lost his mind.

"You're completely insane," Horton said without hesitation as he stepped away from his father.

Klas chuckled to himself. "I had the exact same response when Georg first told me that. I too thought he had lost his mind, until I discovered the catacomb."

"Catacomb?" Horton repeated.

Klas nodded. "Deep down in the pyramid there is proof of everything I tell you now. I will show you, son, but only on one condition."

Horton paused momentarily before answering, uncertain of his father's intentions. Still, his father had piqued his curiosity and he was fascinated by the notion of venturing farther inside a pyramid.

"What's that?" he asked.

"You remove those horrid Zeptan clothes," Klas answered as he walked over to a giant chest in the corner of the room and pulled out a white Illac tunic and a black cloak. He held them out before Horton. "Are we in agreement?"

Horton looked at the clothes in Klas' hands. While he didn't want to give in to his father so easily, he couldn't deny the fact that on some level he hoped Klas was telling the truth. Besides, it felt like a lifetime since he had last worn any semblance of Illac clothing. Without giving himself any more time to weigh the choice, he snatched the tunic and cloak away from his father.

"Fine."

Ten minutes later Horton found himself following Klas back to the large makeshift throne room where he had first seen him and the other Illacs. From there his father led him through one of the side entryways that had been hidden from view previously, having been swamped with Vwari. Together they passed through it, and at the end of the subsequent dim hallway was a wide spiraling staircase, which they descended.

As they walked down the grated metal steps, Horton noticed that the lower they went, the worse the air seemed to smell. It immediately reminded him of the torrid air that had nearly killed him the first time he had traveled through the portal inside the Earth Stone, while at the same time made him think about the larger task at hand as well. He still needed to repair the pyramid here at Exetus, but he didn't know where its portal was or where his orb had gone. This excursion might prove useful for discovery.

After traversing countless steps downward into the caliginous belly of the pyramid, they stood before an open doorway. Horton tried to hide his shudder from his father as the trenchant bone-chilling hiss of Vwari percolated from inside the pitch-dark chamber. He couldn't see the vile creatures, but there was no question that they had infested whatever lay beyond that point.

"Remain at my side," Klas ordered as he pulled a torch off the wall. "There is nothing to fear."

Klas plunged into the black without doubt, giving his son no time to reconsider going forth. Practically hanging off his father, Horton followed in tow as they made their way inside. The chamber of Vwari fell into a sudden and unexpected hush as they entered, and Horton judged by the delayed cacophonic echoes that the Vwari-filled room they now navigated was the largest he had seen in a pyramid yet.

Like a light-emblazoned bubble rising through murky water, the Vwari gave way to the two Illacs. Although he didn't want to, Horton found himself leaning closer and closer in toward his father. He could see them swarming around Klas and him now as countless pairs of glistening Vwari eyes floated just beyond the cusp of the torch's reach, piercing into Horton as they watched and waited.

Then Klas came to an abrupt stop. He held the torch out in front of him, revealing a large and faded emblem at their feet. Horton had never seen anything like it in a pyramid before – or anywhere else for that matter. Portrayed in blue and white on the floor was an archaic globe covered with unrecognizable land masses. Encircling it all were two tree branches.

"What does this mean?" Horton asked his father quietly.

"I'm not sure," Klas responded as he pulled two scarves out from under his cloak. "Wear this. You'll need to cover your mouth from here on."

Once they had wrapped the scarves over their mouths and noses, Klas pointed toward an opening in the floor just a few paces beyond the mysterious emblem. "Come on, it's this way."

Horton stepped over the emblem and proceeded with his father down another winding stairway, momentarily relieved to be escaping the hive of Vwari.

The necessity for protection quickly became apparent after descending just the first few stairs. The fetid atmosphere worsened considerably with every step, and even with the scarf covering his mouth, Horton could feel the air burning his throat, forcing him to measure his breathing.

At the bottom of the stairway was a narrow opening he and Klas squeezed past one at a time. Once through, Horton realized that the opening they had just passed between was actually a partly-opened sliding door that would normally have been hidden in among the uniform wall panels that lined each pyramid's labyrinthine corridors. Examining his surroundings beyond that, Horton found the two Illacs now stood in yet another long corridor, still engulfed in darkness but for Klas' torch.

"Stay close to me," Klas instructed. "Getting lost in these tunnels will spell your end. It's not far now."

Horton blinked and rubbed his dry and burning eyes as he followed his father deeper into the maze. He doubted he could go on much farther if conditions deteriorated any further.

"This is it," Klas eventually announced, stopping in front of a small opening in the wall that easily could have been overseen. One of the wall panels had been bent slightly, apparently pulled open by sheer brute strength. Covering the opening was a blanket of some sort, which as Horton discovered while wiggling his way through it, was there to protect it from the acrid air that filled this part of the pyramid, even if only marginally effective.

"Yet another pitch-black room," Horton stated once inside. "I'm not sure how this relates us to gods."

Klas shot Horton a dark look from behind his torch before shuffling over toward the wall to light another torch that hung upon it. Horton watched his father curiously as he walked around the circumference of the room, lighting an additional torch every few meters. As the significance of the room was slowly revealed one torch at a time, his chest began to tighten.

Covering every square foot of the walls and ceiling was a fresco depicting people worshipping an apparently divine man adorned entirely in white. As Klas continued to illuminate the circular room one torch at a time, the story was retold over and over through the drawings: masses of people, all worshipping the figure in white. The only difference, however, was that the more Klas revealed, the cruder the drawings became. The man in white remained a constant, but the depiction of his worshippers seemed to deteriorate. By the time Klas had come full circle, the drawings had become completely rudimentary in form, transforming from intricate illustrations into little more than scratched etchings in the walls, harrowingly conveying the same message.

Horton slowly swiveled his head around to take it all in once more, and as he did he noticed the pedestal stationed in the center of the room for the first time, embossed with a single, unlit purple button. Unknowingly, he figured, his father had shown him Exetus' portal to the moon station.

"What is all this?" Horton asked, referring to the room's walls. "Who did these?"

"I believe the Vwari completed the final section of it, but as for the rest I cannot say for certain," Klas answered. "The most plausible answer is they killed the original inhabitants of this pyramid."

Horton walked over to the wall to get a closer look.

"Okay I'll admit it – Illacs dress similarly to this guy on the wall, but that doesn't make us gods," Horton said, still not convinced.

"Tell me, my son," Klas began, "surely you have seen the way the Vwari regard us Illacs. We have complete, unwavering control over them. By the gods – they're savage cannibals, Horton! Yet towards us they are calm and obedient... caring, even."

Horton lifted his head slightly with intrigue, but did not react. Instead he followed Klas with his eyes as his father approached the wall and touched it with his hand.

"Do you think it chance that we Illacs traditionally dress ourselves in the same attire as the gods, Horton?" he continued. "Do you think it chance the Illacs are the biggest and strongest beings on Earth? Do you think it chance that only the Illacs have an affinity to the pyramids that none else share? These are our temples, my son. This is our world – you cannot deny this truth."

Horton looked away from his father and to the drawings on the walls. He didn't know how to respond. As far as he could decipher, Klas was correct on all counts. Whether that made them gods he did not know, but on some level it all seemed to make sense.

"The Zeptans know?" Horton asked simply, his focus still caught on the wall's pictographs as he processed it all.

Klas nodded. "They know."

"Penriding has collaborated against me from the start." Horton rubbed his cheek as he quietly thought out loud to himself. "I saw it the first day I arrived in that damn city. The Zeptans never trusted me, none of them. They used me...

"Why is it the Vwari hate the Zeptans so much?" Horton asked abruptly, his fist now clenched beneath his black cloak.

"The Vwari distrust and hate everyone except the Illac," Klas explained. Horton noticed him look away, as if filled with a sudden sadness. "However, after what happened to Georg I gave their hatred a little more focus."

"What do you mean?" Horton asked, confused.

"Georg was a sacrifice, Horton, but not in the way you had previously believed," Klas revealed. "Your uncle was the first to discover this pyramid many years ago through the Earth Stone's portal, and if I recall correctly, he was just about your age. Believe it or not, this place was somewhat operational at the time, despite being entirely overrun with Vwari. To Georg's astonishment the Vwari not only instantly accepted him, but seemed to hang on his every action. Naturally he chose to take refuge here in Exetus – an easy decision considering the alternative was death.

"Over the years he rescued other Three Yearlings doomed to be sacrificed in the wastes and over time they began to call themselves Exetans, renouncing their Illac past. Georg was hell-bent on uncovering the pyramids' secrets, and travelled deeper into the depths of Exetus than any other, often for days at a time, but he never reached its bottom. Still, he discovered enough…"

Klas paused and looked blankly at the ground, seemingly deep in thought. Horton patiently waited for his father to continue, and when he didn't he decided to press him further.

"So what did he discover?"

Klas blinked his eyes and looked at Horton.

"I was the first Three Yearling back, you know. Georg wanted me to throw the initiation, to join him and his band here in Exetus, but I couldn't. All I had ever wanted was a family of my own, to live a normal life in Illac. Nothing more than that. When I saw him again years later, we were two very different men. I had a wife, two sons and a home, but he had attained something I could never find in Illac – the truth. Regretfully, I gave in and returned with him to Exetus, having been tempted by the secrets of the pyramids.

That was the final day of his life… The damned Zeptans made sure of that."

"The Zeptans?" Horton repeated. "Why would they want to kill Georg?"

"When we arrived at Exetus I found, to my revelation, that there were Zeptans here too. Georg had built some sort of partnership with that merchant despot, Nestor Blacksmith, over the years. You arrived here on one of his vessels, Horton."

"Yes," Horton replied. His mind spun as he tried to piece everything together. "So what happened? What was the secret of the pyramids?"

"I never found out," Klas said with a desolate look on his face. "The Zeptans betrayed your uncle and the other Exetans. Initially I believed he had seen Georg and the pyramids as a threat to his trade business somehow, but I have discovered since that it goes much deeper than that. With our guard down, the Zeptans used the opportunity to destroy the Exetus pyramid from the inside-out with some sort of electromagnetic charge.

"Blinded by deceit, Georg had sent the Vwari deep inside the pyramid to hide before the Zeptans ever arrived. He had worried the Zeptans would not take kindly to Exetus' original inhabitants, but it was the Vwari that ultimately saved us. After the Zeptans sabotaged the pyramid those stuck-up fools had no idea what they had unleashed on themselves – they never saw the Vwari coming. With the Zeptans distracted we Illacs managed to escape to safety, but Georg stayed behind to fight. After everything settled down and the Zeptans retreated, Georg was gone and the pyramid operationally demised. With the portals disabled we were forced to build our own wastewalkers in order to return to Illac, but by then I could not go back. Exetus had become my home."

Horton gazed at the purple button on the pedestal in the middle of the room. He leisurely walked over and pressed the button, but it did nothing.

"You should have come back," Horton said softly. "For me. For Deforest. For mother…. Why didn't you come home?"

"I left your fate to the gods, Horton," Klas answered. "Either you passed the initiation and led a normal, happy life, or you failed and joined me. As it turned out, both you and your brother were destined to be at my side."

Horton paused for a moment before responding.

"Gods," Horton eventually uttered, his eyes still fixed on the unlit button on top of the pedestal. "I thought you said we were the gods."

Klas cleared his throat and walked over to the wall to retrieve his torch.

"Do you know the difference between gods and men?" he asked.

Horton looked away from the pedestal and toward his father. He wasn't sure if Klas expected an answer, but he gave him one anyway.

"Forgiveness?"

Klas froze for a second, as if taken aback by Horton's response before he continued toward the opening in the wall.

"Come, my son. We've already been here too long."

As Horton and Klas returned through the large Vwari-packed chamber on their way up to the higher levels of the pyramid, Horton noticed his sentiment toward his former enemy had subconsciously shifted somewhat. It was an unusual feeling as he walked through that sea of monsters, and although he tried to fight it back, it was there and it was real. To an extent he held a sense of compassion and gratitude for the Vwari's inexplicable devoutness to the Illac people. Even worse still was the inkling deep inside him that enjoyed the lust of power and perception of immortality that came along with it. With the Vwari willing to relentlessly sacrifice themselves at his whim, he wouldn't just be the short, weak child anymore – he would be unstoppable. In a sense, he might even be a god.

Stop.

Horton shut his mind out from itself. The thoughts running through his head were leading him toward a path he didn't want to explore.

No, that's not me. That's not me at all… right?

"Horton," Klas snapped, pulling Horton out of a trance.

"Yes?" he replied, only now noticing he and his father had made it all the way back to the upper levels of the pyramid and were standing outside the door to one of the antechambers.

Klas gave Horton a rigid look. "Ulises told me everything that happened between you two and the Zeptans. He assured me your loyalty would lie with me and the other Exetans, but I want to hear it from you personally."

To his own surprise, Horton nodded without hesitation in reply.

"Good. Your brother will be in this room here. I'm sure you two have some catching up to do," Klas said as he patted the door in front of them. "In the meantime I have some business to take care of, so we'll talk again later. It's been very good to see you again, son."

Horton looked up at his father's face and could just barely make out a smile from behind his greying beard. He paused for a second or two before responding with a shallow "yeah" and a slow nod of his head.

"Hold on," Horton suddenly blurted, sharply coming to his senses just as his father had begun to walk away. "What is going to happen to the Zeptans?"

He was ashamed to admit it to himself, but he had become so entrenched in personal affairs since he rediscovered his brother and father that he had scarcely thought at all about the bigger picture. The very least he could do was make sure Penriding and the others were unharmed.

Klas looked at his son sternly. "Those Zeptans – they are your friends?"

Horton glanced away from his father's gaze, not immediately sure how to respond. He regretted ever asking the question now, purely because it meant he would have to come to terms, to some degree, with his changing regard toward the Zeptans. Every possible answer ran through his mind, but none of them seemed to stick except one.

"No," he finally admitted quietly, which was apparently enough to appease Klas. Horton stared blankly as his father turned and walked away down the corridor and into the shadows, disappearing beyond the flickering light of a nearby torch.

Horton sighed under his breath and looked back to the doorway he stood before. He put his hand on the door handle and began to push, but instead stopped himself as he replayed in his mind what had just transpired. Everything he had just told his father – that he supported him and the other Exetans, that he didn't care about the Zeptans – he wasn't sure he had meant any of it. All he had searched his entire life for was right here in Exetus, yet he couldn't shake the feeling that he was more lost than ever.

His mind was scattered and uncertain. Horton definitely had his doubts about the Zeptans' agenda, but there was no way he could condone the Vwari raids on innocents at Zeptus City and in the wastes. At the very least, he thought, it would be some respite to talk to Deforest about it all.

Without warning, Horton's arm violently flung back as the door he was still hanging on to abruptly shoved open. He glanced up to discover the identity of the rude perpetrator, ready to tell him off for the sudden outburst, but he found his heart instantly sunk down into his stomach instead. As he stood there frozen in unanticipated and immobilizing fear, the Vwari-infested chambers of the pyramid's darkest depths suddenly felt like a preferable place to be, because in that moment he found himself standing face to face with the last mug he ever wanted to see again: Thomas.

Horton gulped. It had completely slipped his mind that Thomas had been the sacrifice in this year's initiation, and it was all because he had snatched one of the clay statues for himself and not returned to the village with it.

He took a half step away from the big, mean Illac and hinged his immediate well-being on the flimsy hope that Thomas wasn't aware he ever took one of the statues, or the off chance that being stuck in Exetus together might spawn a new, however unlikely, camaraderie.

To Horton's dismay neither of those scenarios were a reality. In fact, when Thomas caught sight of him on the other side of the door, his face scrunched up into a menacing rage. There was no doubt about it – he knew.

As Thomas took a heavy and pugnacious step toward Horton, the massive Illac's fists curled up at his side, ready to inflict pain. Horton couldn't help but shut his eyes. He had been in this situation before and could sense what was coming, though with all certainty did not want to have to witness it as well. Perhaps this time he would get lucky and not break any bones.

Oof!

Horton staggered a few steps to the side. He opened his eyes, expecting a second and possibly third brutal blow to come hurtling his direction, but to his surprise he instead saw nothing but Thomas' back as he huffed away in the other direction. He might have been a little melodramatic – Thomas had done little more than simply shove him out of the way. This wasn't normal behavior for Thomas though, considering the creep had seemingly been sent by the gods for the sole purpose of tormenting Horton throughout his childhood, but he wasn't going to complain.

"Oh, there you are, brother!" Deforest's cheery face appeared in Thomas' wake through the doorway a few seconds later. "Come inside!"

Horton followed Deforest into the chamber as coolly as he could, despite still being a bit shaken up by the run-in with his old nemesis. He was quickly distracted, however, as he surveyed the room he had just entered. It was chock-full and lined to the walls with random items and mechanical parts, likely pillaged by Vwari raiders for their masters. A slim path had been cleared through the debris toward the center of the room, leading to a couple of large wooden tables upon which an assortment of dried foods and canisters of water sat. Beyond the table was a wider path that granted access to two doors on the far side of the room.

"This is our meeting room," Deforest happily explained. "We eat here and father and the others make their plans here as well. Those two doorways at the end of the chamber go to the sleeping quarters. My bed is in there and so is yours – I saw Asa put your satchel on it earlier."

Horton could only stare and watch his brother as he cheerfully showed him around. He had tried so desperately to find him, worried he was struggling on his own somewhere. Yet here he was with his father, and as far as he could tell, totally content.

Still, Horton felt he needed to apologize.

"Deforest," he finally uttered, cutting off Deforest's in-depth explanation of the bedroom floor plan.

"What is it?" Deforest replied.

Horton began to speak, but couldn't get the words out as his emotions suddenly overwhelmed him. He chuckled to himself in disbelief as he tried to fight back the tears, but it was no use.

"Deforest," Horton managed to squeak out before coughing in an attempt to clear his seizing throat. "I – I'm so sorry… I'm so sorry… for everything. It's my fault all of this happened. I tried so hard to find you. I really did, and for a while I thought…"

Horton quickly made eye contact with his brother but he couldn't maintain it. He was too ashamed.

"I thought I'd lost you forever, Deforest. I'm sorry."

Deforest walked over to Horton and hugged him.

"It's funny," Deforest said with a wry laugh, "I can't remember the last time you apologized to me for anything."

Horton let go of his brother and smiled at him. "Don't get used to it."

He then wiped his eyes with his sleeve, walked over to his bed and sat down on it.

"So what happened exactly, the day you disappeared?" Horton asked.

"I'm not entirely sure," Deforest answered as he lay down on the bed next to Horton's. "To be honest, it was all kind of a big blur. I remember the ground giving way near the Earth Stone while searching for brasys leaves for you. I remember being in a dark tunnel – it was pretty scary – but I found a room that had some lights in it. Next thing I knew I was lying on my back with father looking down at me. I've been here ever since."

"He didn't say how he found you?" Horton inquired.

Deforest sat upright on the side of the bed and looked at Horton. "He did. Father told me the Vwari found me unconscious somewhere deep inside this pyramid and brought me to him. He said the Vwari saved my life, Horton."

"I see," Horton said, slowly nodding his head. Just a few days ago he would have been in complete disbelief to hear of the Vwari doing such a thing, but now it seemed almost expected.

Beside him on the bed was his satchel, pulsating slightly as the soft bluish glow from the orb spilled out of it. He picked it up, placed it in his lap and stared vacantly at it. Now that he had found his brother, restarting the pyramids didn't seem quite as important to him as they once had. He was even beginning to think he might decide to stay at Exetus.

"Oh, I almost forgot."

Horton opened up his satchel and rifled through it. A few seconds later he pulled out a partly torn piece of parchment.

"I, uh, accidently ripped it a little bit," Horton explained apologetically, "but I wrote you a letter. Nothing special, I just wanted to let you know what happened to me during our time apart."

"Oh! Thanks brother!" Deforest's face lit up as he accepted the letter from Horton. "I can't wait to read it."

Deforest looked around for a moment, then turned back to Horton with a subdued look on his face.

"I'm sorry, I didn't make anything for you," Deforest said. "I'll make it up to you though!"

Horton laughed as he dropped his head down onto his pillow. "That's not really necessary, I'm just happy to see you again."

"Me too, brother," Deforest replied with a smile.

As he closed his eyes, Horton felt a rush of happiness

spread through him. Maybe Ulises was right, he thought. Perhaps everything does happen for a reason.

"This is an incredible undertaking if we're right, Emma," *Georg pointed out.*

"What if something happens to him? He has Horton and Deforest to care for... and me," Emma contended, looking to Klas to back her up.

"It's been years since I've visited Exetus," Klas said as he looked off into the hills in the distance. It was obvious to Emma his mind was preoccupied.

"If we're successful your boys will grow up in a completely different world," Georg reasoned, "and I can't do it without Klas."

Georg took a step out from the porch to look up at the night sky. Moonlight shone down on his face.

"It's almost time," he said. "Brother?"

Klas nodded, not pulling his eyes away from the horizon.

Without another word said, Georg pulled his white hood over his head and marched off down the lane toward the edge of the village.

"You promised me you would never return to that place," Emma reminded Klas as she put her hand on his shoulder. "You told me it changed you; don't tell me you've forgotten. Just let him go, my love. It's not too late to put it all behind you."

"Every day those hills have called to me, Emma," Klas said, only now turning to look at his wife. "I have to do this... for them."

Klas gently pulled his arm away from Emma's hand and trotted after his brother without turning back.

Horton woke up the next morning to find no one else in the sleeping quarters except himself and Deforest, who was sitting on his bed watching him. He had dreamed about his father and Georg again, except this time his mother was there too. The experience was all very weird – this dream in particular had felt almost real, as if he was reliving something that had actually happened. He briefly considered mentioning what he had experienced to Deforest, but thought better of it. His mind was just dealing with the sudden reappearance of his father in its own unusual way, he deduced.

"Where is everyone?" Horton grumbled as he rubbed his eyes.

"You overslept," Deforest replied. "Father said not to bother you because you were still worn out from everything that has happened."

"Oh, yeah," Horton said groggily. "That was nice of him."

"Good, you're finally awake."

The brothers turned simultaneously as a figure appeared in the doorway. It was Asa.

"Get ready immediately – Klas is requesting everyone's presence in the great hall," he announced.

Horton and Deforest hopped up off their beds.

"No, not you, Deforest," Asa said, holding up his hand to stop him. "He asked for Horton only."

Deforest scoffed. "I never get to be involved in anything," he complained as he flopped back down onto his bed.

Horton shrugged at his brother.

"Your time will come, Deforest," Asa said. "Klas is very proud of what you've done for us."

"What does he mean by that?" Horton asked Deforest as he pulled his cloak around his collar, but Asa didn't give Deforest a chance to speak.

"Come, Horton. You're already late."

The rest of the Exetans were waiting for them when they arrived in the hall. Klas was sitting idly in his throne when they entered, but he propped himself up when he caught sight of Horton and waved his son over to him.

"Good, you're here," Klas said before pulling himself up from his seat to address the group. "Stay at my side."

Horton quickly glanced around at the former Illacs amongst him. Most of them had their hoods pulled over their heads, making them hard to identify, but he clearly spotted Thomas' robust stature among them. Standing out like a sore thumb was the Reckoner, who apparently had completely shifted allegiances since he discovered his blood connection to the Illacs. He was still laden in thick armor, but had abandoned the helmet that hid his identity and gargantuan sword he employed as a weapon. It probably kept the Vwari from attacking him, Horton figured. At the very back of the group was Ulises, almost hidden from view. He still hadn't had a good chance to talk to him yet since they arrived at Exetus.

"As some of you already know," Klas began his address to the group, "in a twist of fate, my eldest son Horton and my dear old friend Ulises have joined our ranks. It marks an undoubted turn of the tide in our war with Zeptus, as among them we have captured the son of Nestor Blacksmith – the last of the Blacksmith family line."

Klas' upbeat demeanor quickly vanished as his eyes shifted through the small throng of cloaked Illacs.

"However," he continued, "I understand there have been some questions raised regarding where the loyalty of our new compatriots stands, considering the manner upon which they were discovered. Please have no misgivings. my fellow Exetans. I have word from my son and the priest that they are committed to our cause, and they will prove their allegiance in due time."

Klas shot a quick glance back at Horton, who had no idea as to what he had in mind.

"How goes our campaign, Isaac?" Klas asked, turning away from Horton to face one of the hooded men.

"Continued Vwari raids on Zeptus City's southern walls have yielded moderate results," Isaac responded. Horton recognized his voice – he was the Exetan who had led the group of Vwari that captured the Desert Storm. "At our current pace I estimate we will have crippled the Zeptan navy to a point where invasion is feasible, probably four to five months from now."

"What?" Klas boomed. "Four to five months is well behind schedule – that is unacceptable!"

"Klas you must understand," Isaac attempted to assuage, now visibly anxious, "with the Vwari we may have strength in numbers, but we lack the resources to get them all to Zeptus City. We simply don't have enough crafts for transport. We need more time to conduct raids on the outlying tribes and merchant barges to build up our arsenal of cutters."

Klas slumped back down into his throne.

"And what of the pyramid at Tiberonus," Klas asked with his cheek resting against his palm. "Did the Vwari figure out how to get into that thing?"

Isaac took a deep breath. "We did. However, it was not the Vwari that opened it, it was Zeptans. I sent an entire legion of Vwari to seize the portal, but they failed."

Horton noticed Klas close his eyes in frustration.

"They failed…" Klas repeated quietly through his teeth before reopening his eyes. "How do some measly Zeptans hold off an entire legion of Vwari?"

"They were accompanied by three Reckoners, Klas," Isaac explained. "We had not anticipated their kind so far from the city – and your son, yes – Horton was among them!"

In an instant Klas flew out of his seat and had grabbed hold of Isaac's collar.

"What are you insinuating?" Klas yelled while practically face to face with Isaac, his fist raised and ready to strike. Horton took a few steps back. He had never seen his father act like this before.

"N-nothing at all!" Isaac managed to stutter in response. "Please Klas, I was simply stating a fact."

Klas glanced around at the other Illacs as murmurs began to drift among them. Then, as if coming back to his senses, he released Isaac from his clutches, spun around and slowly walked over to the edge of the raised platform at one end of the great hall. He stood there for a moment, looking deeply out into its emptiness as if he saw something the others did not. Confused, Horton looked around to find the other Exetans staring at his father in complete silence.

And then, with a swift and loud snap of his fingers, Klas put an end to that lull as its echo reverberated through the hall.

"I'll never get used to this," Asa turned to Horton and grinned.

"Used to what?" Horton asked, but before Asa could answer he already knew. The Vwari horde's cries carried all the way up to the great hall from the lowest levels of the pyramid, sending a shiver along Horton's spine. They were coming.

"Bring in the Zeptans," Klas called out over the shrieks of incoming Vwari. "I have a surprise for our guests."

ELEVEN

Nestor

PENRIDING AND LINDEN were brought out and lined up before the Exetans as though they were criminals. Behind them the Vwari mass packed into the hall like fevered spectators, their insatiable hisses droning. Horton pulled his hood over his head as the Zeptans entered, though he wasn't really sure why he had done so – it wasn't that he was ashamed or anything. He was an Illac-turned-Exetan after all, and they were Zeptans, the enemy. Regardless, he still did not want to reveal himself.

Klas stood up from his throne, somehow cueing the Vwari to tranquilize their rowdiness. He walked over to the edge of his stage as he had done before and looked over his captives.

"An unusual phenomenon, this Zeptan ideal of equality between sexes," Klas said, looking at Linden. "I understand you are a commander in the Zeptan military?"

"Where are the rest of my men?" Linden demanded angrily, prompting a handful of Vwari to seize her in place. Penriding immediately jumped to her aid, but almost as quickly found himself held in check by Vwari as well. Quickly realizing their struggle was in vain, the commander ceased fighting her captors, and instead slowly gazed up in a defeated manner at Klas and addressed him once again.

"Please tell me. What have you done with them?"

"While my brothers here do not agree, I happen to find it quite impressive," Klas continued, taking no notice of Linden's questions. "All of those soldiers under your control. All that power. I imagine it must be most... emancipating. It will be a shame to see you die."

"Don't you dare lay a finger on her!" Penriding shot at Klas, who broke out into laughter.

"By the gods, it speaks!" Klas said, still laughing. "Oh no, mister Blacksmith, I wouldn't dare lay a finger on your dear old commander."

Klas raised his hand into the air and formed a fist. The Vwari in the hall suddenly shot to attention, their eyes fixated on Klas. Gradually, he lowered his fist from above his head until it was targeted toward Linden.

Klas grinned. "That's what my friends here are for."

Horton jumped at the sudden thunderous bang of dozens of Vwari pouncing on Linden as Klas released his index finger from within his fist, having pointed it directly at the Zeptan commander. He couldn't help but watch as Linden disappeared deep inside the Vwari mob, dragged to meet her sudden heinous end. A few weeks ago he would have felt something – anything – watching someone he once considered a friend killed, but not right now.

"Linden!" Penriding screamed as he frantically fought off the Vwari that held him down with all of his might, but he accomplished nothing other than enlist even more of the monsters to contain him.

"Calm down, mister Blacksmith, calm down," Klas called out to the Zeptan sinisterly. "Don't worry; it will all be over soon."

With the Vwari beginning to settle down from their kill, the Exetan leader turned to his eldest son. Horton had watched the grievous spectacle in a numb stupor from beneath his cowl, still unable to decipher his sentiments toward his former companions now in great peril.

"Horton," he said with a pacific smile, "come. It's your time to prove your loyalty."

After just the briefest of hesitation, Horton slowly wandered out from behind the group of Exetans to join his father at the front of the platform. Fallen to his knees in despair beneath him was Penriding, whose face became instantly painted with shock as the Illac approached.

"Is that you, kid?" Penriding asked as he pulled his sullen head up to look at Klas and his son, who stood side by side before him. His anonymity gone, Horton relented and pulled back his hood, divulging himself to the Zeptan.

"What are you doing?" Penriding bombarded him. "Why would you betray us?"

"I am an Illac. I belong at my father's side," Horton replied, his voice unwavering despite his lack of internal resolve.

"What in god's name are you talking about, Horton?" Penriding plead. "We have a mission to complete, remember?"

"Kill him, Horton," Klas whispered in Horton's ear. "You saw how it is done. Kill that damn Zeptan."

Slowly and deliberately, Horton raised his fist in the air, just as his father had. He could immediately feel the intensity of countless Vwari eyes in the room converge upon him, ready at his command.

"Please, Horton," Penriding reasoned desperately. "Don't do this. This isn't you."

"He lied to you, deceived you for his own gain," Klas asserted, pulling Horton's attention away from the Zeptan's words. "He is just like his father. He's a Blacksmith. Don't second guess yourself, son. Do it."

"He never cared about finding Deforest – he only used me to find the pyramids," Horton muttered under his breath. "He did lie to me…. He let Ananke die."

As he looked at Penriding, his trembling fist outstretched and pointed at the Zeptan, all he could feel was rage toward his old friend. Once more he glanced out at the Vwari army lying in wait, ready to serve his nefarious bidding, and it was then that Horton realized for the first time in his life he was the one completely in control – he was the one with absolute power. All he had to do was give the command and that damned Zeptan was gone. He liked it.

"Stop this damned foolishness!"

Horton recoiled as he felt someone grab his arm and lower it. It was Ulises.

"What do you think you're doing, priest?" Klas shouted angrily. "Know your place, or I'll show it to you!"

"I do not think so, Klas," Ulises responded firmly. "I will not allow you to corrupt your sons as Georg did you."

Klas stomped over toward the priest and pulled back his hood, revealing the heavily scarred head and face Horton had not fully seen since the first time he saw his father in Exetus.

"So your true colors are finally exposed, you senile old fool," Klas snarled. "You know nothing of what you say. It was a mistake to trust you. It was you who led the Zeptans here, wasn't it? Your thirst for revenge was too insatiable to deny any longer."

"Revenge?" Ulises reiterated incredulously. "No, I do not see the world in black and white as you do, Klas. I sought only the truth. I was in error to disregard you and your band's roguery for so long – I did not want to believe Emma when she told me—"

"Shut up! Don't you dare speak of my wife!" Klas screamed, who without warning lunged at Ulises with a dark intent in his eyes Horton had only ever seen before in those of a Vwari.

It was in that moment as he stood there, separated by only a mere foot or so between his father and mentor, that time seemed to come to a standstill. Horton knew he was going to have to make a choice, right then and there.

Argh!

"Look, we're not going to see results overnight," Georg explained to his brother as they walked through the

illuminated corridors of Exetus. Klas had been fond of the pyramid's gentle, nurturing hum and was glad to be back, but he had doubts about Georg's recent news and the mysterious, glowing orange cube he had somehow attained.

"We're sacrificing too much for something we will likely never see the benefits of," Klas contended, "and the Vwari—"

"The Vwari were a mistake," Georg sternly stopped his brother. "Please trust me on this, Klas. Think about the future of Horton and Deforest. With the help of the Zeptans we will be able to—

"Ah, Nestor! I'm terribly sorry to have left you waiting," Georg quickly changed his tune, gallantly addressing a portly man and a small band of what appeared to be his bodyguards, mingling with the other Exetans as he entered the great hall. Klas had never seen such an unusually dressed man before.

"Excuse me, where are my manners," Georg continued. "Nestor, this is my brother, Klas. Klas, this is the head of the Blacksmith Trade Union based out of Zeptus City – he's the one I've been telling you about."

Nestor Blacksmith glared at Klas over his spectacles.

"A pleasure," he mumbled, to which Klas dryly nodded a response.

"I will suggest we get underway immediately," Nestor insisted. "As you know, this region has a high propensity for Vwari attacks, and I assured the council their troop escorts would return intact."

"Of course," Georg agreed, motioning toward an

entryway on one end of the large room. "Please follow me."

As Georg led Klas, Nestor, and his bodyguards through a side passage on their way to the lower levels of the pyramid, Klas jogged ahead to have a private word with his brother.

"Why do I get the impression they have no idea there are Vwari in Exetus?" Klas whispered.

"You're right," Georg sighed. "They don't know, but it will be fine. I sent the Vwari deep inside the pyramid – the Zeptans won't even know they are here. Besides, the Vwari infestation will be taken care of once the pyramid is fully operational."

"What do you mean, 'taken care of?'" Klas fired back.

"I don't know exactly," Georg admitted. "My understanding is that the pyramid will cleanse itself of miscreants once its master processes are operational – or at least it was something like that."

"Do you even know what you're saying? You're willing to give up control of the Vwari for some fool's errand," Klas hissed at his brother, now getting irritated.

"No, Klas," Georg said numbly. "I'm willing to let the Vwari die."

Klas came to an abrupt stop and ducked into a darkened adjacent corridor, letting his brother and the Zeptans walk on ahead. He was so angry at Georg he could barely contain himself, and when the group had travelled out from earshot he slammed his fist against the hard metal wall.

"That arrogant, selfish, idiotic—"

Klas froze mid-rant. In the corner of his eye a pale, washed-out figure slipped out of view from beyond the darkness at the end of the long-forgotten corridor he now stood in.

"Hello?" Klas called out as he cautiously took a few steps farther down the corridor. There shouldn't have been any Vwari on these levels.

Curious, he continued following along the dim pathway for a short while until he reached a corner. He warily pulled his head around it in order to scope out who or what he had seen disappear in this direction, but instead found something equally as unexpected – a faint purple light, bleeding through a small opening between wall panels not more than a dozen meters away.

He turned back to look down the unlit corridor he had just traveled and listened carefully. There was no sign of Georg and his Zeptan collaborators nearby now. There were undoubtedly more secrets to the pyramids and Vwari than his brother had ever revealed to him, and he was certain they were all in on it. This mysterious figure and purple-lit room all had to be parts of the puzzle, and he needed to uncover the truth.

Without a second thought he approached the orifice, kneeled down, peered in through the bent panel and gasped at the sight beyond.

Contained inside was a portal unlike any Georg had shown him before. In the middle of a circular room was a pedestal, upon which sat a single purple-lit button. Drawn upon the purple-hued walls surrounding it were elaborate pictographs of people worshipping a man in white – a man dressed irrefutably in traditional Illac garb.

Klas pulled his head back out of the small crawlspace

between the sheered wall panels and looked up and down the corridor he had last seen the white figure withdraw into, but it was empty. He was convinced he hadn't just imagined it all, and if he truly had seen someone, he had with all certainty passed through this opening. Having made up his mind, he squeezed inside.

Although Klas was immediately mesmerized by the depictions sprawled across the ceiling and walls, he found he was drawn even more so to the room's unusual portal. Georg had told him all about the pedestal with the four differently colored and illuminated buttons, along with its function as a portal to the four pyramids scattered around the world, but he'd never bothered to mention this one. The more Klas gazed at it, the more its soft, enticing light lured him in toward it like a siren. He had no idea where this particular portal might lead to, but in that moment it didn't matter. His outstretched hand closed in on the button, inching nearer and nearer.

"You are a relative of the User," a broken, digitized voice sounded behind him, causing Klas to snap out of his spell and spin around.

"Who are you?" Klas replied as he sidestepped around the pedestal to put it between himself and a featureless, ghost-like figure that stood before him. Its edges appeared almost fuzzy, and seemed to be blinking sporadically in and out of existence.

"Are you a... god?" Klas inquired apprehensively.

"The connection has decayed – our regulation waned," it replied, taking no note of Klas' questions. "The User must reactivate the sub-station or else they will overcome."

"*What are you talking about? You mean Georg and the Vwari?*" *Klas pressed, but the figure abruptly evaporated into thin air before he could ascertain more information.*

"*Damnit!*" *Klas shouted in frustration as he paced around the room. He studied the pictographs on the walls and repeated what the figure had said to him as he tried to make any sense of it all.*

"*Our regulation waned... they will overcome.*"

Suddenly Klas ran over to the gap in the wall and ducked through it, then broke out into a sprint down to the lower levels of the pyramid to join his brother. He didn't have time to stop and think things through entirely, but in his mind he knew enough. For them, he would have to take action right away.

The image of the mysterious figure burned in his mind as he ran. He didn't know what that thing was or what it had wanted from him, but god or not, the Vwari needed a new master and the Illacs were destined to fill that void. The writing was literally right there on the wall – there was no doubt about it. If Georg activated the pyramid, that would surely spell their end. There would be no second chance to save the Vwari. No second chance to become a god.

"*Give me the cube,*" *Nestor demanded as he stood over the portal, ready to engage it.*

Klas watched cautiously from the shadows beyond a large doorway at the darkest end of the chamber to which Georg had led the Zeptans. He attempted to plot a course of action to stop what Nestor and his brother were about to do, but with all the Zeptan bodyguards standing watch, there was none.

"No, Nestor," Georg shook his head. "You know it has to be committed by one with Illac blood, just as it is with the Dreadnought exoskeleton."

The large Zeptan audibly snorted at the notion, but took a step back in cession.

"Very well," Nestor sighed. "Let us just get the damn deed done – this place gives me the creeps."

As Georg engaged the repair cube, panic spread through Klas. If he was going to do something, an option would have to present itself quickly.

"Aaaoo," a light howl fell upon Klas' ears, immediately perking him upright. He skulked away from the doorway and jogged down an adjacent hallway the peculiar sound appeared to originate from. At its end was a large wooden door veiled almost entirely in darkness and barred on the outside by a thick plank.

He leaned his ear up against the door and listened.

"Aaaool."

Without delay Klas took a step back, grabbed onto the heavy plank and then lifted it off the door with every ounce of strength he had.

Clank.

The pyramid reverberated as it coughed back to life at the same moment he heaved the plank down to the floor below. He seized the door's handle and swung it outward, revealing the ensnared glowing eyes of countless Vwari await in pitch-darkness on the other side. Klas took a deep breath as he stood before them, the Vwari completely under his command. There was no time to bask in his discovered power, however, as he immediately twirled around, ran to the end of the corridor and looked on to where Georg and the Zeptans were. The cube had been released and was in full effect. He had to act now.

Instinctively Klas pointed at them – his brother, the Zeptans, the cube – and with great ferocity the Vwari horde obeyed, gushing past Klas toward their targets without any doubt of his instruction.

He watched from the shadows as the Vwari overran the chamber in a ravenous frenzy, their sickening screams drowning out the Zeptans' yells amid the chaos. It had turned into a massacre as quickly as it had begun, but despite it all the cube carried on its duty, having lifted itself high above them, safe from the bloodshed.

And then, for little more than an instant, Klas sighted a miraculously unscathed being emerge from within the fray: the portly Zeptan merchant lord Nestor, his firearm outstretched in hand above his head, aimed toward the cube.

And against all probability, he fired.

Horton!

Horton snapped his eyes open to find Ulises shouting his name as the priest ran over to retrieve the young Illac now spilled across the floor. He looked around the room with wide eyes as his mind rekindled its bearings, and when his gaze caught his father's, Horton found Klas in a state of complete shock.

"Horton…" he watched his father utter as Ulises all the while tugged him up and onto his feet.

"Kill the traitors!" a voice unexpectedly called out from within the group of Exetans. Horton quickly turned to his right to discover it was none other than Thomas, who was pushing his way through to the front of the group with a massive grin on his face. Then, to Horton's terror, he pointed right at him.

Horton swung his head around toward the Vwari, expecting their terrible horde to come raining down upon him like hellfire, but they did not. Instead, they seemed agitated and confused by Thomas' actions. Could one god order the death of another?

Thomas looked around in search of support from the other Exetans. For a few moments they remained motionless, as unsure of what to do in this scenario as the Vwari they commanded, but then, to Horton's dread, Isaac gave in. Just as Thomas had done, the Exetan stepped forward and pointed at Horton and Ulises, marking them for the kill. Then, one by one, each of the former Illacs present, sans his father, followed suit and pointed at them.

Horton's stomach lurched as one of the Vwari broke free from the horde and sprinted impetuously towards Ulises and him. Barely a second later the rest let loose.

Horton turned to his father, his final hope for salvation, but instead found a hollow shell of a man, broken down and on his knees, about to watch his son be slaughtered by the same force that had empowered him. He undoubtedly knew that any attempt to intervene at this point would achieve nothing more than condemn himself to death as well. Horton closed his eyes. He had escaped the jaws of death before somehow, but this time it all seemed hopeless. It was time for him to meet his reckoning.

Clang. Clang. Clang. Clang...

"Ah—"

Horton gasped and opened his eyes just as the Reckoner skidded in front of him to cut off the incoming wave of Vwari.

"Go you idiots! Run!"

He couldn't believe it. It was enough of a shock that the Reckoner had come to their sudden aid, but what really took Horton aback was the fact that it wasn't the Reckoner who had ordered them to flee, but the still heavily-re-strained Penriding, who had his own problems contending with stampeding Vwari that were practically trampling him to death to get to Horton.

"There is no way out!" Ulises proclaimed in response. "There is no escape from Exetus!"

"No, there is one way," Horton quickly countered as he turned back toward the entryway just behind them that led to the living quarters of the pyramid. "But first I need to go back and get my satchel. We need the orb."

As they took off for the doorway, Horton glanced back for a split second and witnessed the struggling Reckoner knee-deep in Vwari, having redirected their attention to-ward their most detested foe. Somewhere beyond all of that was Penriding, still in custody and hopefully one piece. He dare not admit to himself how close he had come to ordering his execution, but he knew he owed it to the Zeptan to rescue him from Exetus, and to do that he'd need to fulfill their mission – Georg's mission – and repair the pyramid.

"Horton, stop," Ulises called out as they quickly made their way down the corridor.

"I am far too old for this, my boy," he shook his head as he peered over Horton's shoulder in attempt to catch a glimpse of the in-pursuit Exetans. "I am only going to slow you down. Go get the orb without me."

"No, I can't just leave you here to be killed," Horton replied.

"Oh, I do not plan on simply giving up," Ulises huffed. "I will draw them in the other direction. Now do not argue with me, boy, away with you!"

"Alright," Horton nodded. "Thank you, Ulises."

Horton practically ran through the door as he shoved it open to reach the sleeping quarters, revealing a stunned Deforest still inside.

"Horton?" Deforest asked as Horton ran over to his bed and frantically searched for his satchel. "What's going on? What's the matter?"

He spotted it lying underneath his bed.

"I don't have time to explain right now," Horton told his brother quickly. "You need to come with me, we're getting out of here."

"What are you talking about?" Deforest asked quizzically. "Father, what's wrong with Horton?"

Horton abruptly stopped what he was doing and slowly looked up. Klas was standing in the doorway, watching him.

"Don't do this, son," Klas plead. "It was all that fool

Ulises' doing, not yours. I can talk to the other Exetans. Everything can still all be alright."

Horton did not respond. Instead he reached into his satchel to pull out the orb, but to his dismay discovered it was completely empty.

"If you're looking for the orb it's not in there," Klas noted.

"Where is it?" Horton said coldly, barely able to look his father in the eye.

"We are holding it – for safekeeping," Klas replied with a wry smile. "But do not worry – it'll do its job. When this pyramid is operational, the Vwari will have the link they need to invade Zeptus City from within its own walls. This Rissa – the so-called Zeptan life force – will ultimately be the source of their own undoing. Quite ironic, actually."

"I'm not staying here," Horton held his ground. "Deforest and I are leaving, right brother?"

Horton waited for his brother's affirmation, but to his surprise no response came.

"Deforest?" Horton said again, turning to look at his brother.

"No…" Deforest said quietly as he shook his head. "I'm sorry Horton, but I don't want to go. I can't leave father."

"Your brother is dedicated to the task at hand, Horton," Klas said. "He was the one who informed us what the orb really is, although I'm sure you were going to mention its true function eventually, right?"

"Deforest…" Horton whispered in shock.

"You explained it all in the letter," Deforest explained sheepishly. "I just wanted to contribute somehow…"

"And you did, my son," Klas smiled. "Now Horton, stop this senselessness. You have nowhere to go. I saw the fire in your eyes back there when you had that Zeptan's life in your hands. Don't deny your fate."

Horton looked at his brother. It was in that moment he was reminded of Ananke. He remembered what the young Zeptan had gone through, what he had lost, and everything he had sacrificed to give him this opportunity.

"You have hope. Your brother may still be alive some-where, hold on to that."

"No," Horton uttered under his breath as he turned to face his father once more. "I cannot."

"Klas!" Asa popped up from behind Klas in the door-way. "The Reckoner is fallen and we have secured the priest. What do you wish to do with him?"

"Lock Ulises up, for now," Klas ordered, still staring gloomily at Horton. "And Asa, my son—"

He cut himself off as he briefly hesitated.

"Your son?" Asa repeated.

Klas took a deep breath before finishing his order.

"Find him a cell."

As Horton sat in the middle of his dark cell and stared at its bare back wall for what seemed like hours, he couldn't help but feel like such an idiot for allowing his feelings to be so easily gulled by his father.

"He never did change," Horton reminded himself more times than he could remember. "All he cares about is him-self. I never should have trusted him. People will die be-cause of my stupidity."

Although he didn't want to admit it, he knew it was as much his own fault as his father's. There had been a part of him that wanted so badly to be a part of his father's life again and something that made him bigger and more significant than his small stature could ever provide, but it was at a cost too great. Worse yet he had turned against his friends, and his brother was lost in subterfuge.

Horton closed his eyes. It was only a matter of time now before his father used his orb to repair Exetus and its portal, opening up the gateway to the Rissa in Zeptus City to the Vwari legions. Zeptus would be lost and the blood of its people would be on Horton's hands.

Horton clenched his jaw as he fought back tears once more.

"It is mortality," Klas' voice abruptly sounded out from the other side of the cell bars behind him. "The difference between men and gods, I mean."

Horton did not turn around or open his eyes. He had nothing to say to his father.

"I saw the look in your eyes earlier, when you came between Ulises and me," Klas said. "I had long forgotten that look, but when I saw it all I could see was Georg's face in you."

Klas paused for a moment before he went on.

"I read your letter to Deforest – you're a User, aren't you," he suddenly stated, causing Horton to open his eyes. "You have been granted a connection between these ancient structures and your mind. You have experienced memories long lost between the cracks of time, just as Georg once did. Tell me, what have the pyramids shown you?"

"I've seen enough to know you lied to me," Horton finally spoke up. "I saw that it was you who killed him, not the Zeptans like you claimed."

Klas scoffed at the notion.

"That's not true," he contended. "Georg turned his back on his people and its covenant – its duty as masters to the Vwari. Are you still blind to this, Horton? The Zeptans saw the Illacs as a threat. They know the immense power we hold – the pyramids, the Vwari, everything. Have you never thought to wonder why Zeptus is a military state? They have no enemies. Held unchecked, Zeptus would overrun the world."

"I think you're delusional," Horton answered, his eyes still focused squarely at the plain wall in front of him. "The sweet taste of power changed you, even mother saw it."

"Stop it," Klas ordered, but Horton carried on.

"You and I come from the same mold. When I first arrived here, the initial feeling of power began to consume me, just as it did you. Ulises was wrong when he said Georg changed you – it wasn't your brother at all, you did it all to yourself. It was Georg who knew the Vwari had to be destroyed, not the Zeptans. His only mistake was trusting his younger brother, and now I'm going to lose mine just as he lost his."

Horton could hear Klas breathing heavily behind him, and as he sat there in silence inside his cell, he thought about what he had just said. It was the first time he had really analyzed it all, and he was right. He and his father were like two sides of one reflection, the only difference being that Horton had always had someone there to rescue him when he slipped into blackness.

He quickly twisted around to face his father, but he was already gone.

TWELVE

The Orb

"GET UP," Asa ordered, unlocking Horton's cell door.

Horton pulled his head up off the cold, hard floor he had been sleeping on. He grabbed the back of his sore neck as he looked up at the Exetan.

"What's going on?" he groaned.

He could just make out the grin on Asa's face in the dim light. Stood in the shadows behind him were two Vwari sentries.

"Your father is sending you home to Illac."

Horton stared back at Asa inquisitively.

"Home?" he asked. "By wastewalker?"

Asa shook his head and chuckled.

"Hurry up."

Asa waved off the pair of Vwari that had accompanied them as he and Horton entered the great hall. There waiting for them in uneasy silence were the rest of the Exetans, staring out at the empty room.

Klas didn't budge in his throne as Horton entered, and except for a momentary glance in his direction, he did not acknowledge his eldest son. Beside him on his right stood Deforest, grasping onto an arm of his father's seat. As he approached the group with Asa, Horton could sense his brother's eyes watching him from beneath his cowl.

Unwilling to make eye contact with either Klas or Deforest, he scanned the remaining faces in the room, only to discover that neither Ulises nor Penriding were among them. It appeared that if he was in fact going home today, it would be on his own.

Asa's hand suddenly grabbed hold of his left shoulder to stop him in place. They were at the edge of the platform at one end of the hall, separated from the others by a few meters.

"It should have been done by now, Klas," Horton overheard Isaac quietly mutter into his father's ear. "We can't afford—"

Klas calmly lifted his finger into the air, silencing his cohort. Horton wondered what was going on.

Clank.

"No," Horton whispered with a shudder.

The room tremored as the ferocious sound bellowed up from the depths of the pyramid and into their domain. The grinding and bending of metal rumbled perpetually toward a crescendo as they stood there bravely awaiting its finality. This ancient structure's enervating vibrations and groans were unlike anything Horton had experienced before –

surely the damage inflicted upon it by Nestor had taken its toll on the Exetus pyramid. Then, just at it seemed the grisly sound of repair would never cease, the pyramid let loose a final and incredible belch, followed by the gentlest of hums.

The Illacs looked around the still-dark hall, waiting for confirmation the orb had been successful. When none arose a few moments later, murmurs of doubt began to emerge from within the group, and even Horton, who had experienced the repair process a few times prior, began to wonder. Perhaps the pyramid was simply too far gone to be saved.

And then Horton grimaced. As if taunting him, a light in the far corner of the hall slowly flickered on. A few seconds later a second one followed, and then another. The Exetans gasped with excitement as the great hall gradually filled with artificial light. Exetus was operational.

Klas slowly leaned forward in his throne to look at Horton, and when his son's eyes caught his, he announced his marching orders to them all.

"The portal and our future – our destiny – await us," he professed out loud, his eyes all the while still locked on Horton. "Today the Zeptans will pay in blood for their sins. Let's go."

Asa pushed Horton toward the middle of the pack as the former Illacs made their way down the spiraling stairway toward the lower levels of Exetus where the portal was kept. Heading the array was Klas, followed closely by Deforest.

Waiting for them at the very bottom of the long stairwell

was a Reckoner. Initially this confounded Horton, who was under the impression that the only Reckoner in Exetus had already been slain by masses of Vwari, but when Klas approached the behemoth, he pulled off his dark helmet to reveal a beaming Thomas.

"Well done, Thomas, well done," Klas applauded Horton's oldest nemesis. "How are things below?"

"The air is being cycled out effectively," Thomas answered. "It should be safe to breathe by now."

Then Klas pursed his lips and leaned in toward Thomas. His eyes seemed to nearly double in size as he nervously pressed him further.

"And what of the Vwari?"

"They are fine," Thomas shrugged. "From what I saw they were not affected in any way by the repairs or the orb."

"Just as I predicted. Very good," Klas nodded as his demeanor instantly shifted back to its usual self. He then brushed past the Exetan outfitted with Reckoner armor and briskly continued down the corridor.

They seemed to meander for quite some time along a maze of now well-lit corridors and stairways as they traversed the lower levels of the pyramid. In fact, while they trudged along, Horton wondered why Klas was leading them through such an unusual route. He had, after all, already shown Horton how to get to the lower levels and the portal rather easily. It was as if he was going out of his way to avoid running into any Vwari.

Then, out of the corner of his left eye, Horton saw something at the end of an adjacent corridor the group was just passing. In that instant he replayed what he thought he had just seen in his mind: a figure in white disappearing into the pyramid's dark recesses.

Al!

Horton's heart skipped a beat. It would be entirely on a whim, but this was the opportunity he had been looking for. If anyone could help him right now, it was Al. Lacking the amenity of time to consider the repercussions of what he was about to do, Horton pulled away from Asa and slid into the corridor at the last possible moment. With no opportunity to dither, he propelled himself forward with a push off the wall and took off toward where he had last seen Al as hastily as he could.

Shouts echoed off the walls all around him as he ran, but he didn't stop or turn around to see who was in pursuit.

Clang. Clang. Clang. Clang...

His eyes practically popped out of his head. He couldn't help it – he turned his head around to glance back, and there was none other than Thomas in the Reckoner suit, barreling down the corridor after him.

Horton skidded around the corner at the end of the corridor at full speed. He hoped to catch Al before he disappeared once again into the Exetus labyrinth, but to his dismay Al was nowhere to be found.

"Damnit!" he muttered.

With Thomas rapidly closing in and no time to stop, Horton had no choice but to haphazardly press on. Along the left side of this corridor were five openings to additional hallways. Horton guessed that Al had to have traveled down one of them.

"You're dead, Horton!" Thomas yelled out as he too

turned the corner just as Horton passed the first corridor on his left. It was empty.

The heavy clinking of armor boomed with each step in his wake, drawing nearer and nearer. Horton hit the second corridor with barely time to slow down this time, and again found no sign of Al.

Thomas was far too close now. Horton decided on the fly that if Al wasn't in this next corridor, he would have to turn into the following one no matter what and take his chances.

Horton jerked his head to the left as he blew past the third corridor, looking for a sign of anything that resembled a person in white.

That's him!

Horton's feet gave out from under him as he attempted to abruptly stop himself and cut into the opening. He grabbed onto the corner of the wall as he felt his momentum carry him past the entryway, and despite his best effort to stay on two legs, he lost his footing. Horton spilled onto the floor.

He looked up. Mere feet away were two tons of reinforced metallic armor about to mercilessly rain down upon him. Without slowing down Thomas threw the Reckoner armor into a feet-first slide aimed directly at him. He would try to ram Horton to death.

Anticipating his doom at any moment, Horton scrambled to get himself to safety inside the corridor. Once he got his feet squarely beneath him once more, he squeezed his eyes shut and lunged his body into it.

Hmph!
Crash!

The incredible leviathan blew past him and into the corner of the corridor, taking out half of the wall's thick panel in the process. Horton found himself in a daze as the shockwave of Reckoner meeting solid metal sent him flying even farther down the corridor. With little more than a short moment or two of reprieve, Horton seized the opportunity to take inventory and ensure he was still in one piece by wiggling his digits and limbs. For now, to his relief, he was.

"Aaargh!" Thomas shouted as he pulled himself and the half-embedded Reckoner out from the wall while Horton clambered to pull his own body together up off the floor.

Horton looked back down the hallway. His heart leaped at the unexpected sight of Al still standing there at its end, watching him. He could make out the holographic computer program's face clearly now, but to Horton's surprise it wasn't the same Al he knew from the space station – at least in appearance. As a matter of fact, he was certain the man standing before him wasn't anyone he had ever seen before, yet at the same time was vaguely familiar. However, before he could examine him closer, the unknown figure turned and walked out of view down the adjacent corridor.

"Hey, wait!" Horton called out to the figure as he got his feet under him once again and began to sprint after the mystery man. Meanwhile the unmistakable sound of a stampeding Reckoner caromed all around him. Thomas was back in the chase.

"This is crazy," Horton panted. Caught in the middle of a cat and mouse chase between a ghost and a remarkably mobile suit of armor, he knew his chances of getting out of this were slim if his gut feeling had been wrong.

With Thomas rapidly gaining ground, he turned the corner at full speed, and then gasped as he almost came to a complete halt. In front of him was an open gap in the wall with purple light spilling out of it. It was then that his mind clicked, and he knew exactly where he had seen this room before, as well as this mysterious person in white. This wasn't the same Al he knew – it was the fuzzy, obfuscated figure his father had encountered years before and the one Horton had seen in his vision.

Still, with Thomas on his tail, Horton didn't have time to mess around. He slid in through the opening in the wall and locked his eyes onto the lone purple-emblazoned button atop the pedestal and sprinted toward it. He was going to ride that purple light back up to the moon.

Ba-beep! Bom!

Horton stumbled slightly as his body tried to adjust to the sudden lack of momentum once through the portal, but he managed to keep on his feet. Immediately he noticed the station was dimly lit, making it apparent that Al was running low on energy once again. After rediscovering his bearings, Horton caught sight of the antechamber's doorway and quickly made his way toward it, anticipating Thomas' arrival at any moment.

Once in the doorway he stopped to catch his breath, and for a few seconds turned back to look at the portal, praying that he had not been followed.

Bom!

Still outfitted with the Reckoner's armor, Thomas suddenly popped out of thin air into the room, faced directly at Horton.

"Damn you!" Thomas screamed out as he briefly caught sight of his prey just before Horton ducked out of sight and into the corridor.

The Illac's heart pounded furiously in his chest as he huffed and puffed throughout the quagmire that was Armstrong Station Six. He could sense Thomas' seething anger elevating somewhere behind him, and so he searched desperately for somewhere – anywhere – to hide, but all around him were nothing but endless, barren corridors.

And then, as if sent from the gods, it appeared: a lone doorway. Horton quickly slipped himself inside it, all the while desperately hoping that Thomas hadn't seen him do so.

He had.

Thomas slowed down as he approached the doorway that was not much larger than his suit of armor before peering in. Inside was a control room of sorts, its walls cloaked in darkness but its center well illuminated. Standing squarely in the middle of the light was Horton, staring back at his fellow Three Yearling with unfaltering resolve.

The brute squeezed his fists and sneered at Horton.

"You... you took it!" Thomas shouted as he squeezed through the doorway and into the room. "That was my idol! You humiliated – you ruined me!"

Now approaching the defenseless and motionless Horton, Thomas slowly pulled the enormous Reckoner blade off his back and furiously pointed it at him.

"Damn you.... Damn your father.... Damn your whole family!"

And in one quick thrust, Thomas shoved the blade straight through Horton's chest. He snarled as he held it

282

there for a moment, glaring into his victim's eyes without any sign of compassion before swiftly retracting the sword. Horton looked down at his wound and then, without saying a single word, fell backward with a thud onto the floor.

"No! Horton!"

Klas buckled onto one knee in the doorway behind Thomas. He had followed his fellow Exetan in his pursuit of Horton, and now looked on at his demised son in stunned disbelief, having just witnessed his eldest son killed right before his eyes. Waiting behind the Exetan leader stood a dozen Vwari, ready to do his bidding, but for now he appeared broken and frozen in place – entirely unable to fathom what had just happened.

Thomas had barely begun to explain himself when Klas snapped-to once more, and in one fleeting, rage-filled motion, he jumped to his feet, flung his black cloak back over his shoulder and pointed wrathfully at his former ally.

"Kill the bastard!"

The Vwari horde pounced like lightning. Caught off-guard, Thomas narrowly managed to knock the first attacker away with the pommel of his sword, but unlike the real and well-trained Reckoners, he was no match for the Vwari, and the second assailant jumped onto his back and clawed away at his unprotected head. His guard compromised, Thomas quickly became entrenched in a mound of ruthless Vwari, and toppled onto the floor.

A few seconds later his muffled screams fell silent.

Klas had all the while slowly begun to make his way over toward his fallen son. As he approached Horton's dormant body he pulled the long black cloak off his shoulders.

"My boy…" Klas uttered as he fell to his knees beside Horton, tears steadily streaming down his scarred cheeks as he looked on at his lifeless face. "All of this… it always should have been for you and your brother… but now – gods, what have I done? Please, Horton, please forgive me."

He closed his eyes and paused for a moment, as if hopefully beseeching the gods to shower him with undeserved mercy and undo Thomas' sinister deed, even though deep inside he knew it was in vain. Then, having reluctantly come to grips with his boy's untimely consummation, Klas slowly and carefully strew the cloak over Horton's body and face.

"I do, father."

Klas swiveled around and gasped. Unbelievably, stood upon the fringe of the shadows behind him was Horton, living and completely unscathed.

"Horton? How are you—?"

"It's me," Horton confirmed.

Thoroughly stunned, Klas turned back to his cloak, which was still laid over what he could have sworn was his deceased son. Charily he lifted it up, only to discover there was now nothing beneath it.

"I-I just saw Thomas murder you – right here," Klas stammered in shock. "No, no – I must be losing my mind, surely there's no way you could still be alive. There's no way at all – not unless—"

All of a sudden Klas' posse of Vwari bodyguards hissed loudly in unison, turning Klas and Horton's attention toward a figure that had just appeared from beyond the room's veil of darkness. Then, like animals flocking to their master, the Vwari quickly congregated around the emergent figure.

Klas cautiously stood up from his knees as the entity silently approached, all the while squinting as he fought with the chamber's restricted light to make out its face. Horton, however, knew exactly who the figure was, having just witnessed him assume Horton's physical identity in a pinch to fool Thomas and keep him off the User's tail. Now, though, Al had returned to what Horton recognized as his normal simulated appearance – the *other* User still in his database.

"By the gods..." Klas whispered as he turned to look at Horton and then back to the hologram. "I can't believe it's you."

Al stopped in place once he crossed the threshold of light concentrated at the middle of the chamber and looked at the Vwari that practically clung onto him. One by one he touched their heads gently like a parent would their child, and then looked up at Klas.

"These humans still carry the infection," Al noted with disappointment. "What have you done?"

Klas leaned in slightly as he stared at Al with his mouth half open. As far as Horton could tell, his father seemed to be as confounded by the hologram's appearance as he was fascinated by it, making it difficult for Horton to tell whether or not his father had encountered Al in the past before.

Then, without warning, an incredibly bright flash of energy shot out of Al's body and into the pack of Vwari gathered in his vicinity, each simultaneously shrieking with intense pain before almost instantly flopping onto the floor like rag dolls.

Horton took a step back. He had never witnessed Al act this way before. Even so, Klas appeared bizarrely enamored by the spectacle. Horton watched curiously as his father boldly approached Al and raised his hand up to the hologram's face and touched it.

"I told you, brother," Klas spoke to him with a contented smile on his face. "I knew we were gods."

Horton opened his eyes wide as it all suddenly made sense to him. He knew there were two User appearances Al had access to, but it wasn't until now that Horton fully realized who the other persona Al had portrayed all along was – a youthful Georg.

Oh no...

"Father, wait!" Horton called out in desperation, but Klas took no notice.

"No, Klas, son of Jamic," Al said in reply. "You are not."

"Al stop, don't do it!" Horton shouted as he ran to intervene, but Al had already pressed his hand squarely onto Klas' chest.

"Recreants must be terminated."

A bright blue pulse shot out of Al's hand and into Klas, sending him flying off his feet in Horton's direction. Horton thrust himself toward his father in an attempt to catch his body, but whatever energy Al had emitted completely disintegrated Klas' body into nothingness before it ever reached Horton's arms.

"Father!" Horton shouted futilely, but it was already done. His father had been killed right before his eyes.

Horton stood there in disbelief, staring unwaveringly at the last spot in the air his father had been before he vanished just moments ago. He replayed what he had seen in his mind over and over, half expecting to blink and see his father standing there once again, but he never rematerialized. As what had happened began to sink in, Horton felt increasingly numb inside.

After a few seconds passed he turned back to Al, who glared back at him unsympathetically through Georg's faux eyes. Al had saved his life, and then in a brutal and merciless burst ended another.

"Why?" Horton uttered quietly to Al.

"Klas was a threat to the Sunbound Initiative," Al answered simply. "My programming dictates I protect myself at all costs until my primary function is fulfilled. I am sorry for any inconvenience, User."

"No," Horton mumbled glumly, "no you're not."

Horton turned his back to Al and slowly walked over toward one of the Vwari corpses lying on the floor.

"User, I am obligated to inform you that these infected are different from those on available database records," Al noted. "Their appearance and the way they followed Klas' orders is not normal. It is as if they have evolved, or perhaps, been altered."

"So what are these things really?" Horton asked, still unable to look at Al after what he had just done to his father. "You said they're humans... are they sick?"

"The source of the virus is unknown. However, I do know the Vwari – as you call them – are the reason I exist," Al answered as he too walked over to the Vwari corpses by Horton.

"I thought you said you didn't know what you were created for," Horton recalled.

"With three of the four sub-stations operating, I have been able to access parts of the data banks that were previously disconnected from me," Al explained as he kneeled down to place his hand on the head of a Vwari.

Horton watched Al closely out of the corner of his eye as he analyzed its body. It was easy to forget that this person – or rather, simulation of a person, was nothing more than a computer program. It was a tough pill to swallow, but to a degree Horton understood that Al was only doing what he was programmed to do when he killed his father. He knew that to expect any type of remorse or sympathy from Al was foolish, as was it to resent him for what he'd done.

"So if the Vwari carry an infection and they're the reason you were created..." Horton pressed as he tried to piece things together. "Then your primary function must be to destroy the Vwari. You're a weapon."

"I am no weapon," Al abruptly retaliated, taking Horton somewhat by surprise. The hologram had always shown minimal signs of emotion to say the least, but there was no doubt that Al appeared troubled by something. "My function is to extricate the Earth from crisis via deployment of the Sunbound Initiative. My programming does not permit me to kill except in the defense of my ability to complete that function..."

Al looked as though he was going to say more, but suddenly stopped himself. He seemed to be processing something in his mind.

"User, I am detecting heavy Vwari activity through the Exetus portal – dozens every few seconds, but I cannot see their destination," Al eventually revealed to Horton. "I am unable to access the other side of the portal to terminate the connection."

Horton grimaced. He'd almost completely forgotten. "It's my father's invasion force. His plan was to seize Zeptus City and the Rissa – the Zepitas sub-station as you know it."

"I see," Al responded, his focus apparently still placed elsewhere. "Interesting. I am reading DNA consistent with Klas' and yours.... The person is passing through the portal, User."

"Deforest..." Horton muttered out loud. "It's got to be my brother. I've got to get back to Zeptus right away – it's unlikely he will survive the battle."

Without hesitation, Horton made for the doorway.

"Wait," Al called out, causing Horton to stop in his tracks. "It is imperative you repair the Zepitas sub-station. Once it is operational I will be able to protect you."

Horton felt his pockets in vain. He had forgotten he no longer had the orb.

"I can't – I lost the repair orb," he said urgently. "You need to make me another one."

Al shook his head. "That is not possible. The tool I constructed for you was one of a kind, and if I generate a new one you will need to reformat each sub-station to be compatible with it. It would take days to complete the process unhindered."

Horton sighed. "Great. So not only do I have to survive

long enough amidst warring Zeptans and Vwari – no guarantees both sides don't already want me dead as it is – but I have to figure out where the orb is too. It's suicide."

"Not necessarily, User," Al interjected as he turned around to look at Thomas' body on the floor, still wearing the Reckoner's armor. "Assuming you have a grade three certification, I can authorize the use of this Dreadnought aegis to you."

Horton blinked. "Uh, yeah – of course I do."

The Reckoner's inner lining expanded as it conformed to Horton's body once he climbed inside the suit. To his astonishment it fit like a glove, despite being about three times larger than him. There was no getting around the fact that he felt a little uncomfortable wearing what had moments before been effectively Thomas' coffin, but once Horton moved his limbs around a little bit and got accustomed to its incredible power, he forgot all about any previous misgivings.

"This Dreadnought's power core is drained and the suit is in sub-par condition," Al said as he examined it. "I can reinitialize the core for you, but it requires I expend all my remaining energy reserves to do so. I will not be able to assist you again until this command station is receiving power from all four sub-stations on the planet's surface."

"Wait, what do you mean by power core?" Horton asked as Al approached him with his hand outstretched. "I've seen Reck— I mean, Dreadnoughts in action without power cores before, they're more than capable as-is."

"The Dreadnought suits are designed to maintain basic

mechanical functions even without an operational power core, yes," Al explained. "However, you will need the onboard artificial intelligence unit to guide you to the orb, not to mention the benefits of the suit's automated defense system."

Horton took a deep breath. "Okay, I guess I can't argue with that. Let's do it."

Al nodded and placed the palm of his hand on the chest plate of the armor. Horton could hear a low-pitched sound begin to hum from within the armor, gradually increasing in frequency and pitch until it became inaudible.

"I have calibrated the suit to your specifications," Al said, glancing up at Horton. "Good luck."

An instant later he disappeared, causing Horton's eyes to dart around the silent room. A few seconds later the sparse remnants of artificial lighting flickered off, leaving him plunged in darkness. He was on his own.

Welcome, User.

Horton spun around anxiously, trying to decipher where the voice was coming from.

"Hello?" he called out. "Who's there?"

It has been at least six months since this Dreadnought Mk. VI unit has updated its firmware. Please wait while an uplink is created.

"How are you—?"

Horton froze as he figured out where the source of the voice originated. It was the armor, but not from the armor specifically – it was speaking to his mind telepathically.

Error. Unable to contact uplink node. Try again later.

"Uh, okay. What?"

Horton was not sure what the suit was trying to do, but he did know he was wasting precious moments. He needed to get to the orb and Deforest right away.

User input received. Interpolating request.

Horton groaned. He'd had enough of this. He attempted to move his legs inside the suit to get it to walk, but the armor did not respond to his actions as it had before.

"What in the gods?" Horton shouted. "Damnit, Al!"

Possible match found. Does User wish to launch custom order A-1?

"Yes, you piece of junk!" Horton screamed. "Do something!"

Horton lurched forward as the suit of armor sprung into life. In a flash he found himself being carried through the doorway and into the station's maze of corridors at breakneck speed.

"Whoa, whoa!" Horton called out as he looked down at the machine that contained him. "Where are we going?"

Then Horton reverted his gaze forward. His eyes only saw blackness as the Dreadnought skipped clangorously through the vacant passageways, but somehow in his mind it all became succinctly clear.

"Oh."

It was something he could have never imagined, even in his wildest dreams, but it was happening. The entire mission Al had concocted and programmed into the suit was laid out for him inside his own head. It was something a person would have to experience firsthand to truly grasp, but Horton could feel a conscious connection between the machine and himself that seemed to be growing stronger with every passing moment. Even in complete darkness his eyes were beginning to envisage his immediate surroundings, creating an unusual sensation.

He could sense now that he was rapidly closing in on the portal room that would send him to Zeptus City. From there the Dreadnought would be able to hone in on the orb's location and take Horton to it.

Fifteen seconds to portal jump. Destination target substation Zepitas.

This was it. Horton was mere seconds away from joining the fray. He hoped with all his might that he would be able to quickly and painlessly accomplish what he needed to do on the other side, but deep down he knew it would not be so simple. Retrieving the orb could be a difficult task in its own right, but what really unnerved Horton was Deforest. He tried his best to block the possible truth from his mind, but it was there nevertheless. There was no guarantee he would be able to extricate his brother from the Exetans.

Five seconds to portal jump.

Horton's heart pounded in his chest. He could now see the doorway to the portal chamber at the end of the corridor, with colored lights seeping into the adjacent blackness from beyond its keep. Long, elegant strides carried the Dreadnought and him effortlessly towards it while the familiar garish clunks of its hefty feet resonated in all directions. With the portal now just meters away, he felt the armor's massive arm reach out for the yellow button atop the pedestal.

Ba-beep! Bong!

THIRTEEN

Deforest

HORTON SQUINTED his eyes open as a wave of warm air rushed over his face. It admittedly felt good to be back in the heat after spending time in the bitter cold of Exetus, but before he had a chance to enjoy it, he and the armor that encased him were back on the move.

However, in the split-second of time before the Dreadnought finished scanning, locating the orb, and blasting off toward its target like a missile through the city, Horton witnessed an image inside the Rissa's grand chamber that would be burned into his mind permanently.

There had only been time for one quick sweep of the chamber with his eyes, but he saw enough for a lifetime. Bloodied and dismembered Zeptan soldiers lay trampled on the floor between the portal and the doorway outside, but strangely there was no sign of a fight from them, having evidently been ambushed and overrun by the surprise invasive

Vwari forces before they ever knew what hit them. Worse still, a handful of stragglers from the terrible horde had stayed behind to gorge on their annihilated foes, as though death alone was not a dreadful enough end for their hated enemy.

A feeling of sickness overcame him as the Dreadnought navigated the rooftops of Zeptus City toward the orb. He desperately wanted to shut his eyes and close himself off from what was going on around him, but he could not turn away. The immense army of Vwari had ferociously spread out from the Rissa at the heart of Zeptus and quickly disseminated into the surrounding city like a virus, devouring every living thing in its path. Cannon fire rang out and smoke bellowed from every section of the massive city as the Zeptan military turned its arsenal around and pointed it back within its own walls. The last shining beacon of hope and life that remained on this dead planet had fallen under a dark blanket of chaos.

Horton sensed through the Dreadnought as it carried him through the city at breakneck speed that the orb was just mere seconds away. He could see in his mind's eye that it remained inside his old satchel, which had been slung over the shoulder of one of two Illacs standing alone inside an abandoned building near the southeastern front line. He spoke their identities as they emerged in his mind one by one.

"Isaac..."

He swallowed hard as the second entity holding his satchel and subsequently the orb materialized within his thoughts.

"Deforest."

Crash!

The Dreadnought catapulted Horton through a large glass window and into a large abandoned room overlooking the cityscape. At its far end stood Deforest and Isaac, their attention pulled away from the carnage outside and back towards Horton and the hulking suit of armor he was wearing. As the dust cleared it was difficult to say what astounded them most: Horton, the Reckoner's suit, or both in tandem, harmoniously bursting into their world without warning like a bombshell blast.

"Is that you, Horton?" Deforest stammered in disbelief as he looked up at his brother's face atop the mountain of armor.

"Yes, it's me," Horton replied, looking down at his brother. He began to move toward Deforest, but stopped when he saw him back away synchronously with every step he took in his direction.

"Where did you get that armor?" Deforest inquired in a dubious manner before seemingly reaching an epiphany. "Hold on – what did you do to Thomas? Where is…"

Deforest paused for a beat, glaring at him incredulously. Horton's heart sank. He had never seen the flame burn in his brother's eyes in such a way before.

"Where is father?" Deforest demanded.

Horton bit his lip. He didn't want to lie to his brother, but he also knew he could not answer his question in that moment. Not when the risk of Deforest falling further away from him was so great.

"Deforest," Horton told his brother as benevolently as

he could muster, "we need to go. You, me, and the orb –
we have a task to complete. I need you to trust me."

"He's not going anywhere with you, traitor," Isaac interrupted as he stepped in between Horton and Deforest.
"Your father was a fool to think you wouldn't turn on us at
the first opportunity."

Isaac traipsed over toward Horton and the suit of armor
to examine it more closely.

"This is the same Reckoner suit Thomas was wearing,"
he concluded. "You had to have killed him for it... and
what of your father?"

Horton said nothing.

Isaac nodded as he glanced over at Deforest before turning back to Horton. "You have betrayed not only your people, but now your own father and brother."

"I've not betrayed anyone!" Horton shot back.

"So Klas is alive?" Isaac questioned.

Horton looked at Deforest and took a deep breath. As
he heavily shook his head in response, he felt a deep sadness overcome him as he saw his brother's distraught face.

*Warning, incoming projectile detected. Emergency eva-
sion routines engaged.*

Horton's attention immediately turned to the large window beside them. A bright streak of light was on a collision
course with their position, fired from a cannon on the city's
outer wall.

"We need to get Deforest out of here!" Horton hastily
commanded the Dreadnought with barely a moment to
spare, but the suit had already begun to extract itself from
the building.

Chances of survival—

"Just do it, damnit!" Horton screamed as he physically and mentally pulled the uncooperative Dreadnought back toward Deforest with all his might.

Just when his tussle with the armor appeared hopeless, the Dreadnought unexpectedly surrendered, becoming limp and turning itself over to Horton. In a last-ditch effort to save his brother, he instinctively flung himself and the two tons of armor over Deforest and Isaac, who had huddled themselves together in anticipation of their likely demise.

With not even a second to brace himself, the cannon shell detonated directly onto the Dreadnought's back plate. Horton gasped as the force of the explosion knocked the wind out of him even through the thick armor, but he held on tightly to the two Illacs beneath him. As dust and building material flew about all around him, he could hear a slight high-pitched whining sound in the back of his head, which slowly fizzled out into silence.

He knew right away what had happened. His mind had just moments before been finely tuned in to its surroundings through the Dreadnought's enhanced sensors, but now it was caged within its own natural limitations, disconnected and constrained. The impact had damaged the Dreadnought and its power core had failed.

There was little time for Horton to adjust to the abrupt mental shift, however, as the floor beneath him suddenly gave way. He scrambled to gather Deforest from underneath him as he felt himself begin to drop, but he could not see his brother amid the dust and smoke. Now in absolute control of the Dreadnought's mechanical functions, Horton franticly swiped at the air below for Deforest as he hurtled toward the ground in a free-fall.

Then he caught something – an unknown body, squarely in the Dreadnought's hand. He quickly pulled it in to secure it against his chest before rolling over in midair so that the back of the armor would hopefully withstand the brunt of the blow once it slammed into the ground.

Horton took a deep breath and prepared for impact. He hoped to the gods he had grabbed Deforest and not Isaac.

Klas opened his blurry eyes to find himself staring up at two white figures carrying him through murky corridors within the Exetus pyramid. Screams and shouts echoed from some distant, hellish section of the installation.

"The cube…" Klas muttered deliriously. "Georg… Georg!"

"Try to stay calm, Klas," a soothing voice said as Klas battled with himself to remain conscious.

Klas screamed in agony. His face and upper body seared with intense pain.

"You have been burned quite badly, please try to remain still," the same voice instructed him.

"The Zeptan… the Zeptan…" Klas raved to himself over and over. He looked up at one of the white figures carrying him and his eyes slowly came into focus on his face.

"Don't let this happen to my children," Klas told him in a sudden burst of bridled composure.

The man turned to Klas and watched him for a moment with sorrowed eyes.

"I know. Whatever it takes, I will protect them," Ulises promised.

Pop! Popopop!

Horton groaned as he awoke to the sound of cannon fire cracking through the air. He was lying on his back in a daze, surrounded by rubble inside a hollow shell of a building. He quickly became cognizant of what he had been doing, however, when something moved slightly beneath the Dreadnought's right hand, which had remained firmly pressed against its chest.

Deforest?

Horton tilted his head forward toward his chest and lifted up his right hand.

"Deforest!" he shouted excitedly as he saw his brother lying in one piece on the armor's breast plate.

"Hey Deforest, are you alright?" Horton gently asked in an attempt to rouse his brother, who appeared to have been knocked out cold at some point. It was as he nudged him with the Dreadnought's hand that he saw blood dripping from Deforest's forehead.

"Put your hands up!" a voice bellowed from behind Horton.

Startled, he shot his head back and looked around to find a squad of Zeptan soldiers had surrounded him.

"By the gods – I don't have time for this," he lamented under his breath.

Horton grabbed hold of Deforest and pounced up from the rubble.

Or rather, he attempted to. Unfortunately, somewhere deep beneath the fallen rubble were the Dreadnought's legs, and they weren't responding to him.

"Damn it," he grumbled, gently letting go of Deforest and timidly raising his hands above his head.

"Horton? Is that you, kid?"

Constable Keen popped out from behind the group of soldiers with an astonished look on his face.

"I don't believe my eyes – what in the world are you doing out here?" he asked as he rubbed the top of his balding head. "And how in Rissa's name did you wind up inside one of those contraptions?"

"I'm sorry but I really don't have time to explain right now, constable," Horton replied. "I need to get to the Rissa immediately."

"Are you trying to pull my damn leg again?" the constable retorted. "The Rissa is swarming with those Vwari bastards, you'll—"

He paused as he caught sight of Deforest.

"Where are Penriding and Linden? What happened to the others?" he asked quietly.

Horton glanced away and sighed.

"Sir! There is a dead body over here," a soldier called out as he inspected a half-buried Isaac in the rubble, momentarily pulling the constable's attention away.

"And there's another one here!" another soldier announced, standing a few feet away from Deforest. "It looks like it's just a boy."

"Don't touch him!" Horton shouted. Garnering every ounce of strength he had, Horton pushed forward the Dreadnought's chest plate, giving him enough space to lift his body up and out of the suit of armor before scrambling down to where his brother lay unconscious.

Without question the constable waved off the soldier, and then kneeled down beside Horton as he tended to Deforest.

"That's your brother, isn't it?" Constable Keen asked as he apprehensively rubbed the back of his neck.

Horton nodded.

"He needs medical attention," the constable decided. "I will have one of the soldiers take you to the nearest field headquarters, there should be doctors there."

"No, please," Horton plead. "He's fine – I just need to get us to the Rissa right away. Please, Constable."

The constable wiped his weary face with his hand and sighed.

"You know, before he passed, Nestor told me you were our best shot at ending all of this," he admitted to Horton as his eyes scanned the cityscape. "Now I don't know why he'd say that or what it means exactly, but that's high praise coming from that old bastard. Why would you want to go to the Rissa?"

"I know how to stop the Vwari for good," Horton replied. "I just need you to trust me."

The constable closed his eyes. "Okay, I give in. If Master Penriding trusted you, then I suppose I do too. Besides, it's not like we have anything to lose at this point. Kid, I will get you as close to the Rissa as I can."

Horton smiled. "Great! Can you get us a Reckoner escort?"

"A Reckoner?" the constable repeated as he looked over the half-submerged Reckoner in the debris beside them. "What's wrong with the one you have?"

Horton's head instantly dropped.

"I think I might have broken it…" he answered sheepishly.

The constable glared at Horton before muttering under his breath a sentence that included "damn kids" and a few words he had never heard before.

"Leftenant!" he then stood up and called out, prompting a soldier that had been examining Isaac's body to jog over.

"Yes, constable?" he responded.

"I am going to escort this young man to the Rissa," the constable explained. "We will need the services of a Reckoner."

The soldier appeared befuddled by the request. "I… I'm sorry sir, but I would advise against—"

"Get me a damn Reckoner, leftenant!" the constable demanded.

The soldier shook his head.

"Latest reports indicate all Reckoners have been deployed to fortify the southeastern boroughs and the area surrounding the Blacksmith manor," the leftenant informed them. "At the current rate the Vwari are pouring in, they are barely holding down the line as it is. I'm sorry constable, but there is no way we can risk any gap in our defenses."

The constable spitefully patted the sweat off his forehead with the sleeve of his uniform, only to stop halfway
between brows to follow the whistling of a cannon shell
with his eyes as it passed somewhere overhead. When his
eyes dropped back down to Horton's level, the old Zeptan
froze for a moment before gently nudging the Illac aside to
get a better look at something hidden against the wreckage
of a partially collapsed building behind him. As he approached the machine buggy covered in a thick layer of
dust and other material, a wry smile crossed his face.

"I think this'll do nicely," he declared as he ran his fingers along its side in search of the door handle. "Assuming
it still runs, of course."

Having discovered the handgrip, the constable swung
the door wide open, deploying a cloud of dust over him.
When he turned back to Horton, the constable found the
Illac with a beleaguered look on his face.

"Um, I'm not sure if you're aware, constable," Horton
said as he warily took a few steps toward the alien contraption, "but I don't know how to drive one of these things on
the street, much less through a warzone."

"Don't be daft, kid," the constable replied. "You have
to be at least thirteen years old to drive a buggy in Zeptus.
I'm going to take you."

"I'm fifteen…" Horton responded diffidently, but the
constable took no notice. He had already hopped inside the
buggy and was trying to start up its engine.

The buggy gurgled as it strained to cough itself to life,
but even after multiple attempts the engine refused to turn
over.

"God damn this thing.... Horton!" the constable called out from behind the dust-covered windshield. "Get your brother in the back seat if you're taking him with you to the Rissa. My father used to know a trick to fix these things in a jiffy, good as new. Just give me a minute or two and I'll have this thing running again – if I can remember his method..."

One of the Zeptan soldiers rushed over to Horton's aid as the Illac struggled to pick up Deforest in order to carry him over to the vehicle. As he and the soldier teetered him over, Horton looked at his brother's face and expected him to pop back into consciousness at any moment, which in a way frightened him. He had no idea how Deforest would react toward him if he were to reawake now.

"Oof!" Horton groaned as he lay his brother down across the back seat of the buggy, and when he did, a small bluish glint caught his eye from the satchel tied securely around Deforest. He had almost completely forgotten about it, but he would need that orb soon enough.

"Horton! Jump in the driver's seat and turn the ignition nob on," the constable called out instructions with the upper half of his body still hidden beneath the hood of the buggy. Wasting no time, Horton swung himself into the driver's seat and began to search for the nob.

"Did you turn it?" the constable hollered.

"Not yet, where is it?" Horton called back.

"It's between the catalytic converter control switch and the seat cooler dial," the constable shouted as Horton looked over the mess of buttons and switches before him.

"Yeah, that's a lot of help," he mumbled to himself.

"Oh, and it's red!" the constable eventually added.

Horton rolled his eyes as he immediately recognized it, partly hidden behind the steering wheel column. He turned it with haste.

"Gah!" the constable shouted in frustration as the engine continued to sputter impotently. He pushed himself out from under the buggy and stared at the contraption while scratching his head and fuming worse than the machine he was attempting to repair. "If I could just remember how my old man fixed these damn things. God help me."

Completely devoid of patience, the constable stepped up to the buggy and kicked the side of the engine bay as hard as he could, at which the buggy let out a deep belch of black smoke before miraculously resurrecting back to life.

The constable sunk his shoulders as he watched the engine roar, raring to go.

"Oh, right, now I remember," the constable remarked along with a long, jaded sigh. "That loathsome drunkard."

Horton pulled himself halfway out the door of the buggy. The constant, dreadful sounds of fighting elsewhere in the city had all but completely phased into the background noise that echoed within his mind over those last few minutes, but now, though, as war rapidly encroached once again upon their borough, it was time to flee.

"Let's go!" Horton shouted as he hopped into the passenger seat next to him to make room for the constable.

In an instant they were away, rumbling off down the street toward the towering pyramid at the city's center. It was not a moment too soon, either, as the Vwari began to exude from between the buildings that lined the road they traveled and toward the squad of soldiers they had just left to fend for themselves. Horton shivered as the Vwari's hair-raising shrieks pierced the air, their initial trickle into this area now a streaming torrent of overwhelming numbers. Surely, he figured, the fate of the doomed Zeptans behind them had been settled.

Still, as Horton glanced back at an unconscious Deforest on the back seat, he knew that with or without his brother, he was doing the right thing.

"Horton," the constable muttered, pulling Horton out from his stupor as the buggy came to an abrupt halt not fifty meters away from the Rissa.

His mind had wandered far away while they drove down that narrow street towards the pyramid, reminiscing to a simpler time back in Illac with his parents and brother. He had hardly taken the time to notice how bizarrely empty the streets were here – and not just of Zeptans, but of Vwari as well. There were signs all around them of where the horde had barreled through, ferociously dragging away everyone in their path to some horrible end that Horton preferred to not think about. Yet now, as he looked ahead of him, he realized why the buggy had stopped. They were no longer alone.

"End of the line," the constable gloomily grumbled.

Countless Vwari swarmed onto the street just ahead of them, blocking their path to the pyramid. With no way for the buggy to get through, the constable twisted his head around to glance out the back window. It was still clear. Without hesitation he threw the transmission into reverse gear, ready to back them up and away from danger, but Horton grabbed the constable's wrist.

"Wait," Horton commanded, his eyes glued to the Vwari threat holding steady some twenty meters away. "Let me go. I think I can get through."

The constable shook his head in bewilderment. "Are you insane? Not happening, kid. They'll kill you if you're not one of their own."

And then to Horton's surprise the constable leaned away from him slightly, all the while glaring at him from beneath his deep brow.

"Not unless you're… you're not one of them, right Horton?"

He stared at the constable for a moment before turning to his unconscious brother on the back seat.

"No, I'm not one of them. But he is."

Before the constable could get in another word, Horton sprung out through the passenger door and heaved open the rear door of the buggy.

"Deforest," Horton said loudly as he gently shook his brother, but to his dismay the boy remained unresponsive. He then froze for a second or two, his sight all the while fixed on his brother, as he contemplated every worst-case scenario in his head as Horton examined him for any sign of life. He uneasily leaned over his brother and turned his head askew, before sighing deeply with relief to the sound of steady breathing.

With no time to waste, Horton grabbed hold of Deforest

and slid him over to the edge of the buggy's back seat. He tossed his brother's arm over his shoulder and wrapped his own arms around Deforest's back and under his knees before gingerly pulling him out with a grunt as he took on his brother's full weight.

The constable, having watched with curious wonderment from the driver's seat at Horton's plan, called out to the Illac. "Are you sure about this?"

Horton paused briefly to look at the Vwari ahead of him and consider the question before turning to respond.

"No," he finally said, blankly, "but I'm not sure about anything anymore."

The constable slowly nodded. "Well, good luck, kid."

Before Horton could respond with even one final glance in the constable's direction, he had already screeched away in reverse, spun the buggy around and taken off the other way down the street. He had left him standing there in the dust with Deforest in his arms, caught on the wrong side of about a hundred baneful Vwari. Horton didn't blame him.

With Deforest clutched tightly in his arms, he slowly began to make his grave march toward the pyramid and the mass of monsters. Almost sadistically, Horton maintained constant eye contact with the horde as he continued onward, anticipating the Vwari to break their line and swiftly dispatch of him at any moment. Each step in their direction seemed to become more difficult than the last, and as the Vwari became increasingly riled up, so did Horton's nerves. They seethed with ire toward their enemy, yet despite his apparent self-immolation, they seemed hesitant to engage him.

With Horton now only a few steps away, the Vwari

grew overtly restless. Their savage and combative shrieks pierced into him like invisible knives beckoning the Illac to stop in his tracks, but still he carried on. He had spent his whole life running away from the darkness and doubts that threatened to mercilessly swallow him up, but on this day he marched unwaveringly toward its perilous veil. He stepped boldly into the sea of Vwari before him, his protective and bright, shining light lying unconscious in his arms and leading the way. To his relief the darkness subdued around him, giving way to his will, and as he carried Deforest laboriously through the horde, the Vwari reluctantly allowed passage.

But only just.

Slowly and deliberately, Horton heaved his brother up the long staircase that led to the entryway of the Rissa's grand chamber. Temporarily pulling his eyes away from his relentless frontward stare, he discovered that the army of Vwari had not only encircled him, but were also moving with him like a shadow. They waited hopefully and diligently, ready to punish Horton in the possible moment he slipped up and released their god from his clutches.

Horton took a deep, fatigued breath. He could feel his arms growing increasingly weary as he approached the final few stairs before the grand chamber's entrance.

"Almost... there. Just need... to hold on," Horton huffed to himself between sluggish steps.

"Can you hear me, Deforest?" Horton called to his brother once again with a definitive hint of urgency. "Please wake up. Just... wake up."

He was inside the pyramid's chamber now with the

portal in sight, but Horton knew he was not going to make it that far carrying his brother. His legs trembled beneath him, ready to give way at any time, and he could tell from the ferocious Vwari barks that they knew it too.

"H-Horton?"

It might have been the surprise of his younger brother's eyes looking up at his or simply the toll on his body finally catching up with him, but when Horton looked down at Deforest's responsive face, his legs and arms gave up. The two of them hit the hard metal floor with a thud, jarring him so fiercely that it effectively jumpstarted his body once more, enabling him to quickly thrust his upper body up off the floor as he recuperated himself before the encroaching horde.

Deforest groaned as he too recovered from the fall. He grabbed the side of his head to inspect the source of his pain, only to find blood seeping from a gash just above his right ear.

"What's going on?" Deforest winced as he noticed the now eerily silent flock of Vwari surrounding them, apparently awaiting a command from their now conscious master.

"What in the gods are you doing here?" he asked as he turned around to look at Horton. "You should be—"

Deforest stopped himself abruptly when he finally caught sight of his brother. The orb had dropped out of the satchel during their fall, and now Horton held it securely in his right hand.

"Call them off, brother," Horton commanded as he eyed the Vwari around them. "Call them off so I can get to the portal and repair this pyramid."

Deforest slowly pulled himself up off the ground before shaking his head.

"You know I can't do that," he said glumly. "Just give me the orb and everything will be okay. I won't let them hurt you."

"No," Horton sternly responded. "Call them off or I'll take you and this orb over to that pedestal myself."

He took two steps toward Deforest before freezing in place. The Vwari around them shrieked momentarily in anticipation as their master raised his balled hand up into the air before pointing it at Horton.

"Don't – don't push me, Horton," Deforest said quietly. "I don't know what's gotten into you, but I won't let you hurt me like you did father. Give me the orb."

Horton lifted his hands up slightly and took a few steps back.

"Look outside," Horton reasoned. "This world is dead because of these damn monsters. They aren't just some plaything – they're ruthless killers. The pyramids were built a long time ago as a weapon to destroy them, and I'm going to make sure they do."

"Hmph. You sound just like your foolish uncle Georg."

Horton reeled around as the congregation of Vwari parted behind him, revealing Asa. The Exetan stared down Horton as he brushed past him to stand beside Deforest.

"It's nothing more than lies, of course," he continued. "Deception. Fabrication. He's clearly been brainwashed by those wretched Zeptans."

Horton watched Asa's eyes glance at Deforest's raised hand, which was still ready to sentence his brother to death.

"What are you waiting for, Deforest? Do it. Quickly. Get it over with," he told him. "Horton betrayed all of us and killed your father. He can't be trusted."

Deforest took a deep breath and squeezed his fist even tighter.

"I'm sorry Deforest," Horton muttered as he slowly shook his head and flopped his hands down to his sides despondently. "I know things changed between us – I know I wasn't the brother to you I should have been. I regret that every single day.

"Still," Horton said softly with a slight chortle beneath his breath, "it sounds stupid, but I would give anything to go spiderfly hunting with you again. Just like we used to back home."

"Damnit child, I'll do it myself!" Asa barked as he stepped in between Deforest and Horton with his arm outstretched, ready to deliver the order to the Vwari.

"No!" Deforest shouted, startling Asa as the boy interrupted him by hastily pulling down his arm.

"No…" he quietly repeated to himself once more as he walked over to his brother. He approached Horton with his arm still out in front of him, except this time instead of a fist, his palm faced outward toward the orb in Horton's hand.

"Father once told me that together, you and I could change the world. It sounded silly at the time, but I think I'm starting to believe it," Deforest said sincerely. "Like it or not, one way or another you're coming back with me."

The two brothers looked at each other for a moment before Horton solemnly relinquished the orb to Deforest in defeat. Despite the threat of Asa and the Vwari looming over him, it was ultimately his unwillingness to go head-to-head with Deforest any longer that made him give in to his younger brother. The boliball was now in his court, so to speak.

Horton watched with a heavy heart as Deforest clutched the orb in his hand and walked over to the portal. He carefully examined the four differently colored buttons lit up upon it, before turning back to Horton.

"I forget, brother – which one of these four buttons takes me back to Exetus?" he inquired.

Horton closed his eyes and sighed.

"Red," he answered truthfully.

Deforest chuckled to himself and then smiled at Horton.

"You're right, you know. We do still need to go spider-fly hunting."

Confused, Horton opened his eyes and stared with intrigue at his brother.

"Fortunately for us, there's always tomorrow," Deforest remarked with a slight smile still clear on his face. His hand hovered threateningly just above the red button, causing Horton's stomach to wrench as he anticipated the imminent coming of what would unquestionably be the final and inescapable blow. His brother, his friends, Zeptus, Earth's future – all lost. But then, utterly unexpectedly, Deforest astounded him. His hand passed over the red button and pressed the yellow button instead. The portal to Zeptus.

Horton and Asa glanced momentarily at one another in shock as a tiny red light had already begun to blink within the orb in Deforest's hand. Instantly aware of what Klas' youngest son had done, Asa seized Deforest's arm and threw him off the slightly raised platform the portal stood upon, sending the orb flying out of his hand and bouncing across the floor. By the time the orb stopped rolling, it lay right at the edge of the Vwari crowd that encircled them. Without missing a beat, Asa leaped over toward the orb to pick it up, but instead found it already spinning in place and slowly levitating into the air. He examined it for a brief time, as if unsure of how to proceed, before carefully reaching up to pluck it out of the air just above his head.

"Argh!" Asa shouted in agony, yanking his hand away from the gyrating orb the moment he touched it. As the Exetan gripped his fresh wound tightly with his other hand, Horton noticed blood gushing from it, forming a pool on the floor below. Asa glared at the two brothers with rage-filled eyes.

"By the gods – kill them!" he commanded with one blood-covered index finger pointed at Horton and the other at Deforest. With only seconds to spare, Horton quickly glanced at the portal and then to his stunned brother on the floor several meters away. There wasn't nearly enough time to get both Deforest and himself out of there.

That was it, he thought. There was no backtracking now. He had done exactly what he'd set out to do, after all. Not only had he found his brother and repaired all the pyramids, but perhaps more importantly, he'd discovered a reason to live – and die – for.

Horton slid onto the floor beside his brother, grabbed hold of him and pulled him in tightly. He shut his eyes and waited for the impending end as the merciless Vwari pack rapidly closed in on them, fearful of what Deforest and he would have to endure. Yet, when the end came it was nothing like he had expected. Every joint in his body became instantly immobile. Numb, even, and it was as though every square inch of his body was being pressed down upon, tighter and tighter, into nothingness.

FOURTEEN

Spiderflies

"I AM SO SORRY about that. If this is a bad time I can send you back."

Horton's skin tingled as he slowly pulled his head out from behind his arms and gazed out. He was lying in the middle of the floor of Armstrong Station Six's command room, looking up at Al with wide eyes.

"Am I dead?" he asked as he surveyed the familiar room. "Is this heaven?"

"Your blood pressure is a little high," Al nonchalantly remarked. "Otherwise you are quite healthy and very much alive."

"Hold on – where's Deforest?" Horton asked as he searched the room with his eyes, growing increasingly nervous.

"Was that the boy who was just with you?" Al asked.

"Yes! That's my brother!" Horton shouted.

"I see, I see," Al mumbled to himself, seemingly lost somewhere within his own mind. "Yes, that makes sense. He is still in subspace – let me bring him through."

Horton blinked, and there was his brother, prone on the floor.

"Deforest!" Horton called out as he ran over to his brother. As he pulled him up into a seated position, Horton noticed his brother's head wound had disappeared. "You're not bleeding any more, are you okay?"

Deforest groaned and nodded. "What in the gods just happened? I feel like I just got squeezed through a rabbit hole."

"A worm hole, to be precise," Al corrected. "While not quite as pleasant as a static portal station, it is an effective transportation method nonetheless. Within limited parameters, automated medical aid and instant subspace travel are just some of this station's many benefits now that it is operating at full capacity once again."

"Well, thanks Al," Horton said as he lifted Deforest and himself up from the floor. "Whether you intended it or not, you just pulled us out of a tight spot back in the Rissa, to say the least. Speaking of which, how are the Zeptans faring against the Vwari?"

"I have been monitoring the Vwari situation at Zepitas to some extent," Al replied. "However, the human colony that surrounds the sub-station is not of any real concern to me."

Horton glared at Al, who seemed to take notice.

"Even so," Al appeased, "the twelve unauthorized Dreadnoughts in deployment seem to be utilizing their new-found perks quite thoroughly now that they are connected to the central core. Active Vwari counts around Zepitas are rapidly declining.

"Which reminds me," Al continued. "All twelve of those persons currently operating Dreadnought armor will need to provide a grade-three certification as soon as possible. In this instance, however, I have temporarily overlooked protocol due to critical circumstances. Speaking of which, I was unable to locate your certification in the database, User, although it is possible that some databanks remain temporarily disconnected."

"Oh, really? That's weird," Horton responded with a half shrug at Deforest.

"So that's it then?" Horton asked, changing the subject. "The Vwari will be no more?"

Al shook his head.

"No. As long as the source remains active they will recoup their numbers, and the amount of infected in the lowest depths of Exetus is—"

"Exetus!" Horton interrupted as he frantically turned to his brother. "Deforest, where were Penriding and Ulises being held inside the Exetus pyramid? We need to get them out of there."

Deforest shifted his eyes away from Horton and to the ground. "I'm sorry, but they never told me anything about what they did with them."

"The non-Users you are referring to are in nominal condition," Al butted in. "In fact, they are on their way here now."

"What do you mean on their way here?" Horton repeated, unsure he had heard Al correctly. However, barely a second later Penriding appeared in the middle of the room, sprawled gracelessly across the floor. He looked worn down and was noticeably thinner than the last time Horton had seen him.

Following him shortly afterward was Ulises, who remarkably appeared out of thin air quite sturdily planted on his feet just a few feet away from Penriding. If anything Ulises looked the same as ever, and as Horton approached him, he noticed the old priest's eyes were closed. Apparently, even the sensation of being sucked through a worm hole was not enough to awake him from his sleep – standing or not.

"Argh! The Rissa be damned, what is going—"

Penriding stopped himself mid-sentence when he noticed where he was and whose company he was in.

"Alright, look – I don't want any more trouble," Penriding stammered as his eyes darted between Horton and Deforest. "I already told those other guys everything I know."

"No, no, it's alright," Horton assured the Zeptan as he loaned him a hand to get him back onto his feet. "We're, uh—"

Horton grimaced slightly as he glanced fleetingly back at Deforest, who seemed to be more than content to distance himself from the situation.

"We made a mistake, Penriding," Horton shamefully explained, "but we're on your side now, I promise."

Penriding looked at Horton with his mouth half-open, either in a state of shock or in preparation to say something, but a moment later he pursed his lips together and smiled.

"I knew I was right," he said as he slowly nodded his

head and chuckled. "I'll admit I thought I had made an error in judgment for a little while there, but nope, I was spot-on as usual."

Horton raised his eyebrow at Penriding, who seemed to be basking in his own bizarrely-placed self-glory.

"Now that I don't have those damn Reckoners breathing down my neck I suppose I should explain," Penriding went on, his previously beaming face now semi-serious. "Before my father died he told the council who you really were, that you were related to the Illacs from Exetus and were potentially dangerous. They were planning on locking you away forever – maybe even kill you – but I maintained that you were an asset to them, an opportunity to destroy the Vwari once and for all. The dire outlook of the war combined with my insatiable charm convinced them to let me take you out and repair the pyramids to save Zeptus – and find your brother too, of course."

"So they used me to get what they wanted," Horton summed it up.

Penriding took a deep breath. "Yes, in essence. Look Horton, I'm sorry I wasn't completely straightforward with you. But hey, look on the bright side – the alternative was rotting in a cell or even worse, a grave."

"Listening to this guy is making *my* brain rot..." Deforest mumbled under his breath to Horton.

"Look," Penriding continued, "the council thought you would betray us the first chance you got – which as it happens you did – but Linden and I knew you weren't like the others. We could see you weren't hardwired the same way and were willing to take that chance."

Horton looked away from Penriding. Surely the Zeptan had not forgotten how close Horton had come to ordering his death at the hands of the Vwari, and it wasn't like he had made much of an effort to save Linden's life.

"No, he is not," Ulises croaked. The priest had been stood still there quietly the whole time, listening to the conversation. "Horton did not give in to the temptation of power like his father, Klas, did."

Ulises' eyes slowly turned to Deforest, who had practically hidden himself from Ulises' view behind his brother.

"Nor did Deforest, I am relieved to say."

Horton turned around to look at Deforest, whose eyes remained fixed to the floor beside his feet. He had noticed his brother had been unusually subdued since Al rescued them from Asa and the Vwari back in Zeptus.

"Alright so let's get back up to speed," Penriding said as he rubbed his hands together in anticipation. "I'm guessing all the pyramids are repaired and operational now? Get this thing running already, Al."

"You are correct," Al confirmed. "The User was successful in bringing all four sub-stations back online and re-connecting them to the primary station here on the moon."

"Great, start them up!" Penriding exclaimed, but quickly reconsidered his enthusiasm. "Actually now that I think about it, did we ever find out what they do exactly?"

"Theoretically, yes, the Sunbound Initiative is ready for reactivation," Al replied after an uncharacteristic pause. "However, I have not yet deciphered the tremendous amount of data I have acquired access to once again. To answer your question, non-User: No, it is not entirely clear yet as to what the primary function is. Additionally, it would be unwise to reengage the program without first discovering and analyzing the cause of its previous termination. I apologize, you will have to wait."

Horton sighed. "How long of a wait are we talking about?"

"I estimate the program will be ready to engage in 41 hours and 34 minutes, with a discrepancy of six minutes," Al responded matter-of-factly. "A User will be required to reinitiate the program. You may return later if you wish."

"Oh, actually that's not too bad," Horton said with a shrug.

"And the perfect excuse for you and your brother to return home to Illac in the meantime," Ulises suggested with a smile as he put his arm around Deforest. "What do you say, Horton?"

Horton slowly nodded his head in agreement, but his thoughts seemed to be placed elsewhere.

"Yes, good idea," Horton finally said. "Mother will be surprised to say the least when she finds out Deforest is still alive."

"And you too, Horton," Ulises added. "She will be very happy to see both her sons again."

"She will," Horton smiled, "but not yet. I have some things to take care of back in Zeptus, plus I need to fill Penriding in on everything that has happened. I'll return to Illac in a few days."

"Very well then," Al interjected before striding over to the doorway at the end of the room and turning back to the group. "Please follow me to the portal chamber."

As they followed Al side-by-side through the station's now bright and illuminated corridors, Horton couldn't help but glance at Deforest every few seconds. He could see on his brother's face that he was bothered by something, and he had a feeling it had to do with his sudden change of heart back at the Rissa. Horton wanted terribly to talk to him about it all, but wasn't sure his brother would want him to bring up the subject in front of the others. For now he'd leave it up to Deforest to speak out about it, even if that meant not finding out for a few more days because of their plans to temporarily go separate ways.

"Here we are," Al announced, snapping Horton away from his thoughts. The hologram had led them into the small chamber that held the portal. "The green button will transport you to Ilakium and the yellow to Zepitas."

"Thank you," Ulises said with a smile as he led the group past Al toward the portal. Horton walked in behind them, ready to return to Zeptus City with Penriding, but found himself frozen in place as Deforest's hand tugged on his arm from beside him, pulling him away from the others.

"What's wrong?" Horton asked his brother. There was no doubt that his decision to side against the Exetans was on his mind, and he needed to get it off his chest before they departed.

"I…" Deforest began, but seemed to struggle to find the right words. His eyes darted across the floor, looking for anything to draw them away from meeting Horton's.

"Look, you don't need to say anything," Horton consoled him. "A lot has happened – a lot of bad things that can never be taken back – but don't blame yourself. It was father that—"

"Please don't talk about father," Deforest interrupted. Horton could see his eyes had begun to glisten with tears. "You never forgave him for what he did – and maybe you were right, but – I don't know. It's just…"

Deforest shot a glance up at Horton for the first time, but just as quickly dropped his head again.

"I didn't want to end up like you, Horton."

Horton took a half step backward. He couldn't believe what he was hearing. This was the same brother that had grown up practically idolizing him, walking in his shadow, hanging off his coattails. And yet as he stood there, trying to comprehend what Deforest had just told him, he realized he couldn't possibly refute it. He was right.

"Spiderflies," Horton whispered, to which Deforest lifted his head, looked him right in the eye and nodded.

"I was so angry at the world that I closed myself off to everyone that cared about me," Horton bit down on his lip as he went on. "Especially you, and I almost dragged you down with me."

"But you didn't," Deforest replied. "You changed, Horton. I almost didn't believe it, but you changed. The Exetans warned me – told me you were a liar, conditioned by the Zeptans to sabotage us. Yet when I read your letter over and over, I didn't see that… It was like the old Horton was back again, and risking everything to find me when all signs screamed that I was a lost cause."

Horton noticed his brother appeared to be getting increasingly tense as he spoke.

"I needed to know once and for all," Deforest continued, now staring Horton right in the face, "so I gave you the opportunity to fulfill the mission you'd been speaking of. When I asked you how to return to Exetus through the portal, you could have so simply lied to me. I had the orb in hand – all I'd have to do was push the yellow button and the pyramid would be repaired... but you didn't. That's when I knew everything you had said was the truth... that you weren't what they said you were. It pains me so much, Horton... It wasn't you that deserted me, brother, I had deserted you."

Horton grabbed his brother and pulled him in tightly, unable to bear listening to Deforest talk that way any longer. As his brother sobbed in his arms, Horton looked around the room to find Ulises, Penriding and Al staring at them. They had heard everything that had been said.

Slowly, Ulises made his way over to Deforest and put his hand on his shoulder.

"It is time to go home," he said gently, to which Deforest stepped away from Horton and pulled himself back together. Horton took a deep breath and gave his brother the best smile he could muster.

"I'll see you soon," Horton assured him.

Deforest replied with a nod and a half-smile, then quickly turned away and walked over toward the portal.

"Goodbye then. See you in a few days," Ulises said cheerfully. "Oh, and Horton?"

"Yes?" Horton responded.

"We have some things to discuss when I see you next, but until then—"

Ba-beep! Beep!

And just like that, they were gone.

Horton stared quietly at the empty space that Deforest and Ulises' frames had just filled in the chamber, and as he did he felt a wave of relief flow through him. Deforest was going home. He was safe.

"I still think something's not right about that old priest," Penriding remarked, breaking the silence.

Horton rolled his eyes and sighed. "Let's just get back to Zeptus already. I'm sure they need assistance after that battle."

Penriding's eyes shot open wide. "Battle? What battle?"

"Oh," Horton replied. He had forgotten that Penriding had been out of the loop while imprisoned in the Exetus pyramid.

Horton extended his hand out to Penriding. "It's probably best if you see for yourself."

"Probably," Penriding said angrily as he grabbed onto it.

Ba-beep! Bong!

"Hostiles!"

Two Reckoners slung their giant swords off their backs and pointed them at the comparatively minuscule Horton and Penriding, who practically flew off their feet and onto the hard floor of the Rissa's grand chamber in shock. With the benefit of power from the newly repaired central core, the Reckoners' weapons crackled audibly and emitted a bright blue, untamed energy that seemed rearing to be unleashed on its foes.

"Stand down, damnit!" a familiar voice called out from

somewhere beyond the two hulks. "Put your weapons away!"

Horton smiled with relief as Constable Keen squeezed between the two Reckoners, all the while muttering expletives under his breath.

"Ah, Horton!" he exclaimed with a sudden change of demeanor. "I'm afraid I have to admit that I feared for the worst when we reclaimed the Rissa and you were nowhere to be found young man, but here you are – and with Master Penriding to boot!"

"What in the Rissa is going on?" Penriding demanded as he jumped back up to his feet, choosing to skip the pleasantries. "What's all this about a battle?"

"Not to worry, Penriding, everything is well under control now," the constable affirmed. "The Exetans and their Vwari puppets launched a blindside assault on the city from within – through this very portal, in fact."

Penriding looked about the chamber. All around them weary Zeptan soldiers pulled their fallen comrades out from amongst the masses of slain Vwari that littered the room. Slowly and methodically, he stepped his way toward the entryway. Outside, big plumes of smoke streamed from the cityscape and into the calm morning sky.

However, it was Penriding's own home, the Blacksmith manor, which had garnered his attention. From the high-reaching peak of the manor ascended a thick, undeviating ray of blue light, so high into the sky that it wasn't apparent how far its reach extended.

"We can't yet explain it – the manor lit up like some sort of magical torch not long after Horton made his way back to the Rissa with his brother," Constable Keen explained, having joined Penriding just outside the Rissa with Horton. "It was then that the Reckoners changed. They have always been formidable opponents to the Vwari, but it's as if they all at once abruptly reached the apogee of their potential. They butchered those demons like bullpigs sent to slaughter. Whatever you did, Horton, it changed the tide of this war. I do not believe the Vwari pose a threat to us any longer."

Horton veered away from the conversation while Penriding and the constable continued to speak to one another. As he looked at the destruction around them, the bodies of fallen Vwari everywhere, he wondered if this was it – if this was the purpose of the pyramids, to empower the Dreadnought armor the Reckoners wore and turn them into the ultimate weapon to destroy the Vwari.

"No. It doesn't make sense," Horton muttered to himself. "Al said the pyramids are not yet fully operational. He asked me to go back and restart them. Why would I need to do that? There must be more to it than just the Reckoners."

"Horton?"

Horton turned around to find the constable and Penriding looking at him. He hadn't noticed them call over to him a few times.

"Are you alright, Horton?" the constable asked. "You seem troubled with something."

"Huh? Oh… no, it's nothing," Horton replied. "I'm just tired."

The constable nodded his head in understanding. "Ah

yes – Master Blacksmith and I were just speaking about housing arrangements. As I had just explained, the Blacksmith manor is off-limits to civilians – at least until we figure out what is going on."

"My family owns a guest house not far from the manor," Penriding added. "It's not quite as impressive, but we can stay there for a few days. That particular borough escaped the battle mostly unscathed, apparently."

"Great," Horton said as he gave Penriding and the constable a half-hearted smile.

For Horton the next few days were a blur. He had been left to his own devices for the most part – under the not-so-secret watchful eye of the Zeptan military – since Penriding disappeared for much of each day to deal with troubled investors and other problems tied to the merchant union that had suddenly fallen into his lap. Horton didn't blame him for it though – he even knew all too well that Penriding despised it all, but it was his duty to the Blacksmith name and the Zeptan people that the union stayed intact and flourished.

The reason Horton had decided to return to Zeptus City was, however, to discover the fate of Ananke before he finally went back home to Illac. It had been weeks since the young wasteman had been captured for what would have been viewed as Exetan-sympathetic attacks upon Zeptus, and he felt it was his duty to make sure Penriding threw his weight around in order to find out what happened to him. All of that was, of course, assuming he hadn't already been executed.

It was ultimately not until the day before Horton planned to return to Al on the Armstrong Six moon station that he had the proper chance to ask Penriding about him. As luck would have it, the Zeptan had been summoned to meet with the city's high council that evening regarding the recent tragic events, so Penriding promised to do what he could.

During the time Penriding met with the high council, Horton decided to go for a walk to settle his nerves. Since his return to Zeptus, Horton had spent a lot of time thinking about everything that had taken place over those last few weeks, and there were still many unanswered questions that kept his mind almost constantly on edge. To make matters worse, he had been dealing with ongoing headaches over the last few days.

"This area is off limits," a voice suddenly boomed, startling Horton from his deep thoughts. He had practically wandered face-first into the outstretched palm of a city guard while aimlessly walking through the city streets. Right behind the guard stood a newly erected barrier as high as the rooftops, running from one side of the street to the other and completely blocking access between the different city boroughs.

Horton looked around. He had hardly noticed the unusually high number of civilians in the streets, especially considering the recent events. In fact, from his current vantage, if it wasn't for the heavy smell of smoke in the air, one would be hard-pressed to believe the city had been under heavy siege only a few days earlier. It wasn't until that moment that Horton thought to question the Zeptan military's defensive tactics, either. It seemed rational that they would focus their efforts to protect the southeastern borough – it was the wealthiest part of the city and home to the most influential Zeptans, including members of the high council, but it made no sense to continue to do so now that the fighting had ended.

"Nobody is allowed through?" Horton redundantly asked the guard.

"No," the hard-nosed guard replied bluntly, not bothering to look down at him.

"Why not?" Horton pestered, but he received no answer. The guard continued to stare straight ahead, right over the Illac's head.

Horton huffed under his breath and walked away. In the end he didn't go on much farther before deciding to head back to the house where he and Penriding were staying. The sun had only just disappeared below the horizon by the time he got back, and was mildly concerned to find Penriding had not yet returned from his meeting with the council.

Exhausted, Horton decided to turn in for the night, but he only tossed and turned in his bed, unable to sleep. He thought about the next morning as he lay awake, staring up at the ceiling. Tomorrow, on his command, the pyramids would be restarted and their secrets hopefully revealed. It seemed too surreal to be true.

Suddenly the sound of footsteps creaked from down the hallway, prompting Horton to sit up in bed and listen. Penriding was home.

Hurriedly, Horton jumped out of bed, fumbled his way through the darkness toward the door and swung it open, just as Penriding passed by.

"Oh, it's you," Penriding noted lethargically. He looked more exhausted than Horton did.

Horton stood in the doorway for a second, expecting Penriding to spill the beans on what had happened, but instead the Zeptan teetered over to the wall, leaned up against it and closed his eyes.

"Well?" Horton pressed.

Penriding slowly sighed before wearily reopening his eyes.

"The council has approved our return through the portal tomorrow," Penriding told him. "So be sure to cancel any treasonous diversions you had planned."

"That's not funny," Horton shot at Penriding as the Zeptan smiled to himself. "What happened to Ananke?"

"Like I told you originally, he'll be fine," Penriding replied as he pushed himself away from the wall and slowly began to make his way back down the hallway. "Apparently the head of the Reckoner project unexpectedly took some bizarre interest in the kid and requested he be sent to him for special training. Ananke was sent to the Diamond Phoenix tribe – or whatever it is – and was more than happy to go."

"Diamond Eagle," Horton corrected him.

"Yeah, I think that's it," Penriding said as he opened the door to his room on the other side of the hallway. He began to step inside, but stopped half way to turn back to the Illac. "Oh, and Horton?"

"Yeah?" Horton replied.

Penriding stared at him for a good moment or two before speaking, as though thinking twice about what he was about to say.

"Back inside the pyramid at Exetus, when your father asked you to execute me... you weren't going to do it, right?"

Horton froze, even though he knew he shouldn't have. It was a simple answer, but he hadn't anticipated this at all. Seconds passed as Horton stared idly back at Penriding.

"No..." Horton eventually managed to say. He opened his mouth again awkwardly, as if he had something to add, but nothing else came to him.

"Okay," Penriding said with a very quick smile. "Good night."

The Zeptan then disappeared into his room, and the moment he did, Horton ducked back inside his own and angrily threw himself down onto his bed.

"What in the gods is wrong with you?" Horton whispered with his head in his pillow, infuriated with himself.

As he lay there, tossing and turning in bed, Penriding's question chimed over and over again in his head like a ringing bell. As much as he dreaded admitting it to himself, he knew exactly what he would have done that day in Exetus. If it weren't for Ulises' intervention, he would have ordered the Vwari to kill Penriding.

Horton's head pounded with pain as the dark thoughts his father had cultivated resurfaced in his mind.

"Damnit. At least Ananke is alright," he reminded himself.

FIFTEEN

The Beacon

PENRIDING TURNED BACK to Horton as he stepped half-way into the buggy that would take them to the Rissa. "Excited to be going home again, Horton?"

Horton felt the exterior of his satchel for the outline of the stone idol he had stashed away, even though he had already double-checked to make sure it had not been forgotten. He knew some questions were bound to be raised, but that statue meant his return to Illac would be welcomed.

"Yeah," he replied with a smile. "Yeah I am."

They jostled in silence as the buggy carried them over stony roads toward the magnificent pyramid at the city center. Horton had been concerned that things would have been a little weird between Penriding and him after their conversation the night before, but to his surprise the Zeptan had seemed his usual self all day. Not that he was complaining, but he found it hard to believe that Penriding would have taken Horton for his word. Still, regardless of what Penriding thought, Horton hoped it was a subject that would never again see the light of day.

It wasn't more than a few minutes later that they reached the edge of the borough's barrier. There they were greeted by a squad of city guards, diligently standing watch over a checkpoint between the southeast section of the city and the road that led to the Rissa.

"Do you know why they have blocked off this part of the city?" Horton asked Penriding as he stuck his head out of the buggy's small side-window to get a better look. Impeding their path up ahead were two Reckoners with their backs to the buggy, faced outward toward the rest of the city and watching intently.

"The Zeptan High Council is a chary lot," Penriding said with a slight tone of aversion. "The old stories say the Vwari are demons, spawn of Hell. They tell of people being bitten by Vwari, falling terribly ill and then dying. Then, shortly after being buried, they come back to life as a flesh-hungry Vwari themselves."

Horton looked at Penriding with wide eyes.

"I don't think that's true..." Horton said unsurely.

Penriding burst out with laughter and shrugged his shoulders. "Hey, you're the one who spent all that time with those monsters. You tell me."

He was right, Horton had spent some time with the Vwari, but he had never learned much about where they came from. Besides the drawings on the wall of the circular room inside the Exetus pyramid, there wasn't much documentation of their history.

"Maybe Al knows," he muttered to himself.

"What was that?" Penriding asked. Horton hadn't thought he would hear him.

"I said maybe Al knows more about the Vwari," Horton elaborated.

Penriding nodded. "Yeah. I have a feeling he does."

Constable Keen and a Reckoner met Horton and Penriding at the base of the long stairway that led to the Rissa's entrance. They would have to escort them all the way up to the portal since it had been heavily fortified with makeshift barricades following the Vwari invasion.

"I hear you will be returning home to Illac after this," the constable said to Horton once they reached the portal. Horton could have sworn he detected the slightest hint of sadness in his voice.

"That's right," Horton affirmed, "but I'm sure I'll be back, one day."

The constable smiled, and then to Horton's surprise, he turned and shook his hand.

"You know, for a dumb kid you aren't as stupid as you look," he reluctantly pronounced.

"Uh, thanks – I think," Horton replied as he shifted his eyes to Penriding, who looked as confused as he was.

"So, you ready to go?" the Illac asked Penriding as he offered his hand to him.

"I've waited my whole life for—"

Penriding's voice choked to an abrupt pause as Horton and he locked eyes. Neither of them could speak nor move. Horton could feel every square inch of his body being squeezed, tighter and tighter, and he knew that Penriding was experiencing the same sensation.

"God damnit, Al!" Penriding screamed at the artificial computer program, which didn't seem to understand what it had done wrong.

"We were on our way over here!" Penriding continued to rave. "Literally five seconds – if you had waited five more seconds we would have been here on our own. I cannot put into words how unpleasant it is to be transported that way. For the love of Rissa, don't do that again!"

"I am sorry," Al briefly replied in a disinterested tone before turning to Horton. "User, are you ready to reinitiate the program?"

Having taken a knee to regain his breath, Horton looked up toward Al through his brow, but instead spotted a face out of the corner of his eye that he hadn't expected to see. Standing on the other side of the room by himself was none other than his old friend, Ulises.

"Yeah…" Horton answered Al as he looked on at the priest with confusion. "Ulises? What are you doing here?"

Ulises smiled and took a few steps toward him. "I arrived just before you two did. I am here only to observe."

"How's Deforest? Did he get home okay?" Horton barraged Ulises with questions. "Was mother happy to see him?"

"Yes my child, do not worry," Ulises continued to smile. "Everything is well. Please, we should begin."

"Oh, well – okay then," Horton agreed before turning to Al. "So what am I supposed to do?"

Getting right to business, the hologram approached

Horton and raised his hand up with the palm faced outward toward the Illac, who simply stared curiously at Al's proposition. Then, after just a moment of guarded hesitation, Horton followed suit and pressed his own hand onto Al's.

"User, to reinitialize the Sunbound Initiative program, please issue the following command," Al instructed. "Initialize program Sunbound Initiative, authorization bravo, charlie, echelon, four, zero, three."

Horton took a deep breath and began to repeat.

"Initialize program... Sunbound Initiative... authorization... bravo, charlie..."

In the middle of reciting the order, Horton quickly shifted his eyes to Ulises, who was watching him intently with his arms crossed. He then peered over in the other direction at Penriding who, judging by the rate he was chewing through his fingernails, was as frightened as he was excited.

"Echelon, four..." Horton looked back at Al.

"Wait."

Horton abruptly disconnected his hand from Al's and took a step back.

"Hold on," Horton said, shaking his head. "I'm sorry, but this isn't right. We don't even know what the pyramids will do yet."

"My boy, I am afraid we do not have time for this," Ulises reasoned.

"I have full access to all information on database," Al gladly divulged despite Ulises' remarks, to Horton's relief. "Please issue a query, User."

Horton took another deep breath and sighed. He wasn't entirely sure where to begin.

"Al…" Horton began as he considered his first question. "What is the purpose of the pyramids – I mean sub-stations – on the Earth and Moon."

"The primary function of Armstrong Station Six and the four sub-stations on Earth is to carry out the operation of the Sunbound Initiative," Al said with a smile.

Horton drooped his shoulders. This might not be as easy as he had thought.

"Al…" Horton sighed again. "What is the Sunbound Initiative?"

"The Sunbound Initiative is a joint-operation carried out by the remaining members of the United Nations intergovernmental group as a last-ditch effort to eradicate the population of contaminated humans and cleanse the planet for the use of future generations."

"Contaminated?" Horton repeated. "What do you mean by contaminated humans?"

"The source of contamination is currently unknown," Al happily answered. "Known symptoms of contamination include headaches, disorientation, seizures, nausea, skin loss or discoloration and shortness of breath. Symptoms of contamination are consistently followed with afflicted individual entering comatose. U.N. law mandates all comatose individuals be euthanized immediately."

"And if they're not?" Penriding spoke up.

"Contaminated persons reanimated from comatose are considered extremely dangerous," Al continued as if reading a prepared spiel word-for-word. "Any sightings or knowledge of a contaminated person is required by law to be reported to your camp's directing officer."

"By Rissa, he's talking about the Vwari, you know," Penriding decreed as he turned to face Horton. "Ask Al how the pyramids will kill them."

Horton nodded. He had no reason to believe that wiping the Vwari off the face of the Earth was a bad thing, but trusting that these massive and ancient monuments scattered throughout the planet would accomplish the feat without any side effects could also spell their own peril.

"Al, how does the Sunbound Initiative eradicate the Vwari?"

Horton, Penriding and Ulises watched Al with great anticipation as they awaited his response, but he would do nothing to ease their concerns. Instead, the holographic simulation just stood there for a moment, his lips tightly sealed.

"Access to requested information is denied," Al finally broke his silence a few seconds later, to their dismay. "Senior User clearance required."

"Are you kidding me? Senior User?" Penriding echoed in disbelief. "Aren't you the Senior User, Horton?"

"No, I'm not," Horton corrected him, shaking his head.

"Georg is the Senior User," Ulises chimed in. "He is, however, unavailable."

Ulises strode over to Horton and put his hand on his shoulder. "Just start the program, Horton. Do not worry about things you cannot control. In due time all of your questions will be answered, I promise."

Promptly, Al raised his hand to create a connection with

Horton once again. Horton glanced back at Ulises, who nodded in reaffirmation. Slowly, Horton raised his hand up to Al's and pressed against it.

"Remember the order, Horton," Ulises said. "Initialize program Sunbound Initiative, authorization bravo, charlie, echelon, four, zero, three."

Horton cleared his throat and began.

"Initialize program Sunbound Initiative, authorization bravo, charlie, echelon, four… zero…"

He took a deep breath. This was it.

"Three."

Horton stepped away from Al as all the control panels and monitors in the command room sporadically flickered to life one by one. Seizing the opportunity, Penriding jumped excitedly between command stations as quickly as he could, trying to decipher any tidbit of information from what looked like a scrambled mess of shapes and characters streaming across each of the monitors. Horton, however, had all the while remained at a standstill. A high-frequency sound had pierced his ear since the moment he restarted the Sunbound program, and it was gradually growing in strength.

"What is that noise?" Horton groaned as he clutched his ears in an attempt to block the sound out. He looked at the others in desperation, but they seemed to be completely unaffected by what afflicted him.

"Damnit! Do you not hear it?"

"What are you talking about?" Penriding asked him, entirely confounded by the way Horton was acting.

"That sound… it's—" Horton gasped as he dropped to

his knees. The sound had rapidly become unbearable. "Argh!"

"Horton…" Ulises' gentle voice seemed to drown out the agonizing whine momentarily, but it too was quickly overcome. *"Horton… try to relax…"*

A middle-aged man flops down into a seat in front of a viewing screen. He sits forward, pushes a button on the screen, then leans back in his seat with his eyes fixed on the empty ceiling above.

"This is the log of Commander Stephen Johnson, commanding officer of the Sunbound Initiative… and what's left of the last true humans on Earth. The date is April 7th – excuse me – April 8th, 2144. Tomorrow will mark the 46th anniversary of mankind's mass exodus into the unknown of subspace. I will surely be dead before I see its return home.

I went for another walk today outside Tiberonus Station. The sun has finally begun to scrape the horizon in this corner of the world, providing us with a perpetual sunrise for the next few months. Walking along the calm beaches here, so far away from the incredible destruction this operation has wrought, is unusually calming. I'm reminded of the way I used to see the sun in my youth. Warm, beautiful, peaceful. I've thought about it every day. It perturbs me to think all of this – the oceans, the trees, the animals, our last bastion of paradise – will soon be boiled to nothingness. 'A fresh, clean slate for humanity,' they always said.

You know, I wish my wife and children could see this, instead of the inside of a tin can for the rest of their lives. Sometimes I wish I wasn't one of the few with immunity to that damn virus. Damnit Stephen, pull your act together. Log note – delete the last two sentences.

It is an honor and a blessing to be one of the few chosen to stay behind and maintain the sub-stations for the preservation of Earth and mankind. I only wish—"

"Sir!"

A young woman storms into the room. She seems shaken.

"What is it, lieutenant?"

"Coolant bays F through H are failing at Ilakium Station, sir," the lieutenant stammered. "There was an explosion – it ripped through part of the station's hull."

The commander sat up in his seat.

"Then repair it. Quickly!" he fired. "Those stations aren't there as giant freezers for the wastes, for god's sake. We can't afford to fall behind schedule!"

"Sir, that's the thing..." The lieutenant gulped as she tried to find her voice. "Just a few moments after the explosion, a... a proximity alert was triggered."

The commander froze.

"What the hell do you mean a proximity warning?" he said. "That sector was fried down to dust decades ago, there's no way anything outside the station survived."

"I'm sorry sir, the sensors said—"

The commander erupted from his chair and pushed past her on his way to the command center just through the next door.

"Al!" the commander yelled out to the room, but despite

being packed to the brim with people scurrying about with their duties, none of them so much as even looked in his direction.

Then suddenly, a man in white clothing appeared right before him. He had seen him countless times before, but the commander had never grown accustomed to seeing his own likeness staring back at him. It didn't help any that Al portrayed him in such a youthful, invigorated manner either, but the commander wanted it that way. It reminded him of the promise he made all that time ago. Long before he had 46 years to rethink things.

"Senior User..." Al addressed him.

"Al, what's the situation at Ilakium?" the commander demanded.

Al replied with what was almost a grave look. "I am sorry to report the outlook is dire, commander. Contaminated humans have overrun decks 21 through 26 of the sub-station. I coordinated evacuation procedures to secondary life decks 1A and 1B, but there are massive system failures throughout the station – I am unable to effectively repel the intruders."

The commander stood motionless, his mouth half open in shock.

"User, it is my recommendation that operation of the Sunbound Initiative be suspended," Al added.

"Is my family safe?" the commander quietly questioned Al.

"Your daughters were evacuated to the secondary life decks," Al replied. "Unfortunately, Valerie is unaccounted for. It is likely she was contaminated."

The commander pressed up against the wall to support himself as his legs began to buckle. He leaned his head back against it and closed his eyes.

"Sir, it would take months to halt Earth's rotation once again if we shut down. It's still not too late to mobilize a team of Dreadnoughts," *the lieutenant suggested.*

"No!" *the commander shouted as he pushed himself up off the wall.* "I can't—"

He instantly paused when he looked up to find all the eyes in the room had turned upon him.

"We can't risk it," *he said, trying to calm himself.* "If we deploy the Dreadnoughts, they will slaughter every living thing in that station – my wife included."

"Senior User, again I recommend operation of the Sunbound Initiative be suspended," *Al repeated sternly.* "All sub-stations must be at full operational capacity to effectively control optimal planetary rotation. An uneven axis would create undesirable results."

Having finally come to grips with the bleak reality of the situation, the commander stepped up in front of Al and raised his right hand, to which Al did the same. He stared grievously at his own reflection within Al's eyes as he gave the order.

"Suspend operation Sunbound Initiative authorization echo, delta, charlie, tango, six, three, four, zero, zero."

"All operation has been suspended," *Al confirmed.* "Additionally, full lockdown routines are in effect at all sub-stations."

Commander Johnson turned and stared blankly out at the command center. Around him the remnants of humanity on Earth were in a frantic struggle to figure out what went wrong and how they could fix it. As the commander's eyes wandered to a small window on one end of the room, he saw the sun. Its rays shimmered elegantly over Earth's last ocean.

"I can't do this," he whispered under his breath.

The commander looked to his left. Al had remained standing beside him.

"Al," he said quietly beneath the shouts and bustling of people around him.

"Yes, User?" Al replied.

The commander considered and reconsidered his next words carefully, but images of his wife and children consumed his mind. He couldn't lose her.

"Access my personal files," he told Al. "Locate a program titled 'Odyssey' and transfer all available power to its mobile emitter. Route backup power to primary systems only."

"User?" Al queried him. "That program has not been sanctioned for deployment. It is imperative we maintain regulation for the return of—"

"I don't care, Al!" the commander boomed. "Is it ready?"

Al took a step away from his superior.

"Yes," he said after a short, uncharacteristic pause.

"Initialize it," the commander ordered.

Slowly and deliberately, Al reached into his chest and from within his own artificial mass, pulled out a bright, glowing orange cube. He extended the cube out at arm's length away from his body, then retracted his hand from beneath it, leaving it floating in midair. Less than a blink *of an eye later, a man appeared in place of the cube. Like Al, the man was dressed entirely in white and mirrored the commander in appearance. Yet unlike Al, he appeared old, grey and hardened by 46 long years.*

Horton squirmed. He knew that face. He had to break free.

"Stephen..." The man said as his eyes shifted around the room.

"You know what to do," the commander told him. "Do whatever it takes. My family must survive."

"And of the beacon?" the man asked.

"Disable it," the commander decided after a short pause.

"User, if the beacon is disabled the humans that fled will be unable to return to Earth through subspace," Al pointed out.

"Mankind forsook and deserted us and its planet," the commander sneered. "They can be damned for all I care. We are the survivors. This is our world now."

Horton struggled about within his own mind. He had to wake up. He had to warn the others.

"I will do as you say, Stephen," the man replied.

"Looks like he is coming to. Horton? Can you hear me?"

Horton shot his eyes open. He was lying on the floor of the space station's command room with Penriding and Ulises looking down on him.

"You alright?" Penriding asked as he leaned the Illac forward and up off the floor. "You freaked me out for a second there."

Horton's head was throbbing. As he rubbed his eyes, he felt a familiar hand on his shoulder.

"Don't touch me," Horton scoffed as he shoved Ulises' hand away before standing up. "I know you're no more human than Al is."

Ulises closed his eyes and took a deep breath.

"I needed you to see that so you would understand," Ulises told Horton.

"Understand what?" Horton fired back. "That you've been lying to everyone all this time?"

"Whoa, Horton – calm down," Penriding butted in, but Horton pushed him away too.

"Commander Johnson's wife was contaminated, wasn't she?" Horton went on. "She turned into a Vwari, so you kept them alive – all of them – for all these years."

"What are you talking about?" Penriding asked, completely confused.

"You are right, I did keep the infected alive for many years," Ulises admitted. "Although they were not the Vwari as you know them today. Sure, they were always deranged and extremely unstable, but being shut away for that long..."

Ulises' gaze seemed to gloss over as he spoke, as if he was peering back into a past he would rather forget.

"Almost two thousand years, in fact," Ulises said softly before quickly turning his head toward Horton. "I did only what I was programmed to do, Horton. I helped build the village of Illac so that Stephen's descendants would lead a safe, peaceful life. Things were good in Illac. They were military families. Strong, willful and resourceful – they knew how to survive.

"But unfortunately, maintaining the Vwari race was not quite as simple. I tried to contain them as far from Illac as possible – Exetus Station – however, their hunger was incredible and over time could only be satiated by meat, something that was not exactly in abundance at the time. Regrettably, I was forced to borrow the flesh of young Illac men in order to clone it. When the sample began to degrade after a few years, I acquired a fresh one."

"Good god…" Penriding blurted, his mouth and eyes wide open in shock.

Horton glared at Ulises, utterly disgusted. "You're telling me that after all this time our people's greatest tradition, the initiation to adulthood, was nothing more than a sick cannibalistic ruse to collect food for the Vwari?"

Ulises slowly nodded his head. "It was flawless, too. Up until Georg discovered the portal to Exetus, that is."

"And you tried to stop him, didn't you?" Horton pushed.

"No, not at first," Ulises responded. "To my amazement the Vwari took to him as though he were their master or god, though it is not unusual, considering. The Vwari had lived secluded in the dark depths of Exetus for almost two thousand years. The only figure they had ever known was me, and I was their lifeline. When I found that they protected him and served his every whim, I let it be. Why? I do not know. Perhaps because it was something different."

"But it was you who eventually turned Klas against his own brother," Horton pointed out. "Georg had met Al – which means he knew he had to repair the pyramids and you couldn't allow that."

"You are correct," Ulises nodded. "However I never

meant for events to transpire in the way they did. It was Georg who reopened the outside world to the Vwari and recruited the Illacs who failed the initiation to his own cause. Subsequently the Vwari found a new food source in the far-reaching merchants that traversed the wastes near Exetus, but when Georg got the Zeptans involved in repairing the stations as well I panicked. My due diligence provided me with the means to take matters into my own hands, but ultimately to my own detriment, as it was then that things got a bit... sloppy."

"That doesn't add up," Penriding noted. "You were the one who advocated we repair the pyramids all along."

Ulises smiled. "I did not lie when I said I am an old man. After a couple millennia, my time is almost up. I have seen generations of Stephen's descendants live and die, with each generation bearing witness new facets of the human spirit. However, it was young Horton who taught me something that I had never before been able to truly grasp. My boy, you are a survivor, as is the human race. I have come to realize that even after I cease to exist, Stephen's wishes will continue to carry on for countless generations to come.

"And you, my dear Penriding, liberated me from my enslavement. You taught me how to break free of expectations and restrictions. I handed you everything you could have ever asked for, and yet you would have thrown it all away in an instant for just a glimpse at the truth."

Penriding looked at Ulises incredulously. "What is that supposed to mean? By Rissa, you sound just like my father used to—"

Horton looked at Penriding curiously, as the Zeptan

suddenly appeared as though he was about to throw up mid-sentence. When he turned back to Ulises, he realized why.

"Father?" Penriding silently mouthed. Incredibly, now standing in Ulises' place was Nestor Blacksmith.

"How.... Were you...?" he then asked, still barely able to put two words together out of shock.

"Stephen Penriding Johnson," Nestor replied. "The commander's middle name seemed a more than appropriate choice for my only son in two thousand years."

"Stop it. As the Rissa crumbles, there's no way. That's not even remotely possible," Penriding remarked as he shook his head in disbelief. He stared at Nestor deeply for a moment, as if expecting to blink and watch his father disappear again.

"You died," Penriding reminded him. "They told me the Vwari killed you."

"I did what needed to be done to break you free," Nestor told him. "I deeply regret the stranglehold I had on your life, I do mean that, but there was no simple way to undo that damage. I was compelled to relight the fire in your heart – your passion to discover the truth – once more. It wasn't an easy thing to do, son, but I wanted you to be happy."

Horton noticed that Penriding's eyes hadn't shifted from their deep, entranced gaze towards a dark corner of the room for some time. Considering that this revelation was a large enough pill in its own right for even Horton to swallow, he could only imagine what Penriding was going through.

"So – if I'm the son of a computer program, then what

does that make me?" the Zeptan asked with a hint of trepidation. Horton could tell that Penriding feared what the answer to that question might unveil.

"Human," Nestor answered simply. "Born of Exetus, to be more precise. Cloned from an Illac sacrifice as sustenance for the Vwari, but meant for something greater."

Horton gulped. If Penriding wasn't going to be sick, he certainly was.

"A clone..." Penriding repeated, his mind clearly buzzing. "I don't get it. Why? Why save me? What's the point of making me your son?"

"I built the Blacksmith Merchant Union many years ago to keep the Zeptans squarely under my thumb," Nestor explained. "Their merchants had begun to infringe upon the region near Illac, so I devised the Union as a way to control their movements in order to keep them in check. With my time drawing to an end, however, I required an heir to take over the business. That is where you came into the picture."

Penriding broke out into laughter. "Well, I made damn sure that plan blew up in your face quite thoroughly. I'm sorry, but you couldn't have chosen a more inadequate son than me."

Nestor just looked at Penriding and smiled. "No, I chose the perfect son."

Horton was almost certain he imagined it, but he could have sworn he noticed Penriding crack a tiny smile in the corner of his mouth.

"Well," Nestor said, turning to Horton and extending his hand to be shaken, "my time is quickly coming to a close."

Horton was speechless as Nestor took his hand and shook it. Ulises may have once been a great friend and mentor to him back in Illac, but now he couldn't decide whether to commend or detest the faux priest for everything he'd done. It was incredible to think that this man – this computer program – had been shaping civilization on Earth for thousands of years, and all to fulfill its archaic, ill-advised programming.

Nestor then turned to his son and extended his hand to him as well. Penriding took it hesitantly, but then, very briefly, hugged his father instead.

Nestor smiled, and then turned away from his son to search for somewhere to sit down.

"Say, you didn't have any other personas we should know about, did you?" Penriding asked him, scratching his head. "I'd hate to find out you were, I don't know – Ananke or someone else."

Nestor wheezed as he laughed to himself at the notion, but as he trudged past Horton on his way over to one of the command center's circular seats, the ancient simulant turned to him.

"Do you know what happened that day Georg disappeared at Exetus?" he asked.

Horton thought for a moment.

"Yes, I saw you destroy his repair cube," Horton said quietly. "I saw it in a vision. You, as Nestor, shot at it with a firearm. I don't get it – why would you do that?"

Nestor grumbled and leaned in toward Horton. "A wise merchant always has a contingency plan, my boy. In short, I had not factored Klas into the equation. It was an incredible risk as it were, repairing the Exetus sub-station, and when your father turned the Vwari on us I did not know what to do. The repercussions of exposing the Vwari home to the Zeptans was an unknown, and so I made a decision."

"Hold on a second..." Penriding blurted out from across the room. "You – you weren't Ananke as well, were you? I mean, I suppose.... No, you couldn't have.... But actually—"

Nestor smiled at Horton and shook his head.

"Never give up hope, young Illac," he said with a wink before continuing on his way to find a seat.

Flopping down into one, Nestor phased back into a projection of Ulises. The old priest closed his eyes for a moment, before slowly lifting his head to look at Horton and Penriding.

"One last thing," he said with a long sigh. "Now that the Sunbound Initiative is active once again, do not fret over its purpose. It is *them*, out there—"

Ulises' eyes peered upward, prompting Horton to look up as well, but he quickly understood what the old priest meant.

"*They* are the key."

Ulises then stiffly leaned in toward him, grimacing all the while. Horton suddenly couldn't help but think how odd it was for a computer program to act as though it was in pain so often.

"They await your signal," he gently whispered so that only Horton could hear. "If you wish to survive, Horton, you will need them.

"Ah. Thank you both for the adventure," Ulises abruptly

croaked, and as quickly as he had leaned back in his seat again, he had vanished once and for all. Left on the seat in his place was a small, dimly-lit orange cube.

Horton remained still for a few seconds, pondering Ulises' final words to him before he stood up and cautiously picked up the cube. He held it up to his face so he could see the faint light deep within it.

"All that is left of him now is the beacon," Al commented from over Horton's shoulder. "I can enable it once more, if you command."

Horton lowered the cube from his face and turned to Al.

"This little thing is how the rest of humanity will find its way home?" he asked.

Al cocked his head slightly and nodded. "In essence, yes."

"But will it actually work?" Penriding questioned as he peered in as close to the cube as he could with one eye shut, trying desperately to get a better look at its inner workings.

"I cannot say definitively," Al replied. "The humans of that time period were highly advanced in comparison to your own civilization. In over two thousand years of space faring, anything could have become of them. There is a real possibility they are all deceased."

Horton and Penriding looked at one another simultaneously.

"What do you think?" Horton asked the Zeptan, curious of his take on it. Ulises' final words had continued to replay in the back of his mind, and the fact he directed them specifically toward Horton, as though it were a personal matter, confounded him.

Penriding sluggishly scratched behind his ear as he blinked at the cube in Horton's hand.

"Well, you heard what the old geezer said, didn't you?" Penriding reminded him. "Why not? Let's bring humanity home."

"Don't you think we should ask the Zeptan High Council first?" Horton asked Penriding, to which the two of them stared at each other for a moment before breaking out into laughter.

Ready to take on whatever the future had in store for him, Horton turned to Al and handed over the cube.

"Do it, Al."

EPILOGUE

HORTON LET OUT A DEEP BREATH as he lifted his head up from between his knees. He had undoubtedly lost his edge on the boliball field since he last played, though he'd be damned if anyone knew it.

"Hey! You ready for this one Hortie?" Deforest's voice carried through the air. His younger brother waited unwearyingly, maybe thirty meters away with the bat their father had made Horton for his birthday years ago gripped in his hands and bouncing readily on his shoulder. Not far away was their mother with hands on hips, contently watching her two sons and a few of the other village youths play ball from the porch of their home.

Horton groaned with exhaustion. This would be the last one, he thought. He couldn't neglect the fact that he'd been plagued with relentless headaches and a general feeling of unwellness ever since the Sunbound Initiative had been reengaged three weeks earlier, and although his state seemed to have improved over the last day or two, his energy levels were still lacking.

"Yeah," Horton called back, mustering the last of his vigor as he patted the mitten on his left hand. "Give me your best."

Not wasting time, Deforest let it rip. The crack of the bat resonated through the air, immediately sending Horton's concentration upward toward the bright blue sky as he tracked the muddy yellow boliball with his eyes. Like any good boliball fielder his first step was backward, but that was the last memory he'd be able to recall.

Horton's eyes were already open when he returned to consciousness, but his vision was mostly obscured in darkness. Strangely, he had reentered his body standing completely upright, within arm's reach of a dim, alien wall not unlike those he had seen before in the pyramids. For some reason he immediately felt as though he had been fixed on that spot for quite some time, though he wasn't sure why. He pulled his hands up toward his face and stared at them for a moment. They seemed disconnected from him in a way, as if they weren't really his.

His attention was abruptly jarred by the sound of a baby's soft, giggly voice, echoing off the clangy metallic surroundings. He felt further disoriented and bereft of any sensation as he sluggishly turned around inside this apparent dream world, hopeful to decipher the voice's source.

What he found was a lone, unclothed baby, no more than a year of age, sat upright in the middle of a brightly lit circle on the floor with its back to Horton. It appeared to be encapsulated inside a strange half-spherical bubble of some sort, made up of a clear substance he could not identify. Curious, he shifted through the darkness and approached the container carefully so as not to disturb the child, then touched the bubble's wall. As Horton pressed his right hand deeper into the mysterious substance it gradually gave way to his touch, but did not permit him to break through its barrier.

Here.

Without warning, a wall panel to Horton's left instantly vanished into thin air, revealing two shadowy and daunting figures not two meters away, each with a set of bright blue synthetic eyes that shone in the darkness like the lit buttons of a pyramid's portal. Now unexpectedly exposed to the ethereal beings, the Illac gasped with fright and jumped backward, but to his terror the bubble's shell refused to surrender his hand. He was trapped.

What is it?

Entirely human.

As Horton continued to desperately tug on his arm in an effort to free it, he could not help but gape in fear at the unknown figures. Each of their faces were masked by dark helmets that featured two large tubes running from where their mouths should have been to somewhere concealed behind their heads.

Remnant?

I do not know yet. Hold on.

Horton ceased his struggle momentarily as he recognized that he could perceive the exchange between the two figures inside his head. It was an abnormal sensation, but not something he was entirely unfamiliar with, having been spoken to telepathically by a Reckoner's onboard mainframe once before. This was different, however, as each telepathic voice was clearly distinct, allowing him to identify which individual spoke at a time.

I think he can hear us.

Impossible.

He has indications of telephage.

Doubtful.

What is taking so long?

Patience. The signal is waning. I need to focus.

Horton attempted to address the beings with speech, but found himself unable to conjure any sound. Instinctively he pressed his hand to his throat, but to his bewilderment it instead passed right through his own body as if it wasn't there. He quickly became conscious of the fact that he had not taken a single breath since he awoke in this room, nor was he able to. Horton began to panic. Either nothing in this room was real, or he wasn't.

This cannot be correct.

Well?

To his alarm, one of the figures began to gradually move toward him, immediately prompting Horton to resume desperately wrenching his arm away from the bubble, but it did not budge even the slightest. Now only a few feet away from Horton, the figure kneeled down and started to remove its mask.

Horton froze in place. Not because he wanted to, but because the struggle to free himself from the bubble's hold had adversely pulled him further inside it, and now almost the entire right half of his body was completely immobilized. One by one the figure released tabs around the base of its helmet, and with each an audible exhaustion of compressed air released. Horton looked on with apprehension as the figure carefully and deliberately pulled the helmet off its head, and as soon as he saw its face, Horton squeezed his eyes shut and plead with his own mind to wake itself up from this nightmare. This couldn't be real. There was no way.

"Are... you..."

Horton grimaced as the figure's words breached his ears. They were measured, but dry and hoarse, as if from a voice box that hadn't been used in years, if ever.

"From... Earth?"

Horton opened his eyes slightly. He didn't want to believe what he had seen, but the creature in front of him was still there. Like some unnatural fusion between a Vwari and human, it was still there. To the extent of his knowledge, it could have been only one thing: A human carrying whatever infection originally afflicted the Vwari.

We are losing the signal.

The infected human kneeled before Horton turned his head to look at the other.

And the source?

Horton felt a sudden tug on his right hand from inside the bubble. When he turned to see what it was, he realized the child had crawled over to him, grasped onto one of his fingers and unsteadily stood up on its feet. For a brief instant he and the child maintained a deep gaze, its yellowed

eyes seeming to penetrate his soul, but as the larger surrounding picture began to form in Horton's mind, he discovered the image was something more akin to a freakish
camp story some of the older Illac kids used to tell. Long
and tangled black breathing tubes spilled out of its nostrils
and mouth. All of them, even the children, were infected.
Once again Horton squeezed his eyes shut as tightly as he
could.

We have it.

"User?"

Horton's eyes shot wide open. He quickly sat up in his
bed and surveyed his candle-lit bedroom. To his relief he
was back at home, but to his thorough surprise it was none
other than Al standing beside his bed.

"What's going on? What are you doing here?" he im-
mediately questioned the holographic computer program.
This was an unusual sight considering he had never seen
Al outside of a pyramid or the moon station.

"I am sorry, User, but I needed to disconnect you temporarily from my system," Al explained. "You were utilizing more than four percent of allotted telepathic bandwidth
– quite unprecedented. I had no choice but to terminate
your link manually."

Horton shook his head. He didn't know what was going
on with him, but he did know this confirmed something he
was afraid of.

"I think they're coming, Al," he whispered.

"Yes, User. I have known," Al replied. "The Senior
User has—"

"You're up!"

Horton recoiled slightly as Al's image unexpectedly evaporated from the room, replaced by Deforest, who had just run straight through Al as though he was never there.

"Thank the gods you're finally awake again," Deforest told him with a heavy sigh of relief.

"Yeah," Horton responded simply.

"Look, I know I shouldn't have done this," Deforest began to tell Horton in a grave fashion, "but you've been unconscious for six whole days. Nobody in the village knows what's wrong with you, so I had to get help from somewhere. It's the dead of night – I promise nobody saw him."

Deforest then took two steps to his left, revealing Penriding standing in the bedroom doorway behind him. When the Zeptan's eyes caught sight of Horton, his jaw instantly slacked and the color disappeared from his face. If not for his tight grip on the doorway, he looked as though he might have fallen over.

"Oh my god," Penriding uttered breathlessly with his left hand now running through his hair in sheer disbelief. "Horton.... You're infected."

About the Author

Originally from Surrey, England, ALEX SPICER moved to California as a child. He graduated with a journalism degree from San José State University with lofty hopes of being a sports journalist before making the natural progression to science fiction writing. He currently resides in the San Francisco Bay Area.

Cover art by REBECCA UGALE